Lost Hunters

By

Deanne Devine

Lighthouse Press, Inc.
Deerfield Beach, FL

Lighthouse Press, Inc.
P.O. Box 910
Deerfield Beach, FL 33443
www.LighthouseEditions.com

ISBN: 0-9676354-3-8

This book is dedicated to my husband, Rick.

Special thanks to Mom and Dad

Prologue

"A pair of hands, Claire, if I had a pair of hands I'd strangle you straight into Hell," said the phantom remains of John Barker.

Claire answered him with a cackle. "Strangle what?"

Cursing their existence in this gray vacuity, Barker tried to turn away, but her presence was everywhere in the milky haze. Strangle what, indeed! She had no neck just as he had no hands. They had no form, yet he envisioned them as they once were; he lean, with dark hair and intense eyes, and Claire, plump and ruddy, her long, red hair in loose curls. Reason didn't allow him to consider what they had become, although he could vaguely comprehend where they were, and he was slowly coming to understand why.

Sanity was a delicate condition in this place, and John Barker's had undergone test after test. For years, the endless, wordless squabbles between Claire and Walter, her dim-witted husband, pushed Barker to the limit. When Walter escaped and fled back into the world, Barker thought he would finally have peace, but it never came. Claire prattled on, bored, prodding Barker for conversation and company, pleading for attention.

Claire alone was enough to keep his ire aroused, yet piled on top of that were the taunts of his captors, the Wethacanwee. They came cooing, calling him names, laughing, their hot coal eyes glowing in the dimness, their snouts wrinkling with delight. Yet, for all their gloating, even they were bound. At least Barker would soon be free again. Even in this empty place, he kept an earthly sense of time and felt the hour near.

1

Beside him, Claire moaned. He must escape before she gave birth. Her whining would become wailing, and the demanding would be intolerable. He flexed and strained, building and storing energy. He was leaving soon, and though he knew she'd follow him, he didn't care because this time she would be coming back alone.

THURSDAY

The girl on the calendar winked.

Ralph Vickers smiled at her. *Aw, Suzie, June is almost over. I'm going to miss you*, he thought, smoothing the hairs on his balding head. *Here's to July.*

"Christopher! Get out of there right this instant!"

The shouting from the kitchen pulled Ralph from his daydream and back into the garage. With a sigh, he continued the search for the camper mattress covers. They should have been *on* the mattresses in the travel-trailer, but when he went out to take inventory, he found only bare foam rubber. He looked in the small camper closet where the sheets were stored, and not only were the covers not in there, but the sheets were missing too.

Their absence was not a mystery. As the father of four young boys, Ralph had learned there were few mysteries. Items disappeared and reappeared all the time. Boys found uses for the strangest things. The sheets may have become capes, or tents or parachutes. Creative uses, yes, but now the sheets were needed to be sheets.

Ralph was airing the little trailer out today because tonight he would be taking it over to his brother's house. Ralph and his brother, Dan, bought the trailer together, and Ralph kept it at his house because he had a much larger yard. It worked out well, for the boys liked to sleep in it during the summer.

Having looked everywhere twice, he gave up and decided to ask Tammy, which to him was much like cheating on a crossword puzzle. Tammy always knew what he felt he should also know, and

3

she often responded to him in the same manner she answered the children. Puffing his thin chest, he went to find her.

She was in the kitchen, doing four things at once: getting the younger boys ready for day care, cooking breakfast, fixing herself for work, loading the dishwasher. It was magical, the way she moved. Suzie the calendar girl faded in comparison.

When Tammy spotted him in the doorway, she raised her eyebrows in that "What do you want?" way of busy mothers as she stirred her coffee and put toast on plates. Her brown hair was pulled back rather than curled, indicating the morning had been particularly rushed.

"Um, uh, have you seen the um, the things that go on the mattresses?" Fourteen years of marriage and she still awed him. "You know, the uh, cover things? The zip-up things? And the sheets?"

She stopped everything. Obviously exasperated, she put her hands on her hips. "I told you last night."

"You did?" Last night. There was a baseball game on television last night. She couldn't have gotten his attention with a loaded gun. "Honey, you know you can't talk to me when I'm watching TV," he whined.

"I had to wash them," she said, pouring milk and counting out spoons. "The boys made a mess when they camped out. Mud and grass everywhere." She stopped once more. "You do remember the boys sleeping out?"

"Um, yeah." He thought he remembered, anyway.

"Breakfast!" she yelled at the ceiling. Then, setting plates on the table, she said to Ralph, "In the basement, in the basket beside the dryer." Somehow, she had filled the juice glasses without him seeing.

He edged out of the chaos of her kitchen and went to the quiet of his finished basement; cool as a cave, insulated from the noise above, the smell of stillness all around. He often fantasized about the basement, about a big television and a wet bar, and maybe a pool table, the air above cloudy with cigar smoke. Not this year, though. Too many children!

Pushing open the door to the laundry room, he had the strangest urge. For some reason he wanted to go to the next door, into the storage room. It was not so much an urge as a pulling. He looked at the door to the storage room, tilting his head like a curious puppy. The mental watch in his head reminded him that he was going to

4

be late for work. Dismissing the urge, he found the basket of sheets and mattress covers, and was on his way upstairs when he heard the crash.

It came from the storage room.

It startled him only slightly because, just as fathers of boys know few mysteries, they are also hard to startle. Sudden loud noises were common in his house. The boys had probably been playing in there, and left something balanced precariously. He set the basket down and went to make sure nothing had broken.

When Ralph opened the door and turned on the light, he was surprised to be startled. Bruce was standing in the center of the room.

He hadn't seen Bruce in years. He hadn't thought about Bruce in years. Bruce, as far as Ralph knew, had been standing in a corner for the past five years, hidden by holiday decorations, swim toys, lawn games, and the billions of other seldom used items that eventually found their way down here. Yet now Bruce stood in the middle of the room, boxes around him lying on their sides, their contents spilling out. At his feet was the brown wig that used to perch atop his bald head.

Ralph recovered. He went in and picked up the wig.

"Did the boys drag you out?" he asked the mannequin, feeling silly and nervous. He placed the wig on Bruce's head. It slid off.

Parenting four boys may have eroded his belief in mysteries and dampened his startle reflex, but it had also heightened his apprehension. Nothing can give the anxieties a better work out than having only three of four kids accounted for after dark, or a phone call from school at one o'clock in the afternoon. Ralph understood apprehension. He felt it now. How was Bruce standing without support? Yes, it was possible; his feet were flat, his legs formed just so, but generally it took more patience than all four boys combined possessed to get Bruce to stand alone. He looked at the boxes on the floor. They hadn't been scooted away from Bruce, as the boys would have left them, but rather they appeared to have tumbled over on either side of his path.

Ralph swallowed a bit too hard, trying to rationalize the alarm he felt. Of course he was unnerved. His initial thought upon seeing Bruce was that a thief had broken into the basement. In this lighting, with one dim, bare bulb casting more shadows than light, he looked very menacing.

Again Ralph picked up the wig. It was a straight, brown, straggly thing. As he again placed it on Bruce's head, he noticed his hand trembling. He even thought, for just a moment, that something was repelling him, as if he were forcing two magnets together.

Trying to control his breath, he pressed the wig in place. When he moved his hand, the wig sprang two inches in the air and landed on the mannequin's shoulder before falling to the ground.

Ralph yelped, backing away, feeling behind him, while keeping his eyes on Bruce. Above the strong jaw, the firm, straight lips, the narrow, chipped plaster nose, Bruce's eyes were deep-set and dark, dark brown. Hard and cold under thickly painted brows, they locked with Ralph's.

Memories came to him in the form of emotions, the way they do when the radio plays an old song. Ralph remembered how much he had once wanted Bruce, how badly he had to have him when he saw him in his brother's garage. He relived the joy of his luck when Dan said, "Well, sure, if you really want him, go ahead." And how, after he brought him home, the feelings were gone. Embarrassed, he was unable to explain to Tammy why, or for what, he wanted Bruce. He brought him down here, where he stayed.

As much as Ralph had once wanted Bruce, he now wanted him out. Not just out, but back to Dan's. The idea of putting him out with the trash made him queasy. *Take me back*, he thought, and immediately wondered where that came from. Sweating, he grabbed the doorframe for support. *Back, back*, he thought. "Okay," he said aloud, but quietly. The queasiness began to settle.

Biting his lip, he approached the mannequin, determined to put him in the trailer and return him to Dan. First, he put the wig in his pocket, enjoying an odd satisfaction. Wrapping his arm around Bruce's waist, he carried him upstairs. It was a light, but awkward load, the unbendable legs bumping the walls.

He carried Bruce through the kitchen where the boys argued and Tammy hovered and no one looked his way. Once he had Bruce inside the camper, he began to question his actions. Did he really think the mannequin moved by itself? Of course not! The boys had made that mess. How ridiculous he was being. He briefly wondered if this is what PMS was like. Well, Bruce was in place and he wasn't going to waste time taking him back downstairs.

He left the camper with high spirits until he remembered the

6

basket of sheets in the basement. Shaking his head in annoyance with himself, he hustled back to the house. Despite the fact he would be late for work, he hadn't felt so good since Tammy's last pregnancy test came back negative.

***

Leslie Vickers sat on the grass, a sun warmed tombstone as her backrest, composing her epitaph:

Here Lies Leslie Vickers
Poet, Humanitarian, Friend To All

Embarrassed, she scribbled it out, afraid she might really die and someone would discover it. Or worse, that she wouldn't die and someone would discover it. She scratched it out totally, checking to make certain it was obliterated before continuing.

Here Lies Leslie Vickers
Here In A Flash, Gone In A Flicker

She liked this. Tapping her pen on the notebook, she studied her mother's tombstone. It was rather plain, small and gray, not at all like the woman it memorialized, but her father was probably not feeling too creative at the time he bought it, so anyone who wandered past Holly Vickers's grave learned only that she was twenty years old and a beloved daughter, sister, wife and mother. There was a round faced, curly haired cherub in one corner, giving by-passers the mistaken impression that Holly was a religious woman. Leslie's father told her he picked the cherub because it looked like Leslie.

Leslie stretched, her back pressing against Hazel Wilder's tombstone. Hazel was buried in front of Holly, here in Section G of Miltonville Memorial Park. Section G was one of what Leslie considered the suburban areas of the garden cemetery. Straight rows of graves with markers that were more or less identical, very similar to the neighborhood Leslie lived in. The wealthy rested in the northern hills and valleys of Miltonville Memorial, under great columns of granite and inside tombs with stained glass windows protected by iron bars. The poor were represented in Section W, also known as Amberly County burial grounds. Many of the markers there were simple flat rocks with names painted on them. Other parts of the cemetery were old and rambling, shady and overgrown with ivy, and Leslie found them oddly comfortable.

She looked around for Anna Redmond, who was somewhere with her own notebook, collecting data for a regional history class. The cemetery was too hilly and full of trees to locate someone with a cursory glance. There might be forty people here, but where she sat, she was by herself. She felt isolated. Lonely, actually. But being here, with her mother, alone in this lonely place, gave her a peculiar satisfaction. It pricked her belly and made her sad. She came here a lot these days, which might have worried her if she stopped to think about it. It was as if she wanted to feel the loneliness, the way some people will press a bruise. Sane people don't do things they know will hurt.

She stretched out on her stomach, propped up on her elbows, and turned to a clean sheet in the notebook, determined to write her feelings to her mother. Instead she stared at her mother's name. She had written letters to her mother daily for years, but now she found it almost impossible to write a simple account of her daily activities. *Because I don't do anything!* she pouted. At the age of nineteen there should be more to life than just work and school—

"Boo!"

Leslie jolted from the ground in one motion, somehow twisting in the air. Her mouth opened, whether to scream or gasp didn't matter because by then she knew it was Anna, and had time to stop herself.

"Anna!" She flung the notebook, and it flew at Anna's face, pages fluttering. Anna knocked it away, laughing. "That's not funny," Leslie said.

"Oh, come on. You would have done the same thing." Anna picked up the notebook, and turned it upright to read what Leslie had written. Remembering the epitaphs, Leslie jumped up and snatched it away.

"No I wouldn't. Well, maybe when I was ten," she muttered, brushing grass from her shorts. "My legs are going to be itchy."

"I guess we can go now," Anna said, readjusting the barrettes in her long hair. It was unnecessary because, like everything else on her lanky self, her hair was as neat as if she'd just brushed it.

"Find anything?"

8

Anna shrugged. "I really don't know what I'm looking for. But I found stuff, yeah." She handed her notebook to Leslie in case she wanted to look. Leslie leafed through it, and having less an idea of what she was looking for than Anna did, gave it right back.

"Let's go eat," Leslie said, but it was more of a plea. This was the third cemetery they had been in today. Anna had come to her house at 8 AM and woke her up, insisting it was a lovely day for cemetery stomping. She was taking a summer class on Monday and Wednesdays, and one of her projects involved collecting names out of area cemeteries. She had eight weeks to work on the assignment, but Anna was the type of student who read through her textbooks before the semester began. Leslie, who often didn't even buy her books until a few days before the first exam, had little patience for Anna's obsessiveness, but cemetery exploration was a different matter. She had an insatiable morbid curiosity, and besides, she didn't really have anything else to do.

"Um," Anna faltered. "Are you ready?" She nodded toward Holly's grave.

"I'm ready," Leslie said, but she didn't move. She stared at the headstone. "Do you know I'm almost as old as she was?"

"Yeah," Anna said. Leslie shrugged. With nothing else to say, they walked back to Anna's car.

***

Leslie lived with her family in one of the cute suburbs that erupted in Miltonville during the 1960s. It sprawled between Highway 20 and Goodenough Road, block after twining block of ranch homes inside small yards. Each house sat atop a slight mound, a small valley separating the properties. Wide sidewalks and driveways displayed chalked juvenile graffiti of hopscotch and four-square. Some homes were lovely, trimmed with pretty colors and surrounded with trees and shrubs; others were plain and battered, with cracked walks and shaggy grass, but most were neat. For a reason never explained, the developer had named each street after some type of food, so the area was commonly called the Kitchen. The Vickers lived on Apple Street, which was in the Fruit Bowl.

With sandwiches and sodas, Anna and Leslie sat on the front porch, relishing the touch of summer on their skin. Actually, it was still spring, summer technically a few days away. But school was out, and so, for Leslie, it was summer. The only thing getting in the way of perfection was her job at Hartmann's Grocery. She didn't hate the job, but she did hate being there. Hard as she tried, she couldn't hold it in the same high regard Anna did, but then, Anna needed the job to help pay for her education. Leslie's father and stepmother were employed by Salem University, which meant she received a tuition waiver. Otherwise, she wouldn't be going to school because she couldn't imagine spending money on books when there were clothes to buy and movies to be seen. Anna, however, didn't mind contributing to her college expenses, because she took her education seriously. As much as she liked her job at Hartmann's, she didn't intend to make it a career.

Right now, neither was thinking about Hartmann's Grocery. They were breathing the breezy, blue-yellow, grass scented afternoon. Plates on their laps, they sipped soft drinks and watched Dottie Geist weed her flowerbed across the street. The sound of the television inside the Geist house drifted over to the Vickers' porch. Mr. Geist hurt his back years ago and seldom left the couch. Apparently his hearing wasn't so good either, because the whole neighborhood could tell who was on Sally Jesse each afternoon. In the distance, dogs barked, children whooped, birds sang and cars whined, but all in all, it was very quiet.

Leslie propped her feet on the porch railing. "I can't believe you're taking summer classes."

"I can't believe you aren't."

"And give up all this?" She spread her arms, corn chips in one hand, soda can in the other.

"You're a porch potato. If you took a few easy summer classes, you could knock off almost a whole semester," Anna said.

"Why rush?"

"Oh, I forgot, Ms. Major: Undecided."

Leslie was about to respond when she heard the squealing brakes of the small Miltonville Activity Center bus as it pulled into the Kitchen. "Here comes Robby." They sat quietly then, too lazy to talk. A moment later, a small man came around the curve of Apple Street, walking quickly toward his home, two doors away from Leslie's house. He held his left arm across his stomach with his right hand as if it were limp. It wasn't, in fact it was very strong, but Robby Canwell had held his arm while walking since he was a boy. He and Leslie used to play together, until they were five or

10

six. After that, Leslie developed along one path with other children, while Robby took his own path and made new friends.

As he passed the Vickers house, Anna and Leslie called out to him. He waved and kept walking.

"Robby! What's the hurry?" Leslie said.

"Thursday," he answered sternly and kept going.

"Thursday?" Anna asked when he had turned up his driveway.

"Work. You wouldn't believe his schedule," Leslie told her.

"He's got a job? That's great. Where?"

"One of those distribution centers out by the airport. I think he helps unload trucks or something. I don't know exactly. They hired a couple of people from the Center for different days."

"Really? I wonder what they pay him?" Anna's voice showed her suspicion.

"Oh, come on. I'm sure he's not being exploited. People look out for that kind of thing. It's part of some program." When there was no sign of approval from Anna, she said, "I think it's a good program."

"I didn't say it wasn't. I'll just bet they'd pay someone else more."

"They wouldn't hire someone else just to unload trucks."

"I'm not knocking it. Why are you being be so defensive?"

"I'm not," Leslie protested, defensively.

"Sounds like he's staying busy, anyway."

"Robby's always been busy," Leslie said with a sigh. In the first grade, Robby joined a class at the Center designed for developmentally challenged students. The group grew together and four of them remained in the area and worked as volunteers at the Center. Robby was a bus captain, hopping on the bus early in the morning and staying on board most of the day, helping to shuffle the latch key kids and summer kindergarten students back and forth. Even on his days off he rode the bus to the Center because many of his friends were there. When he wasn't working or recreating, he kept busy mowing lawns and trimming hedges in the neighborhood.

Leslie thought about her industrious friend, and suddenly felt tired. "He's probably a millionaire, you know."

Anna nodded. For a long moment they said nothing.

"I'm bored," Leslie announced.

"What's new?"

"Nothing's new."

"Are you in a bad mood? You're complaining more than usual."

Leslie thought about it. She wasn't in a bad mood, but she was in a weird one. "I just feel weird today."

"Maybe it's because we were at the cemetery."

"Yeah, probably. I don't know. Maybe." She didn't know why she felt so funny. "I think I'm craving excitement."

Anna laughed. "Excitement? I've got bad news. You live in Miltonville."

"Don't remind me."

"Besides," Anna continued, "you only think you want excitement. People living exciting lives don't get enough sleep and miss a lot of meals."

From the Swift house across the street, next door to the Geist's, they heard Cindy Swift yelling at her son, "Ryan! Get in here. This minute!"

"Man, she's really lost it since Tim left," Leslie said.

"Poor Ryan. I thought they'd be better off without him."

"Let's go uptown and see if there's anyone else hanging around waiting for a life," Leslie said, putting her thoughts of excitement and adventure to bed.

***

Ryan Swift slammed the back door as he entered the kitchen where his mother stood, hands on hips. Neither spoke until he broke the silence with a belligerent "What?" To Cindy it sounded like a challenge.

"This is what." She pointed to the counter where a carton of milk lay on its side. The contents pooled on the floor below, milky paw prints circling it.

"I didn't do it. The cat did," Ryan said.

"Did the cat leave the milk out?" She then noticed the refrigerator door ajar. "And how long has this been open?" She pushed it closed. When she turned, Ryan was gone. Her first instinct was to go after him, but she fought it, holding her hand to her stomach to calm herself. This scene was becoming all too familiar. She had to stop; she needed control. Yelling took them nowhere, and Ryan hated her for it. She knew he thought it was her yelling that made his father leave, but how much could an eight year old understand?

She was the adult, so why couldn't she be patient instead of arguing with him?

The same reason she couldn't be patient with Tim. Because, when she saw that she had lost him, she didn't know what else to do but yell. Soon Tim would begin the fight for custody of Ryan, and with his girlfriend's money paying the lawyers, he'd certainly gain it. Then Cindy supposed that she would have to start yelling at the cat. Unless Tim took her, too!

Dropping a dishtowel into the puddle, she squatted to clean up the milk. Her hair, once a rich bouncy, color-enhanced blond, hung in limp strands in front of her eyes, annoying her. As with everything else, she blamed Tim for this: her hair she could no longer afford to have professionally cut; the milk she could not afford to have wasted; her son, who, in earlier days, would have never run away from her when he was in trouble. She muttered several choice derogatory words and although they were directed toward her ex-husband, she realized too late that Ryan was standing in the doorway, a mop in his hand. His dark eyes were serious, absorbing the brunt of her anger. Cindy noticed for the first time that his shirt was dirty and his light brown hair uncombed. He looked unloved. Cindy sagged.

"I got the mop," he said.

"Ryan, what I was saying, I didn't mean you. I was just ranting. I'm sorry." It seemed she was always apologizing.

He only shrugged, then went back outside.

***

Dottie Geist watched Leslie and Anna leave after their lunch on the porch. She removed her gardening gloves and went inside. Artie lay on the couch, remote control in hand, flipping between Jerry and Sally Jesse.

"There go them girls again," she told him, patting her pink curlers.

"Hm," he grunted.

After pouring herself a glass of iced tea, she joined him at the television. "Some life kids got today, huh?" she said.

"Uh huh."

"By their age, we already had two kids. What have they got to show for anything?" When Artie didn't answer, she continued,

"Weird people, that family. You know Dan and Michele are going camping? They don't much seem the camping type, do they? I'd think she'd be too good for that." She turned in her chair so she could see the Vickers' house through the window.

"Uh huh." Artie's eyes stayed on the television, his arms folded across his enormous stomach.

Dottie stayed quiet for a while, then turned from the window and said, "You'd think they'd ask us to look after things while they're gone. I'll bet they asked the Canwells. Think they'd worry about that retard knowing they were gone. I wouldn't trust that kid. Hey, did I tell you I saw Becky walking with him?" she said, referring to Leslie's six year old sister.

"Look at this," Artie said, gesturing toward the television. "Lesbian nuns." He turned up the volume, then put aside the remote. Dottie, finally silenced, settled down to watch.

***

Anna and Leslie found uptown Miltonville to be every bit as thrilling as Leslie's front porch. A lot of elderly people were out, scattered about the sidewalks and benches, seeming to find plenty to do. Leslie often stated that Miltonville was a terrific town in which to be old. It reeked of yesteryear and looked more realistic when photographed in black and white, as it always was in the Miltonville Cryer.

"There's Ed!" Leslie brightened. In front of the police station, scruffy Ed Philips was enlightening Henry Bledsoe on some matter, maybe county politics, or maybe an upcoming weather pattern. Whatever it was, Henry was no doubt in search of escape, as was generally the case of anyone who fell into a reverie while walking in town, and snapped out to find themselves face to face with Ed Philips. It wasn't that Ed was disliked; the problem was Ed liked to talk. And talk and talk. Sadly, there weren't many people with the spare time required to converse with Ed. Leslie tried to make time because he was always full of interesting gossip and speculation. He had also been a good friend to her mother.

"No," Anna said before Leslie could ask.

"Oh, poor Mr. Bledsoe. We could be nice and rescue him." Henry Bledsoe was nodding and backing away. Ed kept talking, his hands emphasizing every point.

14

"He's a big boy."

"You know, if you're really serious about studying local history, Ed's the guy to talk to," Leslie tempted. "He knows everything."

"And he'd be more than happy to share it with us, I'm sure, but I'm not that bored yet."

Leslie gave up. "Let's go to Hartmann's and get a drink."

It was a true testament to their boredom, going to their place of employment on their day off. They went, intending to hang around awhile (*a la* Ed Philips) but didn't stay long. The third time they were asked what they were doing in the store on such a gorgeous day, they became ashamed of their idleness and took their sodas outside. Hartmann's Grocery was three blocks north of Main Street, so they left the car and strolled back to Main, where they settled on one of Miltonville's many benches.

Leslie had just remarked miserably on how little difference there was between them and the old people when a tiny, white haired woman bustled up the sidewalk, a shopping bag in one hand, books cradled in her arm.

"Hi, Mrs. Lipscomb," Leslie said. "How are you?"

"Fine day, ladies," Mrs. Lipscomb greeted as she passed.

"Oh, no," Leslie dropped her head in her hands. "Even the old people don't want to hang out with us."

Anna's laugh was cut short. "Great," she grumbled. "Here comes the Angel of Death."

Leslie leaned over to see around Anna. "Cool." Maureen Russell was coming out of Mask Backward, Miltonville's only trendy music store.

"Maureen!" Leslie called. Anna gave her a short punch. Maureen saw them and gave a slight Mona Lisa smile, then changed her course and approached the bench.

"What's she doing out in daylight, anyway?" Anna said.

"Shut up. I wish I was that cool." Maureen's hair, which was blue-black last week, was today a blue-burgundy, and hung straight around her fish white face. When she came closer, Leslie could see that she had painted a blue teardrop at the corner of a heavily lined eye. She was wearing a faded black "Meat is Dead" T-shirt and maroon crushed velvet pants. Leslie was embarrassed by her own plaid boxers and souvenir T-shirt until she glanced at Anna's prim embroidered blouse tucked into her pleated shorts. Her straight blonde hair was still held firmly by the barrettes and trim bangs covered her forehead, the antithesis of Leslie's unruly no-color-no-curl-frizz. At any rate, they were both pretty plain compared to Maureen.

"Great day," Maureen said, sitting next to Anna. She had lived in Miltonville her whole life, yet her voice had a tinge of an accent, which drove Anna crazy because, as she pointed out to Leslie on other occasions, before they started college, Maureen had spoken with the same southern Indiana affect as the rest of them.

"Been doing anything interesting?" Maureen asked in her special blend of British and Southern Californian.

"Actually, we invaded your domain today," Anna said. Leslie held her breath, silently begging her not to say anything horrible.

"Just hanging around the cemeteries," Anna finished.

"For real?" Maureen took it in stride. Leslie breathed.

"Yeah. Winston's history class."

"Oh. Did you go to Vanderkellen?"

"Oh, my gosh no!" Leslie let go of her composure. "I forgot all about that. We oughta go," she said to Anna.

"I don't think so."

"Well, if you want history, that's where it is," Maureen said with a shrug.

"Yeah, Anna, history," Leslie said.

"It's too far."

"It's not that far," Maureen said. "I have friends who go out there all the time."

"That's another reason I don't want to go," Anna said.

"Oh, they wouldn't bother you. Besides," she slapped on the Mona Lisa again, "we only come out at night."

"No!" Leslie was amazed. "Are you really into that?"

"Nah. I used to be, but I grew out of it." She reached into her boot and withdrew a cigarette. "They aren't serious about it, anyway. They mostly use it as an excuse to party."

"Wow." Leslie couldn't believe Maureen could so easily admit it, let alone insinuate that the local Satanists weren't devoted enough for her.

"It's no big deal. You'd be surprised who goes out there."

"Who?" Leslie wanted to know. This was not the kind of information she read in the Cryer.

"Don't worry about it." She was sitting with her elbows on her knees, studying the ash of her cigarette, trying to ignore Anna, who was in turn trying to ignore her. She looked past her to Leslie, and seeing her anxious expression, smiled. A real smile! "It's not a big deal. I shouldn't have said anything."

"No kidding," Anna agreed. Leslie glared at her.

"Well, I can see my work here is done." She stood. "See ya later, Leslie. And Anna—" She forked an evil eye to her. For some reason Anna chuckled.

"You're sick, Russell."

"Thanks, Redmond."

"What is the deal with you two?" Leslie asked after Maureen sped off in her Beetle. "She was trying to be nice."

"She's a flake, Leslie. And worse, she flaunts it."

"Well, I think she's right about Vanderkellen. We oughta go."

"No way. Not with your folks going on vacation. No way."

"What're you talking about?" Leslie demanded, although she knew perfectly well.

"Think back. And then forget it."

"Oh, come on, I was a kid."

"It was two years ago! Believe me Leslie, you haven't matured much since then."

"It was *three*! And what was I scared of?" she said, pretending not to hear Anna's comment. "Nothing in the graveyard, that's for sure."

"Yes, you were."

"How would you know? You weren't even there!"

"I didn't have to be! You whined about it forever. You had nightmares. I don't get it. Why do you always want to do this to yourself?"

Leslie couldn't argue. Anna was right. Leslie had an appetite for the macabre. She loved going to Coyle Road to watch for the crying lady, or Pfister Lane to listen for the heartbeat in the well. When a new horror film came out, Leslie was first in line. At Halloween, she went to every haunted house she could afford, once as far away as Cincinnati. Each time Leslie sought to satisfy these peculiar cravings it cost the Vickers family dearly because her nightmares were vicious, and when Leslie had a nightmare, no one slept.

Unable to answer Anna's question, she muttered, "It's just fun, that's all." A thought occurred to her, one that would help her cause. "What difference does it make now? I'm probably going to have nightmares anyway. I already went to three cemeteries."

"Not Vanderkellen."

"No, only the ones you wanted to go to. As usual."

"Don't try to guilt me. It won't work."

"I'm not. It just seems we only do what you want."

"Okay, okay. Geez, we sound like we're married. We'll have to take your car, though. Mom needs hers."

"Really? You really want to go?" Suddenly she remembered what Anna had said earlier about not really wanting the things she wished for. Now, she wished she hadn't begged to go. But begging was most of the fun, and she was so good at it. That and whining, which was how she usually got her way, whether she really wanted it or not.

***

Ed Philips sat on the ledge in front of the courthouse and offered a short wave to Mrs. Pulley as she hurried by. He knew she disapproved of him and that disapproval was based solely on his appearance. He didn't blame her, what with his long, gray hair and scraggly beard. His uniform was a plaid flannel shirt and worn khakis, no matter what the weather. Comfort was his fashion watchword; he needed to impress no one. Not even the pretty widow Pulley.

Watching the traffic passing, he saw Anna and Leslie leaving town. Seemed they were always together. Just like their mothers. He wondered if Anna's mother worried about that, if she was afraid it would happen again. Almost twenty years since the last Itch; whenever he thought about it, his stomach surged as if on the down slope of a roller coaster.

The Redmond station wagon turned from Main Street to Walnut, toward the suburbs of Miltonville. The Itch would be back, probably within the next few years. Not yet though. There was still time.

Every time Ed saw Leslie, he thought of her mother and worried. Then he always assured himself that there was still time.

***

Cindy and Ryan Swift were eating an early dinner when the

phone rang. Ryan moved the canned spaghetti around his plate while his mother answered the phone. He could tell by her tension that it was his dad. Saturday he was going to pick Ryan up for the weekend. He would be more excited if Teena weren't around. ("You can call me 'Teeny', honey," she told Ryan from behind a mask of powder and lipstick. He could almost see the cloud of perfume that enveloped her.) Despite Teena, Ryan was anxious to get away from home. It was boring with his mother gone all morning, and at night he had to stay at the Canwell's because of her second job, and there was nothing to do there. A few times he had gone to the Center with Robby, but sometimes they got on each other's nerves.

"Fine, thank you," his mother spoke formally into the phone. Then, "Yes he is." She held the phone out to him.

"It's your father."

"What does he want?" he asked, afraid to hurt her feelings by appearing too excited.

"To talk to you." She laid the phone on the counter and left the room. Ryan slowly backed his chair from the table and picked up the receiver.

"Dad?"

"Hi Ryan." His dad tried to sound natural, but he hadn't sounded natural since he left. "How's the kid?"

"Okay. Are you still coming Saturday?"

"Sure thing, pal. Think you might want to go into the city? Maybe hit the zoo?"

"Sure," Ryan answered.

"The reason I called is to see if you wanted to go to the truck show afterward."

"Monster trucks?" Ryan smiled at the phone.

"Yeah, that's the one. I'll go ahead and buy the tickets if you want."

"Yeah, I want to go," Ryan said happily.

"Okay, pal. See you Saturday."

"Bye, Dad." Ryan hung up, grinning. When he turned around, he saw his mother watching from the doorway. She looked very tired. Her hair was tied in a loose ponytail, her eyes red, and her pale mouth in a tight smile. He suddenly felt very embarrassed for no reason.

"Big weekend?" she asked casually.

He nodded and she nodded.

"Finish your dinner. I have to leave pretty soon."

He sat back down, his excitement gone, much like the life from his mother's face. It was confusing to be so happy while she was so sad. She hardly ever laughed or smiled or even talked much anymore. Guilt chewed at Ryan's gut. He was consorting with the enemy. He knew it, but it was his dad. Yet, it was Dad who ruined everything. He was the one who left, the reason his mother was always running in from one job and out to another, and hunting for more work in her spare minutes. That hurt Ryan and it also hurt that his father had never shown this much interest in him before he left.

Misty, their cat, put her paw on his leg, so he set his plate on the floor. She hurriedly licked at the sauce. Ryan kept a cautious eye on the door in case his mother should come back. Feeding dinner to the cat would be just cause for another fight, not that it took a lot to provoke her these days. Ryan wished she would be glad for him instead of angry all the time. His room was full of new stuff, even clothes, but she acted insulted that his dad bought things for him.

"Ryan, are you ready?" she called. He was standing at the counter, eating a handful of Oreo cookies. In a near panic he wiped his mouth and pushed Misty away from the plate. When his mother came into the kitchen he was dutifully putting it into the sink.

"I'll walk you down to Mrs. Canwell's," she said.

"Okay," he said, forgetting that his teeth were coated with cookies.

"Ryan!" she said. "Did you eat your spaghetti?"

"Uh, yes," he mumbled, but his eyes were drawn to Misty, and his mother's followed. The little black and white cat sat up in Ryan's chair, her paws on the table, sniffing, spaghetti sauce on her face.

"Ryan!" Ryan flinched, but she wasn't mad. In fact, she was smiling and he was relieved. He smiled with her, and Misty sat innocently licking her nose.

***

Becky Vickers bounced off the walls and Leslie was tired of yelling at her. Uncle Ralph was due any minute, and the arrival of the trailer meant vacation was that much closer. Leslie had conveniently waited too late to put in for time off from work and lost out on the opportunity to go on vacation, which included a trip to Grady's

Galaxy - more commonly known as the Galaxy - southern Ohio's newest theme park. Saturday was Salem University Day, so staff and students would be given a discount on admittance. The Vickers were leaving early Friday, first for Yellowbird, Ohio, to spend the day with Leslie's stepmother's family. Saturday morning they would drive to Colombia (*"It's in Ohio, but it's spelled like the country in South America,"* her father said, trying fruitlessly to give Becky an advanced lesson in both geography and spelling) and stay the night at the park campground. From there, they planned to drive to Piney Grove, West Virginia, where they would swim and hike away the rest of their vacation. Becky, freshly released from the first grade, was unable to contain herself. Jumping up and down, a child without a pogo stick, she sang loudly, "I can't wait! I can't wait!"

"I can't either," Leslie snapped. She was slicing onions, bitterly, because she wasn't staying for dinner. Why should she have to slice onions she wasn't going to eat? Becky hopped and sang, and this, mixed with onion tears, impatience, and an argument with her stepmother, contributed to Leslie's irritability.

"Will you go out? Play or do something. Go away."

Becky kept singing, pulling herself along by her long, blond ponytail that she held high over her head with a skinny arm. "Let's go, hi ho, let's go!" Finally her mother, Michele, a taller version of the waifish child, came into the kitchen. "Becky, if you can't do anything useful, go play in the yard." Still hopping, Becky left the house.

Leslie ignored her stepmother.

"You could at least eat with us tonight," Michele said. "You're going to hurt your dad's feelings."

"He doesn't care if I'm here or not."

Through the window they heard his car, then Becky's shrill "Daddy's home!" A moment later he stepped into the kitchen, sniffing the air.

"What kind of hamburgers are we having tonight?" he teased. For some reason he always teased them about their cooking, despite the fact he couldn't even make decent toast.

"You guys are having plain old hamburgers. I'm going out," Leslie told him. There was a tiny stab at her heart when disappointment clouded his face.

He sat his briefcase on a chair and bent down to kiss Michele. "What's going on? Big date?"

"With Anna," Michele informed him.

"She has a date with Anna?"

"You're all sick." Leslie set the onions and tomato, along with some limp lettuce on the table. "Can I go now?"

"Did I interrupt something?" Dan asked.

Leslie leaned against the counter and crossed her arms. Glaring at Michele, she waited for her response.

"It's nothing," Michele said. "I was just counting on Leslie to help us tonight. I still have laundry to do, there's more packing, I have to go to the grocery. I'd like to leave a clean house—"

"It's my day off," Leslie butted in.

"And I worked all day," Michele reminded her.

"I'm not even going on vacation, so why should I stay here and help?"

"Gee, Leslie, I forgot. In this family we only do things for ourselves. Or Mom does it for everyone." She angrily squished the hamburgers with a spatula.

"Les, what have you got to do tonight that's so important?" Dan asked.

"Oh, this is the good part," Michele said, slamming a lid on the skillet.

Leslie kept glaring and said nothing.

"Well?" her father demanded.

"Anna and I are going to Vanderkellen," she said.

"Oh, for—why? It's dangerous. Besides, you'll have nightmares, and there's not going to be anyone here."

"Dad, I'm a little old for this."

"You aren't acting like it."

"It's not like I'm going to be gone all night. I'll be back in plenty of time to help."

"Yeah, right." Michele set the table, refusing to look at Leslie. Dan watched his wife, biting his lower lip, his forehead creased above his dark eyebrows.

"Dad," she pled.

"I don't want to listen to this all night. Go do whatever you want. I'll help your mother." Michele raised an icy stare to him. He yanked open the silverware drawer.

"Oh great," Leslie said, reading Michele's stance. "Now we get the lecture about how Dad lets me get away with murder."

"No, you don't." Michele laid the napkins down. "I just stupidly thought that you might want to spend some time with us before we left. My mistake."

Leslie turned to Dan for help, but he stood awkwardly with a fistful of silverware. "Geez, I didn't know this was such a big deal." She opened her hands to show her resignation. "Here. What do you want me to do?"

"Go on, do whatever you want," Dan repeated. Michele only shrugged. "Please, though, don't be out late. We have to get up early and I don't want to get woke up in the middle of the night."

It was selfish, and Leslie was ashamed, but now pride was at stake. She stopped at the back door to slip on her moccasins, and left assuring her parents she'd be home before they went to bed. She was opening her car door when Michele came out, holding a pair of hiking boots. Puzzled, Leslie waited.

"You better take these. I'm sure no one cuts the grass out there." When Leslie stared blankly, she clarified. "Snakes."

"Oh, Mom," she started to protest, but realized this was a good time to make up. "Okay."

"Be careful," Michele said, and went back to the house.

Leslie felt much better as she left for Anna's.

***

Anna watched from the kitchen window as Leslie drove her old Maverick, which she affectionately called Bret, up the Redmond's long gravel driveway to the big farmhouse. "I can't believe I let her talk me into this."

"I wish you hadn't," her mother sighed.

"Oh, I'm not worried. I just don't feel like going."

A moment later, Leslie came in the back door. "Hey." She stood behind Judy Redmond's chair and gave her a quick hug. Judy patted her arm and said hello.

"You ready?" Leslie asked, and went to the refrigerator.

"Not really. You want something to eat?"

She shook her head, her mouth full of one of Judy's leftover apple fritters. "Good," she told Judy. "Wish my mom cooked like this."

"I was just telling Anna that you two ought to wait and go out in the morning sometime. It's getting late."

"It's only six o'clock. Besides, I don't plan to be in any graveyard after dark. Or even near dark. Especially with Mom and Dad going on vacation."

"Why don't you stay here while they're gone?" Judy asked.

Leslie squirmed, obviously trying to think of an excuse. "I don't know."

"Well, you can if you want," Judy assured her. "I'll be home by eleven thirty. You'll be home by then?"

"We better be," Anna said. "We both have to work in the morning." To Leslie she said, "I can use the car tomorrow. Want me to pick you up?" Leslie nodded, her mouth again full.

"I'll put some dinner in the oven for you," Judy told Anna.

"Thanks, Mom. Just leave the dishes. I'll do them when I come in."

"That's okay. I'll have time."

"Are you going to work?" Leslie asked.

"Just for a while. I'm covering for Carolyn, and she's taking my shift tomorrow so I can be home when Tom comes in."

When the girls left, Judy sat at the table with a cup of coffee. Seeing Anna and Leslie reminded her so much of herself and Holly Vickers as they were so long ago. It wasn't the physical similarities; except for Leslie's wild hair, both girls resembled their fathers. Anna had Tom's straight light hair and thin features. She and her father looked so serious, until they smiled and their brown eyes sparkled. Leslie was the opposite of Anna's straightness, round like her father, not fat, but rather what the old ladies would call healthy. Her face was round too, a little like Holly's, with eyes that sometimes squinted playfully and other times grew big and dreamy as she went off into one of her own worlds.

Judy worked hard to foster a friendship between the girls when they were young, and with the exception of a few brief periods, her efforts paid off. Now, as the time for a new Itch drew near, she wondered if keeping them together was such a good idea. She wanted to believe Anna and Leslie would be safe, that the Itch picked its victims at random, but she wasn't convinced. Judy had done research and learned that the son of a couple killed in the Itch of the thirties had died during the Itch of the fifties. He, too, was shot, just like Holly. But that family, long gone from Amberly County, had no connection with hers or Holly's. So then, maybe, Judy tried convincing herself, it was a coincidence, all a matter of chance. She could find no patterns, other than those that were common knowledge. The time span between Itches seemed to range from eighteen to twenty-two years. When sixteen years had passed, she began watching for signs: sudden, unexplained deaths, a rash of strokes, murders. The thought caused so much anxiety she sometimes wished it would just come and be done. More and more, her stomach did flips if Anna was late, or if a phone call took her away unexpectedly. She will be safe, Judy told herself over and over. What would she be able to do, anyway? Lock Anna in the house? How do you prepare for the unpredictable, let alone convince others to cooperate when they thought it was all a superstition? She learned the futility of that while trying to convince Tom they should move away before it happened again. He didn't believe in the Itch. Period. But neither did Judy, not in the beginning. The Itch was one of those phenomena that everyone believed in when it happened, but was rationalized and reasoned out with time. Judy suffered greatly during the last Itch, but like everyone else, came to accept the final reports. At least, she wanted to accept them. Finally, she succumbed to curiosity and began to investigate the myth of the Itch. The more she read, the more she wanted to leave Amberly County. By that time, though, Anna was in elementary school, they had the farmhouse they had always wanted, Tom had a good job and Judy was beginning nursing school. It was easy for Tom to convince her that a superstition was not worth the complete upheaval of their lives.

Judy put her cup in the sink, then wiped up the crumbs Leslie left. Messiness, or maybe more accurately, carelessness was a trait she inherited from Holly. With a quick heart skip, she realized consciously for the first time that at Leslie's age, Holly was married with a baby. So was Judy. They had planned it, and part of the plan, the part Judy carried out alone, was that their kids would grow up together. Another part of the plan was to have more children, but that didn't work out. The Itch took care of that. Holly's death had changed everyone's life. In those happy days before the Itch, Tom was a student at Salem, Dan a recent graduate. They became friends because their girlfriends were best friends at Little Easton High School. They married within months of each other. When Dan found a house in Miltonville, Judy and Tom found an apartment nearby. The two couples settled into a routine of card parties on Friday and football on Sunday. Tom went to school around his work schedule and Judy worked part-time while Holly babysat Anna, who was four months older than Leslie. For Tom and Judy Redmond, it was a satisfying struggle. For Dan and Holly Vickers, it was a fairy tale suburban life.

In the heat of July, the fairy tale ended abruptly. It was a Friday, and, as everyone knew, the Redmonds and Vickers would be together. This Friday, Chrissy Michaels and Kevin Lampart joined them, for they were by no means an exclusionary group. They played cards and drank, gossiping and teasing. Around ten o'clock, the phone call came from Margo Gentry. Holly talked to her for a few minutes, making various gestures at the group to indicate the strangeness of the call. Everyone quieted to hear Holly's side of the conversation. It wasn't making sense, but anything connected with Margo rarely did. Since high school, Margo seemed to have lost her way. Like most of their classmates who didn't enter college, she came to Miltonville in search of work, this being long before the new airport brought so many employment opportunities to Westerville. In less than a year, Margo started and left four jobs, and was, at that time, trying to support herself selling cosmetics door to door. To make her situation worse, she had hooked up with Steve Paulin, a man who had been expelled from Salem University ten years earlier and never left the area. Every day was a self-induced crisis and she often called on her high school friends to talk her through her latest problem. Just that afternoon, Judy and Holly saw Margo in town, looking strung out and lost, hanging on Steve's arm.

"I have to make a run," Holly said when she hung up. "She sounds a little loopy."

"What?" Judy asked as if she hadn't heard. Around the table heads dropped into hands and shook at each other among a chorus of "Oh no," and "Oh great," and "I knew it."

"My make-up order is in and she wants me to pick it up," Holly explained.

Dan huffed. "It can wait."

"I don't know. It must be a cash emergency," Holly ventured. "It gets weirder. Remember Cathy Bernett?"

"Cathy Bernett?" Judy asked, her face twisting at the name. "That English kid that talked to herself in class?"

"Margo said she's there and wants to see me. Actually, she said she wants to see you, too. And that's not the weirdest part."

"What?" By now cards were being dealt, and Judy was the

26

only one really listening.

"She said Cathy is dying to see the kids."

"What?" Judy asked again, although it was clear that she heard this time.

"Forget it," Dan said, his attention divided between his wife and the cards in his hand. "Just sit down. She'll be passed out before you get there."

"Just let me run the money over real quick. If she's in trouble..."

"She just wants more vodka, Hol," Tom assured her.

"I don't know Tom," Judy worried. "Steve could have gotten her in trouble. He hangs out with a bunch of junkies."

"If she's in that kind of trouble your five dollars isn't going to help."

Holly bit her lip. "Well, my order was a little more than five..."

Dan laid down his cards. "All right, I'll take you."

"No, you've had way too much to drink," Judy said.

"Yeah," Holly agreed. "This might be a girl thing. She sounds really weird."

"Maybe Steve left her?" Judy offered hopefully.

"Maybe. You want to come?" Judy nodded. "Dan, if we aren't back in half an hour, call. That way we won't be stuck there all night."

"Okay." Dan picked up the cards. "But don't bring her here. In fact, don't let her in the car. It still smells like puke from the last time."

"Okay," Holly promised and Judy nodded agreement. They asked Chrissy if she'd like to join them, but she declined, as they knew she would. She never left Kevin's side.

"If Steve's there don't hang around," Tom said.

"Don't hang around, period." Dan scowled at his cards. "Who dealt this?"

Margo lived over the top of a bakery on Main Street. Holly parked on the street and they walked down an alley to the back of the building, then climbed the wobbly metal stairs to Margo's apartment. A light glowed over the door, but the bare bulb did more harm than good.

Taking each step carefully and holding the handrail, Holly remarked, "Someone's going to fall and kill themselves one day."

They reached the landing. Knocked.

Margo opened the door, smiling, then stepped aside to make

room for Steve. He raised a gun to Holly's chest. She didn't scream, not even when he fired. She only gasped as she fell.

Judy panicked and tried to run, tumbling down the stairs. Another shot. She screamed, hit the ground and ran blindly, slamming full force into a wall. She found her way out of the alley, onto Main Street, into the path of a car. After that, she remembered nothing. There were headlights, a car horn, then nothing. No dreams, no darkness. Nothing.

She awoke to a different world. Six people died that day. Holly had been shot twice, in the heart and in the head. Margo Gentry and her boyfriend, Steve Paulin were also dead of what the coroner eventually defined as aneurysms. Aneurysms had also killed Bill Gurr and Daniel Howe, both residents of Bloomington, who were found behind a tavern on the outskirts of Miltonville. A John Doe was found in a car on Styler Road. Two Miltonville women, Theresa Wehr and Patty Moon were hospitalized, comatose. Theresa lasted three weeks. Patty regained consciousness and howled like a wounded animal. After months of treatment at an Indianapolis clinic, she too died when a blood vessel burst in her brain. Judy, the only witness to Holly's murder, was questioned endlessly, despite the physical pain from the internal injuries, despite her grief over Holly, despite her shame at running away. She told police, reporters, family, Dan, everything she could remember, but it meant nothing, really. Her best friend was gone. Soon, Dan also drifted away.

Dan's family helped him with Leslie while he put things back together. Three years later he married Michele. The Redmonds, whose finances weren't stable to begin with, were confronted with frighteningly high medical bills. Tom dropped out of college and began driving a truck. A generous relative rented an old farmhouse to them that they loved so much they finally bought. Things began to stabilize, and they thought they would have a second child. That's when they learned that the injuries Judy suffered in the accident made pregnancy a dangerous pursuit for her, and when other complications arose from old surgery scarring, a hysterectomy was performed. Once Anna started school, Judy took advantage of financial aid and went to nursing school. That's when she began researching the Itch, searching through old microfilmed newspaper articles when she should have been in the biology lab studying cell slides.

Many in Amberly County agreed, at least for a few weeks, that what had taken place on that July night was the Twenty Year Itch, or John Barker's Itch as it was also called. What they didn't agree on is why the Itch occurred at all. Depending on what you believed, the Itch was either coincidence or a curse - a curse that was said to have started with John Barker in the late seventeen hundreds. The very John Barker who was buried in the Vanderkellen Cemetery.

***

They should have been at Vanderkellen an hour ago. It was only a twenty-minute drive, but Leslie, having missed dinner, insisted on stopping to eat. Anna suggested she eat a burger on the way, but Leslie had a craving for a Shooter's taco salad. The more Anna thought of Shooter's, the better a burrito sounded. This meant heading northwest to Salem. Of course, taco salad is not car food, so they ate at the restaurant. From there it was fifteen minutes south to Vanderkellen. Leslie used the time trying to convince Anna they should get an apartment together.

"No way," Anna argued. "You know I'm saving for a car."

"You can drive Bret," Leslie offered.

"Did I say car? I meant reliable transportation. Bret doesn't meet my criteria."

"Your mom'll let you have her car. You drive it all the time anyway. Or the stink bomb! Hardly anyone uses that."

"Gee, do you think there's a reason for that? Besides, I have to pay tuition. Mom and Dad won't help if I move out."

"But—"

"*But* I don't even want to. And if you thought about it, neither would you. You get free rent, free food, free laundry service. You do whatever you want, come and go whenever you want. Why give it up?"

They rehashed the issue awhile longer; it was one Leslie brought up any time she had a fight with her parents. Anna finally put an end to it by examining the notes she had taken at the cemeteries in Miltonville, leaving Leslie to amuse herself. The closer they got to Vanderkellen, the less she thought of her parents, and the more her stomach fluttered. Excitement or fear? It was impossible to tell. Usually, she relished the excitement *of* fear, which is why she spent so much time pursuing it. Her last trip to Vanderkellen had been too exciting, and was memorable in that it had scared her righteously.

Late in the summer before her junior year in high school, she and seven friends went to the old cemetery in a truck. Gary, Mary, and Barry, whose last names were lost in Leslie's memory, but whose first names she would never forget, were riding in the front. She rode in the open bed with Amy West, Steve Harris, and two other boys whose names were also forgotten. They started out at the drive-in, the last night before it closed for the summer. The same feature had been playing for weeks, and they all had seen it more than once. Barry mentioned a place he had heard of on the other side of Salem where a man was rumored to have been hanged. Supposedly, parking with the headlights pointed at the tree would summon him. Leslie was one of the first 'ayes', and gave the strongest urgings to the squeamish. It took them an hour to find the road, and they were disappointed when they saw how wooded it was. Not wanting to waste the trip, they picked a tree at random, drank a few beers, and waited. Half an hour went by, and they conceded the trip was a waste after all. Then someone mentioned Vanderkellen. It was close, and since they had driven this far, it seemed logical to go there.

Leslie's nerve began to crack on Hopeful Road. Hopeful was the last 'tar' road on the way to Vanderkellen, and it was sparsely populated, mostly flat farmland separated by several stands of trees. In one of these stands, actually large enough to be called woods, was Nepowa Road. Many drivers, who are probably lost anyway, pass by without seeing it. A gravel road with a wooden sign, it was practically invisible, even to those who are looking for it. Nepowa was barely two miles long and ran into Mindell road, Hopeful's slightly off-parallel twin. Vanderkellen Cemetery was on Nepowa, on the west side of the road, midway between Hopeful and Mindell. A dilapidated brick church sat a couple hundred feet off the road. Behind it, to the left, the cemetery rose on a gentle slope, a high iron fence surrounding it. The gates were always open, tilting ominously, the weeds holding them in place. It was a small cemetery, maybe two acres, and old, each tombstone engraved with the date 1798.

As is often the case with oral history, the details of the events surrounding Vanderkellen were sketchy and distorted, and ranged from the mundane to the outrageous. The story taught in school was of a man named John Barker, who in the late 1700's founded a commune in the area. He claimed it to be a utopia, and the settlers practiced a new religion. There were many discrepancies in the tales of John Barker: he may have been a good man led astray by power; he might have been crazy; or he was, in fact, the devil incarnate. The local Shawnee were afraid of him and sent for help, and it arrived in the form of Lucas Vanderkellen. Legend didn't explain why the Shawnee sent for help from the whites who were, at this time, making their lives miserable.

Vanderkellen was a teacher from Pennsylvania. As the story went, he settled just over the hill from the Barker commune. Barker was afraid Vanderkellen might influence his people, and began making threats, but Vanderkellen ignored him. This irritated Barker to distraction, and he started preaching sermons to the commune about the devil over the hill, and the evil he was brewing. He decided that Vanderkellen should die. However, as Barker led the settlers over the little hill to assassinate Vanderkellen, they found him waiting for them. At this point, stories offered the greatest divergence. Some said that Vanderkellen had spent the day digging their graves, and Barker and the settlers fell dead at the site. Other versions mentioned a horrific storm that lasted from three to forty days, killing them all. There were also fire stories, plague stories, and stories of spontaneous combustion. The similarity they all shared was the curse Barker placed on Vanderkellen and his descendants.

Supposedly, after this event, Vanderkellen buried Barker and the settlers next to his church and used his life savings to mark their graves as a reminder to any future cult leaders. Real history refuted this: It was actually a survivor of the commune who replaced the original wooden markers with marble and erected the church. Although historians postulate otherwise, it was widely believed that Vanderkellen stayed in the area and had children. Since that day, each generation of Vanderkellens suffer a plague of death.

Those were the stories Leslie grew up with, and accepted despite the obvious flaws. On that muggy night, the idea of a supernatural massacre seemed very real and very possible to her. What had been mild trepidation on Hopeful Road turned into full-blown terror on Nepowa. It was odd she felt that way; it wasn't the first time she'd come here, however it was her first trip after dark. She began wondering what on earth a bunch of kids from Miltonville were doing out here, on the very grounds that Barker swore his oath. Gravel crunched under the tires, pinging off the sides of the truck. She realized how exposed she was riding in the truck bed. It was wide-open claustrophobia. Everyone was talking, there was laughter, the radio was loud, but all she heard was silence. They pulled off in front of the church. She was trembling, the air around her both still and charged.

Seven people scrambled out of the truck. Leslie didn't move. They hooted and teased her, but she would not get out. They wanted to go into the cemetery. Through the trees, she saw the white head-stones on the hill glowing in the moonlight.

"No," she said, and at last they realized she meant it.

Amy West shared Leslie's fear, although to a lesser degree, and she was also wearing open toe sandals, so she volunteered to stay at the truck with Leslie. They climbed into the cab to wait, windows wound up tightly, the doors locked. Leslie sat on the driver's side because it was farther from the cemetery, yet she leaned forward against the steering wheel so she could see. Amy chattered away, talking about anything other than the present situation while they watched their shadowy friends disappear into the cemetery. Once they entered, trees obstructed the view, but Leslie still watched the gates.

She did begin to calm down, but unbeknownst to her at the time, Barry, Steve, and Gary had found a way out of the back of the cemetery, threaded their way through the trees at a crouch-run, sneaked behind the church and came out the other side. Then they crawled toward the truck from the rear. At the tailgate they split up, Barry creeping to the driver's side, Steve the passenger side, while Gary lingered at the truck bed.

When three figures emerged from the cemetery gates, Leslie recognized her friends and blew a puff of relief. At the same time, Amy said, "Do you hear something?" and then suddenly—

BAM BAM BAM BAMBAMBAMBAMBAMBAMBAM!

The truck was hit from all sides; pounding on the windows, on the doors, something heavy jumping in the bed. Leslie and Amy screamed and screamed, diving under the dash, bumping heads and elbows, inflicting injuries not discovered for hours.

The pounding stopped and gales of laughter filled the night.

Familiar laughter. Although the terror seemed to have lasted an eternity, it had actually taken place in seconds. Leslie climbed off Amy, who lay on the floor whimpering, and onto the seat. Through the window, she saw Steve, on the ground, laughing hard from his belly. Someone else was knocking on the back window, wailing 'boo,' and howling. From the floor she heard Amy say, "I hate them." Leslie opened the truck door, and without getting out - and ignoring everyone, for they were all in on the joke, she figured, which is why they conveniently came back when they did - she screamed at them. No one could decipher what she screamed, least of all Leslie, but it was too the affect of "All right, you ruffians. I've had enough fun and I'd like to go home now."

Amy recovered quickly, giggling as the story was recounted. Not Leslie. She refused to step out of the truck cab until they dropped her off at home. Mary wasn't really happy that Leslie sat between her and Gary, but Leslie wouldn't move.

No one understood why she was so mad, and Leslie wasn't certain herself. Normally, she would have loved their prank; she would have laughed and wished to do it again, like riding a roller coaster over and over. Maybe it was the humiliation, for, although she was deathly afraid of being outside in the dark at Vanderkellen, the main reason she wouldn't get out of the truck was that she had peed her pants.

That was the first night in what would become a long period of severe nightmares. Off and on for the next six months Michele and Dan awoke to Leslie crying out. On occasion Leslie would kick the walls in her sleep, trapped in a dream, until someone woke her up. If she fell back asleep too soon, the dream would return, and so would the shouting or pounding. It became a real problem, but when Dan mentioned counseling Leslie pronounced herself cured. Eventually the dreams did fade, and she learned to control herself when they resurfaced, which they occasionally did. In fact, she had one just last week. She thought about telling Anna now, but the timing wasn't right.

"You're awfully quiet," Anna observed. Leslie turned the old Maverick onto Hopeful Road.

"Anything good in there?" Leslie pointed at the notebook.

"I'm not sure yet. I don't think any of it applies to Vanderkellen. This is your trip."

Leslie's heart jumped at the word "Vanderkellen." Only a little, though, she noticed. Daylight made a world of difference. But the sun was beginning to sink.

The woods were just ahead, so she slowed Bret down. Nepowa was easy to miss. There was a slight dip, and then there it was. Leslie turned slowly onto the gravel road, more out of concern for Bret's delicate condition than any dread. Overhead, branches formed a dense canopy, which broke at the churchyard where Leslie pulled over into the grass, very close to the place where she had once waited fearfully in a locked truck.

"There's been people out here," Anna said after getting out of the car. "Look at all the tire tracks." There were, on both sides of the road, haphazard patterns of mashed grass and dirt ruts.

"Maureen's friends?" Leslie asked. She was relieved to discover she wasn't afraid. Not of ghosts and certainly not of Maureen's friends.

Anna shrugged. "Let's go look at the church."

"It's always locked," Leslie told her, wading through the tall grass. Wistfully remembering the boots that she left on Bret's backseat, she realized she was more worried about snakes and ticks than ghoulish hands coming out of the ground.

She didn't particularly want to go into the church, not out of terror of the unknown, but from a basic fear of rats and rotting floorboards. The original wooden exterior of the building had been replaced by brick veneer not long after it was built. There were no windows, and it was kept solidly locked, although it was frequently broken into. Boards were nailed across the heavy door and a thick chain wound though the handles. Inscribed in a cornerstone was "Vanderkellen House, EST 1798", and beneath that, in smaller letters was "Here shall he, the wicked cease."

"I guess that means stay out," Leslie said.

"Speak for yourself," Anna said. She mounted the steps.

"You'll never get in. I'm going to look for a peephole," Leslie told her. She wandered halfway around the building before Anna caught up with her.

"No luck?" Leslie asked.

Anna shook her head. "That door won't budge. No peepholes?"

"You see me peeping?"

They walked up the slope to the cemetery, both noticing the beaten path through the grass leading to the gates. "What a weird place to party," Anna said.

"There must not have been a lot of people in that commune," Leslie commented, not really wanting to discuss why people partied there.

"More than a hundred, I think."

"Doesn't look like a hundred graves."

"Do you really think they all died right here?"

"Well," Leslie hedged, "what do you think happened?"

Anna squatted to inspect a worn inscription with her fingers. "I always thought Vanderkellen might have been as crazy as Barker. Maybe he killed a bunch of them, shot them or something, I don't know. I don't think they just fell over dead. There're probably as many of Barker's descendants in Amberly County as there are Vanderkellen's."

"That's another thing," Leslie said, reluctant to wander far from Anna. "Why aren't there any Vanderkellens around? I've looked in the phone book and there aren't any."

"I don't know. Maybe he only had girls. What difference does it make?"

"The curse. And that's another thing. How come the Itch only happens in Amberly County? And mostly in Miltonville? You know his descendants are everywhere by now..." Leslie stopped when Anna turned, still squatting, one eyebrow raised.

"So you're saying you do believe in it?"

"Well, I don't know. It killed my mother."

"But you used to say you didn't believe in it."

"I said I didn't know. What's the big deal what I believe, anyway?" Leslie said, then walked off, leaving Anna in her squat, one hand on the tombstone for balance.

Pretending to examine a grave marker, Leslie admonished herself for being snippy with Anna. Confusion was hard enough to live with, let alone try to explain. The truth was she had never been sure what she believed. In Miltonville, Itch believers were considered to be hicks or dim, no matter how closely they were related to a victim. Anna didn't ridicule the notion because of Leslie's mother, but neither did she encourage it, so Leslie rarely mentioned it. When she talked to her father about it, which was less than seldom, he said the Itch didn't kill Holly, Steve Paulin did. Maybe technically Leslie did not believe in the Itch, but being Leslie, she wanted to. It's one thing to be shot by a drug addict, but quite another to die as the result of a two hundred year old curse. It didn't hurt as much to blame the Itch as it did to blame Margo Gentry and Steve Paulin or anyone else. To dwell on Margo actually luring Holly to her house, planning to kill her, made Leslie boil inside. It made her hateful and angry and led her nowhere. But the Itch was inevitable, intangible and her mother accidentally found herself in its path. That was it. Period. No hate. Fate.

Leslie, daydreaming, had trudged toward the back of the cemetery, and was almost to the farthest corner. She had just begun to realize how far away Anna was when something tugged at her foot. Looking down, she saw her foot sinking into a grave. Her stomach leapt.

Screaming, she sank to her calf, and fell forward, scrambling away, leaving her shoe behind. There was barely time for her to rationalize, but once she was free, she had understood exactly what happened. A hand had not reached up through the dirt to pull her into a grave. She had stepped into a weak place, maybe an animal burrow. Just as the thought registered, she saw she had crawled onto a rotting, headless bird.

By now Anna was there, asking over and over "What? What?"

"Look...oh...geez...look," Leslie said.

"Ohmigosh," Anna drew back from the bird. Leslie wiped her knee in grass that was wet with evening dew.

"It's a bird, isn't it? I put my knee in it," Leslie cried, still wiping furiously. "Don't tell me if there are maggots. I don't want to know." It suddenly occurred to her that there may be more birds lying around, and she was missing a shoe. What if she stepped on one? "I lost my shoe!"

"Where?" Anna looked around.

"In a hole, right there," she directed, not wanting to set her bare foot down.

"Oh!" Anna retrieved it. "No wonder you screamed."

"I didn't scream. It was a...a shout," she corrected.

Anna handed her the shoe. "We really ought to be careful, you know. These old graves can cave in—" She stopped, then brushed past Leslie. "Look."

Freshly shod, Leslie joined her. A tombstone had been pushed over and lay hidden in the tall grass. Drawn on it was a pentagram freckled with brown splatters.

"Blood?" Leslie asked

"Probably. Look there." She pointed toward the back corner of the cemetery. The grass was trampled around the sooty remains of a fire.

"Well, let me..." Leslie began, but Anna was tilting her head.

"Do you hear a car?" Anna asked.

Leslie listened, uncertain, but noticing that sky was turning orange as the day grew late. In the distance she heard it. Her heart thumped.

"Maureen's friends?" she gasped.

Without answering, Anna grabbed Leslie's arm and they ran. Leslie, who hadn't run as far as the corner mailbox in years, couldn't keep up, and Anna let go, shouting "Hurry! Hurry!" as she ran. Panic was one reaction Leslie rarely saw in Anna, and it made the situation even more frightening. She picked up her pace in case Anna reached the car first and had ideas of leaving her behind.

Ahead, she saw Anna sprint through the gates and veer left toward the car. Anna was running so fast she could hardly stop, and slammed into the side of Bret. Barely regaining balance, she yanked on the door handle.

"The keys! The keys are locked in the car!" she shouted at Leslie, who was, by this time, well within speaking distance.

Leslie tried to say "No, they aren't," but she was panting too hard. Shaking her head, she circled Bret as quickly as she was able, and was about to open the door when she saw Anna preparing to smash the window with her elbow.

"Stop!" she managed, and pulled open her unlocked door. She crawled across the seat and popped up the lock on Anna's side. This seemed to calm Anna slightly, although she pushed Leslie roughly out of the way.

Once safely inside the car, Leslie began to relax despite her wildly beating heart. It was tempting to pretend Bret wouldn't start, but seeing Anna had been willing to break her own elbow to get inside, she probably wouldn't hesitate to break Leslie's arm.

Bret started on the first try. They pulled onto the road, and were stopping to turn on Mindell when Anna, sitting backwards, said, "I think I see a car. Hurry up."

They turned on Mindell, and after a few miles felt sure they weren't being followed. Soon they were both laughing.

"I can't believe I was so scared!" Anna marveled, not sounding scared at all.

"Me either. How dumb. I mean, what were they going to do to us?"

"Human sacrifice!" Anna laughed.

"Us poor virgins! We don't get any breaks."

"Like you have anything to worry about!"

"I told you I didn't do anything! And you better not let Alan hear you talking about this. Next thing you know he'll say, 'Anna, if you sleep with me, you'll never be sacrificed.'"

"Oh, leave him alone. He's suffering enough. Maybe it's time I gave him a break."

"Excuse me?" Leslie slowed the car too quickly. "You're not! Not with Anal!"

"Don't call him Anal, okay? This isn't a joke. I might marry him, you know. He's mentioned it."

"Well if you're going to marry him, then what's the hurry? Ick, my skin is crawling!"

"I knew you wouldn't be any help."

"I'm trying. Look, you know how well I get along with him. What do you expect me to say?"

"I don't know. Just forget it."

"Forget it? I don't think so."

Anna sighed. "Don't worry. Nothing's going to happen anytime soon. I have to pee, let's go home," she said, changing the subject.

***

Whit Stewart and Rubin Tanner saw the old Maverick turning off of Nepowa Road.

"Who's that?" Rubin asked, driving the truck right up to the cemetery gates. Had the posts been two feet wider he would have driven right in.

"Unh uh," Whit grunted. "Didn't see it good."

They went behind the truck and dropped the tailgate. Whit reached in and tugged at a cooler. Each took a handle and, carrying it between them, they walked into the cemetery.

"When you reckon we oughta get the fire started?" Rubin said, short of breath from the heavy load and the slight hill.

"Soon I guess. It's gettin' dark. He better be grateful," Whit complained. "We didn't agree on no Thursdays."

"Why you gripin'?" Rubin panted. "I'm the one has to work tomorrow. He ever say why the meeting's tonight?" They reached the farthest corner, a few yards from where Leslie fell, and set the cooler down.

"A test of obedience." Whit imitated Troy Ivers's authoritative tone.

"Don't see why it can't wait 'till Saturday." Rubin opened the cooler and raised an icy can of beer. "Oh well, it's his party."

Whit grabbed a can before Rubin closed the lid. For a moment the two of them sat on the cooler, sipping beers, catching their breath. They were both in their late twenties, too young to be so winded. Both were skinny and soft, covered in multiple, poorly done tattoos. Rubin, who had a job, kept them covered at the request of his boss. He also shaved and had a regular haircut, whereas Whit was proud of his long hair and wore a big droopy mustache that added ten years to his features.

"Don't get no better than this," Whit said, finishing his beer.

"I'll be darned," Rubin said. "What is that?"

Whit looked in the same direction as Rubin. Not far away, a cloud was coming out of the ground. An angry cloud, it rose to about six feet, stretching and rolling, as if someone were inside fighting to get out. With the sun barely peeking over the hill, the cloud shone with dull light against the shadowy tombstones around it.

"What the—?" Rubin asked, not expecting an answer.

"Do you think it's some kind of gas leak?" Whit's voice was low and tense, indicating that *he* didn't think it was a gas leak.

Rubin said, "What kind of gas?" just to say something. He regretted it, because of the way his own voice sounded.

"I say we go," Whit said, and Rubin silently agreed. Together they left, not running as Anna and Leslie had, but with more haste than they would ever care to admit. They hurried through the gate, and jumped into the truck.

"Wait!" Rubin said. "The rest of the stuff!" Troy's equipment was still in the bed of the truck. If they took off with it, then, well, it was out of the question. It had to be unloaded.

Moving with quick, quiet speed, it took less than five minutes to pile Troy's tools - his wand, his robes, the gasoline, the candles and the skulls - beside the gates. There were also three cartons of wood and two more coolers. Occasionally one of them would look up the hill and confirm to the other that the cloud was still there.

"Phosphorous, probably," Whit guessed, though he doubted phosphorus would make his heart pound so.

"Or methane," Rubin offered.

"Could be dangerous." Whit tossed the last crate of wood to the ground, nodded to Rubin and they left in such a hurry they didn't even bother to shut the tailgate.

***

Inside the cloud, John Barker seethed. The Vanderkellen had been there, so close. Her presence was more stifling than Claire's, her odor more foul. To his delight, he discovered that, although the Vanderkellen's senses were sharp, she had learned to ignore them. Humans! How did they survive when they taught themselves to bury their instincts?

What a relief to know that he would not need Walter Brandenburg's help after all. Hah! Oaf! His incredible opportunity completely blundered! While he did impress Barker with his daring escape, Walter foiled himself with his eagerness, once again proving to Barker what a fool he was. Just as well. Barker couldn't endure an eternity of being thankful to Walter.

His pleasure grew as the Vanderkellen approached, and the forces that held him weakened. Being close to her gave him incredible strength, and he pulled himself higher, like climbing out of a hole. He was almost disappointed that, after all these years, after all the mistakes and humiliation, it would be this simple. Next to him, Claire trembled with anticipation.

Then, abruptly, it was over. The Vanderkellen sensed him, and her fear sent out a spark so bright it caught him off guard. Her terror pierced his stomach and he struggled to hold onto the place he had reached. He felt himself falling, but he clutched at the darkness. He held. He pulled fiercely.

He saw.

For a brief, exquisite moment, he glimpsed two young women running away. His strength fled with them. How did she know? Did the blasted Wethacanwee warn her? They weren't allowed! It was a rule!

As he slid away from the earth, he heard the familiar drone of car engines, one coming, one going. He realized then her fear had not been because of him. Of course it wasn't. She didn't know he existed. Someone was coming. That's why she ran. Barker knew what went on at the cemetery, things that would frighten most young women, even a wretched Vanderkellen. His opportunity gone, rage burst open his chest. The anger exploded and worked as a fuel. He gained another inch. His frustration built on his anger and he gained yet another inch.

He saw them. Not clearly, but as if looking through water. Two men drinking beer. Another inch, another inch. He begged Claire to help. Another inch and he'd kill them.

To his surprise, they saw him too. They looked at him, then each other, and then back at him, before making a speedy retreat. What did they see? Barker wondered. He had assumed he was invisible until he had a body. How he would have loved to have taken one of theirs! He would use it to kill the other. They were still close, he thought, though he really couldn't see them anymore. He pushed and pulled, desperate to escape, but soon he heard them driving off, leaving him behind to curse and kill them in his mind, over and over again.

***

Ryan Swift sat in the dark of the Canwell's backyard, sulking. He'd just gotten into a fight with Robby, started it actually, and had stomped off. With nowhere to go, he sat on the picnic table. When the porch light came on he flinched, not wanting to be seen. The light bathed him, however, and he looked away when MC Canwell stepped outside.

"Ryan?" she asked. When he didn't answer, she came closer and repeated his name. No answer. She sat on the other side of the table.

"I'm sorry Robby's not wanting to do much tonight. He worked today you know, and he's not used to—"

"Everybody's always working," Ryan cut in.

"Oh," Mrs. Canwell said. Silence, then: "Ryan, do you know why your mom works so much?"

"I guess to get away from me," he muttered.

"No, honey. That's not what she wants. A lot of things have changed at your house. When your dad lived there, there was plenty of money. Now your mom has to make all the money, and until she finds a good job, she has to work these odd hours. It won't be forever. She's having a rough time right now. The car keeps breaking down, and she told me today that something is wrong with the water heater. That's why your mom has been sad lately."

"Dad gives her money. I've seen it."

"Yes, but that's for your clothes, school supplies, food. The things he bought for you when he lived there."

"She can keep that money. I don't need all that stuff. Besides, Dad buys me junk all the time. Why can't she use it?"

"Ryan, have they explained this to you? Any of it?"

Ryan looked at her blankly.

"Well, anyway, it's not easy to find a good job, one that pays a nice salary and has medical benefits. And since your mom didn't get to finish college, it's even harder for her."

"Oh." They were quiet for a while, then Ryan asked, "Mrs. Canwell? Did Mom have to drop out of school because of me?"

"No. Why?"

"I heard Dad tell Teena that."

"She quit to get a job so your father could finish college. It took him a long time. By then, you were here, and all she wanted to do was be a mom. Anyway, my point is that your mom is tired and sad and frustrated, honey. Try not to be too mad at her, she didn't want any of this to happen."

"I know."

"If you need to, you know you can always come here. Okay?"

"Okay."

"How about a can of pop and a game of fish?"

"Okay."

They had just dealt the first hand when Cindy knocked at the door, early, ready to take Ryan home.

***

The argument Leslie and Anna had about Alan disintegrated into distasteful joking before moving on to other, lighter topics. They ended up laughing so hard during their ride back from the cemetery, that they didn't think they would make it to a bathroom in time. They were tired and silly, making up lyrics to all ready ridiculous pop songs on the radio, putting more pressure on their aching bladders. There was no way they could hold out all the way to Anna's house. Leslie's house was on the way, so they stopped there, parking on the street because Uncle Ralph had come and left the camper in the driveway. As they ran inside, Leslie pointed out Mrs. Geist across the street, peeking out her window. Anna slapped her arm down, giggling. "Stop it! I have to pee!"

In the house, Michele Vickers was folding towels at the coffee table while Becky read to Dan. As soon as Becky heard the door she bounced up and down in his lap, and her father's face twisted in agony as she squished and squashed him.

"She's home! She's home," she shouted. Dan put a finger to his lips, and she shushed.

"Where have you two been?" Michele asked, and if Leslie hadn't been so preoccupied with getting to the bathroom, she would have noticed the lilt in her voice, and certainly Becky's gleeful animation at her return. But Leslie had to pee, and right now she needed to beat Anna to the bathroom. Lucky for her, Anna was polite and paused to answer Michele. Leslie took the opportunity and bolted down the hall. Behind her, she heard Becky laughing.

When she flipped on the light switch, she met the reflection of a thin man in the mirror and she screamed for the second time that day. Backing out the door, she understood the situation too late.

Bruce was back. Same wig, same clothes, same chipped nose, same intense eyes. He was leaning casually against the wall, staring at her, an unlit cigarette between his stiff fingers. She felt his eyes, just like before. He hadn't changed.

By now Anna was behind her, and Becky's shrill laughter, mixed with that of Dan and Michele, filled the narrow hallway. There was a strangeness to the moment as old fears resurfaced.

"Is that Bruce?" Anna asked.

"Yeah," Becky said, "Uncle Ralph brung him over. Gotcha Les!" She latched on to Leslie's arm, jumping in circles.

"I'm going to use Mom and Dad's bathroom," Leslie said, ignoring them.

A few minutes later, relieved and a great deal more relaxed, she stood washing her hands and tried to remember Bruce. Why was she so afraid of him, anyway? Did it have something to do with the ouiji, or a seance? She stared at herself in the mirror, biting her lip, trying to force the memory, but it wouldn't come. It was close though, and she was sure it would be in her journal, although in those days she may have called it a diary.

Anna knocked on the door. "Are you about done? I'm in pain."

"Oh," Leslie said, still distracted, and opened the door. "Why didn't you use the other one?"

"Not in front of Bruce."

"What was it that happened to him? Do you remember?"

"You and Lisa said he was possessed, I remember that. I think he just fell over at a bad time or something, and scared you guys."

"Yeah..." Leslie squinted at herself.

Anna bumped her away from the mirror so she could wash her hands. "Aren't we pretty?" Leslie's ponytail had worked itself loose and hair hung every which way around her face. Even Anna's normally tidy hair was straggly, and she used Michele's brush to smooth it. Leslie rather liked her hair billowy, so she left it alone.

"You wanna go uptown?" Thursday night in Miltonville didn't hold a lot of promise, but there would be a band playing at Boonie's Tavern.

"I have to get home. We have to work tomorrow," Anna reminded her. "As a matter of fact, we better go."

As they left the bathroom Anna said, "If you want, you can stay at my house while your parents are gone."

"What?"

"I mean because of Bruce. If you don't want to stay here with him," she said uneasily.

"Thanks." Leslie was not surprised by the offer, but the fact that Anna actually felt a need to extend it was disconcerting. "Does he bother you too?"

"No. Well, yeah. Like you said, he's creepy. I wouldn't want to stay here with him."

Leslie nodded and they went back into the living room where the television had become the center of attention.

"Bruce didn't scare you, did he?" Dan asked them.

"Yes," Anna admitted at the same time Leslie said, "No."

"Bull!" Becky yelled at her.

"Rebecca!" both parents yelled.

"She screamed," Becky said.

"It was a shout," Anna winked.

"I was startled," Leslie defended herself.

"Well, that's over. Now can we get rid of him?" Michele said.

"No, no!" Becky cried.

"Yes, yes," Leslie said.

"Les, you used to like him," Dan said. "I don't understand."

"Me either, Dad, but I agree with Mom." She sat on the arm of the chair and put her arm around his shoulder.

"It's two against two," Becky said.

"Not if you count the neighbors," Michele said. "I don't think they were very crazy about him."

"Is that why we got rid of him? Didn't—" Leslie wondered.

"Robby! It was something to do with him." Dan put a finger to his lips, looking at Becky.

"I hate to break this up," Anna nudged Leslie, "but I have to get home."

"Take care, Anna," Michele said. She picked up a stack of towels and stopped suddenly. "Oh! Les, would you take the trash cans down to the curb?"

"Sure," Leslie said.

"Thanks. We're scattered tonight," she explained to Anna.

"Oh yeah. I'll bet you're excited, Becky."

"When isn't she?" Leslie said, waiting at the door.

"We have to stay at Grandma's first," Becky moaned.

When Anna looked puzzled, Dan said, "We're going to spend the night with Michele's mother tomorrow."

"Then we're going to get up real early and go to the Galaxy. We might stay there two days," Becky finished for him.

"Well, have fun," Anna tugged Becky's ponytail, and Becky put her arms around Anna's waist.

"Take care of Leslie," Becky said.

Anna promised she would, then went out to help Leslie drag the trash cans down the driveway.

***

Dottie Geist peered from behind her curtains.

"There they go again. That's trouble, them two," she informed Artie. He glanced away from the television then right back.

"Yup," he agreed not caring what he agreed with.

"Spoiled. That's what it is. Dan feeling all guilty over dumping that kid off on his folks while he was out living it up."

This wasn't quite true, and although Artie knew it, he learned long ago to nod occasionally when Dottie talked. There was a greater chance she might shut up than if he conversed with her. And absolutely never did he disagree. So Artie nodded.

"What I can't believe," she continued, "is that Judy Redmond doesn't keep a shorter leash on her kid. Probably she can't do nothin' though, with her husband gone all the time doing who knows what."

"He's a truck driver," Artie said, and quickly regretted it. It just slipped out. Now he was engaged in a conversation with Dottie. Great.

"Yeah," she clucked. "We know what that means. We saw that show on truck stop hookers. Remember?"

Artie sighed and nodded.

"Anyway, I tried to tell Dan about that girl." Indeed she had, much to Artie's embarrassment. Once she marched right across the street when she saw Dan Vickers leaving for work. She told him that a reliable source had seen Leslie in Boonie's Tavern. "And what did he have to say about that?" Dottie said while reliving the event. "'Well, she eats there sometimes.' I said, 'Good girls do not eat in a saloon, Dan.' Someday he'll be sorry he didn't listen to me."

Then, as now, Artie nodded, sorry that he did have to listen to her.

***

Walter Brandenburg was so excited he could fancy his heart beating. Fancy was the best he could do because he had no actual heart. Yet, he felt the pulse beating madly in his chest, his neck, his ears. Pounding that grew wilder with her proximity. When her eyes touched him, the pounding increased until he thought the plaster encasing him would explode. The Vanderkellen! No mistake. No wasted time. This morning nasty little Thebis came and told him the guarding forces around her were gone, but he already knew it. After years spent in a near catatonic state, the sensation of her departing protectors felt much like gradually awaking to a far away noise only to find it was actually a knocking at the door. Tonight, she stood close. Finally it would end, and he would be the one to end it. No more would John Barker regard him as a fool.

Anxiety boiled beneath his excitement when he thought of Barker. Behind the presence of the Vanderkellen, as awesome as it was, another power was building, a rageful force, rage focused in part at him. Rage that would soon become the respect - respect he had sought from John Barker since the first time they met. His yearning for that respect bound him to Barker, and it was a stronger bond than either of them had with Claire, although Barker assumed she was the reason Walter had been imprisoned with him.

Walter had no marriage with Claire. If so, she would not be carrying Barker's child. In fact, if not for that baby, Claire undoubtedly would have died long ago.

Inside the mannequin that had been his prison for the last four years, Walter Brandenburg smiled. The ugly wig fell off.

***

Troy Ivers drove Whit Stewart's car up Nepowa Road an hour before the meeting was scheduled in order to make the preparations and have a couple of beers with Rubin and Whit. He could see from the road that the fire had not yet been started, and thought it curious. In the darkness it wasn't immediately apparent that Rubin's truck was not there, but when he pulled up to the cemetery gates, his headlights shone on the abandoned boxes and the coolers. Troy left the car and scanned his surroundings visually and audially. Nothing but moon shadows and night insects. Whit and Rubin were gone. Without wondering why, Troy put his foot on a cooler and leaned on his knee, breathing deeply for control. He was mad, very mad about this. Even more so, he felt the initial prick of alarm. How could he carry this off without Whit? Deep breath. One thing at a time. He surveyed the equipment at his feet, straining to see the far corner of the cemetery. His stomach tumbled. Fear? No, he assured himself, that wasn't a twinge of fear, but rather anticipation. Put it aside, he thought. Right now he had work to do. It was a short distance up the hill, and there would be several trips. Maybe he could wait for the other members to arrive, some were always early. No, that was a bad idea. To ask the members for help would diminish his authority over them. Instead, he retrieved a flashlight from the glove compartment and carried one of the cartons of wood through the dark cemetery. The hand holding the flashlight also stretched around the handle of the gas can, aching miserably, but he did not stop until he reached the corner. He was surprised to find a cooler already there. Maybe someone came while Whit and Rubin were setting up and scared them away. It didn't matter, and Troy didn't have time to worry about them. For now it was enough to know that, wherever they had gone, they were worrying about him.

He found the spot where the last fire had been, dumped the wood, carton and all, and doused it with gasoline. Once it was blazing, he went back for another carton of wood and hefted it to his shoulder, the whole time fantasizing about the various ways he could terrorize Whit and Rubin. He fed the wood to the fire and smashed the carton. The fire looked good. Troy ran his fingers over his lips, smelling the gasoline. Next, he brought the boxes containing his clothes, the books, candles and other supplies. He took the robe and hung it over a tombstone, laid the hood over the top, then checked his watch. Just past ten. Plenty of time, but still he should hurry. All that was left to bring up the hill were the two coolers and another carton of wood. The coolers were heavy, but he managed, at times dragging them, the flashlight leading him around the headstones, the fire his beacon. When he had everything up the hill, he paused to gulp a beer and feed the fire. He still wasn't sure how he would run the meeting without Whit. He held to the hope that Whit would return in time. If not, well, perhaps he would hide in the darkness until the members were stoned and dazed. They would see the coolers and help themselves, wondering at first what was going on, but soon they would relax. He would hide and listen. Let them drink and smoke and talk. Not a bad idea. What did they think of him? What did they think of each other? Their conversation would dictate how he would later present himself. It could prove interesting. Or maybe a disaster! What if they made fun of him? What if—he stopped the thoughts. There would be only serious members here tonight, anyway, with the meeting being on Thursday. Usually it was held on the fourth Saturday of the month, but he had to visit his mother in Toledo for her birthday that weekend.

Looking around, he marked off his mental checklist. Satisfied, he put on the robe and sat on a tent chair to wait. He was beginning to relax, enjoying the snapping fire, thinking of the evening to come, when he realized that he had forgotten the tank. Again, he went down the hill, speedier this time, his hood in hand, aware that any minute a car could turn onto Nepowa. He could not be seen without his hood, his mask. He would lose his dental practice!

From the trunk of Whit's car, he took the tank of nitrous oxide. This would be tucked away until very late, when all but his most special students were gone. It went well with alcohol and marijuana. Troy didn't allow stronger drugs at his meetings; he wanted the group to be mellow with just a tinge of paranoia, not hallucinating or rowdy. That would ruin the mood, upset the tempo. Patting the tank, he sat it on the ground. He had to slam the lid to Whit's trunk several times before it latched. Whit's car was a piece of junk, but Troy had to drive it to the meetings because his Jaguar was too recognizable.

He just made it back with the tank when he heard a car approaching on Hopeful. It had better be Whit, but perhaps, he thought wistfully, it was Jaime. It would be nice to spend some time with her. Smiling at the ideas her image conjured up, he tucked the tank in the weeds along the fence. Then he sighed; even if it was her, it was unlikely she was alone. They traveled in packs, these girls. A couple of them, he had known since they were little children coming in with their mothers for their first dental check ups. Most were from Westerville or went to the university, which is the way he wanted it. The hitch in his heartbeat that came each time he saw one of his flock outside of the cemetery reminded him of how much trouble he would be in should this secret existence be revealed. Discovery might close his practice, but he was more afraid of his other activities being exposed. Not that he was frightened of prison. No, prison would be an island vacation in contrast to the alternative, and more likely event, of being permanently silenced by his 'associates'.

This, however, was worth the risk. He had no idea what he was doing, no formula to follow, no ideology to embrace. It was an act, but it worked. Tonight fifteen or twenty lost and lonely people would come searching for anything to fill their empty hearts and feed their hungry souls. Some were desperate, some were lazy, most were terribly confused and misled. From him they heard answers, prophesies, insights, anything they wanted to hear, because he kept his message general enough to apply to all. In return, they responded to him, respected him, did whatever he wished, and he did have a few fantastic wishes. They submitted, for by the time the ceremony was over, they were too high and too afraid or too enchanted to protest. Most kept coming back. They believed in Troy, or Master, as they knew him. When good things happened, it was because of him; when bad things happened, it was because of him. He pumped them up, brought them down, gave them answers, orders, advice, always whispered to Whit, whom the group respectfully called Messenger. This was done in part for drama and to enhance the mystery, but also, in a much larger part, so that Troy's high-pitched voice could not be identified.

49

Hearing the approaching car, Troy reconciled the possibility that tonight he might be alone, and even if he waited until the group became incoherent, he would still, eventually, have to say something, or else they may never return. He spoke aloud, using different tones and levels. Maybe he would just shout gruffly. Maybe he could fake speaking a different language? Tongues, maybe? Hmm.

Seeing headlights, he tightened his jaw and willed it to be Whit, but again he found thoughts of Jaime interfering. Be Whit, be Whit, be Whit, he chanted silently, though he knew it would not work, and he would be better off practicing his gruff shouts and moody whispers.

"Welcome. Welcome," he rehearsed in a breathy voice. He sounded like a lusty starlet. He lowered his voice. "Welcome, children." Not too bad. He'd say little and use a lot of gestures. It would work. He would have to deal severely with Whit and Rubin later. Even if the evening went perfectly, they must not be allowed to think he would forgive them. He couldn't let them off; he had to keep them in fear, although it wasn't likely that either would turn on him. Not with the information Troy held.

Their relationship began the year before, after Troy learned of the disappearance of a young man from Westerville named Howard. Howard was doing some work indirectly for one of Troy's affiliates and one day Howard didn't come home. His mother reported him missing and his car was found parked at a highway rest area. The police performed the routine missing person procedures, but being familiar with Howard, they believed, as did many, that he was in trouble and had run off. Calvert, the man Troy did sly business with by helping clean up Calvert's income, wanted to find Howard, too. Calvert was to meet with Troy the day Howard disappeared, but called to cancel because, as he said, this kid Howard missed his appointment. Calvert was very angry because the kid was carrying two thousand of his dollars, in addition to a huge rock of cocaine. Troy found this all delightful. Math was not his strong point but he could add two and two. He knew where Howard had been, and with whom he had been. Now, he only had to find out what happened. He didn't share this with Calvert, he only told him to call when he needed assistance and left it at that.

It couldn't be called pure luck or coincidence that Troy knew where Howard would be the day of his missed appointment. Troy spent many hours blending into the background, listening and observing, mostly for entertainment. One particular Monday evening last summer, Troy sat alone in a booth at Boonie's Tavern, drinking a beer and pretending to read a magazine. As was his habit, he scrunched into a corner, his small body pressed against a wall, his plain face hidden in his own shadows, his eyes occasionally rising to look about. The tavern was in its after dinner slump, with only one couple occupying a table and a few men at the bar, Rubin Tanner among them, watching television. Whit Stewart came in and waved Rubin over to a booth. High wooden dividers separated the booths, and Dr. Troy Ivers held his breath, trying to become invisible. They sat a few booths behind him, in the back corner. Casually, Troy took his magazine and went to the bar for another beer. He headed back toward the direction of his original seat, but once out of their eyesight, he slipped unnoticed into the booth closest to them. Troy Ivers loved to eavesdrop. It was a passion, a habit, an obsession that he couldn't let go. A seemingly trivial nugget may later prove valuable, even though he'd never mined anything richer than Luther Noble's affair with his secretary. Still, one should never pass up an opportunity, and on this night he did hear a nugget, though at the time it meant nothing. Whit had set up a deal with a guy named Howard, and they were to meet him at a Westerville rest stop the next day, at ten AM. Rubin didn't want to go because he had to work, but Whit didn't trust Howard and wouldn't go alone. Troy had the impression before ever hearing the conversation that Whit generally had his way, so, after listening to them argue for a while, he became bored and left.

The following morning, Dr. Ivers periodically peered out the window of his Main Street office to the service station on the corner where Rubin worked, curious to see if Whit had won the argument. Around nine thirty, Whit pulled in and had a brief discussion with Al, Rubin's boss. Al scratched his chin, and shaking his head, he went into the garage and emerged a moment later with Rubin. Rubin's hand was on his forehead, and he was also shaking his head. Al patted him on the back, then Rubin climbed in Whit's car and they drove away. Troy wondered what kind of excuse they devised to get Rubin out of the station. Whatever it was, it had been effective. Then the hygienist knocked on his door to let him know his nine thirty was ready and he forgot about Whit and Rubin until later, when Calvert told him that Howard had disappeared with a big stash. Troy kept an eye on the service station, but didn't see Rubin any more that day. The next day, though, Rubin was at work, and Troy had a busy day so he didn't think about it much. A few days later, when he spoke with Calvert on another matter, Calvert told him Howard's car had been impounded, having been left at the rest area and that the girlfriend was afraid something bad had happened. Troy said nothing, only asking if maybe the kid had run off.

"Didn't seem the type," Calvert said. "If he did, he better keep going."

Troy agreed absently, preoccupied with his ideas.

On Friday evening, Troy went back to Boonie's because Rubin was sure to be there. Patti Anne, a pretty woman with puffy blond hair and long pink nails, tended Boonie's bar. Her jeans were tight and her heels were high and everyone knew Rubin was hopelessly in love. He stayed at her trailer most of the time, and if she was on duty at Boonie's, he would be on a barstool. Patti Anne was old enough to be his mother, and he seemed to give her that kind of respect, along with awe and disbelief that a creature as perfect as she would have anything to do with him.

So it had been easy for Troy to find Rubin. He carefully chose a stool close by and ordered a drink. It was early, six thirty, and the tavern was quiet. Patti Anne was watching the news on the television behind the bar and Rubin was watching Patti Anne. He looked very sad.

Playing nonchalant, Troy said to no one in particular, but carefully addressing Rubin, "I'm trying to find someone to fix up an old car for me."

Patti Anne jerked a thumb toward Rubin. "He's a mechanic."

Rubin nodded. "What kind of car?"

"Nova. 72 or 3. It's old."

Rubin took the bait, and started asking questions. It was easy for Troy to act ignorant because he really knew nothing about cars. He teased Rubin with vague information: it had a big block, whatever that was, a V8, and big tires. He told him it was black with white stripes running down the middle and had a jacked-up rear end. He was actually describing a car he used to see loudly cruising the streets of Miltonville. It had made a big impression on other people that reminded Troy of Rubin.

"Where'd you get it?" Rubin was obviously trying not to appear interested.

Troy looked around, embarrassed. "I won it in a card game. Can you fix it? I'm probably going to sell it, but I'm sure it's worth more if it's running."

"I'll look at it," Rubin said with an exaggerated shrug. They arranged for him to come to Troy's house the next morning, and Troy bought him a beer.

"You ain't buying that car," Patti Anne told Rubin, stopping the discussion before it began. Troy left after giving Rubin directions to his house.

The next day, Troy sat on his porch watching Rubin's truck come up the long dirt drive. He didn't get up, but waved for Rubin to join him.

"Beer?" he offered, despite the early hour.

"Sure."

He motioned for Rubin to follow him into the old house and told him to have a seat at the kitchen table. There was a tank of nitrous oxide beside the refrigerator and Troy took pains in making sure it caught Rubin's attention.

"Whoa, is that laughing gas?" Rubin asked hopefully.

"Oh yes. No dentist should be without it. You like it?" He sat a beer in front of him.

"I've never tried it."

Troy was not surprised. Even from across the room he could tell Rubin hadn't seen a dentist professionally in years.

"Want to?" He lifted the facemask and held it out.

"Maybe I should check out the Nova first," Rubin said.

"Oh, this doesn't last. Five minutes after your last hit, you're back to normal." He turned a dial and held the mask over his nose. He didn't inhale. Again he held it out.

"Doesn't it fry your brain?"

"It's not airplane glue. It's safer than that beer you're drinking."

Rubin shrugged. "Okay."

Troy placed the tank next to Rubin's chair and put the band around Rubin's head and the mask over his nose. Rubin looked up, questioningly, and Troy patted his shoulder.

"Leave it on for a while."

Troy sat opposite and lit a joint. He liked the surprise he saw on Rubin's face.

"Don't worry, nitrous isn't flammable," he laughed and passed the joint to Rubin. He pretended to be busy around the kitchen and made small talk. Rubin smoked alone, and soon he was talking and laughing. Nitrous was one of Troy's favorite toys in dentistry. He always fiddled around the examining room while a patient was being gassed and encouraged them to chat. People said the funniest things. It wasn't the same these days, since new laws required an assistant to be present. He used to love to tease the patients, especially the women. Oh, nothing to get him in trouble, just a little patting while he checked the Novocain. "Can you feel this?" he would ask, caressing her cheek, then her jaw, her neck, until she giggled and said, "Yes! I feel that!" And he would chuckle, because it was in fun, and they were not sure it was really happening anyway, not with the amount of gas they were breathing. The men he liked to intimidate by flexing his drill, making it go *whirr, whirr*, while they waited helplessly. It pleased him to watch them squirm, though it wasn't as much fun as tickling the women.

Rubin finished the joint, so Troy lit another and passed it across the table. He kept him talking, telling jokes and work anecdotes; none that actually happened to him, but rather ones he read about in dentistry trade magazines.

When Troy felt enough time had passed, he sat down.

"You know, I saw you the other day. You and your friend, Whit? Is that his name? The hairy guy?"

Rubin nodded, straining to hold a cloud of smoke in his lungs.

"Yes, I always forget his name. It doesn't suit him. But I saw you out at that rest stop, on 42, a couple of days ago. That was you with him, wasn't it?"

"Oh, uh, no." Rubin gagged as he exhaled.

"Hmm." Troy put his elbow on the table and rested his chin on his fist. "Well, according to Whit it was definitely you." Troy casually turned his hand so that his index finger pointed at Rubin. "Did you really do what he said?"

"Do what? Whit said *I* did it?" Rubin tried to stand up and almost knocked over the tank.

"Careful," Troy stood and steadied the tank, then with a hand on Rubin's shoulder he pushed him back into the chair. Rubin fumbled with the mask, but Troy knocked his hands away.

"I didn't do it! I didn't do anything!" Rubin's eyes were wide. Every time he tried to get up or take off the mask, Troy's hands were there to stop him.

Troy bit his lip and sighed, shaking his head. "I didn't say you did. But Whit told us he was there, and believe me, he's in enough trouble because of that."

"Liar!" Rubin tried to shout. Troy didn't know who Rubin was referring to, but he could see the confusion in his eyes. If he had been in the right state of mind, Rubin would have dismissed Troy's claims, and probably would have knocked him flat for suggesting Whit would say such things. But, oh, the power of the blessed drug on a sorry spirit! Troy sighed paternally to show Rubin how concerned he was.

"It was Whit! I didn't do anything. I didn't even want to go," Rubin continued. "I knew this would happen." His head sagged.

"*Whit* did it?" Troy stood back in a pose of shock.

Rubin nodded.

"Oh, but...why would—? I don't understand. What happened?" Troy asked with feigned compassion.

"That kid. Smart mouth punk." Rubin's words stumbled over each other. "I tole him. I din even wanna go! Him and this kid, they fight all a time. I din wanna go, but he came to the station. He tole Al my aunt Rita had a heart attack. You ain't never supposed to lie about that stuff, you know. Something bad'll happen."

"It's okay. Calm down. Take a deep breath, that's good. Calm down. Better?" Rubin breathed deeply of the gas and then Troy steered him back to the point. "Was there a fight?"

"Yeah. A big one. We met him and Whit wanted to try the stuff, but not there, ya know. Ride around. But we had to stop because Whit likes to shoot. So we went to Glencoe Woods." His head fell in his hands. When he raised his head, Troy could tell he was fighting himself.

"Forget what I said, man. I gotta get outta here." But he didn't move. This was so much better than Troy had expected! The least he had hoped for was that they had stolen the product from Howard, causing Howard to run rather than confront Calvert. His idea had been to scare Rubin with the threat of going to Calvert unless Rubin cooperated with him in his grand plan. Now, his plan was grander.

"Don't worry, Rubin. I'll take care of this. But as a friend, I have to tell you...Whit said you were the one shooting up, over by the lake at Glencoe, when it happened."

Rubin tried to clear his head, but it was heavy. "No, we were in the cave. He took one of the kid's cigarettes and took the filter, then stuck it back in his pack. You know, how they use the filter?" Troy acted ignorant. "You heat the stuff and when it's liquid you sop it up with the filter so you can get it in a syringe." He mimed jabbing a drug soaked filter with a hypodermic. Then his hands fell limp.

"So the kid got mad?" Troy guessed.

"Sort of. When he picked up his cigarettes, he saw the broken one, and he might have said something. I can't even remember, but him and Whit got into it. I was telling them to cool it, but they were fighting. The kid had Whit," again Rubin mimed the action, "and alla sudden Whit has this gun and he's holding it up to the kid's forehead and..." He stopped, sobbing.

"So it was Whit." He let Rubin sob awhile longer before he asked, "What did you do with the body?"

"Nothing. He's still there, way back in the cave. We drug him some, but I didn't like touching him." Rubin was talking into his hands.

"What about the money he had? And the rock? Did you keep it?"

"No, no way. I didn't touch nothing of his. I told Whit to keep it. I don't want nothing else to do with it."

"Wow. Well, I think I can straighten this out. You're pretty upset. Let me give you a shot, help you settle down."

Rubin hadn't wanted the shot, and it was obvious to Troy that on some level, Rubin realized he had said too much to the wrong person. He protested when Troy gave him the pentathol, but he was too high to stop him.

Using Rubin's truck, Troy drove to Glencoe Woods and picked up a map at the park office. Two hours later, Troy found the body. It was holding up pretty well in the cool dampness of the cave. He took a mental inventory of the area, then went to Whit's father's house. As Troy suspected, Whit's car was there. Whit was currently, and seemingly permanently, unemployed. Troy pulled into the driveway and blew the horn. The curtains parted. Because he was wearing a hat and sunglasses, and because Whit didn't expect nerdy Dr. Ivers to be driving Rubin's truck, he came out, but not until Troy blew the horn a few more times.

"What's the matter with you? I was sleepin'," Whit said as he approached. As he came closer and realized Rubin wasn't in the truck, he walked around to the driver's side.

"Where's Rubin?"

"He's at my house. We need to talk."

"I don't think so, man." Whit turned to leave.

"I just came from Glencoe Woods."

He stopped and Troy could tell Whit was taking a deep, measured breath.

"So?" he said, his back still to Troy.

"Rubin told me about the cave."

"What cave?" Whit asked, looking back.

Troy smiled. "Wanna take a ride?"

Whit hesitated and Troy saw his fists clenching at his sides. Three clenches, then Whit went around to the passenger side and climbed in.

"Think twice before you do anything Whit," Troy warned in a flat voice. "I recorded my conversation with Rubin and left the tape with an associate. I guess you know the rest," he lied.

"You're a dentist. A dentist! What's Rubin doing with a dentist?" Whit ranted. Troy backed the truck into the street enjoying Whit's disbelief, until Whit began making personal derogatory comments. Troy stopped the truck and grabbed Whit's bicep, squeezing tightly. It was small and soft and his fingers dug in.

"Watch your mouth."

Whit tried to wriggle from his grip, and Troy dug in deeper, finding the sensitive places in the under worked muscle.

"I'm not kidding, Whit. You could be in a lot of trouble. But I'm willing to work with you. You and Rubin both."

"That idiot—"

"He didn't tell me anything I didn't already know," Troy cut him off. "I saw you guys," he added, for no reason.

"But—" Whit wanted to argue.

Troy squeezed Whit's arm tighter. "No more questions. Remember, I'm a dentist. I know how to hurt people."

Later, after Rubin came to, Troy made the offer.

"You guys protect me, I'll protect you."

"Okay," Rubin said.

"No, wait," Whit waved away Rubin's words. "What are you into?"

Troy reached under the sofa and pulled out a Satanic bible. "This is all. I want to start a coven here."

"No way. Forget it. I don't believe in that crap," Whit said.

"I didn't say you had to believe in it. Just work with me. That's not asking much. You're going to get more out of this than you think, more than just my silence. I happen to know someone who is still irritated about that rock you lifted off Howard. Not to mention the money."

"What's the deal?" Whit asked.

"One Saturday a month, you help with the ceremony. That's about it. Let me drive your car, and one of you hang around to take me home. Oh, and Whit, since you were the triggerman, I'll let you be my voice. Don't worry; all you have to do is repeat what I tell you. There will be plenty to drink, beer, wine but no hard alcohol. And nothing stronger than marijuana, either! At the end of the night, you take home the leftovers. Keep my secret and I'll keep yours."

Whit wasn't satisfied, so Troy spent over an hour going over the plan, explaining the procedures. He would be robed and disguised. The dark, the alcohol, the drugs would help keep him hidden. Long ago he had chosen Vanderkellen as the place. Ideally, he would liked to have held the ceremonies in the church, but there were too many problems. For one thing, it was hard to get into and breaking in would draw attention to their activities. Even if they could get in and out easily, he had no idea how the structure was holding up inside. What a mess if the floor collapsed and hurt someone, particularly himself. Eventually he decided the cemetery would be a better setting. John Barker, the area's only cult leader, was buried there, and Troy would emphasize that association.

"What about winter? And rain?" Rubin asked.

"If the weather's bad we'll cancel. And after Halloween, I'll say something like, 'we are going to rest as nature, not to meet again until Spring Solstice'." Rubin thought that sounded impressive, but Whit wanted to know what kind of sissy Satanists they were if they were afraid to get cold. Troy explained that no one, not even evil people, really wants to be uncomfortable. If we want participants, he said, we have to make it attractive.

"Okay, but we still need a better excuse than that springtime crap. We ain't a bunch of flitting fairies. This is for real." Troy agreed to think of a better reason for a winter break. What did he care? He wasn't a Satanist. He didn't believe in devils or demons or even angels, for that matter. He was simply intrigued with the idea of controlling people, influencing them, scaring them. The only reason he chose Satanism was because, having no doctrine to hold, or cause to lead, he thought a pretense of dedication to an imagined being would be his gimmick. After all, it was only an act. Successful cult leaders were actors with a captive audience, and it was immaterial whether the leader actually believed the world was going to end on the fourth of July or that aliens were running the UN. After years of studying various cult leaders, Troy could spot the danger areas and knew he could avoid them. He could handle it, but unfortunately he lacked charisma and would never be able to assemble a group on his own. He needed henchmen. Indebted henchmen.

"So who's going to be at these parties?" Whit asked.

"That's the only other thing I want from you. Bring people. Not local people. Not your friends. Believe me, you don't want them around. Get college students. Clean kids. Not many, either. Five or six to start."

"But I don't know no college kids," Rubin protested.

"I do," Whit said.

"Make sure they don't bring anyone else along until you check them out. Make sure they're legal age, too. I don't want trouble."

"What do you want?" Whit asked, his tone suspicious.

"I'm just looking for a good time."

After they worked out the details they came to an agreement. There wasn't anything to argue about, really. Rubin actually seemed to like the deal, and Troy thought he might have gone along even without blackmail. Whit remained leery, unable to understand why Troy would want to do such a thing. Other than obligating every fourth Saturday night, he couldn't figure out the hitch. Finally he nodded.

"So we have a deal?" Troy asked.

"I guess," Whit agreed.

"I'm in," Rubin said.

Troy extended his hand and Rubin shook it. Whit ignored them and walked to the front door. They were leaving when Rubin turned suddenly and asked, "Hey! What about that Nova?"

Three weeks later Howard's body was discovered. The case was still open.

Now, a year later, as Troy sat waiting in the Vanderkellen cemetery, he saw that the car approaching on Nepowa was actually a truck. When it parked, he could hear Whit and Rubin's voices drifting up the hill. He wouldn't turn them in…surely they must realize that! It was a sad, pathetic existence that brought them back. That and free beer.

***

Anna called Alan the minute Leslie dropped her off. It was after ten, and she was late. She didn't tell Leslie Alan was waiting for her call; she would have driven her around for hours. Anna usually told her everything, but not when it came to Alan Macklin. She tried, here and there, but Leslie didn't understand him. Like tonight. Anna needed a sounding board, and Leslie all but put her hands over her ears. What was the big deal about sleeping with her boyfriend? A boyfriend of seven months. Almost a year, Alan had pointed out. Why wouldn't Leslie just let her talk? Think out loud. Be a friend. But again, she knew before she spoke how Leslie would react. She would have been surprised if Leslie had been anything other than horrified. Mental badminton, Anna called it, because any time her thoughts came close to Alan, they bounced back and forth and never settled. Love was supposed to leave a happy taste, she used to think, but her love for Alan made her uncertain, nervous. If it was love! Of course it's love, she told herself, again in the game of badminton. What wasn't to love? He was smart, planning for medical school once he finished his graduate studies in geriatrics. He was nice- looking, a little pale all over, but he had good hair and teeth. His eyes might be a bit shallow, and that did bother her. Sometimes they seemed vacant, making her wonder whether he cared about what she was saying. But that was silly because he was practically obsessed with her. It was thrilling to be the object of such attention, despite the friction between him and Leslie. He was not happy about the time she was spending with Leslie this summer, so she had lied to him about today. He thought she was shopping with her mother, and that's why she didn't come to visit him in Salem on her day off.

"Where've you been?" he asked. "Surely you didn't shop this late?"

Anna started to lie again, but changed her mind. Why should he be mad? She didn't do anything wrong.

"I was with Leslie," she said, and was sorry right away. What was she thinking when she said that? If she had learned anything from this relationship, it was to be careful what she told him. She could almost feel the heat of his grip on the receiver, and was grateful for the forty miles between them. She hurried to explain the innocent evening, being careful to tell him they ate at Shooter's, in case he found out from someone else. She told him about the cemetery, but wisely left out the part about the dead bird and being frightened off by the oncoming car.

"That was stupid. You know what kind of stuff goes on at Vanderkellen."

"Alan, we were fine."

"You think I'm kidding? I can't believe the stuff you let Leslie talk you into."

"Like what? Are you afraid we'll rob a bank or something?"

"That's not what I'm talking about. You know how boy crazy she is."

She hated it when he acted this way, so with the safety of the distance between them, she didn't hide her irritation. "What are you saying?"

"I didn't say anything. Why are you suddenly so defensive? What's going on?"

Anna said nothing, afraid of how he might twist any reply she made. He had a talent for turning her own words against her.

"I guess that answers my question," he said, using her silence as evidence of guilt. The ice in his voice was frightening. She could picture his angular face growing sharper and the short blond hairs at his temples standing out straight as the blood rose in his head. Sometimes, seeing those hairs stand out, seeing his thin lips press close while his nostrils grew wide, sometimes this struck her as comical, and sometimes, despite his anger, she wanted to tell him he looked like a cartoon.

"It does not," she stammered, then found courage. "Alan, why do you always do this? I haven't done anything wrong. We were in a cemetery. Lots of men there. Lots of them. All dead. Yep, I could have had any one of them, if I wanted. See how stupid that is? Why do you always want me to feel guilty?"

"I'm sorry. You're right. You usually are," he said. "Anna, it's just—oh, I just love you so much, and I get the feeling you don't love me at all."

"Alan—"

"How should I feel? We've been going out for almost a year, and you still keep me away. Do you know what that says to me? It

61

says you must not love me, or else you'd want me as much as I want you. And it says that I must love you a lot, or I would have moved on by now."

"Alan—"

"Here I am, twenty five years old, begging you like some high school kid. We're mature people. We love each other. Or I love you, anyway. I don't know how you feel."

"Alan, you know I—"

"You have no idea how much you hurt me."

"Alan, I can't discuss this right now. Mom's here," she lied. It occurred to her for the first time, at least, for the first time she consciously acknowledged, that the words of his argument never changed. He spoke as if reciting a memorized poem. She was glad she hadn't hinted to him that he was beginning to wear her down, and wondered if she ever really intended to sleep with him.

"Fine," Alan said. "But think about this: I don't have to beg for sex. I could be having it whenever I want it, believe me. I'd prefer it to be with you, but if you keep it up, I can't promise to wait. I wasn't going to mention this, but Jessica Renniger called today."

Anna's heart twisted. Jessica and Alan had dated before he and Anna met. He still talked about her, dropping comments about her classic look, her parents' money, and her mature attitude toward sex.

"She left a message, but I didn't call her back. You know why? Because I love you." He filled his voice with sugar. "And I'm sorry. I'm being hard on you, I know."

"That's okay. I love you, too," Anna sighed loudly

"I'll see you Saturday night?" he asked.

"Yeah."

"Sleep well, pretty Anna," he said, and hung up.

She sat on the couch staring at the wall, her hand still on the phone. Inside, she felt pinched and prickly, wishing she had never looked up from her book that day she first talked with Alan. If this is what it took to have a relationship, she wasn't up to it. She wished the new semester would start so she could immerse herself in cells and molecules and acids.

Mabel stared at her from the floor. When Anna met her eyes, the cat took it as an invitation and jumped into her lap. Anna cradled the old cat like a baby. Mabel purred and lovingly licked Anna's chin.

***

Leslie was beat. It was after ten and she needed to get home to spend time with her parents and hit the sack early, but after dropping Anna off, she was too restless to go home. She decided to drive into Miltonville and see if anyone was at Boonie's. On Main Street she saw Ed Philips shuffling along, tamping a new pack of cigarettes. He waved when she honked. Ed was one of her favorite characters, and he might enjoy hearing about her trip to Vanderkellen. She parked and met him on the sidewalk.

"Hey kid," he said, offering her a cigarette even though she didn't smoke. Neither did he, but he always carried a pack.

Leslie shook her head. "You going to Boonie's?"

"I was considering it. You?"

"I thought about it, but I better not. I have to work tomorrow. But I'll walk with you."

They fell into step, which was more of a stroll. Ed never hurried anywhere. He pointed out Maggie Saylor, who was locking up the ice cream shop. The shop closed officially at nine, but she kept it open later when she could. Ed was telling Leslie the reason. When no one showed up for the late movie, Mr. Reilly would close the ticket window and stop by for a sundae. Miss Saylor was sweet on him.

"How do you find this stuff out?" Leslie marveled.

"You'd be surprised what people tell me," Ed said.

"Maggie Saylor told you that?" Ed only smiled in answer. Leslie laughed. "You just have a way with women, is all."

"I've heard that, too."

"You've heard everything. Oh!" She tapped his arm. "Guess where Anna and I went tonight?"

Ed scrunched his face while he pondered. "Egypt?" he guessed.

"Close. Vanderkellen."

"Hmm. Ghost hunting?"

"Well, as it turned out, no." She told him what they found, and how scared they had been when the car came. "It was a blast."

"You two," he said scornfully.

"Oh Ed, it was daylight. Nothing was going to happen."

"Famous last words."

"Your coolness is fading fast," Leslie told him. They had reached the entrance to Boonie's Tavern. The air around them thumped to the beat of Clabbered Pus, one of the worst bar bands in the county. The door was propped open and Dick the Doorman

63

sat on his stool collecting the two-dollar cover charge. Dick usually let his friends in free, and therefore had a lot of friends because most people were willing to invest a few minutes of small talk with Dick in order to save two bucks.

"Sure you don't want to join me?" Ed asked. "I won't be partaking, but I'm sure I could smuggle a drink to you." Leslie could only have smuggled drinks because she was underage. Boonie allowed this with certain people, like Leslie, who had been wandering in and out of the bar since she was fourteen and never caused trouble.

"It's tempting," she admitted. "But no, I really can't."

"Well, kid, then here's where we must part ways." He peered in past Dick. "Looks like a crowded house."

It was, for a weeknight, but for some reason Boonie's could draw a crowd on Thursday nights, even with a band like Clabbered Pus. Cars lined the curb in front, and the small parking lot in the rear would be full. Boonie's regulars were older, and Leslie liked to go in early, after dinnertime and listen to them talk and fuss about her and her youth. But as the evening grew late, the atmosphere underwent a transformation. Like most drinking establishments, the bar became loud and rowdy, yet the fun seemed strained. People changed before her eyes; pleasant faces she trusted in the daylight melted, smiles felt phony, some eyes tense, others vacant. Pain and loneliness that was ordinarily hidden came to the surface. They didn't see it, but Leslie was acutely aware of it. It scared her a little, and saddened her a lot.

It wasn't the same as when her friends were drinking. They hung out in Salem, at the college bars, or over at the clubs in Westerville. They didn't come in alone, or sit alone. They were young, their laughter sounded real, the bar was only a microscopic part of their existence. In ten years they would be in Boonie's, or a Boonie's counterpart, trying to recapture what was gone, looking for friends, for love, for a life. Leslie preferred to party with them while they were young, before they became wounded, lonely animals.

"I'll probably see you around tomorrow," she said to Ed, smiling dismally.

***

Ed watched Leslie walk back to her car. Under the streetlights, with her hair pulled back loosely, she could have been her mother. Leslie had the same walk as Holly, an aimless amble, as if her feet were continually distracted from their goal. Leslie was a good girl, as was her mother. A little unmotivated maybe, but who was he to judge?

She got into her car and pulled away. He thought about her grandfather. He, too, had been a nice guy. Genuine, like his descendants, friendly and spontaneous. It lent support to a nature over nurture theory, that three people who are related but never knew each other could be so similar.

"Ed!" Pete Etner called from inside Boonie's.

He turned to go in. Dick the Doorman held a hand up when Ed fished for his wallet, and waved him on.

***

At eleven thirty, Leslie sat on her bedroom floor sifting through old notebooks she had dragged from her closet. It would be useless to lie down, even though she was tired, because curiosity about Bruce the mannequin was distracting her. He, or it, was down the hall, still in the bathroom. She had asked her father to remove him, and he said he would when the news was over, but he forgot and went to bed. Apparently no one else minded him, so she pretended not to care about him, either. She cast shame aside when it came to getting ready for bed, though, and sneaked into her parents' bathroom while they were still watching television.

Leslie yawned. She should be in bed, writing in her latest journal, not leafing through these old ones. Her journals were actually letters she had been writing to her mother since she was ten. The first four were diaries, the rest spiral bound notebooks because when she entered junior high she was too mature for a diary. She marked the notebooks 'Math', 'Geography', and 'English', with dates that only she knew were not school terms. One Christmas Aunt Audrey gave her a bound journal, a nice one, but Leslie didn't use it to record her day-to-day activities; she saved it for impressive thoughts and ideas. That way, if she died, or was in a coma and her folks went through her things, they would be astounded by her genius and the depth of her thoughts, not reading rambling accounts of bad days at school, what boy she liked, or who she was currently mad at. The nice leather bound journal lay in her nightstand drawer, with only two pages written on.

Since seeing Bruce tonight, she had been trying to remember exactly what happened with him. She had told the story a zillion times years ago, but she had a tendency to embellish, and after so much embellishment it was difficult to sort out the facts. One thing she was sure of was that he could walk. He could move. That wasn't an exaggeration, but the truth her exaggerations were built upon.

Lisa Richards still lived next door the last time Bruce was here. Because Lisa moved away when Leslie was a sophomore, and because Lisa, who was a year older than she, had been driving, Leslie was better able to determine which journal to look through. It was summertime too, she remembered, because her dad had put Bruce in swimming trunks and laid him on a lounge chair with a radio on the day of the Richards' Fourth of July cookout.

In order to avoid being sidetracked by the other entries, she promised herself that Saturday night she could reread them if she still wanted to. It surprised her how quickly she found references to Bruce. She skimmed back until she came to the entry that marked his arrival. As she read, the memories returned vividly:

Dear Mommy,

Dad pulled a good one tonight! Me and Lisa went to the movies and...

...and the house was dark when she came home. This was unusual; it was only eleven o'clock. She expected her parents to be up watching the news. As was her routine, she dropped her purse on a chair in the living room and headed to the kitchen for a snack. She switched on the light as she entered the kitchen, and was startled by something that didn't belong. The image reached the primal areas of her brain a split second before hitting the cerebral parts, causing immediate panic before anything concrete had registered. A quick glimpse was all she had before she turned and fled. It was all she needed, for in the kitchen, a tall bald man in sunglasses leaned against the counter. He wore a ragged jean jacket and a white t-shirt. The shirt was splattered with blood, evidently the same blood that coated the butcher knife he was holding.

The smart thing for Leslie to do would be to run out the front door, but she ran down the hall instead, to her parents' room. Passing Becky's room, she caught herself on the doorjamb, intending to grab her sister. Then the whole family could climb out the back window. It had not yet occurred to her that it might be too late.

Becky's bed was empty.

Without breathing, she continued to her parents' bedroom, reaching the door in one long stride. The door was shut, and Leslie wrenched the knob and pushed the door just as a vision of her family, scattered in pieces, flashed in her mind. Too late, the door opened.

They were huddled on the bed, basking in the glow of the television, Becky asleep between her parents. Her father looked up.

"Don't you ever knock?" he asked.

"Dad! Shhh!" She held a trembling finger to her lips, scanning the room for something heavy to block the door.

Then suddenly her parents were laughing. Michele reached over Becky and pushed Dan off the bed.

"What?" Leslie demanded.

Her father choked on his words, while Michele warned them both not to wake Becky. "Les, I want you to know I was totally opposed to this," she said, though her giggles caused Leslie to doubt her sincerity.

"What?" Leslie said, louder. This time, her thinking parts were aware of the situation before her primal parts, but the primal urges were overpowering. She ought to be laughing with them, but it was all she could do not to jump on the bed and strangle her father.

"Les, that's Bruce," Dan finally explained. "You won't believe—"

"What?" She stormed out of the room. Usually her father's jokes were funny, but then again, they were generally directed at people other than herself.

Her father followed her into the kitchen, apologizing.

"Les, I swear, I thought you'd think it was funny. It was! You'll see. You'll be laughing about it tomorrow."

"Dad, this is sick." She hesitated before approaching the mannequin, then ran her finger along the bloody knife blade. The knife was held in place with masking tape.

"Ketchup?" she asked.

He nodded sheepishly. He was trying to appear ashamed, but Leslie could tell he was really proud of himself.

"Sick," she repeated. "I don't think other dads do this kind of stuff. I mean, rubber snakes, fake vomit, that stuff, maybe. But this...it's really sick, Dad."

"Honestly, I thought you'd come in, see him, go 'Ooooh'," he held his hands up and imitated fright, "then figure it out and that'd be it."

Upon closer inspection she could see his point. The mannequin had a severely chipped nose and an unnatural stance. Her anger began to ebb.

Michele came in, tying her robe. "He spent the whole evening on this," she told Leslie, rolling her eyes because it was so ridiculous.

"Hey," Leslie had an idea. "Aunt Vicky's coming over..."

So Bruce had a new home, and they lived happily together. Dan kept him pretty busy. Guests would be startled to find him in their beds or buck-naked in the shower. The neighbors grudgingly grew used to him. Sometimes he would wear a trench coat and spy from behind a tree (he especially liked to spy on the Geists), other times he would stand at the front window in his bloody t-shirt. Due to a trick hip and stiff blue jeans, everything he did was either standing up or lying down.

When Dan couldn't think of anything for Bruce to do, Leslie kept him in her room. His bald head made an excellent hat rack and she bought clothes for him, both men's and women's, at thrift shops and garage sales. Bruce had a nice life at the Vickers.

The good times ended the night Lisa Richards brought over her ouiji board. Anna was spending the night, and Carla Moon was there, too. They sat on the floor playing with the ouiji for a while, then watched the little television in Leslie's room. By 2 AM, Anna and Carla were asleep in Leslie's bed. Leslie and Lisa were up watching the Creature Feature and eating huge bowls of cereal. Hyped up on the sugar, they decided to play with the ouiji again, and it was really active. Leslie was sure Lisa was manipulating it, but it didn't matter. It was better than it not doing anything at all.

"Who are you?" Lisa asked.

"W-A-L-T-E-R," it answered.

"How did you die?" Leslie asked.

"M-U-R-D-E-R," it said.

"Who'm I gonna marry?" Leslie asked the all-important question.

"M-E."

They burst out laughing.

"You're so gay!" Leslie accused Lisa.

"I didn't do it!" Lisa insisted.

It went on like this awhile longer, the girls asking silly questions and getting sillier answers. Then Bruce fell over. This was nothing strange, he was always unsteady when he stood on carpet and sometimes needed to lean against a table or a wall. A whisper could knock him over. Leslie got up and propped him against the door.

"Let's ask Walter to do something," Lisa suggested when Leslie sat down.

"Like what?"

"I don't know. Levitate something. Move something."

It so happened that as she said that, Leslie, who was adjusting a pillow behind her, accidentally hit Bruce's leg, causing him to fall against her dresser. Lisa drew back and gasped.

"I did that!" Leslie laughed. She rose on her knees and was reaching out to him when Lisa spoke.

"I know. Let's ask him to do something with Bruce."

Leslie opened her mouth to protest but before anything came out the planchette on the ouiji went to YES. All by itself! Lisa was not touching it. At the same time, Leslie felt a chill. She fell backwards and Bruce came after her. Hard. He was inches from hitting her when he sprang back, slamming into the wall.

Both girls screamed hysterically. Anna and Carla woke up in time to see Bruce hit the wall. A second later, Dan and Michele rushed in. Down the hall, Becky started crying. Confusion reigned for a few minutes until Dan took control. Michele went to Becky.

All four girls piled on the bed, babbling at Dan. Even though they were barely comprehensible, they made it clear that they wanted Bruce out of there. To calm them down he carried Bruce out to the garage. When he came back, Michele was standing in Leslie's doorway holding Becky, who still sobbed.

"It's that thing," Michele said, indicating the ouiji board. Lisa had sneaked it in because Michele would not allow it in the house.

"No," Dan said, "it's four slap happy girls."

"No Dad," and they started again.

"Look," he said, "it's three AM. Go to sleep and we'll talk about it in the morning." He went across the hall to his room.

Michele waited. "You'll be okay?" Satisfied with their grim nods, she took Becky with her to bed. An hour later, after recounting and rehashing, Leslie and her friends fell asleep.

The light of morning lessened the terror. Lisa and Leslie were still jittery, but Carla and Anna, who slept through the incident, were no longer convinced anything odd had happened. They offered explanations and teased Lisa and Leslie over breakfast. When everyone was gone, Leslie asked her father to get rid of Bruce. He said he would, but he didn't. Not then.

A few days later Leslie was watching Becky while her parents were working. She stretched out on the couch to watch a talk show after putting Becky down for a nap, and was halfway to napping herself when she heard a bang from the garage, followed by the sound of a metal garbage can lid spinning on the concrete floor. She sat bolt upright. She had not forgotten that Bruce was into the garage, not at all. Her grip on the couch cushion was tight enough to leave imprints when she finally let go. Slowly, she got to her feet, debating whether to wake Becky and leave, or go peek into the garage. Remembering every horror movie she'd ever seen, she decided looking into the garage would be the ultimate act of stupidity. Wake up Becky, she thought, and go next door. Tell them someone was breaking in.

Becky never did wake up completely, and Leslie carried her on her hip like a wet rag. Quickly, she cut across the yard to the Richards'. No one was home, of course. For one wild moment she had a crazy notion that the whole neighborhood was deserted, and that Bruce was somehow responsible. Then she saw Robby Canwell watering his mother's roses.

"Robby! Robby! Is your dad home?" she yelled, crossing the Richards' yard.

He shook his head and came her way. "Is Becky sick?" He looked worried.

"No. I heard something in the garage."

He passed her and headed toward her house.

"No, no!" She rushed to catch up.

"I'm just going to have a look," he said.

"No, no, Robby. Let's get somebody. Maybe someone's trying to break in." It was a struggle to keep up with him while carrying Becky.

"It's okay," he said with confidence. "I know what to do."

"What? What are you going to do?" She couldn't tell him she thought a mannequin made the noise, so she tried a different tactic. "What if he has a gun?"

Robby stopped and considered this. "Okay. We'll get someone."
They had reached her house and were standing next to the garage.
"Let's look in the window first."

"Why?" She was close to panic.

"Because people will say I'm a stupid moron if nobody's there.
And I'm not stupid."

Having heard Robby called a stupid moron more than once, and
having seen how much it hurt him, Leslie reluctantly followed him to
the garage window. Her heart was pounding and she clung to Becky.
Together, she and Robby peered in.

Bruce was in the middle of the garage, at least five feet away from
the wall where he had been left. He was standing, not leaning. Then,
as they watched, he spun on his heel, faced them, then fell over.

Robby and Leslie screamed at the window, then they turned toward each other and screamed again. Becky woke up and joined them.
Robby grabbed Leslie and pulled her away from the house, into the
front yard. Across the street, the Geist door opened, and Dottie emerged,
squinting in the sunlight. When she saw Robby dragging Leslie, she
started yelling.

"Let them go! Oh my God! That retard's attacking them girls!
Call 911! Call 911." She ran back and forth across her yard, waving
her arms.

Cindy and little Ryan Swift came bounding up the street calling to
Robby and Leslie, and Robby's mother was also coming. They met on
the sidewalk in front of the Vickers' house. Robby and Leslie were
gasping for breath, and Becky was bawling. Dottie Geist stayed on
her side of the street, spouting threats.

"That kid should be locked up! He ain't right!" she shouted. She
had been shouting that for years, so no one bothered to respond. Instead Leslie and Robby tried to explain what had happened. Leslie
and Becky spent the rest of the day at the Canwell's. When Dan and
Michele came home, Robby's mother walked them to the house and
helped Leslie tell them about the afternoon. Leslie took Becky inside
while her parents thanked Mrs. Canwell. She distinctly heard the words
'overactive imaginations,' which is what she expected. Her father promised her that Bruce was history. That evening Leslie went to Anna's
with the understanding that she would return to a Bruce-free house.
And that's what happened. While she was gone, Uncle Ralph had
dropped by, and he took Bruce home with him.

Leslie closed the notebook and rubbed her eyes. What a day

that was, she remembered. No wonder she wasn't fond of Bruce. She went to her door and looked down the hall. The hall light was on; they left it on for Becky. She would be asleep by now. Leslie moved quietly down the hall and closed Becky's door. Then, without looking inside, she reached in the bathroom and pulled that door shut. Back in her room, she shut her own door and wished it had a lock. She turned out the overhead light, kicked the notebooks out of her path, and climbed into bed. The light on her nightstand was burning, her current journal, a blue notebook with 'Psych 126' penned on the cover lay next to the alarm clock. She picked it up and propped herself on her elbows. It was much too late to recount her day, and she was too weary to be inspired, so she wrote:

Dear Mommy,
It's 11:52 and I'm so sleepy. I promise to write tomorrow.
Bruce is back.

She dropped the notebook on the floor and rolled over on her back, raising up to poof her pillow and snap off the light. Darkness closed in. She was so exhausted she felt the bed spinning. She smiled. It reminded her of breathing laughing gas at Dr. Ivers's. He turned it up higher than Dr. Smalley. Maybe that's why Michele changed dentists. Leslie wondered about that as she fell asleep.

***

Cindy Swift staggered from the kitchen, her drink tipping side-to-side, spilling straight vodka over the lip of the glass. She stopped, looked blankly around the living room until she spotted the remote control, then continued her stagger and sat in the easy chair next to it. Pulling her legs close, she stared at the television, which she hadn't turned on. She just stared into it, watching herself stare back.

It wasn't going to work. She had tried, but she could not make this work. People say money isn't everything, but she could only assume the people who said that had money, at least enough to pay the bills. Tonight she was sent home early from her cashiering job because business was slow. Only two hours, but that would be close to ten bucks after taxes. Ten dollars could buy enough macaroni and cheese to feed them for weeks. Ten dollars was a tank of gas. Ten dollars was almost half the phone bill! An entire haircut! Ten packages of toilet paper! Cindy had to hold back tears as she waved good night to Jenny, the nineteen year old senior cashier. Jenny worked as many as thirty hours a week and made fifty cents an hour more than Cindy. She was saving for a car.

She picked Ryan up at nine, intending to spend some time with him. Instead she ended up hiding in the kitchen until his ten o'clock bed time. It broke her heart to be with him because any day now Tim would announce his plans to take custody, leaving her alone, and ultimately, homeless, for the child support helped with the house payment.

She sat in the kitchen drinking and making plans. Tomorrow was payday at both jobs. Two paychecks should be enough for anyone, especially a single woman whose son was provided for with support payments. But those two checks, one for her job as an in-home heath care aide, that occupied her from six AM to two PM, and the other, the part-time, minimum wage cashier position, combined would barely cover the car payment and the auto insurance due next week. She was afraid to put any more on her credit card. She had been relying on it heavily, despite her vow not to use it again until she paid off her Christmas bills. Last week she had a little extra money, but a leaky radiator took most of it. Then Mr. Willus, one of her patients, threw up bright green bile on her only white uniform blouse. Twice through the wash, and it would not disappear. Twelve dollars and fifty cents more on the card! Then one of the lenses fell out of her glasses and cracked. She dug out an old pair of contacts she had put away because they irritated her eyes. Her eyes were red and dry and itchy, and she was sure they were getting infected. She had to get new glasses or go blind. The very cheapest would probably be at least fifty dollars.

Tonight though, tonight convinced her that something was fighting her every step. Jenny was eating pretzels at her register and gave some to Cindy. When she bit down, something gave way, contorting her face with tremendous pain. Probing with her tongue, she found a big hole where once a filling had been, and the tooth was splitting apart. Throughout the night, the pain was constant. She thought the alcohol would help, but her pain involved more than the tooth. Thinking of Ryan, sleeping down the hall, she realized how wrong everything in her life had become. Even if Tim didn't take custody, she had still lost Ryan. She didn't know how to act with him, let alone compete for his attention. Ryan had fun with his father, Tim saw to that. Her house wasn't a home for him, just a place to wait until the next visit. She could tell by how eager he was to leave, and how sullen he was when he returned. Cindy was ruining his childhood. How much better for him it would be if she dropped out of the picture. No more shuffling between Mom and Dad, no more nights at the Canwell's, no more canned spaghetti dinners and microwaved lunches. No more yelling. No more fighting.

There was really only one feasible option. She had dismissed the idea at first, but it kept coming to mind, and she no longer ignored it. She reached in the pocket of her robe and caressed the bottle of pills she had taken from Mr. Willus. She'd had them for a couple of weeks, but he didn't miss them. They were an old prescription for pain from a surgery he'd recovered from long ago.

This weekend, Ryan would be gone. MC Canwell would come by on Sunday bringing leftover breakfast pastries and the Sunday paper. Cindy would leave the door open for her. That way, Ryan wouldn't be around when she was discovered. Then he could go live with his dad and Teena. It was what he wanted, and he deserved at least that much.

***

Ryan Swift kicked off the sheets as he tossed in bed. He was worried about his mother. It was almost midnight, and she was still up even though she had to be at Mr. Willus's early in the morning to give him his medicine. He felt very bad for her tonight, but he didn't know what to say, or even if he should say anything at all. He wanted to, especially after talking to Mrs. Canwell. He understood a little better why she worked so much. He tried to think of something to do to cheer her up. He thought about getting a paper route and decided to ask Mrs. Canwell about it in the morning. Still making plans, he fell asleep.

Twenty minutes later, Cindy paused his door on her way to bed.

It was midnight.

FRIDAY

Apple Street slept.

Barely waking, MC Canwell nudged her husband, and he obediently rolled over and quit snoring. She dreamed she told Ryan Swift what she thought of his father, told him the ugly details of Tim's affair with that young, rich daddy's girl, and despite the shock on Ryan's small face, she couldn't stop herself. Heavy words spilled from her onto him and he broke under the weight.

Robby snored softly across the hall. He was dreaming of his job, which he dearly loved. In his dream, he had finished putting away all of the new inventory, and was ready to go home when his boss told him that another shipment had arrived and he could not leave until it had been unpacked. In the warehouse Robby saw hundreds of boxes, piled all the way to the ceiling.

In the Geist house, Artie and Dottie were once again sleeping in the blue flickering glow of the bedroom television. Dottie turned and mumbled about her sister Belle, whom she was angry with. Artie slept blissfully, his dreams mingling with sounds from the television, full of used cars, carpet stores, and talk shows.

Two houses away, Cindy Swift was not so much sleeping as she was passed out. In the next room Ryan dreamed of running. He didn't fly in his dreams, he ran. He could run all the way to Salem the way most people drove a car. Usually running was fun, but this night was different because he didn't know if he was coming or going. His dad stood in one place, his mother in another, and Ryan ran back and forth, back and forth. He ran away from his crying mother and her problems, then back, needing her. He ran toward

75

his father, his new best buddy, and his apartment with the swimming pool and the game room, then away, repulsed by things he knew, things he had always known. Back and forth, back and forth!

Down the street, directly across from the Geists and two doors away from the Canwells, the Vickers also slept. Becky's dreams were little more than confused images of the weekend she was anticipating, blurry sensations of stomach wrenching rides, color and food. Dan and Michele slept lightly, the fitful sleep of those with too much to do. In her room, Leslie groaned and stirred, trapped inside a nightmare that was just beginning.

Down the hall, the knob on the bathroom door turned.

***

At Vanderkellen Cemetery, the party was almost over. Troy sat off by himself, tired and ready to go home. It was nearing one o'clock, and he had an early appointment tomorrow, a tricky root canal that would take at least two hours and a steady hand. For that reason, he was glad the meeting had been short, but he was also a little disappointed by the lack of enthusiasm. Only ten people remained, two of whom were Whit and Rubin, and another five that had arrived in one car and were preparing to leave. People had to leave early, he reminded himself. He wasn't the only one with a job.

"That was a real good message tonight, Master."

Troy turned to the timid female voice and smiled behind his hood. Jaime, the prettiest of his flock! She came regularly with two other women from Salem. She truly seemed to buy his act; Troy could tell by her attention to the words Whit delivered, and the shy glances she quickly hid when she felt Troy look her way. Troy was actually surprised at the number of regulars that did appear to come for the message rather than the party. They often confessed personal problems to him they probably didn't even tell each other, talking into his stony silence, the hope for an answer visibly evident, even in the fire lit darkness. Occasionally someone would seek out Whit, trying to get a message to, and from, the Master. Whit's standard answer was that he didn't know how to reach the Master and that the Master contacted him only when necessary. Of course, Whit told Troy everything, and Troy had plenty of time to think up broad sermons that each would grasp as his own. Later he would hear of the fights he caused, the break ups, the trouble. It wasn't so much that he enjoyed their problems, but he liked knowing he was able to cause them. A word here, a gesture there, and people did things. He made things happen.

He patted the grass, and Jaime sat cross-legged beside him.

"It's amazing," she told him. "You talked about stuff I was thinking about. You know, stuff I didn't tell anybody." She ducked her head. Troy reached over and laid his hand on her thigh. He wrapped his fingers around it and pulled her closer. She smiled. He slid his hand higher. She licked her lips.

***

In the space between Vanderkellen and the next world, forces were gathering. An entity once known as John Barker prepared to burst forth from his paper-thin prison. Behind him, absorbing his power, Claire was ready to follow. The legion of demons that guarded them watched Troy, giggling at the simple nonsense that so intrigued the world. They barely noticed Barker and Claire's escape.

***

Troy stood and offered his hand to Jaime. As he helped her to her feet he surveyed the remaining crowd. The five who came together were stumbling drunk and picking their way out of the cemetery. Whit lay with one of Jaime's friends next to the fire, making out like teenagers, oblivious to Rubin and the other woman who sat close by sharing a bottle. Troy led Jaime away, anticipation burning beneath his belly.

As they passed the fire Troy felt the ground fall away beneath his feet. It was fast, his heat going to ice as he began to tumble. When he hit bottom there was only blackness around him. He couldn't see, he couldn't move, he was smothering. Someone was sitting on him, holding him down! He flailed about, but touched nothing.

Then he heard himself talking.

"Stay away this time!" he was shouting.

"John! No! You can't mean that!" He heard Jaime cry.

"You are not going to interfere. And be sure to tell that imbecile husband of yours to stay out of my way!" Troy felt movement. He was moving. He reached around in the darkness for a handhold, but found none.

"Walter is not my husband! Not any longer! You are my husband! This is your child!" Jaime sounded desperate.

There was dull pain, and Troy realized his arm had been grabbed. Then came heat, searing, and for a fleeting second he feared he was in hell. Frantically, he tried to get up, but there was nothing to push off of, nothing to push against, even though he was pinned to the ground. It had to be the cheap wine Whit bought. He twisted his head, trying to draw a breath. It wasn't there, there was no air, but there were images against the dark and he had a glimpse of the fire, of a puzzled Whit and Rubin, and two women trying to drag a hysterical Jaime away.

The fire was gone, and again he was blind. He was inside himself, he thought, but he wasn't alone. No, a hallucination! It must be, and it would be over soon. Or was he dead? Dying? What was it? He couldn't breathe, yet his lungs didn't ache. He could move, but not feel. He could see when he strained, and he could hear. He heard his own voice, but he wasn't talking. He felt anger, but he wasn't angry. He began to panic.

***

Rubin and Whit stopped what they were doing when they heard Troy's voice booming across the fire. It wasn't what he was saying that surprised them, but that he said anything at all. Troy didn't speak in front of the members of the group. Whit rose to an elbow as Troy came bursting through the fire, stepping into and out of the flames as if he belonged there. For a moment, Whit thought Troy was someone else, someone bigger.

Then suddenly came Jaime, skirting the fire, her pace quick to keep up with Troy's long, purposeful stride. Waving her arms, she shouted at him, "No John! You are not leaving me again!"

John? Did she think his name was John?

Troy was not listening to her. He pulled the hood from his head. He locked eyes with Whit. His arm came up slowly and he pointed.

"You."

It was more a growl than a word, and Whit began too late to

rethink his relationship with Troy. He tried to untangle from the woman he was laying with even as she tried to untangle from him. He tried to crawl away, then felt the pressure on his neck as he was grabbed from behind. The last thing he saw was the woman crab walking away, mouthing a silent scream as he was lifted into the air.

***

As Leslie slept, she wandered the streets of a familiar, yet unrecognizable town. The streets and sidewalks were buckled in places where graves had burst through from below. Leslie wondered why no one seemed to care about the bulges; they certainly made travel hazardous. Looking down to avoid tripping, she saw an old tombstone embedded in the sidewalk. She wanted to read the inscription, but the light was dim, and the harder she strained, the fainter the letters became. Giving up in frustration, she began walking again, determined to get out of this creepy town, out of this creepy dream. She turned a corner and found herself in a dark, stony hall. There were more graves here, set into the wall, like a mausoleum. A trail of wet footprints made a path Leslie did not wish to follow.

She turned another corner and was at home, holding a photo album. Her father was with her, telling her the photographs were of people from her mother's family. Leslie smiled, her heart warm. The family was scattered across the country and she rarely saw any of them. She eagerly opened the album.

At first she didn't understand. The eight by ten staring back did so with only one glazed eye. The other had disappeared inside a grisly socket. The face was a purple-brown emaciated skull. Raisinish, she thought. The lips were gone; the exposed teeth were broken and rotting. Quickly she turned the page. The next photo was a young man. Leslie could tell by the half of his face that remained. There were blisters on his cheek, and a thick yellow fluid oozed from his closed eye and the ravaged edges of his lips.

A groan rumbled in her throat. "Dad?" she said quietly, unable to close the book.

"That's your Mom's family," he repeated. "That's what they look like now." When she moaned again, he explained, "They're all dead, honey."

Leslie began to wake up before the scream erupted. Conscious-

79

ness intruded enough to remind her to be quiet. *Don't scream, don't scream*, she told herself as she woke. And she almost didn't.

When her eyes opened in the dark, they saw first a thin line of light around her bedroom door. The hall light! The line grew larger as her bedroom door swung slowly inward. Wider, wider, the door opened in direct proportion to her eyes. A figure stood in the doorway; the unmistakable silhouette of Bruce.

Leslie did not let the scream erupt; she forced it out. It was a relief to feel it scratch her throat because it meant this was not one of those dreams where her jaws were locked and she could only grunt and try to kick the wall. This scream was hard and painful, not to mention loud and embarrassingly high pitched. It should have awakened her; it certainly woke her parents. She could hear their voices.

Panicked, she did not wake up. She sat up in the bed, amazed she could move, for so often she was paralyzed in these dreams. Her parents' bedroom door opened and her father stepped into the hallway wearing worn out sweat pants. He stopped suddenly, and backed up into Michele.

Something was very wrong. The dream was starting to seem too real. Adding to its realism, Bruce fell forward and hit the dresser, knocking things over, before he hit the floor. She stopped screaming, not because she wanted to, but because her parents were there. Realizing she was awake, she clapped a hand over her mouth so she wouldn't wake Becky. That would be another nightmare altogether.

"Dan!" Michele was saying. She squeezed past Bruce into Leslie's room, and sat on the bed, pulling her stepdaughter close. "Why did you have to do that?"

Her father stood, open mouthed, shaking his head, while Michele continued admonishing him. After a few seconds of awkward stuttering, and a not-so private exchange with their eyes, Michele's arms encircled Leslie and she firmly patted the back of her head, pressing Leslie's face against her shoulder.

"I told you," Michele said with an insistent voice, "these jokes are getting out of hand."

"Oh, oh. Yeah, I know. I apologize, sweetheart," Her father agreed quickly.

Leslie wriggled out of Michele's grip. "Nice try! Get him out of here! I shut the doors. I made sure. I even shut—ohmigosh," her hand flew to her mouth, "Becky!"

Dan's face paled, and he disappeared down the hall. Leslie felt Michele stiffen.

"Becky is fine. He had to be sure we didn't wake her," Michele said.

"It's okay, Mom. I know Dad didn't do this."

Dan was back. "Beck's asleep." Leslie felt Michele let out her breath. "Really, Les," he continued. "I thought it'd be funny." He picked up Bruce, grabbing him by the arms.

"Are you putting him out?" Michele asked.

"Please!" Leslie added.

"Yeah, out he goes."

Leslie watched her father fumbling with Bruce as he maneuvered the awkward body down the hall. She wanted to yell after him that he should throw the deadbolt, but something in his demeanor told her that he didn't need to be reminded.

***

In the garage, Dan leaned Bruce in a corner, not satisfied at all to leave him there. He didn't put him at Leslie's door. Michele certainly didn't. And Becky couldn't, not without waking the whole house. He couldn't fathom how he got there. Well, he would lock the kitchen door to the garage so there would be no way in. He turned away and was almost at the door that led to the kitchen when he heard something. No, felt something. He turned back and studied Bruce. He hadn't moved.

I'm getting as bad as Leslie, he thought, rummaging for rope. Finally he found a few feet of dirty nylon cord he didn't mind parting with. He wound it around Bruce's arms, binding him tightly. Then he pressed the button to raise the garage door and carried Bruce out to the curb. He emptied one of the garbage cans, stacking the plastic bags around it, then hefted Bruce in, feet first. He would have preferred to put him in headfirst, but the width of his shoulders and the molded bend of his right arm didn't allow it. When he let go the can started to tip, so he pulled the other cans close until he was certain it wouldn't fall over. If the garbage men wouldn't take him in the morning, then he would figure out something else.

Back in the house, he locked and bolted the front and back

81

door, and the door to the garage. Leslie and Michele were now in living room, having watched him from the picture window. Seeing them, he was able to convince himself that he was taking these precautions to appease them.

It was a long time before he was able to fall back to sleep.

***

Miltonville glistened under the streetlights. Above, the wide night sky threatened to swallow the little town. Ed Philips stepped out of Boonie's and paused to relish the sweet air before leaving the noisy crowd. The whoops and hollers grew farther away, and soon he did not hear them at all, even though he was well within earshot. Nighttime was for dreaming, and this he did as he walked alone on Main Street.

Despite the hours spent in Boonie's, Ed had not had a drink. Ironically, he was probably the only patron in the bar who was not driving. He gave up that privilege shortly after he gave up drinking three years ago, and though he often sneaked a drink, he never drove again. It was hard to drive sober; he was too aware of other cars, pedestrians, lights, everything distracted him and therefore he could go no faster than thirty five miles an hour, hands tight, leg tense, ready to pounce the brake at a moment's notice. Motorists flew past, horns blowing, fingers waving, distressing him more. One month after he had quit drinking, he had signed his car over to Red Lampley, and he was never seen driving again. Or drinking. Drinking he kept to himself, during bad times when his stomach bothered him, or his back, which was more and more often these days.

Passing Hartmann's Grocery, he watched his reflection in the big window. Leslie mentioned she would be working tomorrow. Did she go straight home after she left him? Was Judy Redmond relieved that Anna was home safe? No doubt. What about Anna's father, Tom? Was he on the road tonight? Did he call home daily to check on his family? Maybe not. It wasn't that Tom didn't care, he just didn't believe.

Ed Philips believed. He probably knew more of what happened to Judy and Holly than anyone else, thanks to his father's research. How many times had he wished his father had never revealed his findings? Probably as many times as Ed had castigated himself for being drunk the day Holly died. Maybe as many times as he wondered who would be the one to pull the trigger on Leslie!

***

Rubin Tanner drove and drove and drove and drove. He was in Westerville, then he was out, then he turned around and headed back to Miltonville. The horror of what he witnessed at the cemetery blossomed into terror then settled into shock, and he sobbed as he drove. He had no idea where he was going, what he was doing. Whit was the thinker. Where was Whit? Abandoned, oh Lord! Rubin burrowed his face into his sleeve, wiping away tears and sweat. Whit was getting pounded and Rubin had run. He bit his lip, trying to keep control, because he knew Whit was way beyond a pounding. He hadn't imagined that *snap*, or the way Whit hung limply from Troy's hands. And where was Troy now? Probably finishing up the women. Rubin pushed his hair straight back and out of his face. Leaving Whit was one thing - he was undoubtedly dead before Rubin had gotten off the ground - but leaving the women was inexcusable in the redneck society to which he belonged. In the depths of his guilty heart, there was relief that they might never be able to tell how he had run. Even if they got away, he didn't think they knew his name.

Not surprisingly, he headed to Patti Anne's. That wasn't particularly bright since Troy would probably look for him there, but where else could he go? Not his mom's, not after her husband's last violent warning. The thought of taking off to Mexico crossed his mind more than once, but he had no money and the gas sucking truck was almost empty.

Of course, he could go to the cops, and oddly, this idea brought a calm to his belly he hadn't felt in a year. The memory of Whit shooting that kid stayed always under his eyelids, playing and replaying. No matter how Rubin twisted the end, he couldn't pretend it hadn't happened. Whit never had trouble sleeping. Not even after Troy approached him with this weird scheme. Troy was nuts, Whit said, but a coward. We'll play his game, party with the weirdoes, and if he gets antsy, we'll blow town.

Rubin parked in front of Patti Anne's little trailer in the Wafting Winds Mobile Park. She was still at work, and probably wouldn't be home until three. For now, his plan was to sit inside by the front door holding her little twenty-two. Tomorrow, he would go to work as scheduled, and watch for Dr. Ivers to open his dental practice and then calmly approach him in the office. He hadn't yet decided what to say. He would think about that while he waited for morning.

***

Sandy Cornett stared into her beer can while Theresa Hoover paced the kitchen behind her in a cloud of cigarette smoke. Neither spoke, having already said all that could be said. They were tired and scared and waiting for either a brilliant idea or a knock at the door. Who would it be? Maybe the police with their notebooks and questions and handcuffs? Or might it be Jaime, bleary eyed and freaked out? Quite possibly it could be Jaime's new boyfriend, the psychotic little devil-priest who smelled like antiseptic mouthwash.

"I can't believe this is happening," Theresa muttered, not for the first time.

"We didn't do anything," Sandy reminded her once more.

"Fleeing the scene, or whatever," Theresa said. Sandy pushed the beer away and rested her head on her folded arms. She should be more worried about Jaime, but she couldn't muster it now. Too tired. Besides, it was Jaime who always begged them to go to Vanderkellen. Sandy had no interest in devils, but she liked to party. Tonight was so boring she wanted to leave. Jaime was the one who wanted to stay. She had the hots for that creepy little guy.

She peeked under her arm at Theresa, who now leaned against the stove staring through the window into the empty night. Sandy felt queasy thinking of Theresa making out with that greasy hick when the master or devil boy or whatever he was, came out of the fire. What a way to liven up a boring party. One minute she's half asleep, sitting by that gross Rubin guy. Then suddenly here he comes, stomping through the fire, robes burning, pretty cool, actually, Jaime yelling after him. He yanked that guy off of Theresa and Rubin ran off, leaving them behind. Sandy and Theresa tried to drag Jaime to the car, but she pushed them away. Finally she looked at Theresa and shouted, "Go away, pest!"

"Jaime! Let's go! He just killed someone!" they both yelled while the devil man laughed. Jaime continued to cling to his robe. Sandy grabbed her arm and tried to jerk her free, but Jaime hung on. When devil man himself shook Jaime off, she followed him, calling "John, John!"

Theresa and Sandy gave up. They passed Jaime on their way out of the cemetery completely unnoticed. Wordlessly, Theresa started the car and waited. After a few minutes, she opened the door and called, "Jaime, come on! We're leaving!" to which Jaime answered, "Get away! Now!"

"She obviously wants to stay," Sandy said, and they left. Since then they had argued and debated about what to do. Theresa wanted to call the police. Sandy listed a dozen reasons why that was a bad idea. Theresa wanted to go back to the cemetery. Sandy wanted to stay put. They still hadn't reached a decision, and now Sandy was dozing.

***

The Reverend John Barker sat behind the wheel of the late Whit Stewart's Chevelle and searched inside himself for anything Troy may have left behind. Barker was so angry when he took Troy that he knocked him senseless and rendered him useless. Barker couldn't find any of his car-driving knowledge. There were no cars in his day, and his visits since were much too brief to allow him to learn to drive proficiently. He had only driven a few times, using bodies more carefully invaded, tapping their skills. He must be more careful jumping into people. The host's survival was critical in order for him to access what it knew. This body had become nothing more than a vessel to keep Barker from being sucked back into the prison. A body was an anchor, without one he was defenseless. That was a lesson learned by accident, but one that he learned well. That year a ripe Vanderkellen almost escaped, for he hoped to save time by soaring free, disembodied, part of the air and sky, unhindered in his search for the Vanderkellen. One of the Wethacanwee spotted him, and snatched him from the air. Claire and Walter finished the Vanderkellen, but it was too late. It was always too late. The Wethacanwee made sure of that.

Not this time. Not only did they free him before a new Vanderkellen birth, but they let him see her! Either the Wethacanwee were so bored with him that they let him out early just to end the game, or they hadn't been paying attention while they were watching the activities at the cemetery. Barker didn't care why he was out. All that mattered was the last Vanderkellen. One. Female. No children, according to Suruas, one of the few demons Barker trusted. No protected fetus within her, or else he would have felt the repulsion when she was in the cemetery. This would be his last trip. He would not return to his cell.

***

Ed Philips trudged up the wooden stairs to his apartment. For the past twenty years he lived on the second floor of Mrs. Skofield's old house. Mr. Skofield had converted it into a separate apartment only months before he passed on. Ed had been the only tenant, and the rent had never been raised during his stay. Mrs. Skofield had always favored him.

Inside, he greeted himself in the small gold-framed mirror that hung on the wall of the tiny entry. Much as everyone else in town, he was used to his old gray face. Like his rent, it hadn't changed in twenty years. Sometime in his thirties he began to age rapidly, and by forty he looked sixty. Then things stabilized, and finally he looked his age.

Of course, his friends thought his drinking had taken its toll on him, and in his heart, Ed concurred. Yet there were other things he could blame. Wendy, for instance! Then there was that spell with gambling. But mostly, his problems stemmed from the Itch. The Itch started him drinking, which led to the loss of his job, which led back to too much drinking. Eventually he got a handle on it, and, until his retirement he worked as a janitor in the same high school he once attended. Despite the time he spent in Boonie's, most thought Ed had given up drinking.

Unbuttoning his plaid shirt, he went to the kitchen and opened the cabinet over the stove. Reaching into a far corner, behind a dusty jar of Postum and an ancient box of oatmeal, he found his bourbon. An occasional nip was all he allowed himself. Medicinal. Helped with sleeping. He kept it controlled, and kept it secret. He splashed a bit into a cup that held the remainder of the morning's coffee and carried it to the recliner. The apartment was sparsely furnished, but it wouldn't hold much anyway: a small table with one chair that sat half-in-half-out of the small kitchenette, his recliner and a tattered vinyl loveseat in front of the console television. Not much, but more than he needed since visitors were rare.

Normally he would have turned on the television, had his nip, and dozed until two or three, at which time he would wake suddenly, wonder where he was, figure it out and go to bed. But not tonight! He was uneasy, his imagination working overtime. Of course, it was Leslie and her talk of the Vanderkellen Cemetery. He burned to tell her what he knew, to tell her father and Michele, Judy and Tom Redmond, and the Miltonville Cryer. He had known what was going on in this town for forty years, but he couldn't tell anyone. He had tried once, after Holly died, when he was certain his suspicions were confirmed. He talked to Nate Kingston, and Nate warned him to keep his suspicions to himself. Nate was right. What good would it have done? Even if everyone on earth believed him, what could be done about it? Time and time again, Ed resisted the temptation to tell. What would people think if he were to start spreading tales of illegitimate children and rampaging ghosts? They would think he wasn't fit to work in the school system, is what. Holly's family would be mortified. Ed's family would be humiliated. Besides, the whole thing was too fantastic to be true. At times Ed would shake his head at the notion and wonder how he could have ever believed such a thing. It would be cruel to stir up heartache over the silly ideas of his father.

If only he hadn't seen Leslie tonight. She always brought the Itch to mind, especially lately, probably because she reminded him of Holly. Or, maybe because, according to legend, it was nearing the time for a new Itch. He watched the customers in Boonie's, not sure what to look for, but certain he'd recognize it if he saw it. But if he did see it, then what? This dilemma had pained him for years.

He tossed back the bourbon and coffee and rose from the chair intending to put the cup in the sink. The bottle sat on the counter, and using his uneasiness for justification, he poured another shot. He needed to relax. He twisted the cap and reached to put it away, but as it disappeared into the cabinet, he pulled it back and added another inch to the cup. Then he returned the bottle to its hiding place in the dark, behind the Postum.

This time he went to the bedroom. Placing his cup on the nightstand, he sat on the edge of the bed and thought of the briefcase stored on the shelf of the closet. It was full of papers; photocopies, news clippings, old ragged-edged stationary covered with feathery script. Some day he would organize the documents, a job he had started at least a hundred times over the years, maybe twenty times in the last two. He wasn't in the mood to try again tonight. He would, at some point, because it was his aim to turn them over to someone else.

He was always thinking he should keep the case in a safer place. He planned, someday, to buy a fireproof box, or put the documents in the safe deposit, and maybe stipulate in his will that Leslie would get them. But she would have no idea why unless he explained it to her. What would she think if he died suddenly and left her stacks of newspapers and letters written by Virginia Drake? Oh, but they told so much when one *knew.*

Ed scooted back on the bed and leaned against the wall, mentally emptying the briefcase. He had memorized its contents, the tattered, aged photocopies, the tissue-thin letters Virginia Miller Cramer Drake had written to Lucas Vanderkellen and the delicate pages of her journal. Her writing, faint and scratchy, was almost indecipherable, but Ed's father had spent hour upon hour with them, and his typewritten translations were mixed among the documents. There weren't many of her letters left; most had fallen to dust in the Salem University library archives years before his father had stumbled upon them. Some of her writing had been transferred to microfilm at the library. The library also had accounts of the incident at Vanderkellen from several newspapers, but few first hand stories because most of the survivors were too ashamed to talk about it. The documentation one could gather from the library offered more mystery than information, leaving researchers with questions not only about *what* happened in 1798, but *how* it happened. The papers in Ed's closet would answer much of that. The memories in Ed's mind created another mystery altogether.

***

Virginia Miller Cramer Drake had grown up in the same Pennsylvania town as Lucas Vanderkellen, and they had been close since they were children. The Vanderkellen's were of some means, and at sixteen Lucas went away to school. He returned home, tall and broad, handsomely blond, and hoping to marry Virginia. His education, however, had put strange ideas in his head. Being young and eager, he spoke his mind. He wondered loudly about the existence of God, the finality of death; blasphemous utterings, unspeakable, even unthinkable in his hometown. Virginia's father forbade her to see Lucas, and gave Lucas a firm warning to keep his distance. When Lucas could not find a teaching position, he left for Philadelphia. Before going, he begged Virginia to join him, but ladies did not disobey their fathers, and if she were to be honest, she wasn't entirely comfortable with his new attitude. So, he left, and though her life went on, she could not forget him. She wrote him often, friendly, chatty letters, not emotional, always signed 'Yours eternally'.

From these letters one had a picture of a happy girl with many friends. She was not a beautiful girl, but she was pretty, smaller than most, with brown hair and eyes and a straight nose she didn't care for. Her mother was perpetually ailing with something, and in her letters she told Lucas about the newest problems. Her father was a kindly bear of a man who had his hands full with his work, his sick wife, and his two daughters.

Virginia's letters didn't reveal what she wrote in her journal. She didn't tell Lucas right away that Richard Cramer had been coming by often, and her father greatly approved. Richard wanted to go West. The day came when he visited Mr. Miller in private and asked if Virginia might go with him, as his wife. It's hard to determine how Mr. Miller made the decision to allow him to marry Virginia; maybe the financial and emotional strain of his responsibility was too much, maybe he thought Virginia really loved this man, or maybe, this being his first experience in this realm, he just didn't know what to do. But he told Virginia she was going to marry Richard and she could not challenge his judgment.

According to Virginia's later writings, she did not love Richard, not the way she loved Lucas, but she could stand to live with him according to her father's request. She absolutely did not want to go West. She didn't want to leave her friends, her father, her sister, her forever-pained mother, the grandparents and cousins, her town. Being married meant she could no longer write to Lucas so she had written him one last letter to tell him he could write to her no more. Years passed before she learned that he had come to her house and had an awful confrontation with her father, which did nothing to win back his favor. The mail moved slowly in those days, and she was married and heading West with three other families before he ever read her letter.

It was in Ohio that they met John Barker's group. It was small then, only thirty people, but they seemed to be good, Christian people. The Cramers and their companions agreed to travel along with the Reverend Barker. On Sundays he preached, gaunt and handsome in a dark suit that matched his features, his eyes capturing his audience with as much force as his words. At first, Virginia was as caught up as Richard and everyone else, but from Lucas she had learned to question. She had also learned to keep those questions to herself, and so she behaved as those around her, in spite of the fact that Barker subtly twisted the good words of the Bible to fit his own purposes, an easy accomplishment because most of the women and a few of the men were illiterate.

She was never sure whether she was relieved or disappointed when they reached the grassy meadow that Barker proclaimed was picked for them by God. Richard seemed satisfied even though it was only a few days from Fort Washington, hardly the "west" of his dreams. Richard's growing devotion to Barker distressed her, and she wished they would continue west without him. Homesick and depressed, she rarely talked to her husband, unless he spoke to her first. She slept poorly, cried often and quit attending to her appearance. Richard, immersed in his dedication to help Barker build this new community, lost interest in her. Despite Barker's urging to create children, it didn't happen with Richard and Virginia.

There was plenty of work to do, and having been raised in town, most of the skills needed to start from scratch were foreign to Virginia. She realized that to survive, she better start learning. They built and planted and it was terribly hard work, but not enough to keep her mind from dwelling on home, and from time to time, Lucas Vanderkellen. Their settlement was peaceful, close to a river, surrounded by woods. They could farm and hunt and live as they pleased, Barker told them. Up river to the north lived a small band of natives, but they were no threat. Having been moved and chased and murdered by the whites, they stayed clear of the settlers. Everything was ideal; the people worked together, the weather was agreeable, the soil rich, yet Virginia was uneasy. It wasn't only her chronic homesickness. It was also Reverend Barker. Standing apart from the group, she was able to watch his influence over them grow as his theology deteriorated.

Things went so smoothly the first year the group believed John Barker truly was blessed. The community grew, with Barker encouraging them to write their friends, sending men to Fort Washington to mail the letters. Virginia wrote home, but only to tell her father they were settled in a Christian community. She didn't want him to be worried, and she herself wasn't too concerned at that time. Richard cared little for her, and she constantly dropped hints and made comments about how much she missed Pennsylvania. In the back of her mind was the hope that he would eventually send her home. In the meantime, there was plenty of food and firewood and comfort in the fact that the army was close. Surely they would provide rescue should there ever be trouble.

Trouble did come, though only Virginia recognized it. It didn't come from the Indians, or from the weather. The trouble came from their leader, John Barker, and his increasing insanity.

Barker's sermons, always off base, began leaning more toward the bizarre during the first winter. He went from vaguely insinuating his chosen status to outright claiming to be the second Son of God. Preaching fervently by lamplight in the long barn, he told the congregation their good fortune was a result of their loyalty to him, and if they wanted to continue to live blessed lives, complete obedience was mandatory. His voice mesmerized, and as if by magic, he seemed to know their thoughts, their fears and most importantly, their secrets. While he insisted the men care for their wives and children, he also encouraged them to take mistresses in order to boost the population. Barker himself would do his part, of course, and with that announcement, women began fawning over him like never before, hoping to become the mother of his child. Virginia was appalled, not only by Barker's words, but also by everyone's blind acceptance of them. Was she the only one who noticed he no longer used the Bible? Was she the only one who brought one to the meetings? Soon, Richard began staying out all night, and one time she saw Mr. Cox looking slyly her way. After that, while other women spent time fixing their hair and dressing their best, Virginia took special pains to look dowdy.

When the community had grown to approximately a hundred people, Barker officially shut the gates. No more room. Spring had arrived early, and his sermons were delivered almost nightly, held outside with a fire blazing in front of his pulpit. The people, *his* people, were worked into an absolute frenzy. Barker was dangerously close to proclaiming he was God, and his group, isolated from the rest of the world, devoid of reason and sanity, grasped his words and fed. They alone were blessed, and this man who was so close to God loved *them* and no one else. Virginia watched with revulsion as they worked the days like machines and spent nights in abandon. She couldn't bear sitting through another meeting so she did the only thing she could think of; the one thing she detested about her mother might save her now. She took to her bed, sick. Richard hardly noticed, needing her only for feeding and cleaning, and she was able to avoid going to the sermons all together. She believed John Barker forgot she existed. But this was not so.

Somehow, Virginia never knew exactly why, it was brought to Barker's attention that she was ill. It shocked her when she came into their cabin carrying water and found him sitting at the table.

"You shouldn't be working if you're not well," he said with sugary compassion.

"Has to be done," she answered shortly, her heart pumping madly.

"The word says when the body is sick it's due to an illness of the soul. You don't come to services anymore, do you?"

"No, because after working all day, I'm too pained to leave the bed," she lied.

He reached for her hand and guided her to the empty chair next to him. "Miss Virginia, you need a private consultation. You are in great danger, surely you are aware?"

She nodded, keeping her eyes on the floor. She was aware.

"Tonight, after services, and you *will* be at the service, come to my cabin and we'll discuss your problem."

Her stomach doubled up, her face blanched. "I can't go to services tonight. My, uh, my stomach..." She faltered before finishing. "It's a womanly ailment, you understand?"

"Oh." His eyes widened and he nodded. "Well, you will be better soon. I will stop by next week, and if things aren't improved, I will do a personal examination." When he smiled she noticed how pointed his teeth were, and his eyes, she would later swear, had fire in the pupils. He gave her a paternal pat on the hand and stood to leave. Before he walked away he stood behind her and squeezed her shoulders gently.

She sat a long time, biting her knuckles, her mind going in a hundred directions. She hadn't seen this coming. So many nights she lay alone in bed planning different ways to escape this place, why was she still here? Last year, she could have written her father, or, forbid the thought, Lucas, and one of them probably would have come for her. But now, no communication was allowed. She would have to walk to Fort Washington. It was days of travel through wilderness and Indian country, and she didn't know which direction to go, but what choice did she have?

She took her emptied pail and headed to the river. It had to go somewhere. In the woods, she left the trail and walked and walked, keeping the river in earshot. If she floated on a log, where would she end up? Probably crushed in the current. She went to the bank and sat, staring into the trees on the other side. She'd rather die in the river than succumb to Reverend John. Curling up in the dirt, she cried.

Eventually her tears slowed, and when her eyes cleared she was startled to find she wasn't alone. A few feet away a beautiful dark-eyed child stood watching. Very cautiously, she came closer, and laid a handful of berries next to Virginia, then quickly backed away. Virginia smiled and ate a berry.

The child said something Virginia couldn't understand. She repeated it, and Virginia shrugged, trying to indicate her ignorance. The child raised her finger to her eye and drew an imaginary line down her cheek. Virginia nodded. "Sad," she agreed.

Suddenly the child turned and ran away, leaving Virginia alone once more to contemplate her situation. What now? Go back to the settlement? Would the child bring back a group of angry Shawnee? Which fate would be worse? Before she could decide, she heard a rustling in the brush, and the child's voice. The child was back, this time with two adults, a man and a woman. In her depression, Virginia didn't even try to run or hide.

She looked up, resigned to her fate, and was surprised to see the horror on the faces of the natives. The man said something sharp to the child. She diverted her eyes to the ground. The woman said something to Virginia, not crossly, but not overly friendly. Virginia shook her head and shrugged again. The woman took Virginia's hands and held them out from her body. Then she dropped them and searched under her skirt for her legs. Squeezing here and there and speaking words Virginia couldn't comprehend, the woman stepped away, satisfied apparently that she wasn't injured.

The man spoke loudly. When Virginia didn't reply, he spoke again, louder. Still no reply. Then, he said very plainly, "English." Virginia nodded enthusiastically. "Yes!"

He said something to the child, and away she went again. The three adults waited in a silence that was awkward for Virginia, but seemed not so to them. In spite of what John Barker had said about the Shawnee, they did not seem dangerous. On the contrary, they were obviously attempting to help, and Virginia was desperate enough to trust them.

When the child returned she was leading another man. The two men spoke, looking often at Virginia. The second man approached, but did not come close.

"Name?" he asked.

"Virginia." She pronounced it carefully. He repeated it and she nodded.

"Pelenay," he said, placing his palm on his stomach. For a moment there was silence. Finally he touched his leg and said, "Blood?"

It took her a second to realize he was asking if she was injured. "Oh, no, no," she scrambled to her feet to prove it. They stepped a wary pace away, except the child. The woman pulled her close.

Virginia showed her empty hands. "Please, I must get to Fort Washington. I'll pay, please can someone..." She stopped. The only words they seemed to understand were 'Fort Washington.' The adults shook their heads, and the woman began to speak emphatically.

Pelenay interrupted, "No Fort Washington. Your people?"

"My people?" The tears came back and she turned in the direction of the commune. "There," she pointed. "My husband is back there. Not my people. Please." When she looked back, she met icy stares.

"*Matchemanetto*," said the woman, stepping in front of the child.

"Barker," Pelenay said with narrowed eyes. "Man devil."

She nodded in agreement, too frightened to answer. How did he know Barker's name? Had Barker already threatened them? She cried freely, hoping they would take her away, to Fort Washington, or anywhere. Instead he raised his hand to where she had pointed earlier, back toward the settlement. "Go."

"No." Her hands went to her face. "No!" But they were already walking away. Virginia ran after them, desperate. Virginia fell at the woman's feet. "Don't make me go back! Please no!"

They were all silent, and Virginia knew they were casting glances amongst themselves. The woman knelt before Virginia, her dark eyes somber as she tried to communicate.

"Fort Washington. Blood," she said. She laid her hand on her stomach and clenched it into a fist. Slowly her gaze followed her fist to the sky and she gently spread her fingers one by one, giving Virginia a glimpse of all the souls released by the Army. She bowed her head shamefully, but the woman took her chin in her hand and raised her face. Gesturing toward Barker's village, she said, "*Matchemanetto. Pelenay hakeo Virga otayway Matchemanetto. Manuk.*" Now she pointed at the child and again made a fist. She touched it with her lips before sweeping the sky with her fingers.

"But—" Virginia spoke before she understood the danger she threatened. Barker considered the natives a life form deserving of extinction. Imagine the anger he could create by blaming them for Virginia's disappearance.

The woman said something that sounded almost apologetic, then rose. They left her then, the child looking back once. Virginia ached to follow them, but she couldn't bear to be responsible for bringing any more harm to those people. Yet, to get away, she would need their help.

She began the long walk back to the commune. She had been gone hours; Richard would not know it. The possibility of being under Barker's surveillance was more worrisome. If only there were some way to contact Lucas! Above all the regrets she suffered, missing him was her greatest hardship. He would come if he knew what was happening. He would bring the army and put John Barker in Hell.

Maybe she could write a letter and have the natives deliver it. It might be dangerous for them to travel with a white woman, but she knew they could take a letter to Fort Washington. They sometimes traded there, and their tribal leaders dealt with the army frequently, if not futilely. She knew that much from the newspaper in Pennsylvania. Surely she could persuade them to deliver a letter if it would benefit them as well. If only she knew how to explain it to them. Even if she could explain it, it could take ages for the letter to reach Pennsylvania.

She thought about writing instead to Fort Washington, but dismissed the idea. If anyone came, they would talk with Barker and he would charm them and away they would go, leaving Virginia and the natives to deal with the consequences.

Lucas. It had to be Lucas.

Back in Barker's little town, people bustled about, nodding to her, asking after her. She smiled wanly, in response. Just needed rest, she told them with a weak voice. Beside her cabin, children played, children just like the heathen girl who tried to help her. Same thing, different language, different lives. She watched two girls marching tiny dolls in the grass. The dolls were gardening, putting seeds and petals in their aprons, walking to and from their invisible houses. Probably gathering food to feed their big dumb husbands before the evening's orgy.

Suddenly she stopped. Of course! It was so simple! She understood what the children were doing without hearing a word they uttered. Just as she knew the child with the berries was curious as to why she was crying. Could she do the same with Pelenay? Convey to him that a letter had to be taken to Fort Washington so that John Barker, the man devil, could be removed from this place? There was so little to lose she had to try.

Writing a letter would be no easy feat. Barker had confiscated everything, paper and ink included. She would have to reconfiscate a few things, maybe tonight while he was delivering his sermon. The weak smile she wore for the benefit of her neighbors was growing, so she hurried into the cabin.

Having a plan made her nervous. Dinner was unbearable, and being so excited meant it was difficult to pretend to feel bad. Luckily, Richard paid only cursory attention, being that it might ruin his fun if he were to ask about her. For most of the meal she sat quietly, her face resting on her hand, gazing at her plate. Richard ate hastily, asked perfunctorily if she felt up to the service, accepted her answer of decline, and left.

An eternity of pacing seemed to pass, but finally it was dark enough to sneak away. Almost everyone was at the meeting and those who weren't were inside their cabins. The Cramers' cabin was near Barker's, and Virginia slipped in easily. In this commune one rarely shut doors, let alone secured them. Her biggest obstacle would be darkness, for she didn't dare light a lamp. Richard had helped build this cabin, so she was familiar with the layout. Unlike the other one-room cabins, Barker had three rooms, one an office. Stumbling only once, she found the office door open. Like a sleepwalker, she moved, her arms stretched before her until she reached the desk. Here would be quills and ink and paper. There was an inkbottle on the desk, but she didn't want to take something that might be missed. Her fingers located a drawer and tugged. Locked. Another. Locked. Another. This one opened, but it contained nothing to write with. There was paper, though in the dark she couldn't determine if it were blank or not. She took two sheets and tucked them into her blouse. Surely Barker had to have fifty inkpots; he certainly had the Cramers'. But the room had no windows and no amount of strain she put on her eyes could pick anything out of the pitch. Weighing her options against her odds, she decided to take the pen and inkpot from his desk, write the letter at home, then sneak them back. There should be plenty of time.

She encountered no problems on her way back, and once inside her own cabin she went directly to the candle she kept on the table. As soon as she lit it, she thought she heard a noise outside. Had someone followed her? No, she assured herself, it was her nerves. To be safe, she picked up her sewing and piled it on the table. Then she sat facing the door, ready to drop the pen in an instant and take up the sewing should anyone come by. The paper was blank, and the letter to Lucas was scratched out quickly; a short plea for help giving the location the best she knew and asking that he send the army because Barker was devious and dangerous. Again, she heard something. Certainly she heard the same things every night, only they were never so sharp or terrifying. Satisfied that the letter said enough, she folded it twice and neatly printed Lucas's address on one side. Sealing it with candle wax, she hid it inside her blouse along with the extra paper. She rinsed the pen in leftover dishwater and wiped it dry, then she crept back through the night to Barker's cabin. It frightened her that she could not hear him shouting his message. That meant the sermon was short tonight. It was likely they were caught up in the debauchery that often followed. She moved faster.

Barker's cabin was still dark, but she maneuvered through it swiftly. In his office she took the time to place the ink and pen as exactly as she could remember. She was kneeling to open the drawer to return the extra sheet of paper when she heard a woman giggling. Right outside! Virginia dropped behind the desk. The giggling woman was coming inside the cabin!

"So, Reverend," she was saying, "what do you recommend?"

"This might help," John Barker said, and the woman's giggles became wild laughter. Virginia held her mouth shut, pinched her nose. Barker! She mustn't make a sound!

"Perhaps we need a private consultation," he told the woman, just as he had said to Virginia that morning. Virginia panicked. A consultation! She was in the office! Thinking fast, she prepared to give an embarrassed excuse about wanting to see him about their talk today. In the long run, she would pay for that, but she was too rushed to think clearly. She hurried to shove the paper into the middle of the stack, lest it be found in her blouse, and the letter! It too was in her blouse! She mustn't move, or else it might crinkle. She stood stiffly; ready to announce herself, when a lantern was lit in the bedroom. The bedroom. She let out her breath; its sound mixing with their coos. On all fours she crawled from the office. They were talking softly, but she heard their words. He called her Claire, and Virginia bit her lip. Claire Brandenburg! Virginia thought she recognized that voice. She wondered where Walter Brandenburg was tonight, whom he was with. Who was her own husband with, for that matter? What matter? She really didn't care.

She crawled almost the whole way home.

***

The next morning she rose earlier than usual, eager to get about her business. She practically threw Richard out, and he was not very pleased, having been out late the night before. Once he was gone, she picked up the empty pails and headed toward the river. In the cover of the woods she turned off the trail and broke into a run for as long as she could. An hour later she began noticing signs of civilization, and soon after left the woods and walked through a clearing to the village. Already the native people were laying aside their work to stare. Mustering all her confidence she marched boldly into their midst.

"Pelenay?" She said once she was in earshot. A woman bent down and whispered to a child. He ran behind a lodge. Virginia hoped he had gone after Pelenay, and again she was forced to wait in that uncomfortable silence. Keeping a distance, she smiled, but none was returned. All this time she had believed it was they who couldn't be trusted, but now she saw in their eyes herself as the untrustworthy. Humility worked the smile away.

Eventually Pelenay appeared and he did not seem surprised, but his face did show exasperation. He spoke to her in that rhythmic voice she couldn't understand, and a few women laughed softly.

Ignoring them, she fished the letter from her blouse. Holding it in her right hand, she formed an inverted V with the fingers of the left and wiggled them, saying, "Pelenay." Scissoring the fingers, she walked them through the air to the letter, which she then plucked from herself. Using the empty hand she pointed into the distance and said, "Fort Washington." Her left hand bounced up and down toward "Fort Washington." Pelenay grinned, and members of her audience were chuckling. When the letter arrived at "Fort Washington" she released it from her finger legs and let it fall to the ground. Indicating her left hand again, she repeated, "Pelenay," and ran it back to the starting place. Pelenay laughed and said something to a man who stood nearby. But he was shaking his head.

Next, she stepped over and made finger legs with her right hand. "Soldiers," she said, and picked up the letter. The soldiers carried the letter and dropped it. Now her left hand picked up the letter. "Lucas Vanderkellen," she said, enunciating clearly. She mimed reading the letter, threw it down, and ran her fingers back to 'home'. Grabbing her hair, she yanked her head back. "John Barker," she said, and slid a finger across her throat.

They seemed to vaguely comprehend, and she repeated it. More laughing and talking amongst themselves. Getting the letter from the army to Lucas was confusing, but killing John Barker seemed to be not only easily interpreted, but also appealing. Pelenay watched her with interest, although he didn't look quite convinced. She went over it again and again, making sure he understood the details, watching carefully for any indication of agreement. No one was laughing anymore; their discussion was serious. When she began to pantomime delivering the letter again, he waved her hands down, and she was satisfied. Six men and two women walked away, leaving Virginia lost. A woman approached with a bowl of water, and Virginia drank to be polite. Most went back to work. Virginia waited.

Pelenay returned with two young men. The letter was lying on the ground, left from the last time Lucas Vanderkellen had read it. Pelenay retrieved it and tears sprang to Virginia's eyes. He studied it for a moment. "Fort Washington," he promised, handing it absently to one of the men.

Only by using all her strength did Virginia stay on her feet. Gushing, she thanked him over and over.

"Go," he pointed toward Barker's commune. "Birga, go." He

meant it, so she turned and fled back to the woods, running again, but lighter, faster. It could have been a trick to get rid of her, but she could not allow herself to think that way. At this point her trust in Pelenay was all she had. Certainly, he wouldn't lie to appease her; he would simply tell her to get lost. Like yesterday. But maybe he—she stopped herself. The letter would be delivered. It would, it would, it would! Her heart felt healthy, pounding not from fear, but excitement, for not only was she going to escape this place, but she would also see Lucas!

She found her pails where she had left them. After they were filled she returned to the cabin to wait. How long would it be? Two or three days to Fort Washington? Then how long to Pennsylvania? Would they take it? Would he come? How long should she wait before returning to the village to check?

It took mighty self-control the first week. She waited six days before grabbing her pails and heading to the river. When she emerged from the woods and crossed the clearing she again attracted attention, and someone went after Pelenay. He looked annoyed and told her to go. She raced her fingers toward Fort Washington hopefully. Angrily he folded his arms over his chest and planted his feet firmly. "Go," he commanded. Unsure of what this meant concerning the letter, but certain that it meant she was not welcome, she fled back to the settlement.

The next day she paced and chewed her nails. She could not endure the waiting. Barker had not been back, thanks largely to Claire Brandenburg. The biggest secret not being kept was Claire's delicate condition. For all his sexual prowling, this was the first conception, and Claire was now raised to a higher position in the group, probably to encourage other women to aspire to her accomplishment. Claire was extremely demanding, and he was eager to show the rest how doting he could be, even to someone else's wife. Virginia felt safe for the time, but she was still impatient about the letter. Despite everything, she mostly wanted to be with Lucas. She again sneaked away to the Indian village, and in a scene reminiscent of the day before, was again sent home.

On the eighth day she went back. When she arrived she found a delighted group. Pelenay even smiled when he told her to leave. It was okay. The men had returned. Mocking her pantomime, they ran their fingers here and there, and everyone laughed. So did she. Birga, they called her, go. Don't let the man devil catch you here is

100

what they meant. Today it was easier to go home.

Only when she entered her cabin, her face long to fool her neighbors, did she realize that the waiting really started now. How long to get it to him? Would he come? And how would she handle Barker if he came for her first?

***

Ed woke from his doze, images of Virginia within reach. She was very detailed in writing about her memories of life in the commune and the tense, exhilarating wait for Lucas. Once Lucas arrived, she had to rely on second hand information, much of it from Lucas himself, and some from the guide the army had sent with him.

Rubbing his eyes, Ed stretched, thinking of her loopy script that was beautiful to look at, but difficult to read. Although his father had typed much of her writings, Ed preferred reading the originals. The library would be hacked off if they knew he had them. They had been in his father's possession when he died, and no one had ever come for them. They probably never knew they existed.

He should go to bed. Going to bed didn't mean he would go to sleep, though. Not with Virginia on his mind. Best to try and get her out of his head. He carried his empty cup to the kitchen. Resisting a momentary temptation to put it in the sink, he again took the bourbon from the cupboard.

***

Claire Brandenburg plodded along Hopeful Road in the tired body of Jaime Gates. They had been fortunate this time; never before had they emerged to find host bodies so near. In the past they flew off in a frantic quest, terrified the Wethacanwee might catch them before they found an anchor. This body had been inebriated, which, as far as taking possession goes, makes for a fairly simple task. Keeping a drunken body moving was a different story. This girl had resisted only mildly, disappeared for a while, then came back fighting. Claire held her away effortlessly, and eventually the girl gave up and was now cowering in a corner inside herself. Jaime kept guard, but Claire was able to pick at her mind.

Finding nothing useful, Claire ignored the frightened being whose body she invaded and steered it toward Walter.

Poor dumb Walter. Even though they were miles apart she smelled his terror as plainly as she could smell a wet neglected dog under her nose. John did too, and he was certainly heading this direction. She listened for the sound of the motorcar, but it never came. They knew little of these things, but still it surprised her that he couldn't force his host to drive for him. The man was probably dead. Barker was so careless about these things. Not Claire. She used to kill ruthlessly, but anymore the physical pain of the sudden death of a host was more than she could stand. Getting in was hard enough, but leaving them alive required concentration and skill, not to mention practice. She had managed it a few times, but the women were so deteriorated they became little more than raging lunatics. Claire believed that her current host would likely live due to her intoxicated and barely conscious state. Those were the only ones who ever did.

Oh, but this Jaime person must not walk much, she thought. Her lungs strained and feet blistered. The tight pants chaffed her waist, so she unbuttoned them and the zipper spread apart from the pressure. The girl had a little tummy, just like Claire. Was she pregnant too? It might be why she had so many aches. She pressed her belly, but no, there was no baby, just soft flab.

"How far now?" She wondered. Hours. Lights on the horizon and the scent of Walter led her toward the Vanderkellen. Oh, if she could leap into a night bird or a bat and just fly! That was a tough lesson in what *not* to do and they each had learned it personally at one time or another. Unlike humans, an animal's body reacted on instinct. Once inside it was like hanging on to the back of a wild horse, and then, their behavior alerted predators. So far they had yet to experience anything worse than the pain of sharp teeth and digging claws, not even their own deaths had been so painful. A few attempts and they had given up the idea of using animals unless they had no other choice.

A cool breeze lifted Jaime's hair and tickled her neck. Claire enjoyed this, and realized that she really didn't mind the long walk. Years of confinement with John reading her every thought had been stifling. In a few hours the Vanderkellen would be dispatched and she and John would be free. Just in time, because the baby would be coming soon and she didn't want him born in that closet without walls, surrounded by shrieking, taunting spirits. This child, she thought, patting her stomach, will never know darkness.

***

Twenty miles away, in the Wafting Winds Motor Court, Rubin Tanner was literally jerked awake by the hair. Through muddy eyes he saw Patti Anne standing over him. "Sweetheart," he muttered.

"Don't 'sweetheart' me, Rubin. What have you done?" She demanded, gesturing with the small gun. He looked at his empty hand with embarrassment.

"Nothing." He started to get up, but she pushed him back with a palm to his chest. "It's Whit!" he cried. "He's got some dude mad at him. I didn't do nothing."

"Whit! I should have known! What happened?"

"Nothing!" he swore.

"So why are you sleeping with a gun?" She stomped into the kitchen, yanked open a drawer and tossed the gun inside, rattling the utensils. "If you ain't gonna be straight with me, then get out," she ordered, getting a glass from the cupboard and slamming the door. It bounced open and she slammed it again. "I got enough turmoil as it is."

"Baby, I ain't lyin' to you," Rubin wailed, afraid to get up. "I'm just being careful, is all."

"How nice of you to come here to be careful," she continued, ignoring him. "What is it? Drugs? You're messin' with drugs again? I don't want to hear that."

"I'm trying to explain if you'd shut up!" he yelled.

"Explain? Explain what? Whit's a loser. You want to hang around with losers, that's your business. Leave me out of it." Now she slammed the refrigerator door.

"Don't have to worry about Whit no more," he mumbled.

Patti Anne glared at him. "You say something, smart mouth?"

"I said you don't have to worry about Whit."

"Yeah, right, when have I heard that before? Well, boy, until you can prove to me that you're a real man, not one of Whit's little lap dogs, I don't want you coming around." She cut him with that. As sensitive as she was about her age, it bothered him much more that he was almost twenty years younger. Her little digs about immaturity and inexperience were highly effective, and he would never dare retort concerning the fun gravity was having with her.

"I ain't hanging around Whit no more. There ain't no trouble."

"I said go on home." She leaned against the drawer where the gun lay among spatulas and salad tongs. He didn't move. "Rubin," Patti Anne said firmly.

This wasn't how he intended the conversation to turn out. Where was he going to go? He had no 'home', except here with Patti Anne. The only other place he ever stayed was Whit's.

"I'm sorry," he apologized. "Can we just forget it? I promise, there's nothing to be worried about."

"I'm not in no mood for this tonight."

"Please, Patti Anne, don't make me go," he tried again.

"I'm calling the law if you don't get moving."

Still muttering, he staggered to the door. Then out. He heard the locks turning behind him. He climbed into the truck and a moment later the lights in the trailer went out. He sat in the truck and waited for her to come for him. He waited so long he fell asleep.

Suddenly there came a rapping on the window. Every nerve and muscle in his body tensed as he jumped in the seat.

"Whoa, buddy!" A light shined in his eyes for a moment, then raced around the truck. "You live around here?" the officer asked.

"Uh, yeah. In there," Rubin nodded at Patti Anne's trailer.

"Not according to the woman who called. I think you better move along," he advised. Having no alternative, Rubin left the Wafting Winds and drove to the service station in Miltonville where he worked. He had to be there in a few hours anyway.

***

Fright paralyzed Walter Brandenburg far more than the plaster body that encased him. He saw no way out. Even if he could tip the garbage can over, it would take him the rest of the night to creep away, and then where would he go? Barker's anger preceded his arrival. Walter stupidly believed that he would have killed the Vanderkellen before Barker's release. What was he thinking? He had only a few hours to get her and it had taken that long to pull his body the few feet down the hall, not to mention the time and concentration he used turning the doorknobs! Where were all the devils that promised to help? Did they expect him to kill her by throwing the mannequin on her head? He wished they never told him the guardian spirits had left the Vanderkellen, that he had never pulled Ralph into the storeroom to push him into returning the mannequin. The empty sleep state he'd existed in didn't seem so bad now. Not even Gron and Ammak, who came occasionally to inflict torment with their gnawing and ripping, promising him that this was but a taste of what awaited him, even they were preferable to the wrath of John Barker.

Gron and Ammak hadn't been his only company throughout the years he had been trapped in this body. Others came. Filthy, smelly beings that seemed to think the Vanderkellen could be killed. They swore to help when the time came. He should have learned by now not to trust them, but they were such convincing liars, master connivers. Barker himself had been tricked by them many times, not that he would be empathetic. Nor Claire, who was no doubt enjoying herself. They had been competing for Barker's affection since the early days, but Claire, born with attributes that naturally attracted Barker, always had the upper hand. Anytime Walter was able to win some favor, she seethed with jealousy. Had he been able to kill the Vanderkellen her envy would have fumed so hot she would have burnt up and died. Oh, if it had only been so. But no, here he was suffering the utmost humiliation, tied up in the rubbish, while she walked with Barker, valuable to him, carrying his child. The only way Walter could ever win his respect was lost to him forever.

***

John Barker pushed the dead body along. Troy Ivers had departed hours ago. It took a great amount of Barker's energy to maintain the vital functions, which, considering the magnitude of his anger was a good thing. The vision of the Vanderkellen running away still taunted him, and he huffed with each forced step. No car had come down Mindell Road in the past hour; if so he would have stopped it and traded bodies. He strained to see the dark farmhouses, although he was leery of approaching one in search of a sleeping body. He tried three times, but each home was either surrounded by loud, viscous dogs or invisible forces that directly opposed him. Dreadful creatures, they never showed themselves to Barker. Drak, an impish goblin with a face like a rat that Barker ran into often when in the world, Drak could see them. Even the

Wethacanwee feared the places *they* were, Drak told him. Avoid them at all cost. Right now, caution was critical. Barker couldn't risk losing this body; even this one was better than none. He flexed fingers, kept the heart beating, the oxygen in the blood, trying to make it last.

Although he was impressed with it, he had shed the clumsy robe. Now he was playing with the wristwatch. They had changed immensely since his last visit. Instead of hands they now spelled out the time. This watch had buttons all over it and lit up and played tinny music. Three o'clock, it read. It made no difference to him. He would reach the Vanderkellen by morning, he was sure, then he would have all the time in the world.

***

As Claire and Barker walked toward Miltonville via parallel roads, Ed Philips slept, lulled by a combination of bourbon and the dim yellow lamplight. His dreams were of memories he didn't have, memories of Virginia Cramer, a woman he never knew but thought of often. Memories formed from diaries and newspaper clippings, recounting events that unfolded in a time far in the past where a woman named Virginia waited...

***

...and waited. It was more than a month before Lucas came. In that time, Claire Brandenburg continued to dominate John Barker, doing everything possible to distract him from other women. Virginia was grateful. With so many women vying for his attention, he didn't have the time or need to seek out a sickly house bound frump like herself. Richard did as he pleased and she gave him no trouble. She was quiet, almost invisible. She cooked and cleaned and supposed that he assumed she sat home ailing all day. He didn't know that for the last two weeks she had been taking a regular pilgrimage to the Indian village. Every other day she went, and every other day she was told to go. It was not only Pelenay who banished her. Most of them had learned the word 'go'. "Birga go," is what they said, meaning Lucas was not there. What was going to happen when he did come? If he did come? Would he bring the army, as she asked, or would he be alone?

106

Later, she found out Lucas was not alone. He had hired a guide to get him to Fort Washington. Once there, he explained his predicament to a commander and was told that the army was there to control Indians, and so far as he knew Barker was not an Indian. When he realized that Lucas was going on without him, he relented and sent along a man named Jacob who knew the Shawnee in the area and spoke the language. The guide he originally hired opted to wait in Fort Washington.

When they came to the Shawnee village, no one seemed surprised by the sight of him. One by one they abandoned their activities and stood to watch them approach. A man came forward and waited until they were close enough to exchange words. Back and forth he and Jacob spoke in words foreign to Lucas.

In English Jacob said, "The white woman Birga comes often."

"When will she be back?" Lucas found himself anxious.

"He's sure she'll be back tomorrow."

"Can he tell us why she wrote? What is happening?"

Jacob addressed Pelenay, then told Lucas, "We'll eat first and then talk."

After a dinner of fish and mashed berries and something Lucas didn't recognize and was afraid to ask about, he and Jacob were left alone with Pelenay and two others. Through Jacob, Pelenay told Lucas how Virginia was discovered crying in the woods. It was simple to deduce that she came from Barker's village, which was reason enough to keep clear of her. Barker was evil; he played the games of the Wethacanwee and all his village were under the control of the spirits. This woman sought escape. Pelenay's people could not help her without risking attack from Barker. When it became obvious she would not give up, Pelenay consented to send the letter. He told of her pantomime, and how they let her act out the message long after they understood because she was so comical. They spoke considerably more English than they let Virginia know. Her frequent visits made the villagers uneasy. Barker might follow one day, and they did not trust him. He was an evil man with many guns.

"It was kind of you to deliver the letter," Lucas thanked Pelenay. Jacob translated and listened to Pelenay's long reply.

"This is interesting," Jacob grinned. "He delivered it because Virginia promised him you would kill Barker. He wants to know how you plan to do it."

Lucas sat open mouthed, caught totally off guard. Jacob offered a reply to Pelenay, explaining that they would need to speak with Virginia before devising a course.

An hour later, Lucas and Jacob lay under the big sky waiting for sleep. Jacob asked Lucas what he was going to do.

"I don't know," Lucas admitted. "Virginia forgot to tell me I had to kill the man."

***

The next day Lucas waited in the village, watching the tree line. When Virginia finally broke through, he was startled by her appearance. Pale and thin, she looked as sickly as she pretended to be. When she saw him, her face lit and she shouted his name. They ran to each other, embracing while the villagers watched. After a few minutes of small talk, he led her away, and Virginia told him about Barker's settlement. Even with his education and city ways, Lucas was shocked.

"Let's go, right now," he said.

"No, you don't understand. Barker will blame these people. I'm afraid of what he'll do. Besides, there are children in the settlement. I can't even imagine what might happen to them if we don't get them out. What about the army? What did they say?"

He shook his head. "They won't help. This isn't their business."

Virginia covered her eyes to hide her tears. Lucas held her close, so angry he thought he *could* kill Barker. He let Virginia cry against his chest. His face in her hair, he pulled her even closer, intensely, until he was kissing her wet cheeks, twining her hair about his fingers, laying her down in the soft grass of the meadow.

Later, they decided the best thing would be for Virginia to go back to the settlement as if nothing had changed. He and Jacob would meet with the village leaders, and when she came back tomorrow he might have some answers. They said a dangerously long goodbye, and Virginia rushed to get home in time to feed Richard, frightened the glow on her face would betray her.

***

Lucas was unable to meet with the Pelenay and the other leaders until after the evening meal. Their priorities were not the same as Lucas's, having work to do to sustain the village. Jacob warned Lucas earlier that, while he would not interfere, neither would he take part in murder. Nor should he expect much help from Pelenay. It would be suicidal for the natives to assist him in the assassination of a white man. Lucas had no other alternatives, so Jacob explained Lucas's idea of ambush and attack to Pelenay and the other village leaders. The men listened politely. When Lucas had nothing left to offer, one of the Shawnee who had remained quiet began to speak. His name was Wanasteke. Jacob interpreted:

"This man will not die in the traditional way. He has chosen the land of the Wethacanwee for his home, or let them choose him, and they will protect him. The Wethacanwee like this area and are happy to have him living there. Barker is theirs, and their evil will linger in him wherever he goes. His followers are weak, easy sport for the Wethacanwee. The strong ones did not stay."

At this point Lucas tried to argue, but Jacob stopped him. He had his turn to speak, now he must offer the same courtesy.

"White men do not believe in the spirit world, I know, not as we do, but I tell you it exists. Maybe you can go and kill Barker and the settlement disbands, and that will be good. But maybe you kill him and leave his followers so consumed with anger and evil that they want to kill. Maybe they will come here in the dark and kill these people. I refuse to risk their lives for that woman."

"So, what am I supposed to do?"

"I will seek an answer for you." Silently Wanasteke left the group.

"Where's he going?" Lucas asked, although Jacob was already putting the question to the remaining leaders.

"Wanasteke is a spiritual leader, a kind of shaman. He has gone to, I guess, sort of pray," Jacob informed him. "It could take days."

"Pray?" Lucas repeated as the leaders rose and left. Apparently the matter was settled.

Jacob patted his shoulder. "You're going to have to do it their way."

As noble as 'their way' was, Lucas couldn't help but reflect on their recent history. 'Their way' hadn't stopped whites from killing them. Why did they believe it could stop Barker?

***

Wanasteke's sojourn lasted almost a week. During that time Lucas and Jacob ate with the villagers, slept close by, and each day Virginia came as soon as she finished cooking Richard's noon meal. Their hours together were few and dear, and they spent them alone. The immorality of her behavior did not concern her. She loved Lucas, and these moments might be all they would ever have.

Wanasteke appeared six days later, in the early evening. Virginia was already rushing home. Saying nothing, he beckoned Lucas to follow him. Lucas fetched Jacob and they went into the woods with Wanasteke. They walked almost an hour before coming to a meadow on a small hillside. There was a ring of smooth river stones just where the land began to rise. Wanasteke gestured toward the circle and began to speak.

Jacob said, "The settlement is over the hill, through those trees. He says the rocks mark a gate? No, that's not right. I don't know what he means, some kind of gateway. You have to bring Barker here, invite him to step into the circle. Then he will die."

Lucas waited, wondering how to react.

Jacob continued, "That's it."

"This is the help I'm getting?" Lucas started toward the circle, but Wanasteke grabbed him. He told him through Jacob:

"Neither can you stand in the circle. There has been an agreement. Your blood and his cannot walk this land together. In three days one of you will be gone. When that happens, your children will die and the seeds you have planted will shrivel up. There can only be one or the other, a Barker or a Vanderkellen. My people favor you; they hate Barker. The Wethacanwee would like either of you; they don't care which. The Annawah have promised that if Barker stands in the circle, they will protect us from the vengeance of his people. But he *must* be in the circle, it's the only place the Wethacanwee cannot go, and they will try to keep Barker for they like his shallow soul."

Then Wanasteke started walking toward the forest.

"Wait," Lucas cried, but Jacob stopped him. They stared as Wanasteke retreated into the forest.

"This is asinine," Lucas said. "Tomorrow, when Virginia comes, we're leaving."

"You can't do that."

"Why? We don't know Barker will retaliate."

"We don't know he won't," Jacob reminded him. "Listen, I've

been thinking. The commander might intervene."

"But he said—"

"That was before we spoke with Pelenay. The function of the Fort is to control the Indians. That includes keeping peace. This group is not hostile, never has been. It's best to keep them cooperative. If they feel Barker is a threat, then the commander should be aware. Also, his Christian sensibilities would be appalled by what's going on in the settlement. Virginia probably isn't the only one being kept against her will. Perhaps I can convince him to come and free those who want out, and move Barker away from the Indians."

"Do you think he might?"

"I can be persuasive. Give me a week. I'll come back one way or the other," Jacob promised.

That evening, after dinner, as Jacob prepared for his journey back to the fort, Virginia stood in front of her cabin sweeping dirt, grinning. Suddenly her heart went cold as she felt Barker's eyes. He stood at the corner of the cabin, grinning back at her. He nodded and moved on.

***

Virginia spent that night in terror. The night air was still, and Barker's voice was distinct within it. She listened from inside the cabin doorway, and when the sermon was over she huddled under the blanket, clutching her good bread knife. Hours passed and he did not come. Someone staggered in, but she recognized the grunts of Richard and feigned sleep until she was overcome by the real thing.

In the morning, the moment Richard left for the fields, she fled, leaving the mess of breakfast behind. In the Indian village she ran from person to person, and the alarmed natives led her to Lucas. She wept in his arms and told him they were running out of time.

"Jacob's gone for help, but it might take a week," he said, more to himself. "Come with me." He took her back into the woods, back to the place Wanasteke had brought him the day before.

"The Indian says I have to get Barker in there." He pointed to the circle. "But I have a better idea. Do you suppose if there is a witness to the fact that a white man killed Barker, they will leave the Indians alone?"

"We can't suppose anything with those people. What are you planning?"

"I kill him in front of someone."

"And they will kill you!"

"Virginia, I came here to free you. I knew I was taking a risk."

"Frankly, I'm more distressed about committing murder than I am about dying."

"Murder? I don't think of this as murder."

"Okay, assassination."

"Lucas, this is an evil, twisted man. If anything, he's going to get worse."

"Then I'll kill him. My plan was to lure him out here, away from the village. But I need a witness, preferably unarmed. Is Barker armed?"

"I wouldn't know."

"What about everyone else? What kind of defense strategy is there?"

"Well, I know there are rifles for hunting, and there are several guns in the storage barn. But if the Indians attack, everyone is to use their rifles. They're always ready. Most everyone has something. Except the women," she added angrily.

"A woman," Lucas pondered. "Can we lure him here with a woman?"

"What are you proposing, Lucas?" This talk frightened her.

"He comes to meet a woman, I step out, shoot him dead, she runs back and tells everyone a blond haired white man did it." He smiled. "That's it!"

"Except," Virginia interrupted, "what woman?"

"We'll think, lovely lady," and he kissed her. "We'll think," he muttered right into her mouth. They giggled, and after much thinking, came up with a plan.

***

While Virginia and Lucas were busy thinking, Jacob had the good fortune to cross the path of three soldiers the commander had sent. His prolonged absence had caused worry. Jacob told them about Barker's settlement, elaborating on the tension between the Shawnee and the settlement, because if Vanderkellen tried anything foolish to free Virginia the peace would be broken. Two of the men went back to the Fort to request help, and Jacob, along with the third soldier, Daniel, started back to the village.

***

Virginia returned to the settlement by cutting through the small stand of trees separating it from the clearing that held the sacred circle of stones. She carefully marked her trail with bits of thread pulled from her skirt. When she emerged from the woods, barely a quarter mile from where she and Lucas held each other openly, she wrapped the ribbon from her hair around the trunk of a small tree. Getting her bearings, she strolled around the nearest cabin and was pleased to see how close she was to Barker's. The timing worked perfectly; she had wanted to catch him during the noon meal. Poor Richard, she thought, maybe Miss Lynn would feed him again today. Holding her face tight, she knocked on the open door of Barker's cabin. Like the rest of the cabins, there were no windows, so a lantern burned on the table where he sat with Walter Brandenburg. Claire stood behind him, a tin pitcher in her hand. They all froze.

Barker's face broke into a smile. Claire scowled. Walter sat nervously still, as if he had been caught doing something naughty.

"Reverend Barker, please, if I may have a word," she squeaked timidly.

"Of course, Mrs. Cramer," he said, standing graciously. "I see you are feeling better. Please, come into my office."

"Oh, no, out here is fine, please," she smiled shyly. Claire's face was red.

Being inappropriate to argue, Barker excused himself and followed Virginia to the side of the cabin. Unable to control her expression, she kept her face down. Barker misread her behavior as demureness. He pinched her chin between his thumb and the knuckle of his index finger.

"You wouldn't be here to arrange a consultation, would you?" he asked.

She was overcome with the urge to laugh, but only let loose soft giggles.

"Would you?"

"I...I'm not...I don't—" she stammered. It would have been intentional had her giggling not made it natural. She wanted to seem unsure, shy; he would find it suspicious if she suddenly came on brazenly.

She composed herself, then continued in a voice that was almost pleading, "I didn't think you cared about me, until that day you came by." She turned her back to him and said forlornly, "But then you never came back."

Now he stammered, but only for a moment, and apologized. "Please come to the service tonight, and afterward—"

"No!" She spun around to face him. "You don't understand. I'm...I'm frightened. I need to talk with you. I have these feelings—I'm all wrought and confused. The people, they'll see. They'll say things. Please!"

"No one will know anything."

"Oh, Reverend Barker," she sighed. "I know a place. I've marked the path." She took his arm and pulled him to where he could view the hair ribbon. "At dinner time, I'll wait there. Follow me. It's the most beautiful place! And it's private."

The idea seemed to agree with him. He leered openly at her breasts. "Might Richard go hungry tonight?"

"Richard dines elsewhere," she said angrily.

"Oh, I see. Very well then. Tonight we will dine together." He tried then to kiss her, but she ducked, blushing from repulsion. "A delicate blossom, you are," he said, then patted her cheek farewell.

Rushing now, she went to her cabin. Richard was eating hard bread with honey. He had already eaten most of the breakfast remains she had left that morning.

"Oh, Richard," she cried. "I am so sorry! The most horrible thing happened this morning." She babbled on about passing out at the river, an outrageous story only half concocted, for she took it for granted he either wouldn't listen or wouldn't care. In this case it was both.

"I smelled the best aroma from Miss Lynn's. Maybe those girls would be so good as to share a bit with you. They're always so generous," she said absently, clearing away the morning dishes. Richard grunted.

"Will you be in the fields late again tonight?" she asked. His words, muffled by the food in his mouth, indicated that he didn't know. Really it didn't matter, she realized, watching him slobber over his plate. This was the last time she would ever have to lay eyes on him.

***

Virginia thought Richard would never quit eating, but finally he did. With barely a goodbye, he picked up his hat and left. She started to clean up and stopped. It wasn't her mess to worry about anymore. Taking the broom, she went out to sweep the dirt some more so that she could watch Barker's cabin. It was a precarious view, and she could only see from one small spot. She kept that place, sweeping and sweeping. She thought she'd reach China before Barker and Walter finally stepped outside and walked toward the storage barn. Casually, she leaned the broom against the house, and just as casually, she headed toward his cabin. As she had hoped, Claire was there alone, tidying up from lunch.

"What do you want?" she said to Virginia.

"Oh, I'm sorry. Is he gone?"

"Why?" Claire drew herself up straight. "What have you two got going on?"

"Nothing!" she cried, showing obvious shock. Then she gave Claire a concerned, motherly look. "You don't know, do you?"

"Know what?" Claire spat. "Of course I know. Whatever it is, he's told me. I just don't know which thing you mean."

"Never mind, I have to go," Virginia crossed her fingers and before she could turn around Claire stopped her.

"You tell me!" Her tone sent chills down Virginia's back.

"I can't. I promised."

"Oh you better," Claire warned, coming closer.

Virginia looked around nervously. "Really Claire, he'll kill me. I'm scared to death of him. She made me—" She stopped as if realizing suddenly she'd said too much.

"Who? Who?" Claire demanded.

"Claire," Virginia continued to keep an anxious eye open for Barker, "I can't say who, but because you're a friend, I'll tell you this much. Just remember, it's a secret. She's going to meet him, but I have to take him to her because she's afraid her husband will be furious. Supper time."

Claire's face darkened. "He said he'd not be here for supper."

"Watch for me at the tree line behind here. He's going to follow me. Don't say anything or he'll just call it off. If you want to catch him, just follow. Don't let him see you." As she spoke, it occurred to Virginia how ridiculous the plan was. But it was already in motion and couldn't be stopped.

"Okay," Claire said quietly. Virginia thought she heard tears in her voice.

"I'm sorry, Claire." No answer. "Are you all right?"

"Of course I am!" she shot back. "Now go on, I've got work to do."

Virginia, who had not set foot inside, let loose of the door frame she hugged and left Claire alone in the dark cabin. Her skin jumped when Walter Brandenburg stepped around the corner.

"Afternoon Missus Cramer," he said as he passed, his smile uncharacteristically broad and smug, leaving Virginia to wonder whether he had overheard what she told Claire, or if Barker had told him about their supper plans.

***

Waiting, waiting, waiting, always she was waiting. Waiting for Lucas to come, waiting for Richard to leave. All afternoon she sat idly in her messy cabin waiting for the time when the men were called from the fields. Now she waited just inside the trees, questioning her sanity. If this didn't work, the best they could hope for was to be killed, the worst was to be caught. Twice she spotted Claire peeking around a corner. What if Claire didn't follow? Virginia could stay around to act as a witness, then meet Lucas later. Would they believe her, though? She wasn't sure what the others thought of her, but she felt like an outsider. Besides, she didn't want to stay here one day longer.

Where was Barker? Blasted man! Always around when she didn't want him. Was he playing coy with her? Or did Claire stop him? What would he think of the story she told Claire? How would she explain that? Lie, of course. If Claire had confronted him, would he still come? Would he be angry? Then what? She should leave now and forget the whole thing...but what if Claire hadn't told him? Back and forth she went, scared to stay, scared to go, and then Barker stepped into view wearing clean Sunday clothes. He wasn't carrying a rifle and appeared to have only one thing on his mind. This was it. She was going through with it. Making certain he saw her, she ducked into the woods. She didn't go far, she wanted them to go slowly so that Claire could catch up. If Claire was coming...

Barker entered the woods a few yards behind her. Softly, he called her name and she shushed him. Once more he misread her intentions and picked up his pace. He thought she was teasing him. She stayed ahead of him, but they were moving too fast. At this rate it would take only a few minutes to get to the meadow. Could Claire keep up?

When she broke into the clearing, she ran down hill, toward the circle, out of the line of fire. Higher up in the meadow, hidden in the cover of high grass, Lucas waited. The plan didn't entail getting Barker in the circle but rather to draw him far enough from the woods to prevent escape and close enough for a clean shot. Also, Lucas needed to be able to see when Claire arrived. If she did.

Then suddenly Barker caught Virginia. This wasn't part of the plan.

"You silly girl," he chided. "You'll have me so tired with your games I'll have no strength to play!"

"Oh surely you won't let a woman out last you!" Miraculously she broke away. For the briefest instant she saw his anger, but he replaced it with a mischievous grin.

Then, a bigger miracle! Over his shoulder Virginia saw Claire come into the clearing. She was stumbling in a clumsy run holding a shotgun with both hands.

From the middle of the clearing, Lucas shouted, "Lie down Virginia!"

Barker was clearly confused; no doubt that was his intention but not his voice. Virginia dove into the high grass and a shot split the air. Then came another shot! Then another! What happened? She heard Lucas calling to her, his voice in anguish, and somewhere Claire was screaming. Even though it was safest to lie still, she sat up, her eyes just above the grass. Walter! Walter was chasing Claire, shooting at her! Virginia turned around, searching out Lucas. Behind her, Claire's screams grew louder. Virginia went to all fours and began to crawl back up the hill. Again, a shot fired, and it was immediately answered. She froze. Claire was no longer screaming, but there were other voices in the meadow.

"This way! Hurry!" one shouted, followed by gunfire. New voices were calling. Virginia went flat to the ground; the men were just a few feet away.

"What's happening?"

"What have you done?"

POP!

"NO!"

"Reverend Barker! Where are you? Reverend Barker!"

"Claire killed him!"

"No! It was him!" Another shot. "Mark, oh no! Mark!"

"He killed that woman!"

More shots were fired, more shouts and screams. Virginia had lost her bearings; voices were everywhere. She heard nothing from where she thought Lucas should be. Slowly, she lifted herself again to see above the grass.

The sweet and peaceful clearing where she and Lucas had shared their love only hours ago was now filled with men. A battle was taking place around her. She couldn't breathe. What had they done? It just then occurred to her that everyone would have been in the settlement at dinnertime, not in the fields. Of course they would hear the shooting, of course they would pick up their weapons. But they were shooting each other! What was happening? Hank Goodall had climbed a tree and was shooting at his friends! Miles Wilbert cracked Samuel Smithe in the head with his rifle butt! Someone was laughing! Who would be laughing? The laughter was getting louder and Virginia thought for a moment it was all inside her head.

Then she, too, was shot. The bullet hit her shoulder and for a moment she thought she had been punched. She fell back to her knees, but her arm would not support her weight, so she crawled like a snake, not aware that she had been shot.

"Henry's killed the Reverend!" someone cried close by, and was answered by more shouting, more gunfire.

Virginia moved faster, careful to stay low in the grass. "Oh please let Lucas be safe!" she begged anyone who could hear her thoughts. The grass was thinning, she saw she had somehow turned around and was almost to the rock circle where Wanasteke had mashed the grass down. There she would be exposed and vulnerable, so she kept still, holding her breath.

The shooting continued sporadically, the gaps filled with voices. Virginia listened to the accusations being fired with the shots, less frequently now. Even the laughter had died down. She waited for quiet, but another fight began, and another shot was fired. Then came more yelling, more shots, and more of the wildly hysterical laughter. The laughter became louder than the shooting and the shouting. Terrified, Virginia remained pressed against the ground, her hands over her ears, protecting herself from the moans of agony, the shrill cries of disbelief, the pop-pop-pop of the guns, and the laughter that found hilarity in the insanity she and Lucas started.

* * *

Ages of darkness passed. Virginia was safe in the grass, conscious of nothing, until she heard a female voice sighing "Birga." She opened her eyes, and the voice became excited. "Birga! Birga!" Warm hands touched her lovingly, carefully avoiding the wounded shoulder. Brown eyes met hers. The same woman she met that first day, a hundred years ago, was it? Virginia let her head fall back, closing her eyes. Warm hands, now rough hands, picking her up, Jacob's sad, friendly voice asking, "Girl, what have you gone and done?"

She wanted Lucas, but she stayed in the darkness, because it felt like a better place at that moment.

* * *

Was it hours or days? Virginia slept under a blanket of unawareness, but it was a trick she played on herself, for she was fully aware that when she woke, she would be alone. When her eyes were finally forced open by sunlight and hunger, she asked about Lucas. Around her stood Jacob and another white man, Pelenay, the couple who helped her that first day, and many others whose unfamiliar names she could either not remember or pronounce. No one answered. Jacob examined the dirt at his feet. The other men looked out of the corners of their eyes. Only the woman gazed at her steadily. Virginia raised her fist and spread her fingers at the sky. The woman lowered her eyelids, and bowed her head.

If only Claire hadn't taken the bait. If only Walter hadn't followed her. The ifs were endless. Most likely, Walter followed them into the clearing and thought Claire shot Barker, so he shot Claire. He probably had wished for an excuse to shoot her anyway. Apparently the members of the settlement heard the first shots and rushed to the meadow, each mistaking the circumstances, shooting one another in vengeance or defense. There was more to it, she wanted to explain. Hank in the tree, for instance, she should tell someone, but she was too tired. For days Virginia sat alone, trying to get back to that comfortable state of unconsciousness where she could pretend none of it happened; where she was sixteen again

119

and Lucas didn't bring his immoral city talk home to scare the townspeople and he married her and they had babies and their babies had babies and their hair went white and eyes went bad and their bodies went soft. Instead she glared into reality.

Many came from Fort Washington and when they saw the carnage, they sent for even more. The survivors of the settlement walked mutely numb. The spell was broken. Along with their deep sorrow, they dealt with embarrassment and humiliation. They quietly buried the dead on the hill, many practically in the spot where they fell, leaving crude wooden markers and fifty seven mounds as the only reminder. They returned to the Fort with the soldiers, and never spoke publicly of the corruption that had become their lives.

***

Weeks later, Virginia wandered among the graves, reading the names burned into the markers. Names she recognized, people she remembered. Sam Parker, who always fretted in a womanish way over his baby; Thomas Spindler, a cabinet maker whose wife made sweetly scented candles; Daniel Miller, who, like Virginia came from Pennsylvania and could have been a relative. The Brandenburgs lay side by side, sharing one marker. Far off, all alone, John Barker lay away from the others. They buried Lucas in the middle, never asking about him, inscribing "Stranger" on his marker.

In the long days after the self-massacre of the Barker settlement, Virginia and the others slowly pieced together the story. Reluctantly, she told Jacob of her and Lucas's childish plan. Jacob and Daniel were on their way to the clearing when they heard shots fired. By the time they arrived, several men were fighting over who shot who. Then a bloody woman rose from the grass, a gun in her arms and a man in blue britches shot her. From that point on it was pandemonium. Jacob and Daniel hid in the safety of the woods until it was over, risking occasional peeks at the bizarre shoot out. Had it been anything other than murder, it would have been comical. Virginia remembered the laughter and shivered.

Her name was being called; Jacob and Wanasteke were coming. She headed toward them and Wanasteke shouted. "Stop!" Jacob urgently translated. Virginia, still disoriented with grief, obeyed. As they came closer Virginia heard Wanasteke's gently commanding monologue to Jacob.

"Sit down," Jacob told her, and they all sat beside the stone circle. "I'm going to try to explain this, but he uses words I don't know," he began. "Wanasteke is angry with Lucas. He spent days searching for help against John Barker, and Lucas rejected this." He waved toward the circle. Wanasteke spoke again, and Jacob nodded and continued. "This circle is a, I don't know, I think he means like a door, I don't know that word. It was opened especially for Barker. Or Lucas. Or any of their children. When any of them step inside, they cease to exist. Not just die, cease. I think that's what he means. Or maybe he's talking about Hell. I don't know these words. Whatever it does, it's still opened, and before it will close, one of them must be inside. You were about to step inside, that's why he stopped you."

"But, I'm not related to Lucas," she reminded him sadly.

"No, but Wanasteke believes you are carrying his child."

Offended, she opened her mouth to protest, then she stopped. It was possible. Very possible! She hung her head in shame.

"Because the Wethacanwee are from the under regions," Jacob went on, "they are bound by rules, or laws, I guess he means. Out here, out of the circle, your baby is safe from them until it is an adult because the Wethacanwee fear the spirits who watch children."

"What are you talking about?" Virginia interrupted. "I'm not having a baby. And safe from whom? What is he talking about?"

Wanasteke, who Virginia learned later, understood many English words, spoke again, and Jacob interpreted: "The Wethacanwee are spirits who live here. They are lesser spirits, always at odds with the *Matseweehewa*. Those are stronger spirits, I guess, and they don't give the Wethacanwee many privileges, so they are generally bored." He stopped, conferred with Wanasteke, then continued. "They like to find feeble spirited people because they are easy to influence. Like John Barker. That's why some left the settlement after a short time; they probably saw what was coming. Of course, a lot of the women were stuck because of their husbands. Children, however, are always safe from the Wethacanwee, and so will be yours, even though it is a Vanderkellen.

"This is difficult to explain, and impossible to understand, but Wanasteke is a very wise man. He feels that Barker is still here and will always be a threat to you. He is with the Wethacanwee, and they don't give up easily. This is a fun game for them. In fact, Wethacanwee, put in English, kind of means laughing ghosts."

Virginia's head came up. She had only been listening with one ear, her mind more concerned with the possibility of pregnancy. "Laughing ghosts?" Wanasteke nodded. Jacob asked, "What's wrong."

"Laughing?" she repeated. "I heard them. In all the shooting and screaming I heard laughing! I thought I was losing my mind!"

Jacob looked shocked and Wanasteke seemed pleased.

"But," Wanasteke said through Jacob, "no Vanderkellen and Barker shall live at one time. If your baby grows to maturity, it will be in danger, for although Barker exists, he does not live. And he will want to live very badly. I do not know what may happen, maybe nothing. You and your children should be careful. Encourage that child to have many babies, and the same with your grandchildren. In that way, Barker will never be able to live. Because, if he does, his evil will live with him."

"What about Lucas?" she asked. "If he thinks Barker lives on, then where is Lucas?"

Wanasteke spoke at length, but all Jacob translated was, "Lucas did not belong to the Wethacanwee. Don't think about him anymore."

"Why? What is he saying, Jacob?"

"Virginia," Jacob said. "Lucas is gone. That's all he's saying."

She had many questions, but learned little more. Speaking for himself for a change, Jacob said, "We came looking for you because it's time to go. We've stayed behind too long." She agreed.

During the journey home, she wrote all she could remember, much of which would wind up years later in Ed Philips's closet. News of the massacre arrived home before she did, and her family was sick with worry. Her father cried when she appeared on his doorstep. Once home with her family in Pennsylvania, she wrote more. Apparently her mother's condition was not entirely in her mind because she had passed away. Virginia's sister and brother-in-law now lived with her father. They had written, but Virginia had never received anything, although Barker claimed to be sending men periodically to pick up mail.

She fielded endless questions about the massacre. Most were convinced the Indians had started it. Out of respect for those who had helped so much, Virginia tried to defend them, but she discovered that people would think what they wanted.

Her pregnancy was confirmed. It was assumed to be Richard's child, and Virginia did not deny this. She was unsure of Richard's whereabouts, but she told everyone she thought he was dead. He would be too ashamed to come home anyway. Virginia's neighbors wondered why Lucas Vanderkellen was there, and gossip spread the way it will, and eventually died, the way it does. His sister came to visit, politely not asking questions, sweetly presenting Virginia with a box of her letters Lucas had saved. Virginia kept herself occupied with her family and the struggles they had suffered during her absence, busied herself preparing for the baby, and wrote constantly. Jacob Drake sent letters to her often, and she always answered. He was the only one who knew the truth about the baby and the story of the stone circle.

***

At six AM, alarm clocks sounded throughout Miltonville. Obnoxious buzzes and beeps and disc jockeys irritated sleepers and forced them to either wake up or tap the snooze bar. Dan and Michele Vickers would have enjoyed another ten minutes, but couldn't afford it. Two houses away, Robby Canwell sat on the edge of his bed, fighting the urge to lie back down. Today was his day off, but he would still spend it at the Center. Down the street, in the second house from the corner, Cindy Swift, who should be reporting to work, hit the snooze bar for the eighth time. Ten miles away, Anna Redmond reached out and shut off her alarm with confidence, while the cat gingerly touched her face with wet nose wake-up kisses. In uptown Miltonville, Rubin Tanner slept in a car behind the service station. His abandoned truck was parked in the lot, four cars over. Three blocks north, Ed Philips continued to dream a life he'd only read about. Less than two miles from the Kitchen, approaching slowly on very sore feet came Claire Brandenburg, smiling at the sunrise, anxious to find a quiet house and a new body. John Barker was having a more difficult time because of his constant fight with rigor mortis. As Mindell Road had taken him slightly south, he was still five miles away from Walter and the Vanderkellen.

***

The Vickers house was in a state of disarray. The family kept running into each other as they hurried about. Dan and Michele took showers before waking the kids, and while Les and Becky bathed, the parents put together breakfast, one suddenly remembering a last minute something that must be done before vacation could start, which would remind the other of something else.

"The paper!" Michele said, bumping into Dan in the kitchen doorway. "I didn't cancel the paper."

"Les'll be here. It's okay," he assured her.

"No, sometimes she's gone all day. We can't leave the paper out. What if someone saw it and broke in and was still here when Leslie came home?"

"In this neighborhood? With Dottie and her spyglass across the street?"

"Oh, she'd love that, thwarting a crime because we were too stupid to stop the paper. We'd never hear the end of it."

That made sense to Dan, and he added it to the list of things Les was to do. The list hung on the refrigerator door where she was sure to see it repeatedly. "Better put the number down too. If she has to look it up herself, it'll never get done," Michele said, leaving the kitchen. "Oh, keep an eye on the bacon."

In the hall Becky walked out of the bathroom and into Michele. Michele patted her head and told her to report for breakfast. In her and Dan's bathroom, Leslie was bent over, drying her hair. Michele picked her overnight bag off the bed and edged into the bathroom with Leslie, who stopped drying for conversation's sake.

"Can you call and stop the paper today? Your dad's writing down the number," Michele asked, dropping the jars and bottles she had used that morning into her bag.

"Sure," Leslie said, starting the dryer again. She didn't notice the pungent odor Michele was sniffing. Michele followed the smell out of the bathroom, into the bedroom then into the hall. "Dan!" she shrieked. She was answered by the shrill whine of the smoke detector.

In the bathroom Leslie continued drying her hair obliviously.

***

Anna joined her groggy parents at the breakfast table. Her father had come in from Dallas an hour ago. He had driven through the night, hoping to have a weekend at home with his family. He was now receiving the news that both his wife and daughter would be working Saturday, but the grass and gutters might enjoy his company.

"I'm sorry, Dad," Anna said, pouring cereal into her bowl. "I get off at two though, so I can help with the gutters."

"It's okay," he yawned. They asked each other questions about the preceding days during which he was gone, then he excused himself and went upstairs to sleep.

"Too bad you can't be off this weekend," Anna said to her mother.

"Aw, your dad will probably sleep half the day tomorrow, too."

"So what are you going to do today?"

"I thought I'd surprise your father and mow the grass. And the garden needs work. Just piddle, I guess." Judy Redmond defined piddling differently then the rest of the world.

"Well, I better go find something to wear and make my bed," Anna said. Taking her coffee, she went back to her room.

***

Rubin Tanner awoke once more to the sound of rapping on the car window. Someone shouted, "Rubin. Rubin! What are ya doin' in there?"

Painfully he turned his head, forgetting where he was. When he remembered, he sat up quickly, his tight muscles resisting. It was morning. Pete's fat face pressed against the driver's window. "Wassa matter? Patti Anne throw ya out? Get outta there before Al shows up. It's bad enough when you pass out in your own truck round here, but if he catches you in a customer's car he'll can you."

He was alive. One hand rubbing his stiff neck, he more or less rolled from the car. "What time is it?" he asked, his face distorting with the effort.

"Six thirty. I was over havin' coffee when I saw your truck. Thought I'd come over and check if you was here." This wasn't the first time Rubin had slept at the station. Pete stepped back as Rubin passed. "Oh boy, are you ripe. You better run home and clean up. I'll tell Al you're running late." When Pete Lykins told you to take a bath, it must be bad. Rubin shook his head and walked up the alley beside the station to where he could see the dentist office.

"Seen him?" he asked Pete.

"Who? Doc Ivers? No, he don't come in this early. Rubin? You okay?"

Rubin nodded, then walked across the street to the donut shop where Pete had been earlier to drink coffee and wait for seven o'clock.

***

Claire wished she could find a new body. She walked slowly along the highway, cars whizzing by and causing the tired, sore body to stagger. It wouldn't be long, she consoled herself, sniffing the air, puckering at the stench of the Vanderkellen. She must be very close. Ahead, a road came in from the left, and she took it in order to get away from the traffic. The new road began a wide curve, with yet another road running into it, both lined with neat houses. Claire's smile was hopeful; the Vanderkellen may be in one of these houses! Walter's odor was certainly strong, almost stronger than the Vanderkellen's. She was so near to them it was frustrating. The closer one came to such energy the more difficult it was to pinpoint. If she had to, she would walk in ever-smaller circles, spiraling down until she located them. This body was young enough to make it another hour or so, if it took that long. But then, just when she thought she could stretch out and touch Walter, the knees of Jaime's body folded, and they went down. For a few minutes she lay there, stunned. Then she dragged the body off the road, determined to ambush anything that came by, aware or not, prepared to fight to the death, She was too close to stop now.

She crawled into the grass to wait under a shrub, and it wasn't long before Misty Swift came sauntering by on her way home. The fuzzy black and white cat noticed the leaves of a bush rustling, and paused to investigate with cautious curiosity. Of all things Claire did not want to be, a cat would be the first on the list. But she had to take what she could, and the cat could travel fast. This time it was worth the risk, and she jumped.

The cat went wild, bucking and running, yowling frightfully.

Claire tried not to look at the approaching headlights, cringing at the sound of squealing tires and blaring horn, clinging desperately as the cat bounded through yards and over a fence, and headed straight for a door. Claire braced herself for the impact, but felt only slight pressure as the small kitty door swung in. They were in a house! A dark house! Bounding off the walls, claws catching the carpet, the animal sped around the house. Into chair legs, onto window sills, through open doors and into a bedroom where a woman slept. Claire let go and fell into the body, grateful that there were no other spirits nearby to stop her. The cat crashed into the night table, stared at her, then hissed and ran from the room. Claire sighed, relieved, safe in the body of Cindy Swift.

Nausea hit when she raised the head. She lay back down. This body was worse than the old one. The thick, sticky tongue; the heavy limbs; the pounding head and sore eyes! Claire knew the after-effects of alcohol. There was only one thing to do, and she was about to find a place to do it when the most horrible noise came from the clock by the bed. She jumped, and the woman inside of her woke. Hand to mouth, she ran, first into a closet, then back out and through another door; across the hall, into another room, back into the hall, through another door, and there it was! A commode. She collapsed in front of it and vomited.

"Mom," a child's voice called, and the confused woman Claire had possessed became alarmed. Claire continued retching, though no longer producing anything. "Mom! Something's wrong with Misty! Mom?" The child was behind her now. "Are you sick?"

"Go away," Claire said, wiping her face on Cindy's pajama sleeve.

He backed toward the hall. "Your alarm clock...Mom?" Claire tried to stand on Cindy's woozy legs and stumbled. The boy reached to help and she glared at him.

"I said get out." His eyes widened, and he ran down the hall. Grabbing the phone he hit number three on the speed dial, peeking around the corner as his mother came from the bathroom, covered in vomit, trying to find her way down the hall.

***

Robby Canwell found his breakfast waiting when he came to the table. His parents were having coffee, but he preferred juice.

He greeted his father, having already spoken to his mother when she knocked at his door. Friday mornings were always his sleepiest, and without his mother he would undoubtedly have fallen back into his bed, back into sleep.

"Did you remember your lunch money?" she asked him now.

"Yes, Mom," he sighed tiredly. He took out his wallet as if to prove it to her, but actually he wanted to prove it to himself. He was not stupid, but like anyone else, he could sometimes forget things. The wallet winked green, and he was putting it back when the phone rang. The three of them stared at it blankly before MC answered.

"Slow down, Ryan, what is it? It's all right. I'm on my way." MC hung up and announced, "Cindy's sick, I'm going over."

"Is she okay?" Robby asked, concerned. "Should I go and get Ryan?"

"Thanks, Robby, but I think it's okay. Ryan's just scared to see his mom sick," she explained. After reminding Robby to be at the bus stop by 7:15, she hurried out the door, still in her robe and slippers.

***

MC's feet left tracks in the dewy grass as she cut across her lawn to the sidewalk. A man stood at the end of the Vickers' driveway, his back to her, looking off into the distance. It was unusual to have strangers in this neighborhood, and she meant to show him he was noticed, just in case. After all, it was no secret that Dan and Michele were leaving for vacation. Stepping out of the yard, she marched boldly in his direction...then stopped. Her head had become light and she felt something popping inside. Her breath quickened and suddenly she had an urge to see the man. To get close! She took a step. Stopped. Her arms tingled. Another step. He was bald, she saw. He was...he was *in the garbage can*? She shook her head violently, and her marbles fell into place. It was a mannequin: his arm slightly bent in the pose of a model; a dark brown wig sticking out of the breast pocket of his denim jacket like a shaggy handkerchief. Surely not the same mannequin Dan had years ago? She thought he had gotten rid of it. She couldn't imagine him keeping it after it had scared Leslie and Robby so. Maybe this was a different one. At any rate, she was glad to see it in the garbage.

Crossing the street, she decided that if the garbage collectors refused to take him, she would pay the five dollars and take him to the dump herself.

The shouting from the Swift house distracted her from the Vickers' trash. She rushed to the stoop and beat on the door. The knob turned and the door swung open a few inches. MC thought it opened on its own until she saw Ryan, sturdy arms wrapped around his mother's waist, dragging her away. Cindy swore at him, prying one hand off just as another found its grip.

"Cindy! Cindy!" MC said firmly. Cindy didn't acknowledge her, instead she elbowed Ryan in the temple. He barely flinched, holding on tightly. With two strides, MC cornered them and slapped Cindy hard in the face. Stunned only an instant, she raised her head and spat. She missed only because MC had back stepped when she saw Cindy's pasty, sweat soaked face. Strands of hair stuck to her cheeks and spittle ran down her chin. The flesh around her angry eyes was puffy and gray.

"Cindy!" MC said, and Cindy went off again, calling her names in such a steady stream they sounded like one word. MC tried to catch her arms, but they moved like pinwheels, stopping only to claw away from Ryan. MC saw blood on his knuckles and she slapped Cindy again, trying to snap her out of it. Ryan cried, "Stop hitting her!"

"We've got to calm her down." She mashed both him and Cindy against the wall where Cindy bucked like a wild pony. "Can you get out, Ryan? Good! Call Michael," she ordered, trying to be calm for his sake.

He squirmed, but his legs tangled in Cindy's and they all went down. Ryan wriggled from under the women. Cindy rolled over for leverage, trying get on all fours, but MC crawled up her back and put her in a headlock, digging one knee into her spine. The struggling ceased.

"I won't hurt you if you just let me up!" Cindy, suddenly coherent, spoke with authority. "I want nothing from you."

"Don't waste your breath on me right now," MC retorted.

Cindy paid no heed and kept on with nonsense about her purpose. Tired, MC spotted Misty's catnip mouse lying nearby. Taking a chance, she dug her knee deeper, freed one hand long enough to snatch it, and stuffed it into Cindy's mouth.

"That'll hold you," she said, and pressed Cindy's chin into the carpet.

***

John Barker stretched in his comfortable new body. It was a nice one. This fellow, young Professor Mark Reynolds, was captured on his way to Salem University. He had planned to be early today to find some videotapes for his class and had the misfortune to be caught in deep reverie at a stop sign. Sorry, Barker told him, holding him, much like pinning an insect to the ground with a thumb. This time he did not kill his host. The end was inevitable, but the suffering was necessary; as long as the professor lived, his brain kept the vitals going. Whenever a host died, Barker was forced to consciously pump the blood and breathe the oxygen. Often he lost track, and, as with the dentist, the blood thickened and settled, and the limbs grew stiff. So the professor survived, and now paced and pulled at his thin hair in the nether regions of his own consciousness, reasoning with himself, leaving Barker free to track the Vanderkellen. He drove by reading Mark Reynold's memories, pointing the man's car in the direction of Walter's scent, squeezing the wheel. Driving was not his nature, and despite what he stole from the man's memories, he dare not drive fast. Twenty miles per hour was comfortable. Cars sailed by, blowing their horns and making him jumpy. He passed two entry roads into the Kitchen subdivision before he noticed the once strong odor of Walter's fear fading. Carefully he turned around. When he caught Walter's smell again, he took the next road, Hickory Lane, which led into the Nut Valley region of the Kitchen, or the Nut Hatch, as it was often called. Luckily, this area was familiar to Professor Mark Reynolds, who had resided in the Valley for two years. Smiling at the professor's confusion, Barker inhaled deeply in search of the scent.

***

The fire was out at the Vickers' house. It was small, confined to the skillet, but it had scorched the oven hood. When Michele came into the kitchen, Dan was trying to beat it out with a dishrag. She grabbed the skillet lid and quickly snapped her arm over the flame, dropping the lid on the pan and smothering the fire. Embarrassed, Dan concentrated on shutting off the smoke alarm. When it was silenced, Becky's scream continued. Michele, busy opening the door and waving away the smoke hadn't realized Becky was in

130

the kitchen. "Oh, sweetie," she soothed, hugging her gently. "It's just a—"

"What in the world is going on?" Leslie stood in the doorway, hairdryer in hand.

"—greasefire," Michele finished.

"Dad!" Leslie accused. Michele laughed.

"What?" he cried, but then he grinned. "What?"

Leslie sighed, shaking her head. Michele confirmed her suspicion. "I asked him to watch the bacon."

"I thought so. Here's your hairdryer."

"Just lay it by the door with my bag, will you?" she trailed off, distracted by a thought. Wetting down a dishtowel, she flapped it in the air to dispel the smoke. Becky and Leslie opened windows in the dining room.

"Well, we still have the eggs," Michele consoled.

Leslie poked at the grease. "What a mess."

"I was only gone a minute."

"Mom," Becky said, holding the overnight bag and the hairdryer. "Can I put these in the trailer." Becky used any excuse to get inside the trailer. They were barely able to pack for her playing house in it the night before.

"Yeah, if you put them where they belong," Michele said, taking up the eggs before they joined the bacon. While she and Leslie cleaned, Dan was permitted to make the toast, and forced to endure substantial taunting.

***

The night had dragged for Walter Brandenburg. His situation was hopeless, and he was desperate. Both Claire and John Barker were within shouting distance. Seeing no point in discretion, he would try for anyone who passed. No more subtlety, it was time for action, the type of which he wasn't sure, but he thought a quick ride far away might work. Where was everyone? First he had missed the woman. Just barely, though. He thought he had snagged her, but she was determined to get somewhere. Since then, nothing, nobody. Not even the putrid devils who so loved to bother him during his times of failure. He tried forcing himself into the sleeping houses, but he was too far away and nobody heard.

A door slammed and he whirled around inside the mannequin.

The little one was carrying things to the camper. Having been in the house all evening he was aware that the family was leaving and taking the camper for shelter. Of course! He rode in it yesterday when Ralph Vickers brought him over. *Hey, Kid! Kid!* What was her name? He wasn't allowed to hurt children, but they usually heard him.

The clatter of garbage cans distracted him. The garbage! Forgetting the child, he looked behind him, which was actually Bruce's front. Between the houses across the street he saw the garbage truck on Raisin Avenue, the next block over. A man casually picked up a can and tossed the contents into a yawning hole that shut and — what did it do? Chew?

Becky! Becky! He suddenly remembered her name. Her head appeared in the small doorway of the camper, cocked to one side, listening. Walter envisioned himself in the camper, safe on the bed, hidden by pillows and blankets. He waited for her to look his way, and when she did, he forced it at her.

"Becky, breakfast!" a voice called from inside the house.

The kid hitched, as if startled, risked a very quick glance his way then ran to her mother, leaving the door to the camper open. Walter roared in panicked horror. He pressed against his prison walls pounding! *Kid, kid! Come back!*

***

Michael Canwell said little to Ryan when he called the second time. Robby was still home, and he didn't want to upset him. Although he had improved over the years, Robby sometimes had problems controlling his emotions, especially if he was worried about someone he cared for. He assured Ryan he was coming, then went to Robby's room.

"Son, I have to go to Mrs. Swift's. Can you get yourself to the bus?" Michael tried to sidestep the issue by focusing on Robby's task.

"Yes, Dad. Is she okay? Is she sick?" Robby asked, showing his worry, but otherwise not appearing overly distressed.

"Oh, I think so. I may need to take her to the doctor, and Mom will have to sit with Ryan while we're gone. I think it's just a stomach thing. Don't lock the door because I don't think Mom has her keys, okay?"

"Okay," he said, then checked his watch. "Oh, it's almost time to go now!"

Michael leaned over and peeked. "It's seven already? Don't forget to feed the fish. I'll see you tonight."

Once Michael was outside, he picked up his pace, remembering Ryan's urgent voice. MC wouldn't have had him call if it weren't an emergency. Still, he kept his stride steady and casual in case Robby should be watching out the window. He couldn't risk agitating Robby, or they might have two crises on their hands.

Passing the Vickers, he noticed the mannequin in the trash, wondered briefly if the collectors would take it, fought a ridiculous urge to play a trick on Dan by hiding the mannequin in the camper, and forgot it as soon as he was out of sight.

Walking up the Swift's drive, he heard shouting, and hurried to the door. Cindy herself opened it and ran out, oblivious to him. Michael jumped in front of her and she stopped. Her jaw went limp, her eyes grew wide, staring at something distant. Then she went into motion, climbing and tearing her way around Michael.

"Walter! Walter! I see you!" she screamed frantically, spittle flying. MC, nearly as haggard as Cindy, was behind her pulling while Michael blocked her, pushing her back into the house. Pinning her arms to her sides, he kicked the door shut behind him. Cindy writhed in his grip, managing to yell through gritted teeth, "You idiot! Do you have any idea what you're doing?"

"Not really," Michael answered, losing his calm. She was leaning backwards, away from him, so he took the advantage and hooked his right leg behind hers. When she gave the next hard tug, he pushed, and again she went down. Again Misty's mouse went in her mouth.

"Be careful Michael, we've done this before," MC warned. "She tricked me. I thought she was getting sick."

"We better call 911." He was holding her by the throat, straddling her waist.

She nodded. "Let me talk to Ryan."

***

MC found Ryan in the bathroom cleaning up the vomit that had sprayed the walls and floor. It was an ugly job, but apparently he found it preferable to watching his mother manhandled in the front room.

"Ryan, I'm sorry you had to see that." With a silent nod, he kept wiping. "We have to take your mom to the hospital before she hurts herself." Or one of us, she thought. "I'm going to call an ambulance because I don't think she'll—I don't think we can take her in the car." She put her hand on his arm. He stopped rubbing the wall and stared at it.

"The doctors will need to ask you questions. Do you understand?"

"Yes," he mumbled.

"Will you be able to tell them everything?"

"Yeah." Tears ran down his cheeks, and she hugged him while he cried.

"Don't be mad at us Ryan, we're just trying to help."

"I'm not mad at you," he said into her bathrobe. "It's him. It's his fault."

"Whose fault?"

"It's Dad's fault," he cried harder. She knew it hurt him, yet she took a perverse satisfaction in hearing Ryan acknowledge his father's role in their deteriorating situation. Admonishing herself, she patted Ryan's head.

"I'm going to call now. There may be sirens, but I'll ask them not to use them if they don't have too, okay?"

He nodded.

"You want to wait in here?"

Again the nod. It was crushing, but she left him crying alone in the bathroom.

***

Robby never liked being home alone, so he left a little early to meet the bus. Careful not to lock the door as his father instructed, Robby, unlike his parents, stayed on the small walk to the driveway, and went to the sidewalk without hurting the grass. He saw Bruce as soon as he turned out of the driveway. And Bruce saw him, he felt it. Why was he back? But he was in the trash. Good. *I can be brave*, he thought. It's just a mannequin. Besides, he had the strongest urge...*to see him up close*? No, that couldn't be. Brave or not, he was still afraid. *But so was Bruce!* Bruce was afraid, very afraid. Somehow Robby knew this and was compelled to help him. *He liked helping.*

Who said that? It came out of his own head, but it wasn't his thought. He now had the strangest desire to...*to hide Bruce in the trailer*! What? Why would he want to do that? *It would be a good joke, wouldn't it? Wouldn't that be so funny when Becky gets ready for bed and pulls down the cover and sees Walter*? Walter? Who's Walter? *Bruce! Wouldn't it be funny when she sees Bruce in bed? Remember all the tricks her dad played? They would all LAUGH SO HARD! COME ON! DO IT!*

Oh! He wanted to! He really did! Imagine being responsible for such a good joke! For making everybody laugh! Why was he scared? Something was wrong, that's why. *Hurry! Before you get caught! It wouldn't be funny then. Hurry*! Of course, he was anxious, that's what this feeling was. It was like playing hide and seek and hearing the IT kid reaching 95, 96, 97 before he finished hiding.

Smiling, he hurried to Bruce. It was tricky, but he lifted him out of the garbage can quietly and, *faster! Please, please! Faster!* With an increased urgency and a terror, not of Bruce, but *for* him, Robby hurried. Uh oh! The camper door was open! What if someone was inside? *It's okay. The kid left it open. Hurry*! Huh? Where did that voice come from? *Come on! Everyone's going to say you were so smart to think this up, but you better hurry!* Robby's arms tingled with excitement. This was a good idea! He maneuvered the clumsy load inside. The apprehension disappeared, replaced by joy, joy, joy! A quick survey showed Robby the best place to hide the mannequin was one of the beds and it was easy to decide which one. Heart racing, he cleared off the cramped overhead bunk. At first it seemed impossible, but after two attempts he shoved Bruce into the bed, close to the wall. The bunk had been stuffed with bedding and pillows, and he carefully replaced them around Bruce. Grinning, he stepped back to inspect. Not bad! Now hurry and go!

Once outside, he had to fight temptation again. This time he wanted to go in and tell the Vickers, *Watch out! Someone might be going to play a trick on you!* But a glance at his watch stopped him. Closing the door softly, he slunk around the camper and out of the yard. His effort to be quiet wasn't necessary because the garbage truck was growling and groaning its way down Apple Street.

He almost had to run to the highway to meet the bus. The joy of a mere moment ago was gone, the anxiety had returned. A joke, he reminded himself, just a joke. They would laugh, wouldn't they? It was funny, wasn't it? Wondering if he'd done such a good thing after all, he hesitated before getting on the bus.

"Robby? Come on, we're on a schedule," the driver hurried him.

Sighing, he muttered, "Just a stupid joke," and climbed aboard.

***

The clatter of garbage cans turned everyone's head at the Vickers breakfast table. Dan stood up, motioning the others to stay seated. "I'll check."

"He better be gone," Leslie said to her toast.

"He's gone," Dan announced when he returned.

"Are you sure?" Leslie questioned, knowing that Bruce had a way of getting around.

"He's gone. The cans are empty and he's not laying around out there." Dan sat down.

"Yeah, but maybe he was already gone," she worried.

"He was there when we got up," Michele assured her.

Becky, who had been unusually quiet during breakfast said, "He was still there a minute ago, when I was out there. I'm glad he's gone."

"That's a switch. You were pitching a fit before," Leslie muttered.

"I don't care. I hate him now. He looks at people."

"Oh, that's just the way his eyes are painted. It just looks like he's looking," Michele explained.

"No, he can look out the back of his head. He can touch you." The adults stared at the child as she continued eating.

"Told you," Leslie said smugly.

A few minutes later, Dan Vickers stuck his head into the camper to check that all was secure, then thumbed the lock inside the door and slammed it shut. Having hitched it to the car the night before, while Ralph was there to help, they were all set to go. The family stood together in the driveway having an awkward moment as they prepared to say goodbye. This was the first vacation they had ever taken without Leslie.

"Thanks for taking care of the breakfast mess," Michele said.

Leslie shrugged. "No problem."

"Now remember, tonight—"

"I know, today you'll be at Grandma Emily's, tomorrow and maybe Sunday the Galaxy, and Monday night you'll call with the number. I have it," Leslie tapped her head so Michele would know where she was keeping it.

Becky hugged Leslie around the hips, her head resting on her waist. "I wish you were going."

"Me too, Beck. Have fun for me, and don't pull Uncle Lew's finger, okay?"

With a heavy, sentimental heart, she waved her family away, following the car into the street and watching it until it disappeared around the corner. When the moment began to fade, she picked up two of the garbage cans and dragged them to the garage. As she carried the third, the ambulance turned onto Apple Street and into Cindy Swift's drive. Leslie almost didn't notice it; the lights and siren were off. This was more frightening than if it had come wailing around the corner at a hundred miles an hour. A quiet ambulance meant death, or so she thought. Gently, she sat the can down, and drifted toward the Swift's. Across the street the Geist's door opened, and Dottie stormed out in a tattered flannel robe, her hair in curlers.

"I knew something was going on, all that yelling all morning," she was saying, maybe to Leslie, maybe to Artie, whose pale face hung in a dark window, maybe to MC who was directing the medics, or maybe Laura Green, who rushed over on high heels, her briefcase left on the roof of her car. Maybe to all and everyone, but more likely, she was talking to herself.

"What happened?" Laura asked. Leslie shook her head. The three women met on the side lawn of the Swift house. "Wait here," Laura said. Leslie and Dottie followed anyway. MC stood on the stoop, talking to one of the paramedics.

"It's Cindy," she answered Laura's unspoken question once the paramedic had gone inside. "She's had a breakdown, I think."

"What about Ryan? Can I take him?" Laura asked.

"I'm going to take him with me to the hospital."

"What?" Dottie squawked. "You can't expose that child—"

"Dottie, that child has already been exposed," MC said firmly. "He needs to see that she's going to be okay. He's scared to death right now."

"She's okay?" Leslie asked, relieved. "There was no siren..."

"I asked them not to. It wasn't an emergency, but she was too, uh, agitated for us to take her in the car. The sirens would just attract attention, and we didn't want that." MC smiled sweetly at Dottie. Dottie chewed the inside of her cheek angrily.

They were bringing a very sedated Cindy out strapped to a stretcher when Leslie noticed the Redmond's wagon pulling to the curb. Remembering her promise to be ready, and then remembering her promise to clean the breakfast dishes, she excused herself and ran home. She was ready enough for work, and the dishes could wait.

"Geez!" she exclaimed to Anna, "You wouldn't believe the night we had." Then she spent most of the morning telling her about it.

***

John Barker was barely six blocks away when the ambulance left the Swift house. His meandering had taken him out of Nut Valley and into the Vegetable Patch, which blended into the Fruit Bowl. He followed Walter Brandenburg's terror like a hound, occasionally distracted from the target but heading in the general direction. Closer, closer now. The Vanderkellen, too. Now and then he caught wind of her, and the energy was almost magnetic. Claire was likely near, although her scent lacked the distinction of those he pursued. Better if she were there, he decided; he was working on a plan and could use her.

After years of failed attempts he had gathered enough clues to restore his confidence in his ability to stop the Vanderkellen. The last time, his strategy involved killing it and taking the living child to the circle. He preferred not to tangle with the child's protectors, but he would fight them off while Claire drove them to the cemetery. Barker thought the protectors could not enter the circle. He had misjudged the power of the protectors, however, and the moment he killed the mother he was expelled from the world. He went berserk, screaming at the Wethacanwee, accusing them of cheating at their own game, calling them cowards for not giving him a fair chance. It was obvious now; there was no way to end the Vanderkellen line because his release would always be postponed until a new one had been created. The Wethacanwee finally conceded and he was going to win, even if he had to accept help from

Claire and Walter. Ideally, he would have them carry the Vanderkellen into the circle and send them all to Hell.

As he found himself at the end of Carrot Court, another one of those confounding cul-de-sacs, he noticed Walter's fear diminishing. He drove slowly around, came back to Spinach, and turned right. Less Walter, but he still sensed the Vanderkellen. Left on Turnip. Cold, colder. Right on the next street, Cucumber, putting him back in his original direction, where he picked up the scent once more. Not as strong, though. He stayed on Cucumber until it dead-ended at Tomato, the official border of the Vegetable Patch and the Fruit Bowl because no one could agree whether a tomato was a fruit or a vegetable.

There was nothing. He went left, felt nothing, came back down Cucumber, all the way to Almond, where it had been strong. It was gone. *They* were gone! Walter and the Vanderkellen both! Gripping the wheel, he tried to shake it loose with his anger, a low growl scraping his chest, then his throat, and out his mouth in a howl.

A pudgy woman in tight sweat pants strutted by, weights in each hand, arms pumping. Hearing him, she slowed, calling, "Dr. Reynolds? Dr. Reynolds! Are you okay?" His look told her how he was, and she sped up, harrumphing to cover her embarrassment. He pulled Dr. Reynolds hair, and to his surprise, handfuls came out. Tossing it behind him, it wafted down to rest on the body of Troy Ivers. *Calm down!* he scolded himself. These days he thought it important not to arouse suspicion. The townspeople seemed to be catching on to his visits and he didn't want to send anyone into hiding. That is why he put Troy into the back seat when he settled into the professor's body. The fewer bodies lying around, the fewer fears raised.

Alert for the faintest trace of them, any of them, Walter, Claire, or the Vanderkellen, he drove on. Inside him, the little professor, who only a short while ago was contemplating his class and daydreaming about a particular student, now worried about his pregnant wife and all the tracks he had not covered. Notes on his desk, messages on the computer, photos in his drawer. His wife would be devastated and he was surprised by how horrible he felt over that. John Barker had convinced him he was already dead and in Hell, too late to barter or call out to God, Barker said. You're a dead sinner and this is your Heaven. Better enjoy it while you can because it gets worse from here. Dr. Mark Reynolds crouched in terrified resignation, trying not to think of what waited ahead.

***

Dante Masters almost didn't see the leg sticking out from the bush next to her drive, but it was a good thing she did, or she would have run over it. She gave the driveway the usual cursory glance as she backed out of the garage, then diverted her attention to Peach Street. Before she was aware of anything out of the ordinary, her foot hit the brake. Milliseconds later, the leg on the driveway registered. Stomping the brake harder, she opened the door and, without getting out, leaned around to look. It was a leg, all right. She blew the horn. It didn't move. She blew again, longer. Longer. Finally Jim came to the door in his bathrobe, his hair mashed on one side. He worked the night shift at the radio station and had hardly been asleep an hour.

"Jim! Jim!" she called, and with him in sight, found the courage to vacate the car. Pointing to the leg she stated the obvious, "There's a leg!"

"What?" He came out, tying his robe closed, and together they went to investigate.

Once again, an ambulance was dispatched to the Fruit Bowl area of Miltonville's Kitchen.

***

Rubin Tanner took another peek at the dentist office across the street from AJ's Service Station. Eight o'clock had come and gone, but, as far as Rubin could tell, Troy had not arrived. Troy's receptionist, Rose, had opened up the office, and twice he caught her peeking out her own window.

A man stepped onto the curb in front of the dentist's office, flicked his wrist to check his watch, then went inside. Bill Hainey, Rubin thought. Well, Mr. Hainey would have to wait, because Rubin was going to be Troy's first appointment.

***

"Mornin' Rose," Bill Hainey greeted Dr. Ivers' receptionist.

"Is he running on time?"

"Afraid not," she replied honestly.

"Kind of early to be behind." He signed in, surveyed the empty waiting room, then chose a seat next to the magazine rack.

Elaine, the hygienist, poked her head into the reception area. "Well?"

"I'll try again." Rose shrugged, picking up the phone. When the answering machine began its announcement, she hung up, having already left three messages. She buzzed Elaine in the lab.

"Can you cover the phone? I'll drive out there. Maybe he broke down or something."

"Hurry, okay? Mr. Hainey will be mad if he has to wait long."

"I'll hurry," she promised. "Keep trying his mobile phone."

When she returned thirty minutes later, Rose had the unpleasant task of informing Mr. Hainey that his appointment would have to be rescheduled.

***

At nine-ten that Friday morning it seemed everyone in Miltonville was checking the time. Rubin Tanner did, as did both Rose and Elaine in Troy's office. Two blocks away, at Hartmann's Grocery Leslie glanced at her watch again, sighed to see only five minutes had passed since she last checked, and sliced open another carton of baby food. Two blocks northeast, Ed Philips opened his blurry eyes, focused on the alarm clock, then let them close. Across town, at Miltonville General Hospital, the paramedics noted the time during a well-deserved coffee break. Two floors above them, MC Canwell remarked on the time while waiting with Ryan Swift for word on his mother. Seven miles east, Judy Redmond, kneeling in her garden, was disappointed to see she had missed the first part of her favorite morning show, the one hour of self-indulgent, brain deadening relaxation she allowed herself to enjoy when she was off during the week. And miles and miles away, Becky Vickers read the numbers on her pink, plastic watch and frowned.

Like her sister, she checked and double checked the time frequently, bored already despite the toys and books scattered around the back seat. The new watch, a gift from her father, was to keep her from constantly asking if they were almost there. Dad told her they should reach Grandma Emily's before noon, maybe as early as eleven. Then he tried to explain Daylight Savings Time, which southeastern Indiana did not observe, therefore putting Grandma an hour ahead, until Becky let her eyes glaze over. "Noon," he said. "When your watch says 12:00, we're almost there. If the traffic is smooth, of course."

"Mom," she called. "Is the traffic smooth?"

"Yes, sweetheart, it's still smooth. We're on schedule."

Yawning, Becky twisted the head of her fashion doll so that it looked behind itself, then she swung it in circles by its long blond hair. As much as she wanted the car ride to end, she wasn't very excited about spending the day at Grandma Emily's. Her cousins Joey, Elizabeth, Carrie and Amy were nice, and sometimes so was Kevin, even though he was bigger. But Little Ray and Angie were weird, and their dad, Uncle Ray, was mean when he was drunk. Ray lived with Grandma Emily, so he was always there, picking fights, usually right at dinner time. Her father made Mom promise this time that they would leave if Ray acted up. Their vacation was not going to start that way, Dad said.

Well, Uncle Ray, Becky thought, *if you're going to start, do it early*. Then maybe they would go to the Galaxy tonight.

***

It was nine thirty before a young doctor came into the waiting room to talk with MC and Ryan. He nodded and suggested Ryan go to the snack machine for a treat.

"No, it's okay, he can stay here," MC said.

"Well, if you're sure." His lips were pulled tight, indicating that *he* wasn't sure. Sitting down next to them he introduced himself. MC and Ryan did likewise.

"Dr. Reilly? Is mom psycho?" Ryan had worried MC with this question for nearly two hours.

"Uh," Dr. Reilly stuttered at his bluntness. Apparently Dr. Reilly had no children, MC thought. *Of course not. He's a baby himself.*

"Well, no," he recovered. "Your mother is not psychotic. This is an emotional problem. Although we aren't ready to make a diagnosis, I would venture to say that your mother is suffering from a stress disorder, maybe something along the lines of post traumatic stress disorder."

Ryan stared at him blankly. MC shook her head. Dr. Reilly

took a deep breath, then addressed Ryan.

"Well, PTSD is, well, when something bad happens and later, when the bad thing is over, it—"

"But it isn't over," Ryan corrected him. "Something bad is always happening every day."

"Well, um, it's more than that. Besides, I'm not saying it is PTSD, but similar." He struggled away from Ryan's gaze and looked at MC. "Can we—?"

"Okay," she sighed. Digging in her purse, she pulled out some coins "Ryan, you can have a candy bar. Take your time, we're going to discuss insurance." So much for principles.

"But, he didn't say? Is she okay?"

"Basically, I think he means she needs rest. It's like a nervous breakdown. Like Lucinda on Hope for the Hopeless. Remember when she got amnesia and acted weird after Brick left her for Destiny? And remember she got better when her first husband came back? Hollings? The one who was in the plane crash in South America? She was just fine. It's like that."

Ryan smiled and took the money. "Okay. Wow."

"One thing you have to remember," she stopped him. "It takes longer in real life. On the show she got better in a few weeks. But remember Tristan, the baby Charity had last summer? He's in high school already, I think."

Ryan laughed, "I know." He left the room with a remarkably light step.

MC smiled at the doctor, who held her in a disapproving stare. Uncomfortably, she explained, "Sometimes he comes over and we watch that show during lunch."

"Tristan isn't in high school," Dr. Reilly informed her sourly.

"What about Cindy?"

Brief confusion clouded his face before he answered, "It's more complicated than a simple stress disorder. Were you able to find anyone in her family?"

MC shook her head. Cindy's parents were on a road trip this summer, but she did find her sister-in-law in Seattle, who promised to find them. It would probably be Monday before anyone could get to Miltonville. Reluctantly, MC decided earlier to call Ryan's father, and left a message at his office.

"She's very delusional," the doctor continued. "Until we sedated her she was screaming that she couldn't see."

143

"Of course she can't." Once more she dug into her purse, this time withdrawing a pair of broken glasses.

"Okay," he said, taking the glasses. Crossing his arms he leaned back. "Did you know she was pregnant?"

"What?"

"She claims the baby is coming any time now. But the father is not her husband. And her husband, well, he's a dummy."

"Well, he—"

"No, a dummy as in a doll. That's all she would say. Now she's refusing to speak to the point of biting her own lips to keep them shut."

"Maybe I should go in and—"

"She doesn't know who you are. Or Ryan. She only knows you stopped her from killing someone."

"What?"

"And that really made her mad."

After a moment of silence, she asked, "So, what should I do?"

"Can you keep Ryan awhile?" She nodded. "Good, then. Right now there's nothing. She's fighting the sedative, but she's probably asleep by now. I've run the usual tests, and I will consult with Dr. Oliver and Dr. Mick. We'll do all we can. Can you leave your phone number with the nurse? And, if you speak with Mr. Swift, you might mention this could be a long process, so he can work something out about Ryan."

"Oh," was all MC could manage, thinking of Cindy's worries of Tim wanting custody.

The doctor left her, and a moment later Ryan came back with a can of soda and a half eaten candy bar.

"Can we see Mom yet?" he asked.

"Not right now. She's finally asleep. Let's go home for a while and come back later." She gathered her purse and the magazines she had bought and as they walked out she asked him, "Would you want to stay with us until she's better?"

***

Rubin couldn't stand another minute of wondering when and if Troy Ivers would show up in town. At quarter of ten, he excused himself from work and went across the street to Troy's office. Inside Rose smiled at him from the reception desk.

"Hi Rubin. You need to see the doctor?"

He nodded hesitantly, the aroma of dentistry tying knots in his bowels.

"Well, he's out today. Is it an emergency? I'm referring his patients to Dr. Quimly if it's an emergency."

"No, no. Actually it's personal. About a car he wanted me to look at."

"Was he having car problems?" she asked hopefully.

"Um, yeah. He said he was a while back. Is he at home?" He fished for any information.

"No, he's not home..."

"Oh." He faked concern. "Is he in the hospital or something?"

"I don't know. Um, we—uh...we don't know where he is, exactly. We're kind of worried. When did you say you talked to him?"

"Oh, long time ago. Did you call the police?"

She nodded. "They said they'd check his house. His car's there, I checked myself." She shrugged. "I don't know. I hated to call his folks, his mom's so sick, you know, but they haven't heard from him. He's supposed to go visit them next weekend, so the Sheriff thinks he may have headed that way early."

"Probably he is. They live far away?"

"Toledo. He'd need his car."

"Hmm. Maybe he has a ... a friend?"

"Even if he did, why would he go and not say anything?"

"You never know what's going on in people's heads," Rubin said sagely.

***

On the next block, Leslie unknowingly echoed Rubin's words.

"What'cha think the old man's up to?" She held up a bottle of pop for Anna to see. "He bought me this and told me to take a break. He wants something."

Anna laughed, reaching into the cubby under her register, and brought out her own bottle. "I get a break when you get back."

"See ya, then. I'm going outside."

"Ohmigosh, I almost forgot. Did you hear about that girl?" Anna stopped her.

"Yes! That's right by my house. Who do you think it is?"

"They think a student from Salem. Rick Myers was on squad

duty, and he said they couldn't ID her."

"Did he say what was wrong with her?"

"No, he said she looked okay, only her feet were all blistered. She's unconscious."

"She o.d. or something?"

"Don't know. I guess they have to do tests and stuff, but her pupils weren't dilated. Or were they? Are they supposed to be? Anyway, they aren't like they should be for a drug overdose, and her heart rate and breathing and everything's okay. Maybe a head injury."

" I hope Mom and Dad don't hear it on the news or something and freak out."

"They won't. They're way too far away by now. I don't think this would make it to Cincinnati."

"Yeah, that's true. Hey, how about General G's for lunch? I'm dying for a spaghetti burger."

Anna shuddered. "They should give you a blindfold with your order. But I could go for some spud buddies and a squishy fishy."

"Good. Well, I'm going to go enjoy the last five minutes of my break."

"Don't take all day, I'm next!" Anna called after her. Irma Bellamy clumsily steered her cart into Anna's lane, bumping the candy rack. She ignored the shower of mints that came down and began slowly unloading her groceries as Anna began to ring them up.

"Morning, Mrs. Bellamy," Anna said loudly. Irma Bellamy refused to wear her hearing aid in public, preferring to make people scream at her rather than have a tiny lump of putty in her ear.

"Morning Anna," she hollered back. "Did you hear about that girl they found in the Kitchen?"

"Yes," Anna said, but much of Mrs. Bellamy's hearing was done unconsciously through lip reading, and she was busy matching cans to coupons, so she did not see Anna's reply. Not realizing what Anna told her, Mrs. Bellamy continued on with her own version of the story.

***

Claire lay dazed, strapped in her bed in the Amberly County Hospital. Feeling as if she were swimming, no, drowning, she struggled to reach the surface. Somewhere close, Cindy rolled lazily in blessed unconsciousness. Claire forced her eyes open. They were gummy. What had they done to her? What did she tell them? Had they trapped her? Certainly not! She could escape easily. The eyes closed again. She could...escape...easily...

***

Barker drove through the Kitchen, around and around, but the scent was lost. He, also, was lost. Hours went by and at times he thought he was driving in circles, passing the same houses again and again, then he would notice the small differences in the yards, the colors of the shutters, the toys on the lawns. The professor's body was almost dead and therefore of no use for directions. The heart still beat on its own, the lungs still breathed, but it wouldn't be long before he expired completely, and rigor mortis was so unpredictable. Troy Ivers's body had lasted almost the entire night, but during the last hours, it had grown distressfully heavy, now was fairly pungent. Barker was occasionally brushed by the ripe odor whenever a draft lifted it from the back seat where Troy lay in a balled up state of decomposure. The smell was bad, but nothing compared to being inside a body when it began to rot, and with the professor so close to his exit, it was time to start watching for potential replacements. But first he must concentrate on finding his way out of this labyrinth of boxy mirror-image houses.

Driving had become more comfortable, and he meandered in and out of Nut Valley and the Garden Patch and now entered the Fruit Bowl for the second time. Down Strawberry Lane, right on Watermelon Circle, *whoops!* that's one of those turn around-circle streets. Back on Strawberry to Cherry Street to Orange Boulevard then Apple Street. As he passed the Vickers' house he felt it. Something. A twinge so faint that any minor distraction would have caused him to miss it. He pressed the brake he had been riding. There was nothing. He reversed and aha! There it was again! Not strong, but surely the residue of a Vanderkellen. He fumbled with the door latch. One button lowered the window, another moved the mirror, but how did the door open? Where was the handle on this car?

"Can I help you?" a nasal voice called. Her tone belied her words, and he looked up to see a squat woman in hair rollers strid- ·

ing into the street, her expression showing suspicion.

"No. Go away," he dismissed her. Finally he located the door latch.

"Are you looking for someone?" she persisted.

"Go away!" he repeated, pushing open the car door. It hit her as it swung outward, knocking her aside. When Barker removed his foot from the brake to get out, the car lurched forward, and the door hit the woman again. This time she went to the ground, screaming in pain or rage or both. Barker's foot went back to the brake. He pulled on the gearshift. 'R' rolled it backward, 'D' went forward, this much he knew. Already he appreciated the automatic transmission, but he didn't know which letter would stop the car. There was an OD, a 1st and a 2nd and a P. Maybe it was the key? The key started it; maybe it stopped it.

"Dottie! Dottie!" The man's shouting interrupted Barker's experiment with the gearshift. "Help somebody! Call the police!"

"Artie! Oh Artie! Help me! This madman ran me over!"

Again Barker pulled at his hair. For a moment he considered trying for one of them. Both would be easy to take in their agitated states, but he himself had been caught off-guard and couldn't think. Besides, if he took either of them he'd have to deal with the other. Once more he let off the brake and hit the gas, speeding to a dangerous thirty-five miles per hour, leaving the hysterical couple behind. He would return once he calmed down. Turning down Mulberry, he found his way out of the Kitchen and onto the highway. Around the next bend he unwittingly turned back into the Kitchen when he took a left on Oat Road, in the Grain Bin. He crept the car around the Kitchen, plotting his next move.

***

Ed Philips rolled over and opened his eyes. 10:30. He shut his eyes. When he next opened them it was 10:42, and he again closed them. Now it was 10:51. He raised slowly, his hand touching his head in case it should fall, and the way he felt, having his head fall off might be a blessing. Pushing off the bed, he stumbled out of the bedroom. Thankfully, the blinds were drawn letting in only enough light to allow his eyes a gradual adjustment. There was no window in the bathroom, and even though this was a feat he could have easily executed in the dark, he flipped the light switch out of habit, bringing forth a full assault on his sensitive eyes.

This was not going to be a good day.

A few moments later, while making coffee, it dawned on him that he was still sleepy, so he lay down while it brewed. The smell of the coffee gagged him. How could he drink it straight after using it as a mixer last night? That's probably why he felt so bad, so thick and heavy. He was afraid that the horrible taste in his mouth was there for the day - the gargle that could clean the dry sticky morning after mouth had yet to be invented. Ed would have scraped his tongue with a butter knife if he thought it would work. There was only one thing that might, but he refused to start the day with a bourbon mouthwash. Not again.

At 11:15, he admitted defeat. Sleep would not save him from this quasi-hangover. On the night table sat his empty cup, its odor painful to his nose. Leaving it, he went to the kitchen for a clean cup of hot coffee. He turned on the radio for background noise, then prowled around for something to eat. It occurred to him that toast might be helpful in soaking up the paste in his mouth, so he dropped a couple of slices of bread into the toaster. As he waited for it to reappear, the news began, so he turned up the radio. The radio station was west of Salem, and most of the 'local' news was actually from Bloomington, so Ed was surprised to hear Miltonville mentioned.

"*...unidentified woman found on the west side. She was taken to Miltonville General where she remains in stable condition. In other news...*"

Ed froze for a moment, remembering the summer nineteen years ago when he heard about a body discovered on Bryce Road. But this isn't the Itch, he assured himself. Sometimes people pass out at peculiar times in peculiar places.

Hadn't he thought the same thing nineteen years ago? And suddenly six people were dead, including Holly Vickers, one death he might have prevented.

The toast popped and he jumped.

He thought of the briefcase. Maybe he should get it in order. Turn it over to Dan Vickers. Let him decide if anything should be done. That thought led to another, which led to another, which led to Virginia Miller Cramer Drake, and Ed sat in the kitchen to finish his coffee.

***

For two years after the massacre on the hill, Virginia Cramer and Jacob Drake exchanged letters. Because Jacob knew about her and Lucas's plan, and that her daughter, Elizabeth, was Lucas's child, Virginia could truly express herself and their correspondence was therapeutic. When her father passed away, Virginia left Pennsylvania and married Jacob. No longer in the military, he worked in Cincinnati where he and Virginia lived happily. They had more children, a boy, Thomas, and two girls, Celia and Ruthie.

They often traveled to visit Jacob's brothers in the territory that was now called Indiana. They lived within a day's ride to the site of Barker's commune, and Virginia's curiosity was overwhelming. Using military maps, they located the remains of the settlement. It was called Nepowachung, or The Hill of Death. Little was left, a few cabins and some decrepit furniture; enough to evoke painful memories. Virginia could close her eyes and run the path she'd worn from the settlement to the now vacated Shawnee village. Through the woods, the meadow of rotting markers sloped gently toward the stone circle. At Jacob's insistence, he and his brothers erected a building over the circle.

Because of their trips to Indiana, the Drakes were aware of how rich and affordable the land was. Jacob was an outdoorsman and longed to work the land, and Virginia was quite attached to his family, so once they had the money, they moved west. The children were thrilled, having come to equate holidays with visits to cousins, fishing and romping about the woods and helping in the fields. Jacob worried about the proximity to the old settlement, but Virginia swore she was more concerned about the distance to the market. Her life was too happy to linger over a sad memory.

Her baby Elizabeth married at seventeen. She had known her husband, Steven, since they'd first come to Indiana. Steven was bright and curious, and reminded Virginia of Lucas. He had big city dreams, and he and Elizabeth lived in Ohio where he continued his education. Virginia missed her daughter, but she and Jacob were relieved to see their restless child so happy.

Elizabeth died two years later. It happened in the summer, when she and Steven brought their new son home to visit. The family was celebrating, for not only did Elizabeth recently have a baby, but Celia, her little sister, had just been engaged. They had planned a dinner for Saturday and were busy with the preparations that very morning. Virginia and Elizabeth sat on the back porch shelling beans while Celia and Ruthie worked on pies in the kitchen. Baby Steven Jacob slept on a blanket in the shade of tree, and the men were just coming in from the fields.

The peaceful scene was shattered by a scream in the kitchen. Celia burst through the backdoor, staggering to catch her balance, a bloody knife in her hand. Elizabeth and Virginia jumped up, beans falling from their aprons. Celia's eyes fell on her mother and she grinned. "Virginia Cramer!"

Virginia's heart almost stopped. Her children did not know her name had ever been Cramer.

"Celia," Elizabeth was saying, "what's happened? Where's Ruthie?"

"Virginia!" Jacob yelled, running toward the house, followed by Thomas.

"Elizabeth!" Steven passed them both, rushing into the yard.

Celia held the knife up, her grin wider, her eyes glazed. She ran toward her sister. Elizabeth tried to duck away, but Celia moved with lightning speed. She stabbed her once, twice, three times, before Virginia stopped her. She struggled mightily, and Virginia screamed for Jacob to hurry. The back door opened once more. Ruthie, her apron covered with her own blood fell stumbling onto the porch. Stunned by the sight, Virginia lost her grip, and Celia sprang toward Elizabeth. Steven bounded onto the porch, moving to block her, but Celia stopped on her own, leaning on a porch post, panting.

"What's happening?" she asked, her hand over her eyes. "Why...?" Then she collapsed.

That evening, the gathering took place, but not as planned.

It was a sad, sad time in Amberly County. Celia and Elizabeth were not the only ones to die that day. Three others died, including a young woman Steven found beneath the kitchen window of the Drake's home. Thankfully, Ruthie recovered from her injuries, but she bore the scars for the rest of her life.

Before the winter of that year, Jacob and Virginia bricked up the building over the stone circle to preserve it should anyone ever need to find the stone circle. Their friends thought this a strange way to deal with their grief, but no one protested.

The few diary entries Virginia wrote after Elizabeth's death were twisted and frightening records of her fears. She was certain John Barker wanted to kill her children and grandchildren, especially baby Steven. Ed Philips did not know what happened to the family after that year.

***

Ed shook away his daydream of Virginia. He thought of her so often her life seemed like his own memory. This brought a wry smile, because long ago his father had been the same way, and Ed used to think he was crazy.

***

The Philips family came to Amberly County in the early 1930's, when Ed's father, a professor of history, accepted a position at Salem University. Ed was three years old. Ed's sister, Susan, who would one day become a professor herself and die at forty-two of cancer, was an infant, so it was natural that when their neighbors, Jerry and Molly Templeton, announced their pregnancy, his mother made herself available for help and advice. The Templetons were terribly young; Molly was barely eighteen, and her husband was only two years out of high school, working at his father's insurance company. Jerry's family, Miltonville natives, generously rented a house to the couple, and tried to ease the nervous Mrs. Templeton with gifts and shopping trips, but as the pregnancy advanced, she became more listless. Ed's mother, thinking Molly missed her own mother in New York, spent time with her, talking while they did their baking and sewing. Ed's parents agreed that Molly was awfully immature, but once the baby came Molly proved to be a capable mother. She and Jerry positively beamed when they took Jerry Jr. out for their evening strolls. They were a charming, happy family for two months.

One Monday in June, Molly and little Jerry Jr. came knocking on the Philips' door. The neighborhood was buzzing, Molly said, and women were warned to stay in, as there was a madman loose. Three people had died the previous night in a manner that was still being investigated. Curious, they gathered the children and headed to town, making the excuse that they needed to do some shopping, even though it was not their usual market day. Mrs. Philips said later that an old man in Woolworth's was comparing the deaths with some that occurred years before. Another man had nodded and said, "Yup. It's the Itch, I betcha." The clerk shushed them and told them to quit scaring the customers. Later, as they pushed their carriages home, a neighbor told them another body had been found in a motorcar on Salem-Vinton Road. Molly stayed at the Philips' until it was time to go prepare supper. When she left, Mrs. Philips watched her from the porch until she and Jerry Jr. were safely inside. That was the last she ever saw of Molly.

Early in the morning, what most would call the middle of the night, the first shouts started. Shortly after, the alarm sounded. The Templetons' house was burning. Ed's father helped the fire fighters, and the women made coffee. Only baby Jerry survived, his room untouched by the fire. Highly suspicious, said the officials, but the Philips and other neighbors had already come to that conclusion. The fire, it was confirmed, had been intentionally set, and recovered along with the bodies of Molly and Jerry Templeton, were those of Gertie and Byrum Henderson, an elderly couple who, as far as anyone knew, had no more than a nodding acquaintance with the Templetons. What were they doing at the Templetons' at that time of night?

Days later, at the funeral, the Philips met Molly's parents, Rebecca and Donald Bennett. Molly had spoke often of the Philips and the Bennetts thanked them for helping Molly through her pregnancy. They were invited to dinner and came the next evening. The following day, Donald left for New York, and Rebecca returned to the Philips' home again for dinner. She was staying in town for two more weeks to help Jerry's father finalize Jerry and Molly's affairs, including the custody issues of baby Jerry. During that time she ate many dinners with the Philips, as they had been close to Molly and had much to tell Rebecca about her daughter's last days. Rebecca asked many questions, and was so emotional that before the two weeks were over she had confided a great deal to them, extracting promises of secrecy from both. Her story piqued Ed's father's interest in the Itch.

It surprised the Philips to learn that Rebecca's father, Molly's grandfather, was Edgar Edmonds, a prominent figure in Salem, and a major contributor to the University. With a full belly and two glasses of wine, Rebecca relaxed and began to tell the truth of how life was growing up in his household. A stern, inflexible man, Edgar wanted control of everything. Coming from a meager background, he managed to accumulate a fortune and, along with it, the power it wields in a small town. He used his money to manipulate others, contributing heavily to the University to keep those beggars at his heels. He kept his wife under his heel in much the same way. But his daughters were another story. Instead of going to the University or marrying, as expected, Rebecca left for New York to visit cousins and never returned. Dora, the middle sister, toed the line and started college, met her husband then disappeared with him forever. The youngest, Francine, did not make it so easy on Edgar. She was a hellion from the start, and the more he sat on her, the more she squirmed. She was fifteen when Rebecca left, and the next time she saw her was when Franny showed up on her doorstep, homeless and pregnant. Rebecca fretted; the situation was awkward enough, but Rebecca had married only three months before, and had barely told her new husband anything of her family. Rebecca wanted to call her parents, but Franny threw a fit.

"What about the father? Does he even know about this?" Rebecca asked, knowing Franny too well to envision her as a victim in the situation.

"He doesn't know about it," Franny admitted. She said he worked on a farm not far from the Edmond estate. Gorgeous, Franny said. Blond hair, dark skin. She saw him first in the spring, while walking with a friend, and each day she made a point to walk past the fields where he worked amongst a crowd of young men. At first she regarded him coyly, and she and her friend giggled hysterically over the way he smiled shyly.

"They're from the boys' school," her friend told her, and right then, Franny said she knew she had to have him. The boys' school was for orphans and bad boys. It was way over on the other side of Miltonville, and they rarely came to Salem, but in the spring and summer, the older boys worked the fields.

"His name was Mason. Oh, Rebecca, he was so handsome! His hair was yellow-white and his eyes were sky blue. And his shoulders!" She stretched her arms to show how wide. "Can you imagine what Daddy must have thought?" Franny quickly made his acquaintance, and put forth no effort to hide their blossoming friendship from her father. When it became apparent everyone was afraid to tell him, she did it herself, and to her delight, he blew up. He confined her to her room, but every night she sneaked out the back door.

"It was so romantic in that smelly old barn. We were going to run away together. I might have really done it, I think. He was beautiful in the moonlight."

"So where is he?" Rebecca demanded. "Where is this beautiful man who left you to travel alone in this condition?"

Franny looked out the window and said, "He's dead," as simply as if saying, 'He's taking a walk.'

"He was stabbed with a pitchfork by one of the other boys," she continued, still looking out the window. "That boy died too. He was still holding the pitchfork when they found him. He was lying right beside Mason. They don't know who killed that boy. They think something in his brain burst because he was bleeding from his nose and ears. Other people died, too. James Smithey, remember him? And a college boy! Lots of people died that week." Then she turned back to Rebecca and said, "I don't care if they say that boy did it. I know Daddy did it. I know he did. The whole town knows it, I bet." That's when Rebecca realized her sister's problems went beyond pregnancy.

It was a tense time for Rebecca and Donald. He was a sweet man and he graciously opened his home to Franny, but Franny made life difficult for them. They had no control over her, she came and went like the wind until she began showing. She was irritable and hateful, never happy. Rebecca had called home and spoke to her father briefly. He said he had reported her missing and assumed she was gone for good. He would like to still believe that. They argued, she demanded to speak with her mother, and he hung up. It was clear that Franny was her and Donald's problem. A few weeks later a sizable amount of cash appeared in their bank account.

"Is this compensation?" Donald asked.

"I think perhaps a pay off," she answered.

Donald and Rebecca had no idea what Franny had in mind, but it hadn't taken them long to agree that she could not stay with them. Her unpredictable behavior and strange moods caused too much stress. During dinner one night a few weeks after her arrival Donald pressed the issue with Franny.

"What do you plan to do with the baby?"

"Why, I thought you two should have it."

"What?" They were astonished.

"Well, I certainly can't keep it. Mum and Dad...well, that's out of the question. Dora's at school. Who else can take it? I won't have him in an orphanage, like his father."

Despite their protests, Franny insisted they keep the baby. Even when Rebecca discovered that she, too, was pregnant, Franny persisted. Donald argued that his wife was not going to bear the load of two infants.

Not long after, Rebecca fell sick, and suddenly Franny was to the rescue, cooking, cleaning, caring. The doctor came and went, puzzled by this illness. Rebecca slept constantly and had severe stomach pain. For two weeks she languished in bed, and then one day she was awakened by Franny screaming. Struggling, she made it into the hall on unsteady legs. Franny stood at the head of the stairs, her eyes wide in horror, her mouth covered by her hand. Seeing Rebecca, she pointed wordlessly down the stairs. Rebecca hurried.

"What?" she asked, holding to the banister. Franny, reaching for her sister, cried, "I saw a rat!" As she reached, Rebecca would later swear, Franny pushed her. Lightheaded, on wobbly legs, she felt the slightest pressure on her back as her feet became tangled with Franny's. Did Franny's foot step in front of hers on purpose? Rebecca fell face down and slid on her belly to the bottom of the stairs. Behind her Franny screamed again, and then she was next to her, crying, "Oh no! You've lost the baby! Oh no!" Then she was up and out the door shouting for help, shouting that Rebecca had fallen down the stairs and lost the baby.

The baby was not lost then. Several days passed before she delivered the tiny dead fetus. Rebecca became so ill after the fall that it was feared she would follow her son. Donald could not stay home every day, so he asked a neighbor to care for Rebecca. She did not tell him what happened on the stairs, being too weak to talk, but Franny's attitude raised his suspicion. She seemed no longer concerned with her sister's condition, and ventured as far as to suggest her baby as a replacement.

With her neighbor's help, Rebecca recovered. To her relief, Donald took her hand tenderly and asked, "Did Franny cause you to fall? Be honest, please."

"I can't be certain," she said sadly, but her tears answered his question. He called her father. After briefly explaining the circumstances, he demanded the old man provide Franny money on the condition she move far away. If not, then he, Donald, would drag the girl kicking and screaming back to Salem where she belonged. He meant it, and Edgar knew he meant it. The money arrived shortly. That very day he went to Franny's room while she was still dressing.

"Get out!" she screamed, hiding inside her robe.

He shook his head, tossing the money on the bed. "Pack your bag. There's enough there to hold you for a while. Contact your father when you run out, he'll supply it on one condition: That you never, ever show your face around here again. If you do, he has promised to take you back to Salem," he lied.

She was gone within an hour. He would not allow her to say goodbye to Rebecca. Months later he discovered a near-empty box of arsenic in the basement.

Three months after she had gone, he came home from work to find his wife holding a baby. Mrs. Morely, the neighbor who had cared for her during her illness, was visiting when they heard crying, and upon investigation discovered the little girl in a wooden crate on the back porch. A tearful note was attached, from Franny, of course. *Please call her Juliet*, she begged.

There followed days of intense discussion. Donald did not want to keep Franny's baby. She would come back to take her away. Or try again to move in. She was a conniver. But it wasn't the baby's fault, Rebecca argued. They could start legal proceedings right away. This was a clear case of abandonment. If Franny showed up they could prove her unfit. Donald held the baby. It was such a tiny, sweet smelling thing. He thought of their child, now buried on the hillside of his parents' home. Could Rebecca survive him forcing this child away? Maybe not, but could she, in a week, a month, or maybe a year, survive Franny coming to wrench the child away? Soon the neighbors were in on the debate, swearing an allegiance to the Bennetts. It wouldn't be wise of Franny to show her face in town, they assured him. The days of discussion had turned in to weeks, then months, and they, the Bennetts, were a family of three, and two years later, of four. Later, they had two more children. Franny never returned. Three times they received cards from Tennessee. She was married. She had a baby. She was divorced. Nothing more. No questions about Juliet, who was now Mary Bennett, or Molly, as most called her.

Rebecca knew nothing of Molly's father, only that his name was Mason, but she surmised that Molly must have inherited his nature, for she was nothing like Franny. Always at Rebecca's side, she was every bit a little helper. When the other children were born, she fussed and spoiled them as if they were her own. At two years old she was trying to change diapers. By the time the last one arrived she was eight and very adept at changing, not to mention feeding and bathing. A natural, Donald called her. The other children minded and respected her. Sometimes her parents worried that she took on too much responsibility, but no matter how many chores they delegated to the other children, Molly took on more.

When Molly was fourteen, Rebecca's mother died. None of the children had ever met their grandparents. Christmas and birthdays they received gifts of cash, and they always wrote to thank them, but that was the extent of their relationship. Rebecca was going to Salem to attend the funeral and assist her father and she and Donald decided to ask the children if they would like to come along. Only Molly and Jeannie wanted to go; the boys weren't interested. It was summer and they had better things to do. It would be a holiday from the women for them. The girls were excited to be rid of them, too. They packed their prettiest things for their first train trip.

Needless to say, they were more than a little disappointed. The trip was long, and of course, their destination was a funeral for someone they had never met. The grandfather was softer than what they had been led to believe, no doubt because he was old and alone with no one left to torture. Molly and Jeannie spent a lot of time just walking around town and visiting the University. That was how Molly met Jerry. He was older, almost eighteen, and handsome in an aw-shucks way. At first they only looked at each other in the park where he stood around with his friends. Too timid to approach her, he sent another girl over to talk to her, and she introduced them. Grandfather Edgar was livid when she excitedly recounted the story. Rebecca warned him to calm down, then he started shouting about Franny. The girls wanted to know who was Franny, and Rebecca chased them out into the yard. When she returned Edgar was sobbing.

Not long after she and the girls went home, Molly received the first of many letters from Jerry. The next year, when he graduated high school, he came to visit for a long week, staying with Donald's parents. When he went home Molly moped in her room all day. Soon came a letter to Donald asking for her hand. Donald politely told him no. Then another, this time adding that he took a job at his father's insurance firm. Now can they marry? Again, Donald said no. One day Molly came up with the idea that Grandfather Edgar might be lonely and need help. Could she go stay awhile with him? Both parents said no. Other boys came to call, and Molly always turned them away. A year passed before Donald and Rebecca finally relented. On the eve of Molly's seventeenth birthday, Jerry showed up unannounced with flowers for Rebecca and a birthday present for Molly. Again, he asked for Molly's hand, this time backed by Donald's mother, who was caught up in the romance.

As when Molly first arrived as a baby, there was much discussion between Donald and Rebecca, and once again the neighbors became involved. Molly was young, yes. She should meet other boys, yes. But they had been courting two years. By post and by wire, Donald reminded them. On what was to be the last night of Jerry's visit, Donald and Rebecca sat on a neighbor's porch, joined by others who also loved Molly. What to do? Edith Eckert, somewhat of a suburban rebel with her hand rolled cigarettes and long pants, stood up and said, "I say let them go. Don't, and she'll resent you. Her grandfather can tell you what that's like. If it doesn't work she can come home. Bob and I'll take her in."

The discussion continued as neighbors compared their ages at marriage and the ages of their parents, and what they would tell their own children, or what they had told their children. Later, walking home, Donald and Rebecca considered all the advice they were offered. As they approached the house, they saw Molly in the upstairs window looking up into the night sky.

"She's not much interested in school," Donald commented.

"No. I wish she were."

"Seems all she's ever wanted was to keep a house. And kids."

"She's so young."

"Lots of girls marry at her age." Donald stopped and pulled Rebecca around to face him. "I don't want her to resent us. I see how it affects you. Your whole family."

"We're hardly like my parents." Together they watched Molly watching the moon. "She's never really asked for anything, has she?"

"No."

"And if it doesn't work? If she goes back to Salem and finds him unbearable?"

"Then she comes home, I guess."

"You'd allow that?"

"Rebecca," he sounded disappointed.

Jerry happily delayed his trip home in order to marry Molly. The morning wedding was small, followed by a backyard reception. The newly married Mr. and Mrs. Templeton planned a short trip to Niagara Falls before returning to Salem. The last time Rebecca saw her daughter was that teary, miserable rainy day when the family gathered at the train station to bid her farewell. She had only letters and the Philips family to fill in the gaps.

"I told my father she was here, but he never tried to contact her. I don't know if she ever called on him. If so, he wouldn't admit it now, I'm sure."

The story came out in bits and pieces over several evenings. On this last night she brought an expensive gift for the Philips, and toys for the children. She wasn't staying for dinner because it was her final night with Little Jerry. Everyone agreed that he should remain with his paternal grandparents. She thought it horribly unfair for her to try to take the child they had known and loved for two months. They had no children but Jerry, and she had three yet at home. There would be holidays, and when he was older he could spend summers with them in New York. So she had come to say thank you and goodbye.

Rebecca would never know the curiosity she stirred in Dr. Philips. Having heard plenty of talk about John Barker's curse, he wondered if Molly was possibly a descendant of Lucas Vanderkellen. It was easy to get Molly's father's name. Using the birth date on the memorial card, he dove into the stacks of old newspapers and found the story in barely an hour. It was a front-page item on June 27, 1917. He skipped it for the moment and pulled out the June 26 issue. The first article he found told of two people, Mrs. Annalee Henson, 27, and James Smithey, 31, whose bodies were found on Harmony road. Their feet were in poor condition said the article, but otherwise there was no obvious cause of death. At the bottom of the page was a small piece that he almost missed; a local farmer, Russell Wilke, 65, died in his field. Possible heat exhaustion.

The next edition carried the article concerning Mason Collier, Molly's biological father. The headline screamed "Amberly County Boys' Home Killer Dies in Action", followed by a bit of sensational reporting bearing too much detail. Again, at the bottom of the page was a smaller headline that almost escaped his attention. "Amberly County Curse Blamed for Recent Deaths." The article was short, only a paragraph, and it cited a claim by a local citizen that 'the same thing happened around 20 years ago in rural Miltonville.' The article also stated that the Amberly County Curse, sometimes called John Barker's Itch, began in the 1700's when Barker was murdered by a rival with the aid of local Indians, and manifests itself every twenty years. The same issue reported the mysterious deaths of two men in other parts of the county.

By mid-July, there were no more references to the Itch in the newspapers, but one obituary in August caught his interest. A woman named Mildred Sneed, age 27, died in a mental hospital in Chicago after falling ill in June. He checked the county records for a death certificate, but it wasn't filed in Amberly County because she died in Illinois. Neither could he find any information on Mason Collier's parents, but Mason's presence in the boys' home was a fair indicator that they were dead.

From there, he dug deeper, searching public records, old military documents, gleaning them for information on John Barker or Lucas Vanderkellen. He spent hour upon hour in the university archives, scanning handwritten artifacts and delicate letters. When the librarian noticed his persistent visits, he told Dr. Philips about the storage attic where dozens of dusty boxes sat waiting to be sorted. Among a box of books and photographs donated years earlier by the Teasdale estate, he found a volume of Virginia Miller's writings. At first, while skimming the pages of her journal, he thought it was only an account of life in Pennsylvania, interesting in itself, material he'd save for later reading. But leafing through it, the name John Barker jumped at him. He sat huddled in the spot reading until the librarian closed the archives. With permission, he checked the box out, thrilled to discover more journals and several packets of letters. Over the next ten years, Dr. Philips transcribed the scratchy pen, resigning the box out so many times, the librarian told him he could have it on permanent loan, unless someone else requested it. By the time an archivist was hired to maintain the growing collection, there was no longer a record of the box of books.

When Ed entered Salem University, Dr. Philips developed a chronic case of pneumonia that turned out to be lung cancer. The cancer spread, and the Philips family worked to come to terms with their sad future. Dr. Philips, realizing his research must be passed on, called Ed to his bedside. It was a heavy secret to hold, but he trusted Ed with the responsibility. If Jerry Templeton Jr. were indeed a Vanderkellen, then he must be protected. Thankfully, Jerry had been sent to boarding school in New York, where Dr. Philips believed he was safe.

"With any luck, son, Jerry will stay in New York with the Bennetts."

Ed listened with respectful skepticism that his father acknowledged.

"I know it's hard to believe, but it's all right there. In black and white, as they say." Dr. Philips indicated the briefcase on the bed where he rested, his eyes glassy with morphine, spindly limbs across his swollen belly.

"If it's so obvious, then why hasn't anyone else figured it out?" Ed challenged. His father might be wasting away, but he wasn't dead, and despite the pain and the morphine, his mind was remarkably lucid. Ed counted on mental exercise to keep the cancer away from his brain.

"Who knows that Donald and Rebecca aren't Jerry's grandparents? The people in New York? They never heard of the Itch. The Edmonds? You can bet they kept that secret."

"What about Donald and Rebecca? They know."

"Yes," his father conceded. "But do they know about the Itch? It's really little more than a folktale."

"Rebecca's probably heard of it. They probably both heard about it when they came to the funeral. From what you told me, the whole town was talking about it," Ed said.

"I suppose they must have heard something. I didn't ask."

"Maybe you should ask them? Warn them?" Ed suggested, already knowing his father wouldn't do such a thing. At least, he hoped he wouldn't.

"I've thought of that, telling the Bennetts. Like you said, they may already suspect. But think about what this means. Jerry Jr. might die in a few years. What good would it do?"

"Maybe he won't come back to Amberly County if they know."

"I'm hoping he won't come back anyway, but that's not likely, not with the Templetons still here. Besides, how do we know Jerry's safe in New York? If there really is a curse, I'm inclined to believe it's more a family thing than a curse on Salem or Miltonville. So what good would it do to tell them?"

Ed nodded. "Do you really think there is only one living descendant of Lucas Vanderkellen?"

His father smiled. "Son, with all this morphine thinking for me, I'm not sure. I'd like to think, if John Barker can reach out from the grave, that there must be some power that will allow me to—" He shrugged. "I'm talking foolish, I know, but the closer death comes, the more straws I grab for."

A month later he was gone, and two years later Ed had put aside much of this father's notions. Then one day, in the spring of his junior year at Salem, as he sat in the library half asleep with an open book between his elbows, he was jerked into consciousness by a whispered shout "Hey, Templeton!" Across the big room a young man stopped and turned, scanning the tables. His face broke into an easy grin as he changed his course and took a seat at a crowded table. Heads bent close for a moment, then broke apart as the young man laughed loud enough to elicit glares from other tables. It was a testy time in the library; the semester was almost over and there were deadlines to be met. Realizing this, the young man offered an apologetic grimace to the room before resuming his quiet conversation.

"Is that Jerry Templeton?" Ed asked.

Pete Vaughn looked vaguely over his shoulder and shrugged. "Dunno." Pete was from Tennessee, so he wouldn't know. Ed reached across the table and tugged Gordon Bales sleeve. "Hey, do you remember Jerry Templeton?" Gordon thought for a minute and shook his head.

"He was younger. In my sister's class. His folks sent him off to boarding school when he was a kid. You remember?"

Gordon squeezed one eye shut to show Ed he was thinking hard. "Nope. Why?"

"I think that's him over there."

"Oh," Gordon said, and went back to his book.

Ed stared at the young man, comparing him to his memory of Jerry. Six years was not a long time unless it's the six years between twelve and eighteen. There was nothing spectacular about this guy, which was also true of Jerry Jr. He had short, wavy brown hair and a roundish, pleasant face. It could be Jerry. But then again—

The young man stood up, saying his goodbyes. "Watch my

stuff," Ed said. Pete and Gordon grunted. Ed hurried across the room and caught up to him outside the library.

"Hey! You wouldn't happen to be Jerry Templeton?" he asked. The young man regarded him carefully before drawling "Why?"

"I think I used to go to school with you. Or you were in my sister's class, I think. I mean."

"Oh, you do look familiar. Hope your sister doesn't look like you."

"Her name's Susan Philips."

"Oh! Doc Philips was your dad. My grandparents liked your folks a lot." After a short, respectable pause, he added, "Sorry about your dad, man."

"Yeah," Ed paused a moment too, not necessarily out of respect for his father, but because he suddenly realized he didn't have anything else to say. "Sooo, you came back to Salem, huh?"

"Yeah, my grandfather set me up here."

"Hmmm. Well, good to see you." Ed shrugged.

"Jerrrryyyy!" a girl called impatiently as she climbed the library steps. "We're going to be late!"

"No we won't. Hey, this is Sherry. Sherry, this is uh? I'm sorry?"

"Ed Philips." He extended his hand.

"Ed's an old family friend," Jerry explained.

"Long story," Ed told her, sensing her urgency to get going. He began backing away. "Anyway, I just wanted to say hi."

"Great. I'll see you around. You ever go to Dale's? Maybe I'll see you there sometime."

"Maybe," Ed said, as Sherry pulled Jerry away, complaining, "I hate Dale's."

"And tell Susan hi!"

Ed nodded and waved. He heard Sherry ask, "Who's Susan?" before he went back inside the library.

Over the next year, Ed stayed in contact with Jerry, partly out of curiosity and partly because he liked the guy. He was fun and impulsive, too full of life for Ed to ever believe he would die any time soon. When Ed graduated, he took a position at an architectural firm in Cincinnati. Most weekends he came home to visit his mother and sister, and get his clothes washed, so he still ran into Jerry occasionally at Dale's. Jerry and Sherry remained a couple, and the more Ed got to know them the less he thought about the Itch.

The summer before Jerry began his senior year, Ed was given a promotion and was doing well both financially and socially. Thin and handsome, he had thick dark hair and eyes that drew women with their illusion of innocence. There was barely a time that Ed didn't have a girlfriend, but despite his semi-steady relationship with Cathy and his off and on relationship with Marie, he went home on the weekends often because he worried about his mother and sister being alone. On this particular Saturday evening, Cathy had to work, so he gathered his laundry, and an hour later he stepped through his mother's kitchen door.

Clearly she was surprised. There was no dinner fixed, she explained, because Susan was out with her friends. "But I'll get something going," she said nervously, hiding her face in the icebox, in the cupboard, always turning away.

"Is something wrong?" he asked. "Are you okay?"

"Oh, no, everything's fine. I just wasn't expecting you," she said into the oven.

"You don't have to cook. I'll tell you what! Let's go out to eat. Maybe a movie, too. Let's do that, instead."

She stood up and looked at him full for the first time. Sighing, she put a hand on her hip and finally, his real mother was in the room. "No, no. I'm okay, just flustered. It's been a strange day, and I'd really rather stay home. But you can help, how's that?"

"Great," he agreed. He reached over the counter to turn on the radio, but her hand flew out to stop him. The nervous mother returned for an instant.

"No music," she said. "Just talk. Where's Cathy? Working? She has terrible hours, doesn't she?"

Together they chatted, slicing and frying and tossing. They ate slowly as the kitchen cooled with the evening. Later, while his mother washed and Ed dried sloppily, Susan burst into the house. "Mom! Eddie!" she shouted. "Ohhh! I missed dinner! Did you eat everything?" She walked right past them and opened the refrigerator door.

"I'm fine, thanks. And you?" Ed said. Susan's retort was muffled, her mouth stuffed while she continued rummaging.

"Why don't you just climb in and shut the door?" he said. "See if the light stays on."

Magically she whirled away from the refrigerator with her hands full and slammed the door closed with a casual swing of her hips.

"Oh, here! You're going to make a mess!" Mom cried, taking a bowl from her. She slapped at a hand. "Don't eat out of there! Get a plate! I swear you act more like an animal every day!" Ed snapped Susan with his towel, and she spun to show him her tongue, which was liberally coated with partially chewed ham. He gagged and she laughed. Susan was a grown woman, but around Ed, she was always a big kid.

"What are you doing home anyway?" Mom asked, already busy preparing a second dinner.

"Everybody's in tonight. They think it's the Itch going on." His mother froze. Ed said, "What?"

"Yeah, you know, the Itch. That thing—"

"I know, but why?"

"I don't want this nonsense repeated in my house," Mom warned.

"Didn't you hear?" Susan continued as if their mother were invisible.

"Susan!"

"Mom, what's the big deal?"

"People have died, Susan. I don't want that made light of."

Ed and Susan looked at each other in shame while Mom busied herself filling Susan's plate. Finally, she spoke. "They found a man this morning. A dead man in a car in Salem. Then Craig Thorton turned up dead behind his garage. This afternoon Grace Pebble collapsed right on Main Street in Miltonville—"

"She went hysterical first, then she died," Susan clarified.

His mother turned to Ed and confessed, "That's the reason why I've been acting this way. I thought you came back to...well, I know what you think, what your father told you—"

"What?" Susan asked.

"I don't want you going out and scaring folks. I want you to stay here tonight. Me, you, and Susan. We can play cards. I'll make fudge. Whatever." But it was too late. Ed was going to go out to find Jerry Templeton. "Oh, why didn't you stay in Cincinnati this weekend?" his mother said.

"What's going on?" Susan demanded.

"I won't say anything, I promise. I just want to stick with him and make sure he's okay."

"No!" his mother said, tears forming in the corners of her eyes.

"Mom, I'll be okay." He smiled and tried to lighten things up. "You said yourself it was nonsense."

"There's still a killer out there!"

"Nobody was murdered, Mom," Susan said.

"See, it's okay." He took her head in his hands and pulled her forward to kiss her forehead. "Don't worry if I'm late."

As he pushed at the screen door, his mother stopped him.

"What if your father was right?" she asked quietly.

"Then I'm safe. It's Jerry that's in trouble."

"Then why wasn't Jerry's father safe? And Grace? All the others who died? Please don't go."

"Mom," he smiled. How could he make her understand when he didn't himself? He wasn't sure why he was going out. Did he really think Jerry was in danger? If so, was he going out to protect him or to watch him die?

He left his mother crying in the kitchen doorway, Susan behind her demanding answers.

***

The parking lot at Dale's was almost full, not unusual at nine o'clock on the weekend. Unlike the bars in Salem, Dale's did not hibernate throughout the summer. It attracted a fair number of students while school was in session, but it also was far enough from Salem to be popular with the local crowds all year long. Because of this sometimes incompatible mix of students and townies, Dale's had been the site of a few brawls and earned a rough reputation. Reputations being worth what they are, the folks that frequented Dale's went there for cheap beer, greasy food, decent dance music and a good time, while those who never bothered to visit kept it in infamy.

Ed spotted Jerry at the bar. Beside him, Wendy Daniels spun idly on a barstool. They both smiled when they saw Ed, Jerry happily, Wendy miserably. Ed wondered why she was here; she lived somewhere in Illinois. Maybe taking some summer classes. Her current boyfriend, Mark Cline, lived in Westerville, and so he was probably here somewhere. Whatever the case, it was a good thing Sherry was home this summer. For some reason, she hated Wendy Daniels and she'd be steamed to see her next to Jerry, no matter how innocent the situation.

"Hey! Did you come for the Itch party?" someone called, and Ed's back chilled. Did Jerry hear that? How much did Jerry know about his parents, anyway? He was sent away when he was young, but still, the kids would have told him.

"Whatta buncha idiots!" Jerry answered. "Like a buncha igno-rant peasants!" He threw his arm around Ed, "Eddie! We were just about to blow this pop stand."

"We still are," Wendy moaned. "Can you help me get him out?"

"Sure. Where's Mark?"

Ed saw her hold a breath, then she relaxed, ready to answer when Jerry interrupted, "Yeah, where is good old Mark?"

She crossed her arms and looked away. "I knew I shouldn't have come."

"Nobody invited you," Jerry said.

"You're drunk. Ed? Help please?"

Ed nodded, ready to comply. He reached around Jerry's back to steer him out when he was struck by a sudden image of him driving Jerry and Wendy away from the safety of all these people, of an accident on the road, of Jerry becoming hysterical, like Grace or the man who killed Mason Collier. Maybe here, in Dale's, Jerry might keel over unexpectedly, but Wendy would be safe. Ed re-fused to admit the part his cowardice played in the decision to stay at Dale's.

"Let's get him some coffee first, okay?"

"Oh, Ed. I'm so bored. And this Itch-business is creepy. I want to get out of here," Wendy moaned.

"Wendy, Wendy, Wendy," Jerry said. "You always want to be somewhere you aren't. Have you noticed that? Ed, have you no-ticed that?"

"That's it."

"Wait," Ed stopped her from walking off. "I'll take care of him. Do you need a ride somewhere?"

"No," she stewed. "I have Jenny's car. I'm staying with her this weekend. She's out with her boyfriend."

"Yeah. That's where you should be, too," Jerry turned away from her.

"Is he driving?" Ed asked Wendy.

"Not like this, he isn't. Give Ed your keys, Jerry," she said sternly to his back. When Jerry turned and just stood, confused, she reached brazenly into his pocket and pulled them out.

"Hey!" Jerry said. "j'you see that?"

"I'll take him home," Ed said, accepting Jerry's keys.

"I don't care what you do with him." With that, she spun and marched through the crowd.

"For two cents man, sometimes," Jerry swore drunkenly as she disappeared, unaware that this was his last ever glimpse of her.

He turned to the bar and waved. "Hey! Give me another—"

"Coffee. And fries," Ed interjected. He met Jerry's hurt angry face. "I need you to sober up. What are you doing with Wendy, anyway? Sherry'd kill you."

"Yep. She's going to."

"Hey, what's going on?"

"Long story. Thanks for shaking Wendy."

The coffee arrived. "Drink it," Ed ordered.

"I'm not drunk," Jerry muttered, but he drank. "I'm just...I'm just in a real bad mood today. I came here to have fun, but they had this stupid Itch stuff going on. I mean, it's all crap, I know, but still it makes me mad. I shoulda left. Seen a movie instead. Then she shows up, out of nowhere." He finished the coffee and Ed signaled for another. The fries came with the second coffee, and Jerry seemed calmer, if not sober. He sat on the stool and faced the crowd.

"What's with her, anyway?" Ed asked about Wendy.

Jerry shook his head. "Not now."

Ed shrugged, helping himself to a french fry.

"So, how is Ed? Still drawing pictures?"

"They aren't pictures..." Ed began to explain for the umpteenth time, but he and Jerry both caught sight of something. An odd thing. Addison Kleimier, Dr. Kleimier, was staggering around the tables.

"He needs this coffee more than I do," Jerry said.

"What's he doing here?"

Dr. Kleimier scanned the room, stumbling, all the while his mouth moving as if in conversation. When his eyes fell on Jerry he grinned. And laughed.

Jerry laughed back. "He's bombed!"

Dr. Kleimier headed their way.

"Oh my God," Ed said under his breath. Was this it? Logic told him that Kleimier must have once had Jerry in a class and was happy to see a familiar face, but his gut asked why an elderly, stuffy, psychology professor like Dr. Kleimier would be stumbling drunk at Dale's. No, not drunk. He was mad, like a rabid dog. Ed's gut stopped asking questions; it, along with every nerve fiber, every strand of hair, every inch of skin and spine were demanding action! Flee! Flee!

"Jerry! Run!" Ed said and the world slowed down.

Jerry was laughing, shaking his head as if to clear it, ready to say something to Ed, when someone screamed. Ed and Jerry looked at the same time. Kleimier stood a few feet away, a pistol raised in front of him, waving it toward the bar.

"It's one of you," said Kleimier, and Ed backed away, leaving Jerry alone. "Hah!" Kleimier said, pulling the trigger. It was that simple. Mere seconds after Jerry fell, Kleimier did the same. Dale's was pandemonium. The bartender hurried to attend to Jerry. Kleimier lay on the floor, alone, trampled, the gun still where he dropped it. His mouth moved. Ed fell to his hands and knees beside him. There were tears on the old man's face.

"Dr. Kleimier?"

"No, no." Ed knelt closer to hear his weak voice. "I'm sorry. I...I didn't...*I tried.*"

"Why? Why?"

"No, no, no," Kleimier wept.

Steeling all his courage, which wasn't much, Ed forced himself to ask the question his father would have wanted him to.

"Who then? John Barker?"

The old man's frightened eyes found Ed's, but he spoke no more.

***

The visitation and funeral were as horrible as Ed feared. He went with his mother and sister, aching with guilt and bourbon. Rebecca and Donald Bennett came in from New York, staying close to the frail Templetons. Ed was not surprised to see Wendy Daniels, but he avoided her. Jerry's girlfriend, Sherry, and her family were also there. Jerry's best friend, Steve Dunlevy, stood next to Sherry throughout the two long, bizarre days. Numbly, she leaned on him, her face dull and translucent as they approached Ed. She looked at him blankly, but Ed felt the accusation and blame behind those dazed eyes. *Why didn't you take him home? He didn't need coffee! He needed to get out of there!*

Sherry mumbled something about Jerry having a good time in his last hours, and moved away, hanging on Steve. Ed only heard what he thought her eyes told him. What Rebecca and Donald's eyes were telling him. And the Templetons, and Heaven help him, even his own mother's eyes were saying these things to him.

Ed stood uncomfortably at the visitation, amazed at the numbers waiting to sign the guest book, shake sympathetic hands, and suffer the strange agony of the sight of Jerry's photo next to the closed casket. The funeral the following day brought an incredible amount of mourners. The Philips family sat together in a packed room in the same building where they had once come to say farewell to Dr. Philips. Ed's head throbbed from the previous night's binge. It was good this way. He couldn't think, nor did he want to. Thinking provoked his feelings of guilt, hitting him as hard as it did the minute he saw the gun in Kleimier's hand. Harder, really, because at that time the thought was fleeting—*Ohmigosh! It's true! Why didn't I get him out of here?* Now, after the fact, he caught that thought, and held it. Studied it, and reasoned. How could he have known Dale's wouldn't be safe? Where could he have taken Jerry? What could he have done to stop Kleimier? It wasn't his fault. He defied the guilt and pushed it away, but it came back, again and again. It knew it was home.

Two days later, Rebecca came to the Philips home to return a casserole dish and have coffee. Ed, still in Miltonville, indifferent to the fact that he was expected back at work the day before, discreetly laced his coffee with bourbon and listened while his mother and Rebecca talked. Rebecca asked him many questions, including the one he had already answered over and over, "What did Dr. Kleimier say before he died?" ("He just apologized," Ed said.) The flesh on Ed's head tingled as he tried to follow the conversation.

"It's over now at least. The Itch, I mean," Rebecca said.

"What?" his mother asked, her face concerned.

"It was us. The Edmonds. I believe in the curse, and I think it's us, my family." Rapidly, she blinked her tears away. "Franny had only one more child, a girl, who died at four. Fever, is what Franny said, though we always doubted that. Now maybe, I don't know. Dora's children were adopted, and I don't think they will ever have a reason to come here. My children, well, their grandfather soured them long ago, and when Jerry died, I told them about the curse and begged them to never come near Amberly County. That's why they didn't come to the funeral. I know they are trying to pacify me, but I don't care, as long as they stay away." She quickly bowed her head into her hands and pinched back the tears.

"Rebecca," Ed's mother consoled, "the Itch did not kill Jerry. It was a drunken old man. A mean old man!" The tale of Dr. Kleimier's funeral had drifted back from his hometown of Westerville. It became a dark circus when his son, enraged at the outpouring of sentiment, stood on a chair and announced to all that this honored saint who had snapped, (or, as some murmured behind their hands, had become possessed) was in fact a tyrant who abused his family, cheated on his wife, berated his children, and considered himself far superior to everyone. "Admit it!" he shouted to his timid mother, who stood by wordlessly, her eyes closed, as she had throughout her marriage while she was bruised and humiliated, while her three children had their arms twisted behind their backs and were told how worthless they were. "Tell them!" he demanded his brother and sister, who looked on with a terrified anger they had not known since childhood, a buried anger painfully exhumed. "Go ahead!" He pointed at his aunts and uncles, neighbors, minister, teachers. After an eternity that lasted only a few minutes, he descended from the chair, kicked it over, and pushed through the crowd, swinging a flask to his lips, determined not to follow in his father's footsteps despite the fact that he was taking the same path.

"It doesn't matter. He was used to get Jerry." Rebecca held her hands up to ward off the argument she felt coming. "Look, I'm only telling you this because you are the only ones who know about Molly, the whole story. I'm hoping the curse was only following Father and Franny because they were both so, so evil!" she spat the word.

"Rebecca," Mrs. Philips cooed, not knowing what else to do. She stabbed Ed with a warning glance. She needn't worry. He would not speak of the foolishness his father had handed down. Verbalizing anything at that moment, even something as innocuous as, "Nice day," was dangerous for Ed. He sipped his coffee.

"I know you think I'm a silly old woman, ready to believe anything. Maybe I am, but I will never come here again. No more funerals in Amberly County. Sorry, you will all have to die without me." She tried to smile. "Maybe this way, the curse will be over."

And so it was for her. For Ed it never ended.

***

Forty years later he looked up from his bourbon laced coffee and felt the guilt all over again, like new. A lot had happened in the years since, more thinking, more bourbon. He scrutinized and rationalized, but it always came back to the same place. He went to Dale's knowing that Jerry was in danger. He should have tried to get him out of town. Maybe he would have died anyway, it was at least worth a shot, especially since Ed was fairly sure Jerry wasn't safe in Amberly County. Yes, the odds of escaping John Barker may have been slight, always uncertain of where he was, *if* he was, how far he could reach, and what to do if they met. Bad odds indeed, but better than the ones he faced in trying to escape the guilt; from that he would run forever, and yet it would always be on his back.

***

After recovering from his disastrous encounter with Dottie and Artie Geist, Barker eventually found his way out of the Kitchen and drove slowly on Route 20, toward Miltonville. His first angry impulse had been to go back and make the nosy fat couple suffer, but the more distance he put between them, the more he thought against it. To begin with, both bodies were obviously in poor shape. Also, the Vanderkellen was gone from there, and who knew when or if it would return. It occurred to him that it might have gone to the university. She was the right age, and odd as he thought it was, he knew many women attended the school. He decided to turn around and head to Salem, but first, he had to find a body. The professor had died and he was a miserable fit.

Coming up to where he remembered the town of Miltonville to be, he saw two squat buildings, one garishly bright, the other a dull brown and yellow, both surrounded by asphalt parking lots. Around them, people sat in their cars, seemingly doing nothing. He chose the bright building, the one with a big blue, red and yellow soldier holding a sword of skewered sandwiches under a sign reading "General Goodburg's" because it was on his side of the road. He pulled the car into the lot in a slow wide arc, and the car behind him blew an aggravated horn and sped away. He stopped behind a line of cars and studied the occupant of the car ahead.

Female. No good, but Barker could contend with the oddness of being a woman long enough to get to the university. Elbow out the window, head on hand. Bored? Fantastic! He put the car in park, having taken some time after the fiasco with the Geists to teach himself how to stop the car, though he hadn't quite figured out the difference between park and neutral.

"May I take your order?" a voice squawked, and he jumped. He looked back and forth, but no one was there. The car ahead inched forward. He followed, needing to stay as close as possible.

"Have you decided?" the voice came again, and he saw that it came from the post beside his car. How did they do that? Like the telephone, he supposed. The car ahead moved on, the woman inside tapping the car door with her fingernails. Barker decided too late to give up and go elsewhere. A car had pulled up behind him, trapping him in the line. In front of him, the car moved farther away. It's occupant held an arm out, a green bill in the hand.

"Have you decided yet?" the scratchy voice asked again, less patiently.

Barker fumbled with the gearshift, accidentally reversed, and went back into park. A horn blew.

"Can I take your order?" The gearshift stuck in park because he forgot to put his foot on the brake. He yanked at it viciously.

"Hey idiot!"

Barker jumped again. This was not the voice from the post. He saw in the side mirror a figure approaching from the car behind him.

"What's your problem? This is a drive *through*. Get it?" The figure, a young man, leaned close to the window. Barker stared at him with the professor's blue white, slack jawed face. The man pulled away, but Barker grabbed him with his eyes. The man's eyes were red, the rims almost bloody. Barker could see the loose grasp he held on his consciousness and easily knocked him out of reach. The man stumbled as Barker overtook him. The professor's body fell forward.

Barker now stood next to the car, taking a moment to collect his thoughts and get his balance. The man, barely out of boyhood, cowered and cried, the tough guy gone. The driver behind them honked and shouted, "What'sa problem Lutz?" Barker walked on unsteady legs to the honking car, where the smell of burning herbs hung in a cloud.

"What'd ya do to the guy? Is he crying or something?" the driver asked. In the crowded backseat a girl giggled.

"Move this car."

"What?" The driver squinted.

"That man is ill. I'm going to take him to a doctor. Move this car so I can drive out of here." Barker spoke in a monotone, having no feel for this man's natural voice.

"What?" The driver repeated, pushing his head out of the window for a better look. From inside the car someone asked, "What is he talking about?"

"Just do it!" Barker demanded and stomped off, leaving a chorus of "Hey, Lutz!" and "Come on, Paul, get back in the car." Ignoring them, he opened the car door and pushed the professor's torso into the passenger seat. He worked angrily on the professor's legs but he couldn't position the body while he himself was half in and half out of the car. Rolling the professor, he pushed him headfirst to the floor. His legs stuck up, and Barker, overpowered by rage and a fresh lungful of Troy Ivers's odor, tried fruitlessly to break them off. Growling and swatting, he gave up and climbed into the driver's seat, seething.

The car behind him finally backed away, and Barker, recklessly pulled out. From inside himself he heard faintly, "You moron! You don't even know how to drive." Barker took a deep breath and *pressed* until the man quieted. They drove away, toward Salem, leaving Paul Lutz's puzzled friends in the parking lot.

***

Less than ten minutes after John Barker left General Goodburg's, Anna and Leslie pulled in for lunch. A battered car bounced out of the lot, music blaring.

"Get a job," Leslie muttered, waving at her former classmates.

"Yeah," Anna agreed. She pulled up to the post and placed their orders.

"Hey, why don't you stay all night with me tonight?" Leslie said suddenly, as if the idea just occurred to her. "We can go to the movies or something and that way your mom and dad can be alone or whatever."

"This wouldn't happen to have anything to do with Bruce would it?"

"No. He's gone. Really," Leslie said, before conceding, "Okay, maybe it has a little to do with him. So what? It's still a good idea. We can eat out and all that."

"Yeah, okay. Just don't tell Anal-er-Alan. He'd be mad that you got me to stay the night with just dinner and a movie."

"You are so disgusting." Leslie handed over her money, and they took their food into Miltonville to eat in the town square.

***

Judy Redmond stretched in her garden, shadowing the scarecrow. He was a handsome thing, though not too fearsome. She and Anna and Tom made it a few weeks ago, more for fun than protection. Leaning this way and that to relieve the kinks, she made her way to the house, and Mabel, the cat, ran to catch up.

"Lunchtime girl?" Judy asked. Her own stomach rumbled in answer.

They went inside, Judy shushing the anxious cat. Tom was sleeping, and would be for hours, having come in so early that morning. She took Mabel's bowl and a box of food to the porch and fed her there, then went in to make a sandwich and think about dinner. Earlier she had laid a roast out to thaw, and next to it, yeast bread was rising. There would be mashed potatoes and gravy, along with vegetables she had put up last year. All things Tom would appreciate after four days of fast food. Oh, and a dessert! Maybe a cheesecake? No, she was too tired to throw together a cheesecake. There was frozen apple pie. He wouldn't know the difference between that and a fresh pie, especially when it was dressed up with ice cream.

The evening was fairly well planned out in her head: Tom would probably wake up around three or four, and she'd have a pot of coffee ready for him. They'd stroll around the property, and she'd show off her garden and the flowers. Back inside they would chat, watch the news and prepare dinner. Being Friday, Anna would probably go out after dinner. Then she and Tom would sit out in the evening, she with wine, he with a beer—

"Uh oh," she interrupted her own thought. Opening the refrigerator she realized there was no beer for Tom. She finished putting her sandwich together and took it and the handset of the cordless phone outside. Sitting at the picnic table, she punched in the number for Hartmann's Groceries. Holding the handset to her ear she heard dead air. Grumbling at it, she poked the big blue button. The bright sun made it impossible to see if the red light was lit, signaling the phone was turned on and ready to dial. Holding it to her ear, she heard the dial tone and tried again. This time it worked but Anna was at lunch.

"Can I give her a message?" the cheerful voice asked.

Judy was too embarrassed to ask her to have Anna bring home beer, especially because Anna was underage and would have to have someone buy it for her. She asked that Anna call her back. Then she started to call Donna, but had barely pressed the first number when she remembered it was Friday, and most everyone would be at work. Laying the phone aside, she finished her sandwich, then headed back to the garden. It had been neglected lately, and was pretty choked up, but she was almost done weeding. She wanted to work a bit with her flowers before going in and cleaning up. Halfway to the garden, she remembered the phone and went back to get it. When Tom slept, she turned off all the ringers, and lowered the volume on the answering machine, but if she expected to talk to Anna she better hear the phone ring. Switching on the ringer, she set it in the crook of a tree. With the gentle breeze and the sound of birds and squirrels against distant lawn mowers and airplanes, she didn't hear the faint hum of the dial tone

***

In Salem, the ringing telephone broke the silence in Theresa Hoover's apartment. On the couch Sandy Cornett rolled over and pulled the pillow over her head. From down the short hall she heard murmuring. "Sandy," Theresa called, "it's your mom."

Sandy rolled again to her back and took a second to compose her thoughts before reaching over her head for the extension on the end table.

"Mom?"

"Thanks for calling to let me know you weren't coming home," her mother started in immediately.

"You knew where I was."

"I assumed. Now with that news about that girl—"

"What news?" Sandy interrupted. She and Theresa were up for the six AM news, but nothing had been reported. They didn't lie down until Theresa's roommate got up for work. She thought they were just getting in.

"You're still in bed, aren't you? What time did you get in last night?"

"Mom, what news?"

"They found some girl in Miltonville. Unconscious."

"Is she okay?" Sandy asked, trying to keep her voice measured.

"I guess. You can imagine what I thought! I think the time has come for us to have a talk."

"Mother, I'm nineteen years old."

"Fine. If you consider yourself an adult, then today would be a good day to get a job."

"Mom—"

"Not now. I'm at work. You be at the house when I get home."

Sandy didn't answer.

"Sandy?" her mother said sternly.

"Okay. Goodbye," she said, hanging up before her mother said anything else. For a moment she lay back into the pillow before she remembered the girl in Miltonville. "Theresa!" she shouted, rummaging about the rubble on the coffee table in search of the remote. "I think they found Jaime!"

Theresa bolted from the bedroom, her hands buried in the thick tangle of her hair. "What? Where?"

"Miltonville, I think. I didn't get any details. Mom was too busy griping."

Theresa sat next to her on the couch and picked up the phone.

"Who you calling?" Sandy demanded to know.

"Shhh…Jaime's. Maybe that's not her. Maybe she made it home."

Jaime's brother answered. "She stayed all night with Sandy last night. Try over there," he said.

From the television they learned nothing. They turned on the college radio station and waited for the next news broadcast.

"Do you think she's in the hospital? Should we call?" Theresa suggested.

"Are you crazy?" Sandy said, shocked.

Theresa stared back, equally shocked. "Are you?"

The question hung in the air. The silence was broken by a broadcaster announcing there was still no word on the identity of a woman found unconscious in a Miltonville suburb.

"She is described as blonde, with dark roots, about five feet six inches and approximately one hundred and fifty pounds. If you have any..."

"That's Jaime," Theresa stated.

The broadcaster continued, *"...is listed in stable condition at Miltonville General, although the cause..."*

"Maybe it's Jaime. Whoever she is, she's okay," Sandy said.

"We better call. That guy probably did something to her."

"No, no. Not a good idea. We'd have to tell them what we were doing last night. I don't know about you, but I for one, do not want to be associated with that mess."

"Mess? This is Jaime we're talking about!"

Exasperated, Sandy raised her hands and exclaimed, "Have you forgotten that we are accessories to murder?"

"You said yourself we don't know if he was dead or not."

"Oh, come on! I only said that because you were making out with him! His neck broke like that!" She snapped her fingers in Theresa's face.

"Then we should of went to the cops last night!" Theresa shouted.

"Well, we didn't! And we aren't!"

"Why not?"

"Hey, we're lucky he didn't come after us last night. Maybe he doesn't know who we are and I want to keep it that way. Besides, *we* don't know who *he* is!"

"No, but that guy Rubin does. We can call in an anonymous tip."

"No way. Rubin'll know it was us. He'll tell the cops and devil man."

"You just said he might not know who we are. Maybe he'll think Jaime told."

"He'll still end up telling the cops about us being there."

"They'll probably find out anyway. Jamie was supposed to be staying at your house last night. Have you thought of that?"

"Look, I have to think this through. We have to be careful. Think of what devil man might do if finds us, or thinks we're going to the police. Maybe you aren't worried about yourself, but how would you like to come home one night and find Carol dead because he thought it was you?" Theresa drew back at the thought.

Sandy continued. "Maybe we should call the cops, but first we better think of everything. For now, if it comes up, I'm just saying that we went to the party, saw two guys fighting, and Jaime wanted to stay with her boyfriend. As far as I'm concerned, that's all we know."

"Can I think about this, too?" Theresa asked, still mortified at the image of a murdered Carol.

"Yeah. Just don't do anything yet, okay? We really don't know what's going on. That Whit guy is probably okay."

"But you just said—"

"Forget what I said. I was just trying to get a rise out of you." She stretched out on the couch.

"I'm going to take a shower," Theresa said, stunned by Sandy's attitude.

"What time do you have to be at work?"

"Four."

"You should call in."

"Are you kidding? I get like a week's worth of tips on Fridays..." she trailed off, amazed they were even having this conversation. She left Sandy watching TV and shut the bathroom door. It irked her to think of Jaime lying in the hospital while Sandy lounged on the couch. Sandy didn't care about Jaime, or Carol's safety. The only thing important to her was keeping peace at home. Her only leverage against her mother was her father, but even he would be angry if he found out where they were last night.

Theresa reached into the shower and turned it on. Then she opened the nearly empty bottle of shampoo, filled it with water and poured it into the tub. "Terrific!" she said, loudly and caustically, then turned off the water. Fetching a pair of shorts off the top of the laundry hamper, she pulled them on. Wearing the t-shirt she had slept in, she went back into the living room.

"What's wrong?" Sandy asked, barely looking away from the television.

"Carol used all the shampoo..." She let her voice fade as she dug into her purse for change. "I'm going to run to the corner. Want anything?"

"Nah, I don't think so."

Theresa slid her feet into her sandals and walked the two blocks to the Quick Sale where she paid too much for a bottle of shampoo. On the way out she stopped at the pay phone. Miraculously, there was a phone book, although she was prepared to go through the operator if she had to, and she almost did have to, because her nervous fingers had trouble picking out the numbers. For a moment she felt like she was dreaming, one of those dreams where she had an urgent call to make but kept punching the wrong number, or there weren't enough numbers on the phone—

"Miltonville General," a happy voice greeted. "How may I direct your call?"

"That girl you found," Theresa gushed. "There's a guy named Rubin. I don't know his last name, but he knows what happened to her." Then she hung up and walked back to her apartment.

***

It did not take long for John Barker to declare Salem a dead end. He navigated the campus using Paul Lutz's memories. Paul, while not a student, did cruise the college often. "Looking for a girl, huh? Or maybe not. I figured you were one of them," Paul taunted. He was becoming more courageous, convinced that he was dreaming. Barker ignored him at first because he needed him for driving, but he wouldn't shut up, accusing Barker of all manner of perversion, calling him names, *pushing* back at him. Irritated, Barker pounded him to death. Once again, he was stuck inside a dead body.

Frustrated, he headed back to where he first smelled the Vanderkellen.

***

In Yellowbird, Ohio, the inviting warmth of Grandma Emily's kitchen had chilled. When the Vickers arrived at noon, Grandma Emily was busy preparing a light lunch and a huge dinner simultaneously. Tonight Michele's brothers and sister and their families would fill Grandma's home, eagerly dining on fried chicken, fried potatoes, fried tomatoes and fried cabbage - Dan always said the Everette family gave special meaning to the phrase 'blood is thicker.' Dan and Michele spent a pleasant afternoon chatting with Emily as she continued slicing, peeling, and rinsing at the sink, refusing help as always. Outside Becky swung on the tire, talking to herself non-stop. Emily was talking about Aunt Marion's gall bladder when Michele's brother, Ray, entered the room to break the peace.

"Mornin' folks," he mumbled, rubbing his eye loudly with the heel of his palm. The doorframe got in his way, and he staggered a moment. With an impish smile he sat down at the table and laid his stubbly cheek in his hand, his fingers kneading his temple. "Nice trip?"

"So far," Michele said, her voice pleasant.

"Rough night?" Dan asked, not caring to be pleasant. Ray didn't seem to notice. He smiled broader and raised a suggestive eyebrow. Michele gave Dan a warning pinch under the table. Grandma Emily chatted on, barely pausing as she poured coffee for Ray. The air was heavy as they waited to see which direction Ray's mood would take them. To the relief of all, he was surprisingly civil and in sharp humor. When he left to shower, Michele released an audible breath.

"I told you he was getting better," Grandma Emily said quietly, not wanting to be overheard. Dan repressed the urge to ask why he wasn't working. Where did he get his money? Who paid his child support? Instead, he bit his lip. Emily blamed Ray's behavior on the loss of his father, even though Ray was seventeen when Big Joe died, and his behavior patterns were already in place. He possessed the lethal combination of a quick temper and poor alcohol tolerance. The youngest of four, his weary parents dealt with him the way they had his older brother, once also a wild youth, assuming Ray would eventually settle down.

Ray, comfortable in the coddling of his mother and the absence of his father, continued his rowdy high school behavior long after his peers had outgrown it. The family was at a loss. He turned Emily's gatherings into events of dread and trepidation. Would he be sober? Would he be there at all? How far would it go this time? Many times over the years, Dan vowed to never return, yet here they were again. It was likely, too, he knew, that before the day was over he and Michele would be pretending everything was fine while the brothers brawled and children cried and Grandma Emily kept dishing out food and begging everyone to please sit down and eat.

Sometimes, though, as if just to show Dan how unpredictable life could be, a sober Ray would show up, full of jokes and tricks for the kids, helping with dishes and playing his guitar. Today appeared to be one of those times, so Dan relaxed. Michele's sister, Audrey, showed up around one with her boys, and soon after, Little Joe arrived with his kids. He owned his shop, so he had the liberty of taking off early. His wife, Olivia, would come after work.

Grandma Emily took a break, having finished her pies. They all went out to the yard to sit and rest. Ray was antsy and having trouble making conversation. Finally, he spoke up.

"You know what'd be good tonight? Watermelon."

"It's kinda early in the season, isn't it?" Dan said.

"Dwight has a truck load out by McGarvey's."

"Olivia'll probably pick one up. She passes right by," Little Joe said.

"Oh, no. I'll get one," Ray offered. "I'll be back in a little while." He fished his keys from his pocket, not hearing Grandma's weak protest. As he left, the small group passed nervous glances to each other. Grandma Emily went back inside.

"Well," Little Joe said cheerfully, "he probably won't be back." Dan grit his teeth and hoped Joe was right.

Though the afternoon was pleasant, the weather right for a picnic, the kids happy to be together, a cloud had appeared to threaten the day. They tried to ignore it, but it wouldn't dissipate. It disgusted Dan that Ray left it behind.

***

At Miltonville General Hospital, Marsha McBerry stared at the brief message she had written. An elderly woman walked to the window of the reception desk and knocked.

"I'm looking for Marty Shelton's room?" she asked.

"Oh, uh, certainly," and she typed the name into her terminal. "205. Down the hall to the left is the elevator." The woman thanked her, and Marsha watched her go down the hall and to the right. A moment later she reappeared and took the other route. Marsha called upstairs.

"Intensive Care," a voice announced.

"Wanda, it's Marsha. What's the word on the Jane Doe?"

"She's doing better. We're going to move her off the ward, but she's still unconscious."

"Well, I just got a call. A girl said a guy named Rubin knew her."

"Rubin? Rubin Tanner? That's the only Rubin I know."

"That's all she said. What do you think?"

"I think you better call the police and tell them."

***

It was almost half an hour before a policeman arrived at the hospital. Miltonville's small police force had been especially busy. They may have found one girl, but they had lost two men. Troy Ivers had not yet shown up for work, and a professor from Miltonville did not make it to his class. Oddly, the description given by Dottie Geist of the man who hit her with his car door matched the description given of Mark Reynolds. Dr. Reynolds had been seen driving around and around the Kitchen all morning, so the police couldn't classify him as missing, but they needed to talk to him about the Dottie Geist matter. Not exactly big city news, but enough to keep the Miltonville PD busy!

Marsha found someone to cover her post when Officer Fred Wendell arrived. He rephrased the same question over and over, trying to trigger a lost memory.

"She just said there was a guy named Rubin and that he either knew her or what happened to her. She was talking so fast I really didn't hear the last part."

"How did she—" Wendell started when the door to the break room flew open. A breathless aid ran in smiling.

"Wanda told me to tell you! Jane Doe woke up! She opened her eyes and said 'John'! Plain as day! I heard it!" and she whirled out again. Marsha clapped her hands. Wendell stood up and thanked Marsha before following the aid. He could barely keep up with her, and all the way to Jane Doe's room he questioned her. "Did she say anything else? Are you sure it was John? Not Don or Tom? Or Rubin?"

Wanda stopped them as they entered the intensive care ward. She was a big woman, as big as Wendell, and much sterner.

"She's out again. Please don't go in there."

Over Wanda's shoulder, Wendell saw the prone Jane Doe through the glass walls of her room. She looked as if she were in a peaceful sleep, much better than she did this morning. Her color was back, and someone, had brushed her hair. At the foot of the bed her heavily bandaged feet stuck out from under the sheets. Wendell asked a few more questions, found out nothing new, then left to go to AJ's service station to see what Rubin Tanner was up to.

Wanda gave the aid some files to take downstairs. She hadn't told anyone but Dr. Katt that Jane Doe had sucked juice off her finger. In less than an hour they were going to move her downstairs for observation until the test results came back.

***

John Barker was so incredibly mad. His hopes of victory were fading with the day; everything was working drastically against him. In the distance he could hear the laughter of the Wethacanwee and he boiled inside.

Once more he was walking. The car he had driven all morning had sputtered and sputtered and finally stopped. He had been on his way back to the Kitchen to visit the street where he felt the Vanderkellen strongest, and not until he passed General Goodburg's did he realize he had gone too far. Then the car quit, forcing him to walk, huffing and gritting the teeth of the dead, heavy body.

He went toward Miltonville, ready to pounce any body who crossed his path. Fortunately for whoever that might have been, Barker saw five or six cars behind a dingy white building. A car. That would do, and not a minute too soon, either, because he was practically dragging Paul's body. The body wasn't in such bad shape, but the hours of aggravation had worn Barker out.

Car to car he went, locked door, locked door, locked door. An old truck. Unlocked. He pulled himself inside. How to start it? He beat at the useless head, rattling the dead brain. How? How? He only knew keys, but there were no keys in this truck.

A faint stench began to register. He raised his nose to catch it. Could it be? He sniffed. Barely there, but definitely Vanderkellen! He couldn't trick her into coming with him in this horrible body, and he certainly couldn't grab her right in town. He needed a new body immediately! A female one, she would trust. Or someone who knew her! And where was Claire? He needed her, too! What happened to his plan? He'd been so overcome by his misery that he forgot he actually had to get the Vanderkellen! He was about to pound his head on the steering wheel in misery when he saw someone. Someone he knew. "Oooh," he said, and the wickedness of the moment warmed him.

***

Rubin had been a zombie all day. Terror had worn off and sleepiness became his biggest problem. He had no doubt that Troy had fled, afraid to face what he had done. Rubin stopped worrying about him. That is, until about two thirty when he emerged from the bathroom to see a Miltonville cop pull into the lot. The panic he thought was gone exploded and he backed against the wall. Hoping he hadn't been seen, he crept along side the building to the back lot where his truck was parked.

What was that? Someone in his truck? Paul Lutz! Great, just who he didn't need to be seen with.

Paul looked up and grinned. Rubin saw his pale face, the purple under his eyes and around his mouth, and stopped.

"Hey! Rubin Tanner!" the cop shouted coming around the building.

Confused and tired, he looked from Paul to the policeman, then back to Paul, and then he was slammed into the wall, not by the cop, not by anything he could see. Like a blast from an explosion! The last thing he saw before passing out was Paul Lutz leaning sideways and falling out of view in the truck.

***

Fred Wendell knew he was onto something big the second he saw Rubin Tanner trying to slink away. Whether or not he had anything to do with the girl's condition, he most certainly was guilty of something. Wendell followed Rubin around the station.

What was that? Who was in the truck? Paul Lutz? What were these two up to? Drugs, maybe? Is this what he had wandered onto?

Paul tried to hide under the dash and Rubin stumbled. Wendell ran to him, saying, "Whoa boy! Wait just a minute!" and grabbed his arm. Rubin didn't try to make a break, he simple stood, shaking his head and blinking his eyes.

Big Al, followed by several employees, came running around the corner. "Oh Rubin! What have you done now?" Al shooed the others away.

"Rubin, I just have a few ques—" Wendell began to explain, but Rubin jerked away. His strength surprised Wendell. "Come on, don't make this hard on yourself."

Rubin turned and started to walk off. Wendell, remembering Paul was hiding in the truck, pinched the button on his collar mike. "244 requesting back up at AJ's Service on Main and Poplar." He didn't wait for the dispatcher's response, and quickly caught up to Rubin.

"You better go," Rubin warned in an unnatural voice.

"No, buddy. You better hold it right there." Once more he grabbed Rubin's arm, this time prepared to hang on. As Rubin tried to jerk it away, Wendell twisted it and pushed him against a car. "Spread 'em. I'm placing you under arrest."

"Are you out of your mind?" Rubin bellowed. "Do you want to die?"

"That's it," Wendell leaned against Rubin, trying with all his might to hurt him. He dreamed of moments like this, longed for the days when he could knock a little wise acre around, the days before criminals had more rights than citizens. Wendell would not be in trouble this time; this was legitimate. The punk was fighting back, had threatened him, and there was a chance his buddy would jump him from behind.

Rubin fought like a crazy man, and Al tried his best to help, but only got in the way. Wendell managed to cuff him, and directed Al to hold his legs. Sirens screamed in the distance, and more officers appeared. They shackled Rubin's legs and finally managed to get him in the cruiser. Wendell tapped the window. "You have the right to remain silent..." He read the Miranda with ill-concealed glee while the other officers gathered their composure and thanked Al for his help.

"Geez, he's foaming at the mouth," Officer Mike Jones said.

"Man, this town is full of lunatics today. I'm glad my shift is almost over."

"Is it a full moon?" Officer Petrie asked, leaning into his cruiser to call the dispatcher.

"Oh, wait, I just remembered," Wendell said. "Paul Lutz is hiding in the truck over there."

"Oh, bet he's long gone," said Officer Beemer, hitching his pants and accompanying Wendell and Jones to Rubin's truck.

Paul Lutz was still in the truck. The gravity of the situation slowly dawned on the officers. This boy didn't die a few minutes ago. Miltonville may be small town, but people died there like anywhere else. They knew the difference between fresh dead and hours dead.

"Oh, man," Officer Beemer moaned. "This paperwork will take all day."

"Hey, Beemer. Jones." Petrie approached the truck. "Wendell and I will finish up. Get on down 20, quarter mile south of here. There's a car abandoned with two people in it. Paramedics are on the way, but dispatch says it may be too late. Way too late." He looked at Paul Lutz for the first time. "What's going on here?"

***

Leslie kneeled in aisle seven of Hartmann's Grocery, bored, filling in soups. The afternoon was dragging, as usual. Again and again she checked her watch, as if magically it would be three o'clock and she would have fifteen refreshing minutes in the sunshine. Two ten. She sighed and continued rearranging the soup to make the shelves look fuller and prevent another trip to the stockroom.

"Why Leslie! Happy summer!" A low, rich voice said from behind. Immediately she recognized it, and turned happily to stare up at the tall woman.

"Hi Dr. Loomis," she said, getting to her feet. Dr. Loomis was by far Leslie's favorite professor at Salem. Her lectures, combined with her smooth accent, held Leslie's complete attention, and as a result, she received the first A of her college career. Leslie was not certain if she earned that A because cultural anthropology was so intriguing or if she was trying to impress Dr. Loomis. Leslie, never sure about her own direction, often swayed under the influence of others, but Dr. Loomis was her first academic role model. The last person to be held in such high esteem was Gary Gearlock, the front man for Intestinal Backwash, a local band currently touring clubs across the country. Leslie met Gary at a party, went to hear him at the Crimson Crypt in Salem, and was in rapt awe of his talent and sensitivity. He wrote down the lyrics to a song he was composing on a napkin, folded it gently and kissed it before laying it in her palm and closing her fingers around it. That folded napkin was in her jewelry box, the old box, not the one she actually used. She occasionally took it out and carefully unfolded it, studying it as if looking for something she may have missed the thousand other times she read it. Though months had passed since she thought of it, she could recite each scribbled word of the incomplete song:

Acid Rain
by
Gary Gearlock
Acid Rain
eating a hole in my umbrella
through my skull
into my brain

Acid Rain
melting the birdbath in my yard
melting bird feet
bird puddle stain

Acid Rain

Once, she showed it to Anna, who laughed hysterically and began adding her own lyrics: *Acid Rain will open drains, derail trains, knock down planes; Acid rain will cause you pain! Bad, bad Acid Rain! Made Gary Gearlock go insane!* And she laughed more, going on and on about mutated grain growing on the plains in Spain while Leslie fumed and told her to forget it because she would never understand someone as tender as Gary Gearlock. "Geez Les!" Anna said, "He's not sensitive. He's writing about acid rain because it rhymes with about every other word in the dictionary." Leslie kept the napkin, not admitting Anna's mimicry had knocked Gary Gearlock down a rung or two on her ladder of legends. This left room for another, and Dr. Loomis, being the most elegant and interesting person Leslie ever met, climbed right over the back of Gary Gearlock.

"I'm a little disappointed in you, Leslie," Dr. Loomis admonished. "I thought you were going to take Western Civilization this summer. Is there a problem?"

"No," Leslie tried to think quickly of an excuse, but nothing came.

"Just being lazy maybe?"

"No, um, you know. I have to work," she said lamely, gesturing to the soup cans.

Dr. Loomis pursed her lips slightly and shook her head gracefully. "If I didn't know your tuition was waived because of your parents' position I might accept that." She tapped her chin with a long, coffee-brown finger. "It seems to me that a woman who lives at home and is so close to campus should have time for one class. Especially when she promised the instructor she would be taking it."

Leslie's gut clinched, but then, unexpectedly, Dr. Loomis smiled.

"Leslie, are you ever going to become a serious student? Or are you determined to fly by the seat of your pants? That's a terribly unflattering posture, if you think about it."

Leslie smiled back. Around the corner came Tara Crum, and seeing Tara in the same field of vision as Dr. Loomis caused Leslie to marvel again that such an amazing person as Dr. Loomis chose to live in Miltonville. Tara came closer, her short, round body stuffed into black knit pants that fit like a sausage casing, revealing each and every lump, bump, and ripple. Her frosted, perm-frizzled hair contrasted with the short, natural style of Dr. Loomis and Leslie realized again, sadly, that it was Dr. Loomis, not Tara Crum, who was out of place in Miltonville. Fingering her own wiry hair and looking down at her own pudgy knees, she was even sadder to realize that she was only a few years from becoming another Tara Crum herself.

"Hey Leslie!" Tara seemed excited to see her. Dr. Loomis gave Leslie a farewell shoulder pat and went on with her shopping.

"What's going on in your neighborhood? Have you heard?" Tara asked.

"Yeah, it's pretty weird." Leslie settled back to her work. "Have you heard anything about Cindy? Is she okay?"

"I don't know. I was hoping you knew something. What about Dottie?"

"What about her?" Leslie asked. But they were interrupted by Tara's boys who came tearing into the aisle, something in each hand.

"Put those back! Everyone of you!" Tara yelled at them.

"But Mom!" they chorused.

"Now!"

The kids, three of them, all barefoot and filthy, persisted and it became an argument. The middle boy scrunched his face and said, "I hate you!"

"What about Dottie?" Leslie kept asking, but Tara, wearing a flustered face, said, "I gotta get these brats outta here. They drive me crazy!" Then to the boys she said, "Okay, okay! Just shut up!"

Leslie waited for them to disappear and then she took a different route to the check out where Anna was busy filling in candy.

"Hey! Have you heard anything about Dottie Geist?"

"Yeah," Anna shook her head.

"What?" Leslie asked impatiently.

"Nobody told you? I saw Tara Crum running around yapping about it."

"About what?"

"Well, first I heard she was run over by a car, but then I heard, and this I believe, that some guy was lost out there, and she came running out, acting like she does, and he tried to get away from her but she was hanging on to his car door or something and got knocked down. She wasn't hurt or anything." Anna shook her head again. "What a dingbat."

"Oh my gosh!" Leslie cried. "I would have loved to have seen that!"

Anna nodded, continuing her work, overstuffing the gum on the rack.

"I hate being stuck here. Everything happens when we're at work," Leslie said. "Oh well. Did you call your mom back?"

"I tried. Phone's been busy."

"She screwed up the cordless again, didn't she?"

"Looks that way," Anna said. She rearranged the breath mints in order to fit more into the boxes. The ones she added rolled to the floor. "Poop."

In the next check out, Dr. Loomis gathered her groceries into a net bag. "Goodbye," she waved.

"She is the most beautiful person I've ever seen," Leslie said, waving. Anna raised quizzical eyebrows. "Oh, come on. I'm not, like, some latent lesbian or something."

"I didn't say anything," Anna grinned.

"No way," Leslie said, heading back to the soup aisle. "I'm secure enough in my womanhood to admire beauty in all others, regardless of gender." Then she turned around and came back, very concerned. "Do you think—?"

Anna laughed, "Will you go back to work?"

Leslie returned to aisle seven to wait for her break.

***

191

In Miltonville General, Claire thought the medication might be finally wearing off, and she forced herself to remain calm. The last time she felt herself emerging from the drugged stupor, she had gone wild seeking escape, and they injected her with more. For most of the day, Cindy dozed, but Claire resisted. At first she didn't understand why the drugs were affecting her so. She never had problems like this before. It must be the baby. He weakened her. What was a baby, anyway, other than a parasite sapping its mother's strength?

There was movement in the room. She opened Cindy's eyes just enough to see. Three nurses were bringing someone in on a rolling bed. Working together, they moved a young girl into the next bed. She squirmed and groaned. The nurses leaned over the girl.

"Honey, can you hear me?" said one. Another groan.

"She's responding!" The nurses seemed to rejoice and for some reason this made Claire angry. She opened Cindy's eyes wider. "Oh," she tried to say through Cindy's slack jaw. She recognized the girl. In fact, she had *inhabited* her. So the pathetic thing survived. Claire listened to the cheery nurses and wished she had killed her.

The girl muttered something, and her head rolled on the pillow. Her eyelids fluttered, then snapped fully open. "No!" she cried softly, and her arms and legs thrashed weakly under the sheets. The nurses' joy was gone. They worked to try to calm her.

"Let's get her out of here," a male nurse said, and Claire saw him looking at her. Without realizing it, she chuckled. Quickly, they wheeled the girl out of the room.

***

Tom and Judy Redmond sat together in their large kitchen, sipping coffee and filling each other in on their last three days apart. Neither had anything major to report, and a dripping bathroom faucet was the closest they came to a problem.

"I think I might get to that before dinner," Tom said, refilling his coffee cup. "Shouldn't take long."

"Great. Will you need anything from town?"

"You have to go to town?"

"I was going to have Anna pick up some things, but she hasn't called back. It's just as well, because I thought of a dozen other things I need since then. Let me have a few minutes to shower before you start on the faucet."

He looked over her grass stained knees and elbows and picked a leaf from her short red hair. "A few minutes?"

"Smart aleck," she grumbled. As soon as he took his coffee to the backdoor she fished an ice cube from her tea and hooked it down his pants. Then she ran like crazy up the stairs.

***

"The squad's going out again?" Wanda asked, looking out the window of Miltonville General's nurses' lounge. Beneath her, the ambulance wailed into the street.

"I'm glad my shift's over. What's that? Third time?" Ellen Flannery slammed her locker shut. Anxious as she was to get home, she needed a smoke more, and she dug into her deep bag.

"Be thankful you're not in ER," Wanda reminded her.

"What difference does it make? They're sending them all up-stairs."

The door opened, and Marsha McBerry poked her head in. "Anyone else here?"

"Just us babes," Ellen told her.

Marsha came into the room. "The squad just went back out. Now this is a rumor, so don't say anything, but they might be bringing in three more. All DOA."

"Oh, no. What happened?" Wanda asked. Ellen waited tensely.

"Well, like I said, it's not certain. I just talked to Pam." Pam Banks was Miltonville's police dispatcher. Between her and Marsha, they knew everything that was going on.

"She got a call about a disabled vehicle on Route 20. We got that too, because there were two men inside. But then, Fred Wendell called in and said Paul Lutz was dead behind AJ's, in Rubin Tanner's truck. Fred went there to question Rubin about that call we got, and Rubin went berserk. Then they found Paul."

"Oh no." Wanda whispered. "We better call Judy." Ellen nod-ded.

"I tried," Marsha said. "Her phone's busy."

"I'll go out there," Ellen volunteered. "It's close—"

"No," Marsha said. "Just go home. Probably her phone's busy

because of everyone calling. She won't answer the door with all this going on. Let's go home and stay there. If someone calls begging for help, hang up and send the cops."

"I can't do that." Ellen stood, grinding her cigarette into the ashtray.

"Ellen," Wanda warned, "that's how it happened to Judy."

Marsha nodded. "You can't trust anyone. It's the Itch."

***

At three o'clock, Ed Philips was sleeping off the morning's binge. He had started the day full of good intentions, but his memories threatened to carry him away, so he reached for an anchor. By noon, he was pretty well anchored. Not so much a fall down drunk as a lay down one, necessary after the ordeal of remembering Jerry Templeton. Usually when these memories crossed his mind, Ed cast them aside. Practicing the same visual imagery technique his sister used to deal with cancer pain, he learned to picture himself with a broom sweeping Jerry away. Sometimes, though, it backfired, and his broom became a vacuum cleaner, sucking in every bit of information, searching under every rug for any scrap of detail he had hidden. *My brain is a dirty sweeper bag*, he thought, *and my head is as big as a house*. Bourbon couldn't stop the vacuum cleaner, but it eventually allowed him to shut the door on its incessant whirring. Still, there were windows, and he had to peep because there was so much to see and it wasn't going to go away until he looked. And this time, when he looked, Wendy looked back.

***

Nearly forty years earlier, Ed had returned to his job a week after Jerry's funeral. His employer and co-workers were sympathetic, so no one complained about his prolonged absence. With Jerry gone, and no more Vanderkellens, he threw himself into his work. John Barker had no one left to curse. It no longer mattered whether it was real or simply his father's creation. Even if a ghostly John Barker were roaming the earth, who cared? At least he didn't seem to be killing anyone anymore.

Actual time and distance mimicked the cerebral time and distance, and by concentrating on his work, he survived the next twelve years successfully. Cathy left him not long after Jerry died. Ed couldn't blame her; he was drinking a great deal and was extremely moody. His other girl, Marie, hung on longer, but she, too, finally gave up when he announced he was taking a job in Indianapolis. A few years later, he moved on to Chicago. There were other women, none too serious, though. He spent his days working, his evenings with a TV dinner and a glass or two of bourbon, his weekends either in Miltonville or out with friends. It wasn't an exciting life, but it suited him.

The October of the twelfth year after Jerry's death, Ed was home visiting during Salem University's homecoming weekend. Friday evening, he and Susan went out to Dale's for the Go-Go Knights' party honoring the Salem University Knights football team. They were going up against their arch rivals, the aptly named Winchester Dragons, the next day. The place was filled with alums and locals, and Ed and Susan split up, each finding old friends.

Twice during the evening, Ed noticed a woman staring at him. She looked familiar, about his age, maybe older, and definitely not a local. It wasn't her high-heeled leather boots or ultra short skirt, the pricey kind the girls from Amberly County bought imitations of that set her apart. It was her eyes, dark and mocking under her teased black hair. She sat on the barstool watching the crowd like a Martian scientist sent to observe primitive human life. He barely had time to give her a flickering thought before being distracted by former classmates.

By midnight, he was pleased to be somewhat sober, yet still having a good time. On the way to the bar with a drink order memorized, he felt a tug at the back of his shirt. He turned, grinning, prepared for a friendly face. Instead, it was her, the black haired woman.

"You don't remember me, do you?" she asked, still regarding him as a lower life form.

Caught off guard, he couldn't come up with a witty response, so he stood there looking every bit like the insect she assumed him to be.

"I said, 'you don't remember me, do you?'," she repeated. "But why would you?" She stuck out her hand. "I'm Wendy Beckman. Daniels, I guess, you'd know me by."

Ed let his jaw drop, and he took her hand, stammering an incoherent reply.

"You do remember me, don't you? I was here with Jerry Templeton the night he was killed. Right over there." She turned to point.

"I remember," Ed managed to stop her. "I just don't want to talk about it."

"Who said I did?" She shrugged. "So how're you doing these days? Wife, kids, all that?"

"No. I live in Chicago. Still single." He was anxious to get away.

"Chicago? Wow. That's a great place. Well, I'm single, too. Again. I've been single a few times. Just one kid, though."

"Kids are nice," Ed said to be polite.

"Well, she's almost twelve, so I guess she's not much of a kid anymore."

Ed nodded, never sure what to say when people started talking about their children. The bartender came to take his order.

"Well, it's been nice," Ed attempted to excuse himself, but she touched his arm.

"Say, do you happen to know what happened to Jerry's family? Are his mom and dad still around?"

"I think they retired in Florida or Arizona or somewhere."

"Yeah, they were pretty old, weren't they? What about other family?"

"I really don't know. Hey, I have to order—"

"Oh, yeah. Sorry. I have to go anyway. My kid'll think I got lost."

"Well, it was good to see you. Maybe I'll see you at the game tomorrow."

"Maybe." She held his eyes a moment, as if she didn't want to leave. Then she tilted her head and gave him a tight smile before turning to go.

At four a.m. his eyes snapped open. He had done the math subconsciously. No, he assured himself, it couldn't be.

He didn't see Wendy at the game the next day. Four years would pass before he saw her again.

The call came on a Thursday evening, just as he and Gail finished dinner. Gail surprised him by being in his kitchen when he came in from work, and though he was terribly uncomfortable about that, he tried not to show it. He intended to have a word with the building supervisor who let her in. This kind of thing always happened to him, women trying to control his life. A few dates and suddenly they were hinting about marriage and babies. Fortunately, Ed discovered several ways to make them mad enough to leave, be it drinking, flirting around, or changing his phone number. It was always a drama.

Tonight, throughout dinner Gail fussed over him, refilling his plate and asking about the food. "The meat's not too dry, is it? Is the wine okay?" When the phone rang, he snatched it up eagerly, hoping for any reason to cut the evening short.

"Is this Ed Philips?" asked the female voice.

"It is."

"Did you go to Salem University? In the fifties?"

"Yes." Ed watched Gail hovering close, dishrag in hand.

"Do you have any idea how many Edward, Edwin, and Edgar Philipses are in the Chicago book?" the woman on the phone continued.

"No," he answered, not paying as much attention to the question as he was to Gail.

"Are you going to ask who this is?" the voice asked.

"I thought you were getting to that."

"It's Wendy. Cline. Beckman. Hill. *Daniels.*"

"Wendy?" he repeated, and Gail frowned.

"Yeah, Wendy." When he didn't answer, she asked how he was doing.

"Um, fine," Ed answered, doing a quick mental assessment of which woman would be the least trouble. He could cut Wendy off and spend the rest of the evening with Gail, and then Gail would try to make plans for Friday, then probably hang around all weekend. Or he could chat with Wendy, and make Gail angry, perhaps leading to her hasty departure. He chose to chat with Wendy.

Gail did leave, but not as hastily as he hoped. She asked a lot of questions about the conversation she blatantly eavesdropped on, and the dinner invitation he indiscreetly accepted in her earshot. He didn't want to have dinner with Wendy, but he did want to get rid of Gail. Besides, it wasn't really a date; he only wanted Gail to think it was.

*****

When he arrived at Lequini's, Wendy was waiting at the bar,

drink in hand. Her hair was short, but still an unnatural black, matching the thick liner around her eyes. She looked terribly skinny in her low cut red dress with see-through sleeves. They made a lot of small talk, avoiding the topic of Jerry Templeton. She was staying with a friend and looking for work. Her spirits were good, having just come from a promising interview.

"It's just waiting tables, but he said I could learn bar tending. That's where the real money is, you know. Especially for a woman," she told him.

"That's great. What about your kid? Daughter?" Ed asked, recalling their conversation four years earlier.

"Oh, daughter. Holly." Wendy blinked rapidly, looked away, then back, smiling. "She's staying with her grandparents."

"Mmmm," Ed nodded, not knowing what to say.

"Not my mother," Wendy went on. "I wouldn't do that to a kid. Mark's parents. They live in Little Easton. Mark's father teaches at Salem. He's a dean, or a chair or something."

"Oh," Ed nodded again, still not sure how to respond.

"Yeah. My lifestyle isn't conducive for child rearing. I can't stay in one place, you know. I get restless. It bothered Holly. She's a real homebody. Sure took good care of me!" She paused, shaking her head.

"Hmm, yeah," Ed uttered nonsense syllables in place of speech, once again at a loss for appropriate comments concerning children. Wendy sat quietly for a moment, her gaze roaming the restaurant.

"Her grandparents do love her. I think she's happy now. She has best friends, and everything. She's a good kid," Wendy smiled. "And she's so pretty, even though she looks like her father."

Ed drained his drink and signaled the waiter.

"Anyway," Wendy said, sensing Ed's discomfort. "What about you? What do you do with yourself?"

He shrugged and told her about his job. She listened attentively, asking questions; by the time the food arrived, they were settled into a chatty conversation. Ed asked about Mark Cline, her first husband.

"Mark? Oh, I guess he's still overseas. He's military. Has been since we married. Lucky for him he's not in the war. Directly, anyway. Funny, I couldn't stand moving from base to base, but I couldn't stand being in one place, either. You know, we had to get married because of Holly, so I guess I really wasn't ready. Mark said I was a screwball," she sighed.

Wendy went home with Ed that night, and stayed most of Saturday. She was relaxed and funny and they spent the rainy morning watching old movies on television. Ed dozed off in the early afternoon, and woke to an empty apartment and a ringing phone. It was Gail, wanting to know what he was doing. She asked if he enjoyed his date with Wilma. Ed told her he had errands to run and hung up. There was no sign of Wendy.

He did have things to do: laundry, groceries, call his mother… Instead he stayed home, watching more TV and thinking of Wendy. Three days went by before he heard from her. She had started the waitressing job and worked late hours, but on her night off she came over and stayed around a few days, before disappearing for a few more. Before long, they fell into a pattern of her coming and going. Ed didn't mind, instead he became intrigued by her mysteries. Where did she stay when she wasn't with him? He didn't have her phone number, but he supposed he could reach her at work if he needed. Why didn't she bother him with talk of commitment? Not even a hint of it. In fact, she wouldn't commit on Tuesday to a movie on Friday. Day by day they went, usually hiding in his apartment when she was around, getting drunk or stoned or both. She introduced him to many new habits and he accepted them easily. Gradually, her friends started showing up, bringing an array of pharmaceuticals, and several mornings he woke to find strangers sleeping on the couch or sitting around a bong in the kitchen.

Six months went by before it occurred to Ed that, once again, a woman had taken control of his world. Since meeting up with Wendy, he had used most of his sick leave and all of his vacation time because he couldn't cut the late nights. His performance at work was sliding and he was minutes from a second reprimand. He was nervous and stressed, but she always had something to soothe him, a pill, a drink, a smoke and then everything was fine. Even if he lost his job, there were others, she said. They'd make it.

"But are you happy like this?" he asked her once. They were both barely coherent, but he remembered her answer.

"Happy? I don't know. I never thought about it. This is just how I am. I never know where I'm going, but somehow I always get there." She rolled closer to him on the bed and giggled. "I'm not really in control of what I do. If I were, I would have picked a faster way to kill myself."

Eventually, his second reprimand at work came. He wasn't fired, but he was being watched. Ed lied about problems with his health, and after rambling about that, he made his mother ill, for good measure. His boss knew he was lying, and Ed knew he knew. Humiliated, he resolved to make the necessary changes, the first being to end his relationship with Wendy. He went home that day ready to resist anything she might offer, but as it turned out, Wendy made no temptations.

The odor in his apartment assaulted his nose when he opened the door. Foul, like a dirty animal cage. The drapes were pulled, filtering the late day sunlight. Wendy lay on her side, naked, on the floor, covered in feces and vomit, a rubber tube around her arm. Beside her, snoring loudly, slept a man Ed vaguely knew as Andy, or Randy.

He approached cautiously, afraid. Carefully, he touched Wendy's face under her nose. She was breathing. He rolled her head toward the floor, and thick vomit oozed from her mouth. It was all he could do not to throw up himself. He prodded Andy or Randy with his foot several times until he groaned. Ed grabbed his scrawny shoulders and shook him awake. "What did you do to her?" he demanded, shaking harder until Andy or Randy was semi-coherent.

"Get dressed," Ed ordered, disgusted. Andy or Randy crawled away, reaching about for his clothes. Dragging Wendy to the bathroom, Ed put her in the tub and turned on the shower. She made little noises, but didn't wake up. He left her there and packed what things she had at his apartment, while Andy or Randy swayed in the hallway, professing his innocence.

"Man, I didn't know she was your old lady. We were just messin' around," he sniveled. Ed ignored his whining, commanding Andy or Randy to assist him dressing Wendy so he could take her to the hospital. Beneath his urgency was an unsettling hostility, not toward the scared, skinny man, but toward Wendy, not only for this betrayal, but for stepping in and almost ruining his life.

Tiny sounds came from her lips and her eyes opened partway. Ed took the bag he'd packed, put one of her arms over his shoulder and told Andy or Randy to do the same and they stumbled their way down to Ed's car.

Half an hour later, they hauled her into the emergency room of the county hospital. Ed sat them both in waiting room chairs and told Andy or Randy to wait while he talked to the nurse. At the counter he pointed out Wendy to the nurse.

"See that girl? I think she's overdosed on something. You'll have to ask her boyfriend what happened. I just gave them a lift."

The nurse asked him to stick around. Ed said sure, and asked where the bathroom was. He nodded at her directions, began to follow them, and ducked out another door.

The next day he called to ask about Wendy's condition. She was still there, doing better, recovering. The nurse on her floor all but begged him to come visit. Ed made a noncommittal comment and hung up without giving his name.

Later that week his sister called. She asked how things were going, and needing to talk, he told her what happened. He was still anxious about his job, but assured her he was making every effort to rectify the situation. Susan expressed a fear that Wendy would come back when she was released from the hospital. Ed told her he had the locks changed and was thinking about moving.

"You mean you'd move to avoid telling her to get lost?" Susan marveled.

"Yeah, I guess I would. She's a psycho, Susan."

"No, you're the psycho!" she laughed. "Ed, someday you are going to have to get tough with people. It really is easier than running from them. Or moving."

They had a good talk and Ed's spirits were lifted. Susan was a professor now, like their father, working in Connecticut, but she was still his goofy kid sister and she knew how to make him laugh.

That same evening, his mother called. It was odd that she was calling so late on a weeknight. Surely Susan didn't call and tell her about Wendy!

"Susan told me she called," his mother started. "She had something to tell you, but she lost her nerve." He heard the quiver in his mother's voice.

"Mom? What is it?"

"Honey, she has cancer..."

"No..."

"...very much like your father..."

"...no..."

"...better prognosis..."

"...no..."

"...new technology and better treatments..."

Ed stopped listening.

That night he got very drunk. He made it to work in the morning, fuzzy-eyed and numb. His boss gave him the eye. Nothing was said.

Over the next week he made several calls to friends at Salem University, explaining about Susan's illness and his need to be at home. Within two months he quit his job and moved home with his mother, accepting a position as an instructor at the university. Susan refused to leave her job in Connecticut, but despite his mother's optimism, it would only be a matter of time before she, too, returned to Salem, and Ed wanted them to be together.

While Ed was poking around the basement for mementos to spring on his sister when she eventually came home, he found his father's leather briefcase. He waited for his mother to go out before he brought it upstairs. It was well organized, enough so to stir his curiosity. Remembering that Wendy's daughter was staying with her grandfather in Little Easton, Ed decided to call him. He was, after all, a friend of Mark's.

It took a couple of weeks to get to it, but when he did call, he told Dr. Cline he was back in town looking up old friends. Mark was in Germany, Dr. Cline said, but he took his number and promised to tell him he called. That was all, and Ed let the Itch go. But in December, Dr. Cline called on him. Mark was coming home for the holidays, and the Clines were having a party. Would Ed like to come?

He accepted, still mildly curious about Wendy's daughter, but more than anything, he was happy to be going out. It was a nice party, mostly a family gathering although there were a few faces he recognized. He met Holly briefly as she flitted about the guests. Wendy was right, she was pretty, even if she did look like her father. She looked so much like her father, in fact, he wondered if Mark Cline ever questioned his paternity. Mark's dark, straight hair and narrow features were sharp against Holly's softness and her halo of untamable mousy brown curls. Her light, barely-there-freckles danced on a face that smiled easily.

Over the years, Ed cultivated a careful relationship with the Clines, first by helping them build a barbecue in the spring, then by introducing them to someone who helped them with an electrical job. When Mark came home for his infrequent visits, he was pleased to see Ed. They weren't close in college, but it was nice to see a familiar face. Mark had a new family in which he was never able to completely incorporate Holly. Wendy had taken off with her when she was a toddler, and at the time it was difficult to do anything legally. According to Mark, Wendy had a history of drug abuse, which led to an ugly court case forcing custody of Holly to the Clines.

Holly was, as Wendy said, a good kid. She did okay in school, had a lot of friends and enjoyed herself. Her boyfriend was older, in college, but met the approval of the Clines. Her best friend, Judy, had a serious boyfriend in Miltonville. By the time the girls entered their senior year in high school, they were making wedding plans.

Ed gave them brochures from colleges all over the country.

"I can't get in to any of these," Holly said. "Besides, I'm getting married."

"Me, too," Judy chorused.

"I wish we could do a double ceremony."

"No way. Not with those colors you picked."

The Clines sat nearby, chuckling at the girls. They would be no help to Ed. They came from an era that considered women old maids at twenty. Ed's apprehension was not due to the girls youth; it came from Holly's recent announcement that her boyfriend, Dan, promised to take a job near Little Easton when he graduated. Holly was very attached to her friends and family and Dan would do anything to make her happy.

Ed didn't give up. He persuaded Dan so hard to shop around before choosing a place to settle that Holly finally asked why he was trying to get rid of them.

He wished he could tell her, but he couldn't imagine how. First, he'd have to tell her he thought Jerry Templeton was her real father. Once he did that, the ire of the entire family would prevent him from seeing her again, even to protect her. No, he decided, he'd wait, he'd watch, and if the time ever came when he thought another Itch may be occurring, then he would tell her.

Ed attended both weddings, sent gifts to both babies. He kept an eye on the papers, an ear to the radio, but as time passed without event, he turned his attention to his sister, who finally came home to die. Her good cheer, her persistent, pitiful faith in God, distressed him. Every Sunday, he took her and his mother to church, never sure why, but always mindful of their peaceful demeanor, as if they actually thought God was going to save Susan.

That nagged him. Many things nagged him. With no classes in the summer, he had little to do but help around the house. His social life was dismal, his home life heavy with Susan's worsening condition. Alcohol proved a satisfying escape now that he no longer used drugs. The day Holly died, he was recovering from one of his lengthier escapes, a night where he combined beer, whiskey and gin while losing a week's pay at Neal Reedy's card table. He stayed in bed that day, telling his mother he had the flu, and she made no mention of the news about town. He didn't know the Itch happened until it was over.

Holly's death tormented him. The funeral played like a dream, her white coffin floating down the aisle like a bride. Ed searched for Wendy, desperate to tell her all he knew in order to unshoulder his guilt. Wendy's affair was to blame; it was her fault Holly existed. Wendy was not there; the guilt was his alone. He was supposed to be watching, waiting, but he forgot.

He drank constantly now, without the good sense to be embarrassed about it. His buddies rallied for him, talked to him, yelled at him. His sister needed him, his mother, they said in their ignorance. One late afternoon, while Nate Kingston and Jim Erwin tried to sober him up, he tried to disclose his guilt. His drunken, muddled story upset Jim and Nate, and they warned him to shut up. The Cline's had been through enough.

After much cajoling, several attempts with a 12-step program, and a year of Sundays at church, Ed professed to have regained control, but not before he lost his job. He was hired by Amberly County School District as a custodian at Miltonville High School. He helped his mother bury Susan. He terminated contact with the Clines. He moved into his tiny apartment, and there he stayed.

***

There was a knocking at the door. Persistent.

"Ed? Ed? You in there?"

His heavy eyelids fluttered. More knocking. What time? Morning? The room was hazy, the curtains drawn. Oh, yeah. A nap. He was waking from a nap. He sat up and held his head. More knocking. Harder. He stood, steadied himself, and crossed the small dark room. At the door he pulled back the curtain, squinting against the sun, and saw a shiny brown head as Nate Kingston descended the stairs. He jerked open the door. Nate turned around.

"What are you doing? I was going down to get Mrs. Skofield. I thought it'd got you!" Nate came back to the landing and followed Ed inside. "You aren't holin' up, are you?"

"What are you talking about? I was asleep—"

"Oh, man. I smell what you've been doing," Nate said, calmer. He picked up the coffee cup from the table and sniffed. "I should have known."

"Will you tell me?"

"Well, I came to see what you were going to do. I guess this answers my question." He pushed Ed aside on his way to the door.

"Wait," Ed grabbed his arm. "What're you talking about?"

"You've not seen the news today?"

Ed shook his head. "I've been busy."

"You've not heard about the girl? About that lady out in the Kitchen? Paul Lutz?" Ed kept shaking his head. "Ed, we're having an Itch. I remembered what you told me about that Vickers girl. Do you still believe it? Are you going to tell her?"

Ed had no answer. "I don't know."

"Maybe you should. She's old enough. Get her to leave town."

"But how?"

"You mean to tell me after twenty years, you don't have a plan?"

"I had hoped I'd never need one."

Outside, a car horn honked, and Nate looked toward the door. "That's Frieda. She's nervous. We're on our way to Bloomington."

"You better get going."

"But what are you going to do," Nate said.

"Don't worry. I kind of have an idea," he lied.

"An idea? What idea?"

"Never mind right now. I'll tell you when it's over. Right now, you need to get Frieda to Bloomington."

"You sure?" Nate frowned at him. Ed nodded assurance, although he had never been less sure of anything in his life.

***

"Is it a full moon?" Barney Boyd asked Russ, one of the paramedics who delivered Troy Ivers, Paul Lutz and Mark Reynolds to the morgue.

"Not sure," Russ said. He was busy filling out paperwork at the coroner's secretary's desk. Barney, the coroner's assistant, had responded to the scene in his personal car, so the squad, having no one to transport to the hospital, brought the bodies to the morgue.

"Well, thanks for droppin' em off, Russ. Saved me one unpleasant ride." The paramedic handed a clipboard to Barney.

"Sure," Russ agreed. Being a fairly quiet man, he didn't feel it necessary to enter discourse on Dr. Ivers's keen odor.

A door opened and another paramedic, Pete Holmes, appeared from Hank Gabbard's workroom. "Well?" Barney asked.

"Don't know," Pete answered.

"I'll lay money that Paul's early departure was chemically induced. What cha say, Pete?" Barney said.

"Barn, I told you already, I won't bet on cause of death. It's not respectful."

"Gruesome, really," Russ added.

"Aw," he started to wave them off, but stopped short and clapped his hands together. "Okay. I got something better. How *many* will there be?"

"What?" Russ asked.

Pete pointed a stern finger at Barney. "That doesn't deserve a reply."

"Oh, don't take everything so serious. It's just a myth. Fun."

"Barney, I'm going to ignore that because you haven't lived here long enough to know anyone who died from it, so you don't know any better. But now you do."

"Hey, I'm sorry, really. I mean, I really thought it was some kind of a joke or something. Really."

Pete smiled, but only a little. "That's okay."

"Are you guys coming?" A young woman called from down the corridor.

"Yeah, Kim," Pete answered as Hank Gabbard stepped into the lobby.

"Are you still here? I'm paying by the hour for your time, you know," he reminded them.

As Russ and Pete returned to the delivery dock where Kim waited, Russ asked, "Was he talking about the Itch?"

"Yep."

"Well, I've lived here three years and never heard of it. Today, that's all I heard. Mind filling me in?"

"Just a local superstition that happens to be real."

"Oh," Russ said, and seemed satisfied.

***

Barbara Mann did a classic double take when Judy came into the personnel office. "Judy," she greeted. "What are you doing here?"

"Something's wrong," Judy began, talking on as Barbara's red head bobbed in agreement. "I just came from the bank, and they didn't get my check again. They said we didn't complete all the paperwork for direct deposit—" Judy paused because Barbara's concerned expression flashed surprise, then confusion. "Barbara, are you all right?"

"Uh, yeah. I'll look into it." She removed her large glasses and bit the stem. "Um, has Wanda talked to you? She tried to call you earlier."

"Oh, no. Please don't ask. I can't work tonight. Besides, I'm on first tomorrow, and Tom is leaving Sunday. Sorry."

Barbara waved her off. "No, no. Have you heard the news today?"

Judy took a step back. "What's happened?"

"Some things. Unusual things."

"Define unusual, Barbara," Judy said sternly.

"As in not usual." She tried to smile. She pointed to a chair and Judy pulled it up to the desk as Barbara continued, "Actually, not everything's been on the news. It started this morning when they brought a woman in from the Kitchen. Hysterical. She's stable now, but still zonked. Well, they no sooner brought her in when we had another call out there. Someone found a girl in their driveway. Knocked out, but not like she was assaulted or OD'd. Like she was asleep. Couldn't wake her up. No ID. She's started to come around, but not much."

"Did they ID her? Who was the other one?"

"No ID yet, but the first call was Cindy Swift. She's been in for Aid training, does agency home health care, I think."

"Cindy? I know her. I helped with her training." Judy scooted closer, her eyes wide and fearful.

"MC Canwell called her in. Cindy was going nuts. Really out of control. MC literally sat on her, and we had a heck of a time here. Last I heard, she was coming around. Doc says it's stress."

"I can see that," Judy agreed.

"Anyway, all these little things started happening. Pam, at the PD says Dr. Ivers is gone. No trace, just didn't show up for work this morning. Then, Rubin Tanner went nuts in town, and they found one of his friends dead in his truck. Some guy named Paul Lutz," Judy shook her head indicating that she didn't know him. "So then, just a while ago, they found two dead men in a car on the highway. We don't know who yet."

"Oh, it can't be," Judy said quietly.

"We're acting on the assumption it might be."

"Where's Cindy? Can I see her?"

"Second floor. She's okay. Why don't you go home?"

"I will. You said she was coming around? Maybe she'll talk to me."

"She's probably asleep, Judy. You can see her later, okay?"

Judy smiled sadly. "I may not have that opportunity."

"Do what you have to, but hurry home."

"I will as soon as I get the girls from work. You do the same," Judy advised, and left the office, her direct deposit problems completely forgotten.

***

The nurse at the desk on the second floor gave Judy the same startled expression as Barbara. Apparently no one expected Judy to be away from home.

"Hi Stacy. Where's Cindy Swift?" Judy asked.

"203. But Judy—" Stacy said, but Judy was already on her way to the double room where Cindy slept, the late afternoon sun brightening its starkness.

"Cindy," Judy stood next to her, speaking quietly, "it's Judy Redmond. Remember me? I taught you how to give a shot to an orange." Cindy's eyelids twitched. "Can you hear me? Can you try to wake up, sweetheart? Try really hard." The eyes opened, and fell shut again.

"Tired," Cindy muttered.

"That's a good girl. Keep trying." Judy watched the peaceful face and wondered how long she would last. Actually, she looked quite healthy. Nurses who had cared for past Itch victims reported that their patient's complexions were pasty, that their eyes and mouth and fingers and toes were purple. Maybe Cindy wasn't an Itch victim; maybe it was a coincidence. After all, her very public divorce and subsequent struggles could cause a breakdown. She would go have a peek at the Jane Doe. First though, she better call Hartmann's and catch Anna before she left. They would fuss about staying in on a Friday night, but not much. Tom and Anna usually humored her when the subject was the Itch. Squeezing Cindy's hand, she started to leave, but Cindy returned the squeeze.

"I'm still here, honey," Judy assured her. She would wait a moment in case she woke up, then she'd signal for Stacy so she could go. Across the bed was a large window, which afforded a view of the backside of Miltonville. In one of those alleys, almost twenty years ago, she and Holly had gone to check on their friend. It was this time of year, too. And a Friday. What were the odds of it falling on a Friday again? The Itch of the fifties was on a Saturday. Was there a sequence? No, the one before was on a Monday or Tuesday...

"I know you," a groggy voice said.

"Huh?" Judy said, coming out of her reverie. She glanced at the bed where Cindy lay, eyes now wide open. Suddenly, incredibly, the room went dark, and Judy felt herself being thrown against the wall. Oh it hurt! She tried to pick herself up, but there was nothing; no wall, no floor, just dark. But not dark. A fog? Haze? What was it? Nothing she'd ever seen before. A woman was there, Judy couldn't see her, but she felt her pressing, pulling at the arms she had protectively wrapped about her head.

"I knew it! My, my this is a small town!" She heard. Her arms were being tugged, but she held tight. "Oh, bother! Like you have anything I need!" Then she felt movement, like riding fast over hills. Her stomach surged. She heard her name, voices she recognized: "Hey, Judy!...You okay Judy?"; "Don't worry, just go on home."; "Everything'll be okay." Then, in her own head she heard, "How do we get out of this place? There! Can you drive? Do you have a car? Come on, answer me!"

Judy held on, stunned, unable to think. She felt the heat of the sun as they left the hospital. "Help me find my way back!" the woman demanded. Back where? She saw it, then, just a flash. A tiny bit of the woman's memory filled her and she could see paramedics, MC Canwell and her husband, Dottie Geist and across the street, Leslie's house. She wanted to go to Leslie's house? Why?

"Who's Leslie?" the woman snapped. Judy again covered her head, and again, the woman began pulling at her. Judy concentrated on swatting her away, feeling as if she were playing tennis with ten balls coming at a time. She hit them away with one hand while her other arm protected her head.

She opened her eyes. It took a great effort, but she found she could see if she strained. Everything was blurry, like looking through frosted glass. There was too much going on. Even while fighting off the woman's probes, she heard things, saw things, learned things about the woman, but these images and thoughts didn't register in her panic. They passed the old stink bomb in the parking lot and to withhold information about the car, Judy bit her lips. Did she even have lips? *Keep thinking about that*, she told herself. *There's a distraction. Do I have lips?* She kept her eyes open and slapped the enemy away again and again, repeating the question: *"Do I have lips?"*

***

John Barker sat sullenly beside a desk in the Miltonville Police Department. Inside him, Rubin cowered, his arms tight against his head. Unlike Judy Redmond, he kept his eyes shut, but he heard the questions being shot across the table. No answers came from his mouth. Barker had forgotten him and was concentrating on something, no *someone*, else. He was getting ready to leave his body, and Rubin was eager to be rid of him. Then again, he was extremely afraid because he was at the police department. He didn't know if he'd been charged with anything, if they had found Whit, or worse, Troy. He might be able to weasel around what happened to Whit. *Dead? What do you mean? They were just horsing around. Honest. Whit's my best friend. I wouldn't leave him if I thought he was in trouble. That guy? Oh, I don't know. Supposed to be a big secret. I thought it was stupid, but hey, it's a party, right?* That's what he'd say. Say it and pray Troy was a million miles away. So far they were only asking about Paul Lutz and some girl they found out in the Kitchen. *Paul?* he thought, *how did Paul end up dead in my truck?*

Meanwhile, Barker sat in Rubin's tired, dirty body as Rubin's thoughts buzzed about like insects. Rubin had immediately taken the defensive posture, crouching with his arms over his head. Over the years, Barker noticed that most did that, and some, feeling the probe of another stealing their minds, fought protectively against him, trying to hide any incriminating thoughts. Silly people. Barker had no interest in their indiscretions. He only wanted simple information: directions, names, instructions. Barker didn't care about the boy Whit killed last year, or about their devious ties with the dentist. Oh, Rubin had done well to cover these thoughts, but thoughts dart like flies, and keeping one's mind to oneself was akin to putting those flies in a five gallon bucket and trying to cover it with your hands. Some escaped, especially when people like Rubin guarded a few in particular. While he held on to those, Barker tried to find something useful. There was nothing, and Barker decided, if he had time, to torture Rubin before he left. He was still angry with him for frightening the Vanderkellen out of the cemetery the night before.

The officer and detectives were getting tired of him. They were going to take him to a holding cell until his attorney arrived, they said. He grinned, sending his chill. Behind them, through the open door, he could see Officer Fred Wendell sitting at a desk, writing. Barker stared at him hard, ignoring the detective who pelted him with questions. Occasionally Wendell looked up and Barker would reach, but never fast enough. Wendell stopped writing and seemed to be drifting with his thoughts. *That's it, that's it*, Barker urged. He needed Wendell to let his mind roam.

The pen in Wendell's hand hovered, then fell limp as he gazed off into space. Barker drew together his energy, pulling everything within him. Then—

BAM! The detective slapped the desk. "Pay attention, Rubin!" he shouted. Wendell jumped. Barker wheeled in anger. Rubin shrank into a tighter ball. Barker rose, his jaw clenched. His frustration ignited his anger, raw and intense. He leaned across the desk and pierced the detective with his eyes. No, he couldn't get into this one, but he could see into him, see his ego, his vanity. Detective Horn felt he was smarter and far more capable than his peers. Barker saw that, but so could anyone else who was perceptive. Detective Horn knew he was smarter than his captive, and this made Barker grin because Horn didn't know diddle, and he certainly didn't know about the fat demon that just appeared on top of his head.

"Mohar!" Barker said.

"Shhh. They can hear you, idiot." Mohar grabbed Detective Horn's hair and tugged. Horn reached up absently and scratched his head. "I'm here to make a deal with you."

Barker leaned back, not noticing the fire in Horn's eyes, or hearing the threats he made. Barker tilted Rubin's head, distrusting fat little Mohar. No one from that world could be depended upon.

"Trust me," Mohar read his thoughts. "I mean, look at me! I obviously can use some help. And you—well, psshhh! There's a few of us. We're as trapped as you. Well, maybe not that trapped, but we still have to latch on to these dumplings. But we can get around and maybe help you get this thing, whatever it is. By the way, you have to kill it in that circle thing, in case you haven't figured it out. Don't screw up and kill it somewhere else."

"Why would you help?" Barker asked, interrupting Detective Horn's questions.

"Why? Buddy, maybe you've been too busy to notice, but things are heating up. I don't know what goes on in that corner of wherever it is they keep you, but it's getting ugly out here. Rumor is, the big one is coming. Those other ones, the invisible ones, they're showing up all over. I'm surprised you can't see them. There's one over there, by that dumpling on the phone. I see it—aw, shut up!" Mohar made a gesture toward something Barker couldn't see, then turned back toward Barker, leaning forward so that Horn's hair fell into his face. "Whatever it is, something's about to happen, and when it does, I sure don't want to be attached to one of these dumplings."

Barker shook his head, careful not to speak aloud.

"You want that guy over there?" Mohar pointed to Wendell. "He'll be easy. He's been dreaming about knocking your head off. I'll make sure he takes you to the cell. I'll keep him down there until he's ready for you. But," he said, putting a finger to his mouth to keep Barker silent, "what we want in return is freedom from the dumplings. You get to the level you're heading for, you'll be able to grant it."

"If I don't grant it?" Barker said out loud.

"Then you become our dumpling. Trust me, there are enough of us to make you regret it," Mohar said, and bit Horn's ear. Horn shrieked and grabbed his ear. Mohar laughed, then whispered into Horn's other ear, "You're an intelligent man, aren't you?" Wendell

212

and another officer were coming to his aid, having seen him swat himself. Mohar kept talking: "Enlighten us, please. Tell us all you know. Write it down. Volumes. Please." Horn's face lost all expression. He picked up a pen. Barker started to laugh.

"Rubin," someone said.

"But he's so smart," Barker said.

"Rubin, you were doing a lot better for yourself before you decided to open your mouth," a young policeman told him.

"Detective Horn? Are you okay?"

The detective was busy writing. *The grass is green. Green is a color. Blue is a color. I know all the colors, red, yellow, orange, purple...purple is blue and red together. Roses are red, sometimes, sometimes yellow. Or pink. Pink is light red. Red and white mixed makes pink.*

An officer pulled Barker away. Barker smiled. Another officer joined them. Suddenly, Fred Wendell appeared, and offered to take Rubin to the holding cell. Barker followed, straining to hear the confusion as they left the squad room.

"Horn, what's wrong? What are you doing there, buddy?"

"Look what he's writing. About colors..."

Barker then heard Horn say, "Yes, colors...I know about colors and...and I know that I know about colors! I know that, Steve! And I know you're Steve, and your wife is Kate and..."

"Quit it! Stop writing!"

Barker laughed, and took a stick in the ribs from Wendell. The big, dumb officer led him down a stairway, cursing and calling him names. Barker gnawed Rubin's smirking lip. Any minute the officer would again be reminiscing about the excitement of the afternoon. Mohar would see to that, then Barker would have another chance.

***

*Tick...tick...tick...*the second hand swept slowly around the dial. Finally, it rounded the top. "Hot dog," Leslie said. She had been pushing a cart around, picking up misplaced items and reshelving odds and ends. Summoning the energy she had stored all day, she pushed the cart through the swinging doors into the stock room and abandoned it. Wasting no time she ran her finger over the time cards until she found her own and pushed it into the time clock.

From her locker she took her keys and slammed it shut. It was rarely locked. She never brought a purse, her money was in her pocket, and no one in their right mind would steal Bret the Maverick. She rolled her apron into a small ball so customers would not recognize her as an employee and ask her for assistance, then went out to find Anna. As she thought, Anna was still counting her register drawer.

"Will you hurry?" She begged.

"What's the rush?"

"We've been here *nine* hours! That justifies rushing."

"I'm coming." She took the drawer to the service booth. "What are we doing, anyway? Movie?"

"Yeah, we can. I don't know. Let's go over to Salem or something." Leslie followed Anna through the store.

"Okay. I tried to call Mom again. I bet you're right about her not hanging up the phone because it's still busy."

"That's aggravating," Leslie said.

"Yeah," Anna agreed. Leslie waited as she punched out. She folded her spotless apron neatly, then withdrew her purse from her locker and put her apron in its place. "I think I can get another day out of that," she said to herself.

Leslie clenched her own apron tightly, not caring that she had to wear it again the next afternoon. "Anyway, just drop me off and I'll change and come get you. Okay?"

"Sure." Anna led the way out of the store. Leslie wasn't paying much attention, so she bumped into Anna when she stopped suddenly in the parking lot. "Oh no," she grumbled. Ed Phillips hurried their way, waving.

"Oh, lighten up," Leslie said. "Hey, Ed."

"I was hoping to catch you two," he said, and then stood awkwardly. After a moment of silence Leslie said, "You were?"

"Uh, yeah," he scratched his head. He scratched his chin. "Uh," he scratched the back of his neck. Then he blurted, "What are you two up to tonight?"

"We're going to Salem," Anna said.

"To the movies, maybe. Why? You want to come?"

"Um, well. Actually I was wondering. Well, I need...you see, there's something..."

"Ed? What's the matter?" Anna asked.

"Yeah, Ed. Spit it out," Leslie said.

Ed smiled. It was genuine, but nervous. "I really need to tell you about some things. About the Itch."

"Ed," Anna began, but Leslie interrupted.

"What about it?"

"Look, I know you think I'm a crazy old man. I guess I am. No point in arguing. And after I say what I have to, you're going to have me put away. I have to risk it because that's how serious I think this is."

"Well, what is it?" Leslie urged.

"Les, this is one of those sit down talks. Kind of a long story," he said sadly.

"What could you possibly have to say that we haven't already heard? Keep in mind we've heard it all," Anna said.

He shrugged. "Actually, an awful lot."

Leslie held up a finger to Ed and pulled Anna away. "We don't have anything better to do. And you know...I mean, I guess I know you don't believe, but I kinda do. I think. Besides, if nothing else, you might get something out of him for your history paper."

"Les, he's just going to scare you."

"He won't. Besides, with all this going on today, aren't you a little curious?"

"Okay. But I'm not so sure about this. I have a creepy feeling you're just being morbid." They walked back to Ed and Anna apologized. "I didn't mean to be rude, but we hear too much about this Itch thing sometimes. People don't realize—"

"I do," he assured her.

"Can we do this later though? I have to run home. I don't want Mom and Dad waiting dinner on me."

"Yeah, Anna's going to drop me off to get my car, then I'm going to pick her up. You want to meet uptown in a little bit?" Ed looked uneasy. Leslie had a dreadful feeling that he wanted to come along, and she couldn't imagine what Anna's parents would say. "An hour?"

"Well, truthfully, I'd kind of like to talk to your parents, too."

"Mom and Dad are on vacation," Leslie said.

"And I don't want to get my mom stirred up. She drives me crazy as it is with this Itch thing."

"All right, but promise you'll come back. I'll wait in front of the courthouse and if you aren't back in an hour, I'm going to call your parents, Anna." He held up his hand to ward off their protests. "And, stay together. Don't stop for people on the road, even if you know them. Get back here as fast as you can, and I'll explain it all."

"But," both girls tried to argue as he turned and began walking toward Main Street.

"Hurry," he called over his shoulder.

Anna and Leslie stared from Ed to each other, then back to Ed. Anna shouted, "Don't you at least want a ride uptown?"

"No!" he called and kept walking.

"It may not be so bad," Leslie consoled. "It's definitely different."

"I don't know," Anna said, still watching Ed. "I sure hope he doesn't call Mom. This Itch crap will ruin her night."

***

Dinner at Grandma Emily's had not even started before it was over. Michele Vickers clenched her fists in her lap and bit off words that begged to be said. On the stove, four pots heated, filling the room with steam and the aroma of potatoes, corn, cabbage, gravy. On the counter, an electric skillet fried the chicken, the platter next to it already full. In the oven, homemade biscuits warmed next to a sweet potato casserole. On the buffet, apple and cherry pies waited for vanilla ice cream. Around the table sat family, most everyone there but Audrey's husband, Lew, who worked second shift, and Joe's wife Olivia, who was on her way from work. From the yard came the sounds of playing children. At the counter, Grandma Emily nervously turned the chicken. This should have been a happy, slow time, full of chatter and clatter and teasing. Not this silent, stressful eternity.

Ray had come home with the watermelon.

He leaned in the doorway with glazed eyes, pretending to almost drop the melon, laughing at his own antics. Ray had, quite obviously, spent the afternoon in a bar, and Michelle didn't need a psychic to predict what was going to happen.

"Don't wanna drop that!" Ray slurred with a put on happiness, fumbling with the watermelon. "That'd be a big mess now, wouldn't it, Mom?" He set the melon on the counter and put his arm over his mother's shoulders. Michele saw her draw back slightly.

"Mom, can I mash the potatoes?" she volunteered.

"Why sis," Ray said, drowning out her mother's response. "Now why you wanna go and do that all'a sudden after sittin' there on your lazy butt all day?"

No one spoke. Michele grabbed Dan's knee under the table and squeezed.

"'sides," Ray continued, his grin maniacal, "ain't nobody whips a tater like Mom. She gets them taters and she *whups and she whups and she whups!*" For emphasis he pantomimed whipping his mother. Joe stood up. Emily turned around.

"Now, quit your playing around, Ray," she said, watching Joe. Her hands were shaking. "You should have picked up Little Ray and Angie."

Ray's eyes went blank, and Michele braced herself until he refocused, the petrifying moment passed. "Jo Alice wuddn't home." Michele could tell he was lying. If Ray really wanted his kids and couldn't find them, he would be tearing the kitchen apart by now, letting everyone know what would happen to his ex-wife when he caught her. Poor Jo Alice didn't weigh a hundred pounds, even with her stringy, dyed hair soaking wet. Jo Alice with her big eyes and harshly aged young face. Jo Alice and Ray, with their matching drinking habits. Oh, family gatherings had been interesting when they were together. What to do when a pregnant woman staggers and stumbles through the house searching for an ashtray? What to say about those fingerprint bruises on her skinny arms? The same kind that sometimes graced her neck like love bites? How many times did Jo Alice blacken her eye by walking into a door? Two babies they had together and no one asked why. The only luck she had with Ray was when he let her go.

"Well, you know it's a pretty day. They probably all went to the park," Emily said. "Now go wash up, dinner's almost ready."

"Wash up? Okay Mommy, I'll go wash up so you can talk about me."

It took some time for him to find his way out of the kitchen. Once he was gone the family let out their breath. After an awkward moment of silence Michele's sister, Audrey, said, "It's too bad he didn't get the kids. They never come around much." She said it, but Michele knew she didn't mean it. Michele, too, had been grateful to hear they weren't coming. It wasn't nice to think ill of children, but there was something very wrong with Ray's kids. Becky was terrified of them, and Michele had to promise her that if Little Ray and Angie came, she could stay inside. Becky never said why she was afraid, and it worried Michele. Maybe some day she would be able to tell it to a therapist.

They passed small talk across the table. Very small, and very quiet. Perhaps if they sat perfectly still Ray would fall asleep. No sound came from upstairs, so possibly Ray decided to have a nap. *Oh please, Ray,* Michele begged, *please be unconscious.*

They stiffened at the sound of an approaching car. Olivia, Michele thought. Everyone's eyes fell on Joe, as if he could silence his wife's car. Emily began to take plates out of the cupboard. *Quiet!* Michele thought. Next came the silverware. Michele should be helping set the table. Audrey rambled on about the kids, but she spoke softly. No one seemed to be listening to her. Outside a car door slammed. Children called. In the kitchen the family smiled falsely and let Emily set the table as if she were oblivious to the tension.

Joe stood up. "This is ridiculous." Emily flinched as he brushed by her and went to greet his wife. He stopped at the screen door. "Look out," he said.

Two grimy children burst through the door: Little Ray and Angie. They barely paused before heading to the living room.

"Children!" Emily called them back. "Where are your manners?"

"Grandma, we wanna play Torture Train!" Little Ray whined.

"Look here what Olivia brought," Joe grinned, holding the screen door while Olivia maneuvered past carrying a huge watermelon against a bosom that was almost as large.

"Hi!" she greeted, happily. "Did you see who I found at the Quick Mart? We'll have to call Jo Alice and let her know where they are. Here, Joe, take this. They were selling—" She stopped when she saw Ray's watermelon on the counter. "Whoops. Oh well. You can never have too much!" She rolled the melon into Joe's arms and went to hug the waiting Michele.

"We wanna play Torture Train!" Angie interrupted.

"Outside," Audrey ordered. "Your father is asleep." The kids stomped out, scowling and grumbling.

"Shelly! Hi, Dan!" Olivia embraced her sister-in-law, ignoring the nephew who bumped her as he passed. The chill in the room finally caught up to her, and she slowly released Michele. Her enthusiasm gone, she shook her head. "Oh, no. Please tell me Ray's not drunk."

Joe leaned close and said, "Never guess who brought the other melon? Of course, he'll start in about how what he buys isn't good enough."

Olivia made a pained expression. "Can we just sneak out—" She was cut off by the distraught face of her mother-in-law. "I mean, sneak *it* out."

"Good idea," Audrey said.

"Good Lord," Dan said. Everyone stared at him.

Emily pushed Joe. "Hurry before—"

"Before what?" Ray said from the doorway. "Well, looky here. Big Ollie made it to dinner." Olivia's face fell, and she held Joe's arm to keep him from jumping to her defense.

"Hello, Ray," she said, her cheerfulness as forced as his smile. "How're you?"

His mouth moved as if he were going to answer but lost his words. Instead he grinned harder, his eyes remaining cold and vacant. He took a careful step into the kitchen and was attempting another when he noticed the watermelon Joe held. His cold eyes went to ice and his wicked grin dissolved.

"Wasn't it nice of Olivia to pick that up?" Emily babbled desperately. "She didn't know you already got one! Maybe Michele and Dan can take one with them for their camping trip."

Ray feigned surprise. "Wha...I figured Ollie'd want one all for herself."

Joe stiffened and Olivia squeezed his arm hard. Ray held up his hands in a gesture of surrender, showing his good humor. "No, no, Ollie, we must let Princess Michele take the leftovers. But wait! Leftovers are too good for her."

"That's it," Dan stood.

Ray's face went instantly red. "Oh, screw you! All of you and your too pure to puke selves! Come on, college boy. You too good to get your hands dirty?" He advanced toward Dan, and stumbled, his foot caught on a throw rug. Distracted, he kicked at it, shouting. "You buncha...you think you're all better'n me! You think your kids are better'n mine. You can't even eat the food I buy. It ain't good enough!" He left the kitchen, but returned immediately. "You're a bunch of losers. You know the truth? I'll tell you the truth. You're a bunch of white trash." Again he left them. This time he didn't come back. They heard him ranting and stomping his way upstairs.

For an awkward moment, the kitchen was quiet. Then Dan

simply said, "Michele?" She nodded at him.

"Mom, I'm sorry, but I can't let Becky see this again. We have to go."

"Oh no, Michele!" her mother cried. "He's gone back upstairs. He'll go to sleep now."

"No, Mom. No he won't." She looked around for support. Everyone glanced away. Joe set the watermelon on the crowded counter and went to the window.

"I told you," she continued, "if you let him do this, then, well, I guess that's your choice. Don't expect us to put up with it."

"You don't understand. He has problems. What am I supposed to do? Throw him out?"

"That would be a start," Michele said, and heard Joe sigh.

"She's right," Olivia spoke up. "I can't believe you would defend him after the way he treats you. Why do you put up with that?"

"She's afraid of him," Audrey said.

"I'm not afraid of him—"

"You better be," Ray was back in the kitchen doorway. "All you better be very afraid of ol' Ray."

"Let's go, Michele," Dan said.

"Hold it there, college boy," Ray said, casually raising his arm. He held a pistol, cocked and pointed at Dan.

***

"You can go on," Leslie told Anna. "I'll change and come on over."

"No, we can't disobey Ed. Besides, if the Itch gets you, I want to see it."

"Thanks for your concern." Leslie unlocked the door. "Hello, hello," she called into the house.

"You are spooked!"

"Uh uh. I'm just being cute. Hey, do you care if I call Grandma Emily?" she said as if she just thought of it, though she had wanted to talk to them all day about what was going on in town. "You know, this Itch stuff may be on the news. I don't want them to be worried and come home or anything."

"I doubt Miltonville made news in Ohio, but sure, go ahead. Won't they be having dinner now?"

"Not this early."

"They're on Daylight Savings Time aren't they?"

"Oh, yeah. Oh well, we're not talking Buckingham Palace here. We eat on the phone all the time."

"Don't I know."

Leslie flopped into a chair and punched Grandma's number into the cordless phone. It rang a couple of times, and for a moment it sounded as if it were picked up, but then there was a loud popping sound. When she heard voices she spoke, uncertainly, "Grandma? Grandma? It's me, Leslie." She was answered by several clicks. After a second of silence the dial tone sounded.

"I hate these phones," Leslie grumbled. She went to the kitchen to try again on another phone while Anna thumbed through a magazine. A moment later Leslie came back.

"Well?" Anna asked.

"No answer. Probably too many birds sitting on a wire somewhere. Let me change and we'll get going. I can't wait to hear what Ed's got to say."

***

Dan and Ray regarded each other coolly, the pistol taking up the space between them.

"Who's the big man now, college boy? Who's better'n who now?" Ray's lip twisted into a sneer.

The phone rang. Everyone jumped, including Ray. Impulsively, Emily reached for it. It rang again.

"Don't!" Ray ordered. But she did. Ray shot into the ceiling. Joe shouted, and leapt for Ray, but Ray went for the phone. With amazing strength and agility he pulled the phone off the wall.

"Don't even think about calling the cops! You think the cops could handle me? No one can handle me! Not you! Or you! Or you!" He pointed the gun here and there and it settled on Michele.

The phone upstairs began ringing. Again Ray shot into the ceiling and a rain of plaster fell on him. Furious, he left the kitchen. The family, too stunned to move, listened as he loudly made his way upstairs. There was another shot and the phone stopped ringing.

"Everybody out," Joe said calmly. "Mom, you too."

Olivia took her sobbing mother-in-law in her arms and led her out the door. In the yard, the children had stopped playing and silently watched the house. Little Ray and Angie stood apart from the others. Becky and Carrie held hands.

"Is Uncle Ray drunk again?" Carrie asked in a timid voice.

"*Is Uncle Ray drunk again?*" a voice mocked, and everyone looked up to where Ray leaned out of the upstairs window. Then he slammed the window shut. Below, mothers gathered their children. Emily didn't move.

"Dan, are you all right?" Olivia asked. Dan nodded, kneeling with Michele to comfort Becky.

"Mom, you are going to stay with us," Joe told Emily.

"I can't do that. This is my home."

"Just for a while."

"What are you planning?" she asked, her voice low.

"I'm calling the Sheriff, Mom," he said. Immediately her frightened face became agitated. Her arms went out and she pushed away the air as she dismissed his idea.

"No! I'll not allow you to have your brother locked up! This is not his fault. You older kids don't know how it was for him to be raised with no daddy!"

"Mom," Michele said, "he was seventeen years old when Daddy died!"

"And he didn't have Daddy to send him away to some fancy college, like you did. Or trade school, like Joe," Emily reminded her.

"He didn't even finish high school," Joe said.

"Well, you can settle this among yourselves," Dan stood, holding Becky's hand. "We're leaving."

"Oh, no, Dan. Please!" Emily begged. "He's asleep now. He'd of been down here otherwise. Maybe we could just bring dinner out here on the picnic table, it's so nice, and that way he won't be disturbed. Please don't go." The same woman who had earlier cheerfully prepared a meal for fifteen now crumbled into herself, withering.

"Emily, he pointed a gun at my wife. Your daughter! He pulled the phone off the wall. He *shot* the other phone. Frankly, I can't believe you indulge him at the risk of the rest of your family."

"I know," the old woman whimpered.

"So you'll come with us tonight?" Joe asked.

Emily's body hitched, but she didn't answer. "I made all this

222

food...please. The kids need to eat. You know he'll sleep for hours..." Her voice trailed into the air as she tried to compose herself.

"What if he isn't sleeping? He might be aiming at us right now," Dan said.

Without a word Joe left and went into the house. Michele busied herself with Becky while Olivia and Audrey did the same with their children. A long moment later, Joe reappeared.

"He's out," he announced sourly. "Like always, come in like a hurricane and sleep through the consequences. Tomorrow you'll fix him breakfast and ask how he feels and tell him to go lay back down awhile and that'll be it."

Emily bowed her head. It was true.

"Maybe next time he'll shoot something that can't be fixed. Like you. Or one of the kids."

Her head went lower.

"Mom, if you come with me tonight, if you let the sheriff take him, you know they'll put him in detox. That's what he needs."

"I can't let my baby wake up in jail. I can't," she said.

"You have to make a choice, Mom. You have three other children who hate coming here. You have three other children who don't tear your house down or shoot guns at each other. He'll go too far one day, and *you'll* be partly responsible. Think about that," Joe said.

"Or someone else'll kill him," Audrey said. "You don't really believe he lost those teeth falling down the stairs, do you? That was Ross Jacobs done that. And Ray was lucky that's all he done."

"Okay. I'll go," Emily said without raising her head. "But please...all this food..."

"I'm hungry, Daddy," Becky said. Dan glanced at his mother-in-law, remembering how in control she was a few hours ago, how he marveled at her abilities and energy. He looked at Michele, who shrugged half-heartedly.

"I guess we can stay. But not long," he said. Relieved, Emily regained a little of her former poise, but her confidence was gone.

One by one they went inside and came out with tablecloths and food. The chicken was no longer hot, the potatoes had set too long to mash, the gravy was congealed. The food in the oven survived because Emily had turned it down earlier. They sat to eat without appetite. The kids were better. They sat on a blanket like a real picnic. At one end of the picnic table Joe and Dan talked quietly.

"Another historic Everette get-together," Joe said.

Dan nodded. "One for the books. When did he get a gun, anyway?"

"Beats me. I looked for it upstairs but he must be sleeping on it."

"You're going to have to get it away from him."

"I'll tell the sheriff about it. I'm sure it's not legal."

"You're really going to do it this time?" Dan asked.

Before Joe could answer, there was a crash of glass as a window broke. All heads turned to see one of Joe's high school track trophies fall to the ground. Then it was quiet again.

"That's it. Michele, get your stuff. Becky, in the car. Now!" Dan ordered.

"You too, Mom. Olivia, get the kids."

Audrey was already collecting her children, along with Little Ray and Angie. Incredibly, Emily began gathering dishes.

"Mom, leave it," Michele said.

"I can't have a mess like this with the sheriff coming," she argued.

The flurry of activity was stopped by the sound of gunfire. Ray was at the window laughing.

"Daggone!" he shouted. "I missed. There he is!" He pointed the gun at a tree and fired again. "That little bugger is fast! Come back here, you rotten nutjawed tree rat!"

"Come on, Ray," Michele called. "You're scaring the kids."

"Aw. I forgot you got a city kid. Ain't seen a gun before. Well don't you worry. Uncle Ray knows how to handle a gun." With that, he leaned out, juggling the gun. He almost dropped it, and hurried to catch it, fumbling, and he appeared startled when the gun fired into the crowd below.

***

In the trailer, a relaxed Walter Brandenburg strained to hear the commotion outside. Being safely away from Barker, he found himself content to the point of boredom. The gunshots and screaming caught his interest. People could be so entertaining.

***

Ryan Swift peeled potatoes in the Canwell kitchen, careful to do it the way his mother taught him, a little proud to have this grown up job. He was glad to have something to concentrate on after his tiresome morning at the hospital, and his miserable afternoon at the Canwells. He recently learned his father was coming for him tomorrow, even though Mrs. Canwell practically begged him to let Ryan stay with them in Miltonville. Ryan overheard the conversation, but pretended not to know what Mrs. Canwell was about to say when she joined him in the family room.

"Your dad is worried about you. He wants you to stay with him until your mom is better," she told him.

"I don't want to go," he said.

"I know," she said, and that was all. That's what he liked about Mrs. Canwell. She didn't try to convince him it would be better to go with his father because she knew it wasn't the truth. She didn't lie to kids.

Mrs. Canwell stopped chopping carrots to check his progress and exclaimed, "You're some peeler! I think you can stop now, there's only four of us."

"Sorry," he muttered.

"Don't apologize for over-achieving." She took the pot from him, leaving him again with nothing to do, so he wandered to the front room and stared out the window. Four doors down, across the street, was his house. It looked so sad and empty. The grass needed mowing. His mother's pretty shrubs were scraggly and this year they had no flowers. The small garden plot in the back was grown over. Ryan swallowed the lump in his throat, and then almost choked on it when he saw Misty sitting on the porch washing her paws. Waiting.

He went back to the kitchen. "Mrs. Canwell, I have to feed Misty. I forgot this morning. And her litter box needs to be cleaned." Real bad, he thought, trying to remember when he had last done it.

"Okay." She reached for a box on top of the refrigerator and fished out a key. "Here. Maybe you'll meet Robby. His bus is due soon."

"Can I wait for him at the corner?"

"Sure. He'll be happy to see you."

With the key in his pocket, he made the short walk with long stretching steps. He saw Anna and Leslie backing out of the Vickers' driveway and waved. They didn't see him. Both of them had babysat him at one time or another when he was little. Anna read books to him and helped him build puzzles. Leslie made cookies and talked on the phone. She let him talk to one of her girlfriends, and then she helped him write a letter to her. Her friend's name was Heidi and he wanted to marry her. He smiled at the memory. He was such a dufus back then.

Misty met him in the drive. She did fast figure eights around his ankles, almost knocking him down. He stumbled up the step to the small porch and they went in together.

Gosh, it was hot in here. Since Dad left, they hardly used the air conditioner because it was expensive to run. There was a fan in the hallway and one in his bedroom window. He turned them on before feeding Misty. The linoleum in the kitchen was cool, and he lay next to the cat while she ate.

"No wonder you waited outside. We'll get it cool in here, don't worry," he assured her. Having heard the gossip at the hospital today, he locked Misty's cat door to keep her inside. He wished he could take her to Robby's, but Mr. Canwell was allergic. He wanted to stay here, that's what he really wanted. If his dad was taking him tomorrow, when was he coming back? Who was going to take care of Misty? What if his mom came home and he was gone? He knew his mom was afraid his dad wanted to keep him. That's why he always had his way. That's why the grass wasn't mown and Misty's litterbox was dirty. His mom didn't have time and was afraid if she forced him to do chores he would go live with his dad. She worried so much she went crazy. That's what happened. It was his fault. What would she do if she came home and found out his dad had taken him?

He squeezed his eyes shut to keep away his thoughts. He couldn't go with his dad. He would hide somewhere, run away, until they gave up looking. That'd be easy. His mom would be better soon, he was sure, then he would come back.

Misty finished eating and pushed his hand with her nose. He scratched her head and rubbed her belly whiled she rolled from side to side, unable to choose what she liked best. When she started to nip at him, he tickled her and ended the game. "I have to go meet Robby. His bus'll be here in a minute." On his way out he paused to raise the living room window. Outside, a policeman stood across the street, between the Wilson's and the Vickers'. Probably checking on the Vickers' house since they were on vacation. Ryan wasn't very interested until he heard a woman shouting.

"John! John!" Her breathless voice called. The policeman turned and frowned. Ryan saw a woman running up the street. She was familiar to him, but he couldn't place her. "She was here! I felt her! I *still* feel her! And Walter! I saw him this morning! Here!" She reached the policeman, John, Ryan supposed his name was, and bent over to catch her breath.

"Claire," John, the policeman said. Ryan could tell he was not pleased to see her. "Where have you been?"

"In a hospital! Drugged all day! They trapped me! But first I was—" She turned and faced the Swift house. Ryan ducked. Her voice came closer. Ryan peeked. The woman was dragging the policeman into their yard. "There! This is it. I was there, and I saw him..." she paused to get her bearings, "there!" She pointed at the Vickers. "I didn't think I would ever find my way back, but this woman knows this place—"

"Walter was here? What was he doing?" the policeman asked.

"Huh? Oh. He was standing in a barrel. I couldn't do anything. The woman I took was fighting and screaming, it was all I could..."

"What? What do you mean, standing in a barrel?"

Ryan heard a door slam. "Excuse me, Officer," Dottie Geist's voice chimed in.

The policeman seemed to clench his jaw. "You'll like this woman, Claire. She reminds me of you."

"Are you looking for someone?" Dottie asked as she joined the couple in Ryan's yard. "I know everyone."

"Yes, I am looking for someone," the policeman said. "I'm looking for whoever lives in that house." Ryan saw him point to Becky's house. Uh, oh. Was Leslie in trouble? Mrs. Geist always said she would be one day.

"The Vickers? Why, they're on vacation. They left today," Dottie told him.

"Vacation?" he repeated.

"Yeah. They went to that new amusement park; I think it's called the Galaxy or something like that. You know, the one over in Ohio. Columbus, or somewhere like that. Is something wrong—" she put her face close to his chest to read his badge. "Officer Wendell?"

"Did the girl go?" the woman named Claire asked.

"Well, of course...oh, wait, Leslie—"

"Is her mother dead?" the policeman interrupted.

"What? What kind of question is that? Oh, you mean Holly? Lord, she's been dead twenty years. Wait a minute...you're that Redmond woman aren't you? What's going on here? You know she's dead - you were with her when she got shot. Officer, she can tell you more about Holly Vickers than I can."

"Did you see the mannequin?" the woman said.

Dottie was stumped for only the briefest second. "Yes I did. And I wanted to report that, too. That retarded Canwell boy was messing with him this morning. I think he stole him. I was going to tell Dan just as soon as I was dressed, but then there was all this commotion. It's the Itch, again, isn't it? That's why you're here, too, isn't it? I'm sorry, I can't recall your name. You're Anna's mother. Boy, you and me oughta have a talk—"

"Excuse me, about the mannequin?" the woman reminded her.

"Oh, I'm sorry. I guess I shouldn't go on about the Itch like that, huh. I guess it was real hard on you. Weren't you in the hospital a long time? Seems I remember that. Shame," Dottie clucked, oblivious to the puzzled and frustrated faces that watched her.

"What about the—" the policeman started to repeat his question.

"Oh, that. Anyway, I was having coffee this morning, sitting by the window, and I notice Dan has this mannequin, real creepy, standing in the garbage can."

"Garbage?" the man asked.

"Rubbish?" the woman laughed.

"No, really," Dottie misunderstood. "So this retard comes by— he's trouble, that one. Those kind are supposed to be locked up. So he picks the dummy up, and right about then, Artie starts screaming that there's no toilet paper. By the time I got back, the kid was gone and so was the dummy. Both dummies were gone," she snickered. "Get it? Both dummies?"

"Where is this boy?" the policeman asked.

"Oh, who knows." As Dottie launched into a spiel about how he rode a bus somewhere every day, Ryan glanced at his watch. Robby's bus was due back any minute. Was he in trouble? Ryan decided to run out the back door and try to cut Robby off by getting to the bus stop before the bus did.

Speeding through the kitchen, he almost tripped over Misty. Out the back door, over the Garner's chain link fence, across their yard, a quick pat on the head to Goober, the dog, then over the fence again. In the distance he heard the squealing bus brakes. Maybe there still was time. Ryan cleared the Keneski's fence. Two yards left. Too late! He'd have to catch Robby on the sidewalk before he rounded the small curve and someone saw him. A quick change of course put him between the Jergen's and the Simpson's, right on the curve. Hiding in the shrubs, he saw Robby striding quickly past.

"Psst! Robby!" he called. Robby looked over, just as Dottie Geist shrieked, "There he is! Robby Canwell! Get down here right now! You have some explaining to do."

Geez, Ryan thought, what'd Robby do, anyway? Probably nothing. One time Dottie almost slapped Robby just for coming in her yard to pick up a candy bar wrapper. She hated him and wanted to get him in trouble. Bravely, Ryan came out of the bushes and ran to catch up with his friend.

***

John Barker stood confined between Claire and the obnoxious woman, Dottie, wondering what he had done to deserve this. Both yapped at him, each wanting to know what he intended to do. Across the street, another woman appeared, calling, "Robby? Ryan? Come on home!"

"MC! That boy of yours has been into mischief again. Now the police are here!" Dottie said, gleefully. The other woman marched across the street. From the other direction came a man and a boy.

"What, Dottie?" the other woman said. "What did he do now? Pick his nose in public? Chew gum with his mouth open?"

"No. He stole. I saw him," Dottie announced proudly.

MC disregarded her and looked at Barker with horrified eyes. "There must be some mistake. Robby would not—there he is. Robby!"

"Mom? What's the matter?" the young man asked. He regarded Barker warily, putting a protective arm in front of Ryan to keep him back.

"You took that mannequin—" Dottie started to accuse, but Barker cut in.

"You're not in trouble," he said. "I'm looking for the mannequin. The one that was there this morning." Barker pointed to the Vickers'.

Robby took a step back, not hiding his fear.

"Robby," his mother said gently, "it's okay. I'm sure it's a misunderstanding. Did you see the mannequin?" After a moment, he nodded. "Did you take it?" He shook his head.

"I saw—" Dottie started but stopped when she felt the sting of their glares.

"I didn't take it," he said, speaking in an uncertain, but steady voice. "I...I was playing a trick."

"A trick? On who?" MC prodded.

"On the Vickers. He wanted—I put him, *it* in the trailer. I put *it* in the bed in the trailer and covered *it* with blankets. I thought it would be funny when they found him. But I didn't take him—*it*. I promise. I went right to the bus."

"I believe you, Robby," she said. To Barker she explained, "The Vickers have a camper they take on vacation."

"A camper?" He didn't understand.

"Yes. You know...a trailer. They pull behind the car? To sleep in? You know what a camper is, don't you?"

"You mean like a wagon?"

"I guess. It's a trailer. Why are you asking about this, anyway? Did Dottie call you about that?"

"No," Dottie sneered, offended. "Dottie did not call. Dottie has better things to do." MC ignored her.

"Ma'am," Barker said, trying to talk to her the way he heard the other officers speaking at the police station. "There really isn't a problem."

"Well, if that's all then," she waved at Robby and Ryan to join her. "It's just about dinner time." As they walked away Barker heard her say that Dad would be home soon. The youngest boy broke away and said something about not locking the door. He made a wide circle around the trio and went behind the house.

"There's another one—" Dottie said, ready to tell them all about it, but Barker cut her off once more.

"Thank you very much for your help." She wasn't to be so easily dismissed, and Barker had to tell her several times to go away. When she finally did, he and Claire both sighed audibly.

"That woman gave me a headache," Claire said.

"Yes," John said. "I know exactly what you mean."

230

Claire disregarded his statement. "What do we do now? The Vanderkellen is traveling and Walter is with her. Is he following her or running from us?"

Her use of the word 'us' grated on his nerves. "I can find them. They haven't been gone long, the odor is still here. I want you to go back to the circle and work on getting that door open."

"It will take me all night to get back there. Besides, what makes you think you can find them?"

"My dear, our mouthy friend told me more than I need."

"She's in *Ohio!* It'll take days to get there," she whined.

"It used to take days. This man I have is alive and cooperative. He's already assuring me we can get to Columbus by midnight and that the park will be easy to find." He took her by the arm and led her to Wendell's car. "I'm confident that this is it. I've never felt so sure. I'll drive you to the circle. It will likely take you longer to pick that lock than it will for me to drive to Ohio and fetch a Vanderkellen and a Brandenburg."

"You're going to put Walter in there, too, aren't you?" she asked eagerly.

He answered with a smile. *Right behind you,* he thought.

"Oh, I'm so excited! Please let me go with you!"

"No, no Claire. I need you here. You'll do the greatest service by opening the door. Besides, I'll just be worrying after you if you come along. The graveyard is the safest place for you," he said, pretending to be stern.

"But John—"

"No more arguing. In the car."

She paused to look at the Swift house. "That little boy, it was his mother I took this morning."

"Yes. So?"

She shrugged. "I suppose his father can look after him."

"Claire, are you going soft?"

"Of course not," she said, seating herself in the car. "I just don't want our world overrun with orphaned brats."

***

Inside the Swift house, Ryan sat at the open window, hearing all but Claire's last statement. *What were they talking about?* he wondered, and what did Mrs. Redmond mean about taking his mother?

231

***

"Dad!" Anna called. Leslie followed her through the house.

"Out back!" he answered. They found him on the glider, book in hand, iced tea on the table next to him.

"Hi," Leslie said. "Good trip?"

"Average. No excitement."

"You just don't know how to stir it up."

"This coming from the Queen of Boredom?" Anna said. "Where's Mom?"

"I was going to ask you. She had to go to pick up a few things for dinner. You didn't see her?"

"She probably went to Thrifty's," Anna sighed. Thrifty's was five miles farther down the highway than Hartmann's, and it was cheaper, bigger, and faster. Compared to Thrifty's, Hartmann's was a large convenience store.

"Naw, she wouldn't shop the competition," her father said.

"Why not?" said Leslie. "My folks do all the time."

"I'll be right back," Anna said. "I have to change. We're going out tonight. I'll probably just stay at Les's, so I brought the car back for Mom so she doesn't have to drive the stink bomb."

"Oh, she'll be disappointed," Tom said.

"You two should be alone," Leslie said with an exaggerated wink.

"Leslie!" Anna's face was red.

"Come on, Anna!" To Tom she said, "She can't accept that her parents are anatomically correct."

"Oh! Like you think yours are!" Anna countered.

"Geez, Anna, that's disgusting."

Anna gave up and left. Leslie sat on the edge of the porch.

"So what have you two got planned?" Tom asked.

"Aww, I don't know. Not much to do around here. Probably go to a movie. Maybe go over to Salem or something."

"You don't want to hang out with us old people?"

Leslie remembered just yesterday when old people didn't want to hang out with them. Now it seemed all the old people wanted them. Oh well. Ed asked first.

"Don't take it personally," she said.

A few minutes later, Anna burst out the back door, her neat cotton blouse and slacks replaced with neat cotton shorts and T-shirt. "Where's the cordless?"

"It's not in the living room?" Tom asked.

"No, and it's off the hook, I think. I tried calling home all day."

"Uh oh. Your mother was doing yard work today." The three looked over the large, freshly mown back yard, lined with weeded flower beds and trimmed hedges. Beyond the fence grew an incredible garden that demanded most of Judy's spare time. "Guess I better look for it. You two go on."

"Tell Mom I'm sorry I'm missing dinner." She picked up his tea and took a big gulp. She offered it to Leslie, who shook her head.

"Give me that," he took the glass away and examined it's contents for germs. "Now get out. And stay outta trouble."

"Yeah," Leslie muttered as they went around the house. "Like we have a snowball's chance of getting in trouble around here."

***

Ed was sitting on the courthouse steps.

"There he is," Anna said. "You realize he's going to talk our ears off."

"Hey, we should make a night of it. Let's take him to dinner." Anna started to protest, but Leslie continued, "He's always nice to us. Probably nobody else does anything for him. We're gonna be stuck with him all night anyway."

"I don't care," Anna caved. There were worse things, she supposed. "Just let's not do General G's again, okay?"

Leslie parked the car in one of the diagonal slots. Ed was hunched over, elbows on knees, examining his hands. He hadn't even seen them. "He really looks worried," Leslie said, and Anna had to agree.

***

Ed really was worried. He had worried about this moment for years, had rehearsed and fine tuned it so much that the words should flow from his mouth like rain from a down spout. Now the moment had arrived and his mouth was dry, his words like sand, clogging his throat. Did he really think he could tell Leslie her grandfather was not Mark Cline, but Jerry Templeton? That her mother, like her father, and his mother, and her father and so on through the years had died at the hands of angry spirits? That she was next? Any minute someone, maybe a stranger, or maybe a friend, could walk up and stick a gun in her face? Maybe that person would be Anna? Maybe he, himself? He had envisioned this task to be difficult, but he foolishly believed that all parties involved would see the light and he would be redeemed.

What on earth had he been thinking?

Delusions, that's what he was having, and that's exactly what these girls were going to think. Say he could talk them into leaving town, how would he know when it would be safe to return? And if they survived the Itch, what would it prove? "Hey girls, it's over and you're alive." "Uh huh," they would reply, with those irritating sidelong glances they were always giving each other. Then he would have the wrath of Dan to deal with for telling Leslie such nonsense about her grandparents. Even if they all survived, if the Itch didn't get Leslie and Dan didn't kill Ed, what then happens in twenty years? How old would he be when it returned, that is, if he still *was*. If he was this helpless now, what good would he be then?

He noticed them parking, but didn't raise an arm. He wished they would keep driving. Then he could stand up, brush the concrete dust from his pants and say, "Well, I tried." What a coward. If only he had this discussion with Dan and Michele years ago. If only Leslie had gone on vacation with her folks. If only there were some way to get her away from here without telling her.

"Hey Ed!" Leslie called as she climbed the steps to join him. "We're hungry. Why don't you have dinner with us?"

"Huh?" He was bewildered.

"Yeah," Anna said, "we were thinking about trying that new place in Westerville."

"Everybody says it's really good," Leslie continued. "There's supposed to be a live elephant in the lobby. I have to go to the mall anyway to take back some shoes. Are you okay?" She changed her train of conversation because Ed's cloudy face was suddenly beaming.

"Westerville? On the other side of the interstate?"

"We don't have to," she said.

"No, no!" He smiled. "That'd be great. My treat. Maybe we can even go to the movies or something?"

Leslie and Anna exchanged one of their glances. "Don't get too excited," Leslie said. Ed laughed.

"I've been stuck in Miltonville a long time."

"Jeez, and I thought I had it bad," Leslie muttered as the three walked to the car. "Do you guys care if I run by my house and get those shoes?"

"Can we stop by my place too? I just need to run in. It won't take a minute," he promised.

"Sure," Leslie said. "I'm anxious to hear what this is all about."

"Yeah, well," he waited as Anna climbed into the backseat of the old Maverick. "It can wait until dinner." He wanted to put it off indefinitely.

They chatted casually for the few minutes it took to drive to his apartment. Originally he planned to bring them here and show them the history the old briefcase held. Even though the plan had changed, he wanted the briefcase with him so there would be no reason to return to Miltonville.

He tried to insist the girls accompany him inside his apartment, but they said they would wait. He didn't want to scare them, but he did make them swear not to leave. Again, they glanced at each other. He went as quickly as his worn legs would take him, and was relieved to see the old car still idling when he returned.

"What's in the suitcase?" Leslie asked as he passed it to Anna in the backseat.

"There's some things in there I need to give you," he explained, and folded a light flannel jacket over his lap.

On the way to Leslie's house, they heard more about the afternoon's events on the radio. Two bodies were found in a car on Route 20 were not named, pending notification, but in a separate incident, Paul Lutz had died behind AJ's Service in Miltonville.

"Holy cow!" Leslie exclaimed. "Paul Lutz! I wonder if he was with Steve and them today."

At the same time, Anna was saying, "Was Paul at General G's today? I can't remember if I saw him."

Ed shook his head. He didn't say anything, but he had heard a rumor that another man had also died, a prisoner at the police station.

"Maybe it really is the Itch," Leslie said.

"That's why I think Westerville is a good idea," Ed admitted.

They had barely pulled into the Vickers' drive before Dottie Geist was upon them. The woman was ready to spew information like a fountain until she saw Ed get out of the car, then she froze like ice.

"Why, Ed Philips. What are you doing with...here?" she asked, not masking her suspicion.

"We're going out," Leslie interrupted what was certain to become a barrage of questioning.

"How nice. Anyway, what I came over for...I thought you might want to know what Robby Canwell was up to this morning. He was messing with that dummy. I know you're just going to say 'Big Deal,' but—"

"What?" Leslie was confused. Anna, climbing from the backseat, echoed Leslie's question.

"—it is a big deal when the police come out. And your mother, too, Anna. Worried half to death I'll bet," Dottie plowed on without stopping for breath.

"Oh great," Anna moaned. "She thinks it's the Itch."

"Well, of course she does. Don't you know all the stuff going on around here? Cindy lost her mind—"

"A breakdown," Anna corrected.

"And that girl they found. And that man that ran over me! And whatever that sneaky kid was up to this morning with that mannequin."

"Mannequin?" Leslie asked.

"Yeah, that horrible thing. He put it in the camper. For a joke! What kinda sick sense of humor is that?" Dottie seemed pleased with the concern she stirred.

"He did what? Anna did you hear?"

"Les, come on. Let's talk to Robby, okay," Anna said, and started across the yard toward the Canwell house.

"I know that doesn't sound like much," Dottie continued as if anyone was listening, "but what kind of sneaky things has he done that we don't know about? Well, I told the policeman, I did...uh...Leslie?"

"Excuse me," Leslie called, following Anna and leaving only Ed to listen to Dottie.

"Excuse me," Ed said, and left Dottie alone by the car.

"Well! Excuse *me!*" Dottie huffed, and stomped home.

***

The Canwell's were eating dinner when the doorbell rang. Robby laid his napkin aside, but his mother motioned for him to sit still. His father went to the door. Ryan was staring into his plate, and Robby knew he was worried about his mother, even more so now that his father was going to make him go to Little Easton. Robby's stomach knotted when the bell rang. What if Mr. Swift had come early? Please no, he thought. They planned to take Ryan to the hospital to see his mother after dinner, then they would go to Floogie's for ice cream. If his father came early, Ryan would be so upset.

"Robby, Leslie's here. She's out front," his father announced.

"Uh oh." He pushed away from the table. "She's mad at me about Bruce, I bet."

"No she's not," his mother assured him. Ryan said nothing. He was elsewhere.

Robby made slow tracks to the door. He was aware that his mother was behind him, and he was embarrassed, not because Leslie would see her, but because his mother would be witness once more as he admitted what he had done. Not that she thought he had done anything bad enough to call the police over, but she was concerned that the Vickers' would have to find somewhere to dump Bruce. He didn't know how to tell her how wrong it was, what he did. He felt it in his stomach, in his head, even in his skin. *"He frightened you before. Are you not afraid of him anymore?"* she had asked. *"No,"* he lied, but lying wasn't comfortable, so he corrected himself. *"Yes."*

"So, you were afraid and you played a joke anyway?" His mother seemed interested that he had conquered his fear, but she didn't understand. How could he explain that Bruce was still bad, but he, Bruce, was also afraid, more afraid than Robby. Even if Robby could find the words, it would probably upset his parents, so why bother? Besides, how *did* he know Bruce was afraid? He had doubted himself all day, but when he saw the policeman tonight, he was certain that Bruce had indeed been terrified.

In grade school there was an old janitor with scaly skin who used to let the older boys smoke in the boiler room. He was friendly with many of the boys, but Robby was afraid of him. The janitor was nice, always grinning and still Robby didn't like him. One day Robby was in the bathroom by himself when the janitor came in behind him. He offered Robby a candy bar and told him to come to the boiler room after school and he'd show him some really neat magazines. Robby's heart pounded with terror as he stared into that smiling, wrinkled face. It was his eyes, those yellowed, runny eyes. Robby managed a squeaky "no, thank you," and fled back to class. Terror, deep down and unreasonable. The same way he felt when he faced the policeman today.

He was disconcerted to find not only Leslie, but Anna Redmond and Ed Philips waiting on the porch. Les must have mistook his reaction for fear, because she said, "Don't worry Robby, I just want to know if you put Bruce in the camper this morning."

He nodded. His stomach hitched when he saw her face tighten. "I'm sorry. I didn't know everyone would get mad."

"No, no, Robby. I'm not mad," Leslie reassured him. "I just wondered what happened. Snotty Dottie, you know." She smiled. "Does this mean you aren't afraid of him anymore?"

"No, but he was scared of—" Robby quickly stopped himself. Anna and Ed were looking at him funny.

"Scared? Of what? What makes you think he was scared?" Leslie pressed. Robby couldn't think fast enough. He stood there staring dumbly into their bewildered faces. If he told them he heard Bruce in his head, he knew what would happen. Susie Chez, at the Center, she heard someone in her head and now she was on medication. All she ever did was sit at the window working puzzles. Sometimes she got mad, but mostly she just sat there, quiet. Not smiling or talking. Like she was empty. "That's the medication," someone once told him. "It keeps her from hearing the voices. The voices make her do things." Things like putting mannequins in campers. Robby finally shook his head.

"I meant that *I* was scared," he said, honestly. "But I thought it would be a good joke on Becky." Everyone nodded, though Ed was scratching at his beard. "He isn't real, you know," Robby said carefully, trying not to let his true feelings show.

"I know. It's okay, really. It would be a funny joke, too," Leslie said. Anna smiled at him like he was an idiot. He hated that, so he didn't smile back. "I'm glad you told us though, cause Mom and Dad would have yelled at me for scaring Becky. Now I can let them yell at you!" she laughed nervously. He knew she was kidding. "I hate to spoil your joke, but I think I'm going to call and tell them. Okay?"

Again he nodded. "I think that's a good idea. It really wasn't funny."

He stood in the doorway after they left. If Leslie had been alone he could have told her exactly what happened. Anna was usually nice, but she wouldn't believe him. Ed, he didn't know about.

Gosh! This was one of those days he wished he had stayed in bed! He went back to the kitchen, trying to be upbeat for Ryan.

***

"I really don't want to pry," Ed jumped into Anna and Leslie's conversation, "but who is Bruce?"

"He's a mannequin," Anna sighed.

"I was afraid you'd say something like that."

"It's a long story," Leslie said. "Let me call Grandma Emily first."

"And let me call Mom," Anna added. "I can't believe she called the police."

They went inside the dark, cool house, each one aware of the watching eyes of Dottie Geist. Leslie flopped into a chair and picked up the phone while Anna opened the drapes to let in the light. "Want a pop?" she asked Ed and he shook his head, taking a seat in the chair opposite Leslie. "Anyway," Anna explained, "Leslie thinks Bruce is possessed."

"If you're gonna tell it, tell it right. Oh, man, they still aren't answering."

"Check the number," Anna said, and Leslie handed her the phone.

"The condensed version of the story is that, once, a long time ago, Dad brought Bruce home, only he wasn't scary. Then one day a bunch of my friends were here, including Anna, and we were playing with the ouiji and we told it to do something with Bruce and Bruce started moving." She had pulled a thin book from a desk drawer and started flipping through its pages. "Here it is."

"Wait. You lost me," Ed told her.

"They still haven't hung up the phone," Anna said.

"So then, Bruce got real creepy, and once me and Robby saw him move in the garage and the whole neighborhood went nuts, but that's another story. Anyway, Uncle Ralph took Bruce home with him. Then all of a sudden he brought him back. And then, last night when we went to bed, he was in the bathroom. I woke up and he was in my doorway. Dad even freaked out. He put him in the trash...this is the number I was calling." She took the phone from Anna and carefully pushed the number. After a moment she said, "Something's wrong. There should be a bunch of people there."

The conversation left Ed behind, and impatiently he wished Leslie would make her connection so they could leave town. An evil mannequin? He wondered if it had anything to do with the

Itch. Not likely, since it was now miles away from Miltonville...

"Now who are you calling?" Anna asked.

"Audrey's."

No answer again. She tried Uncle Joe's. Nothing. She punched in another number.

"Yellowbird, please."

"What are you doing?" Anna asked.

Leslie held up a finger. "I need the number of the police department that serves Yellowbird, please." Her finger went down and picked up a pen. "Uh, huh," she was saying, "No, that's fine. That'll do. Thanks." Immediately she began to punch in the new number. "Nobody's answering anywhere. I just want to check," she finally answered.

"Oh, Les. That's taxpayer money you're wasting," Anna complained. It was too late. Leslie was already speaking to someone.

"Yes, I just want someone to check on Emily Everette, out on...excuse me?" Leslie's eyes went wide. "What call? I'm her granddaughter, Leslie Vickers. What happened?" Ed and Anna moved to the edge of their seats. "When? Did someone get shot? But nobody answered. Yes...uh huh...but my parents—yes...okay...I will." She took the phone from her ear and pushed the button to disconnect.

"What?" Anna prompted.

"What happened?" Ed asked.

"She thought I was calling to report gunshots fired out there. Someone already called the police. She wouldn't say anything else." She laid the phone in its cradle and stared at it.

"Gunshots? Could they be goofing around?" Anna asked.

"It must be more than that. They sent someone out and they wouldn't do that just for gunshots. Not out there. People hunt and shoot stuff all the time." Her head fell into her hands.

"Maybe Uncle Ray?" Anna offered. To Ed, she explained, "Every time they get together her uncle gets drunk. Really drunk. Him or his kids are always starting fights."

"Yeah, Ray's kids. The poster children for the genetically challenged," Leslie muttered the old joke into her hands.

"The police can handle him. It may not be anything anyway."

"Maybe not. But they have Bruce with them..."

"So? You don't think Bruce has a gun do you?"

"No. I don't know what I think. The Itch thing has me creeped out. And Bruce has me creeped out. And Uncle Ray, he's just a creep. If someone is shooting guns out there, it isn't target practice. Not with all the kids there."

"We'll wait an hour, then try back."

"I can't wait an hour!"

"What choice do you have?"

"I don't know, but I can't just sit here. I can't stand this."

Ed couldn't stand it either. Every minute they stayed in Miltonville put her that much closer to danger. How could he propose they go on to Westerville now? What kind of moron would do that when she was so worried about her parents?

Eureka!

"How far is Yellowbird?" he asked.

"I don't know. It takes four or five hours to get there."

"And when did Bruce show up?"

"Last night."

"Bruce could be exactly what you think he is," he blurted. "I think we should go to Yellowbird. Right now."

Both girls stared at him. But when Anna turned to give Leslie the 'glance', Leslie didn't return it.

"Are you nuts?" Anna cried.

"No," Leslie said. "I want to go."

"It'll be eleven o'clock before we get there! Just how would we explain that?"

"We'll just tell them we were worried! Anna, I can't stand just sitting here."

Neither could Ed. "Let's go."

"But what if Mom and Dad call?" Leslie asked.

"Can you check your machine from another phone?" he asked. She nodded. "Then we keep checking in. If your folks call, and they're fine, great! If, well," he faltered here, more for emphasis than to pick his words, "if there is a problem we'll already be halfway there."

"Okay, and I can keep calling Grandma's on the way, too. Let's go then," Leslie said.

"Right," Ed said, with less enthusiasm. What if she found out thirty minutes into the trip that everything was okay?

"You're *both* nuts," Anna said. "Besides, I have to be at work at eight in the morning. We may not be back by then."

"You don't have to go. Maybe you can stay and answer the

phone?" Leslie suggested. Ed nodded in agreement.

"This is stupid. Try your grandma's one more time, okay?" Leslie did so immediately. "This is ridiculous. Bret will never make it." She stopped, realizing her argument wasn't working. It was two against one. "Okay. Will you promise to let me sleep? If you promise, then I'll go."

"Of course," Leslie said. "There's still no answer. Are you going to try your house again?"

"Are you kidding? Mom's caught wind of what's gone on to-day. You think she'd let us go anywhere but home? You know, she's looking for us now. I hope she talks to Dad soon so she won't worry all night." She shook her head wearily. "I don't believe this."

Ed bit back his smile, trying desperately to appear concerned. Leslie brought a pillow and blanket and Anna scavenged the kitchen for snack food, the idea now being to conserve money for gasoline because Leslie's car gobbled fuel by the minute, not the mile. Leslie found a few road maps, and took the detailed vacation route Michele left on the refrigerator should Leslie need to find them because it had all the phone numbers listed. Anna decided to drive because of Leslie's agitated state and because Ed didn't drive. It didn't matter to Ed who drove, as long as they got moving. He couldn't help but feel pleased with himself. It was luck, actually, pure dumb luck, but it worked in his favor. Of course, once he got them out of town he might have to keep them out. If nothing else, he could tell them the story. It would be a last resort. For now he was just happy to be putting miles between Leslie and Barker.

In the car Leslie fretted aloud while Anna calmed her. Ed rode in the backseat grinning inwardly at the irony! Bruce, the entity Leslie so feared would save her life. Ed intended to use that fear to distract Leslie from thinking of any alternative to driving to Yellowbird. He was already concocting a plan in case she learned along the way that her family was fine. He patted himself on the back, not realizing they were driving the same highway John Barker traveled only thirty minutes earlier as he too made his way toward Ohio.

*****

Six-thirty came and went and Tom Redmond was worried. After Leslie and Anna left, he had walked around in the yard, half searching for the phone. He truly believed Judy would be home soon and she would go right to it. When it occurred to him that if Judy was having a car problem she wouldn't be able to reach him, he went in and unplugged the base of the cordless phone. By then it was after six, so he settled in to watch the news. The station was two hours away, but one of the first stories concerned Miltonville. The anchorwoman prattled on about an unidentified coma patient, dead professors and dentists and hoodlums. Did this signal the coming of the Itch? she asked.

"Oh, crap." That's why Judy wasn't home. He went to the kitchen phone and called the hospital. She would have gone there to find out what was happening. "Personnel," he said to the friendly phone operator.

"I'm sorry sir. That office is closed. Would you like to leave a recorded message?" the woman chirped.

"No, can you connect me with the second floor ward clerk?"

"Why certainly sir!" and suddenly a phone was ringing.

"Second floor. Rhonda speaking,"

"Ronnie. It's Tom Redmond. Has Judy been in?"

"Hi Tom. She was, but it's been a while."

"Wanna give me the low down? I just got up and heard the news."

"It's been busy, that's for sure." Her synopsis of the day varied in places from the newscast, but not by much.

"Did you talk to her? I need to know where she went."

"I'm sorry. I didn't see her go. She came in to visit Cindy. Try Wanda. I know she tried to call Judy a couple of times but the phone was busy."

"I will." And he did. Then he called a few other places, including Hartmann's to see if she'd been in shopping. Last, he called the Vickers and left a message for Anna suggesting she and Leslie stay the night at the Redmond house. He checked the answering machine, even replaying old messages, just in case. Only Alan Macklin's dry voice came over, asking for Anna. He stood at the window, then at the door. It certainly must be as Wanda said; Judy was out looking for Anna. He decided to give her another half hour. If she wasn't home by then, he'd ask his sister to come and phone sit, because he already knew he could not pace the floor much longer.

***

After hanging up with Tom Redmond, Rhonda 'Ronnie' Settles decided to check on Cindy Swift. Her son was expected back this evening, and it might not hurt to see what kind of disposition she was wearing before letting Ryan visit.

Cindy was sleeping, her breathing natural and even. An IV feed kept her hydrated, and her chart was encouraging, but Ronnie knew the woman was worn ragged. She put a dab of petroleum jelly on Cindy's lips and arranged her hair, wishing there was a way to add color to her pale face. Making small talk, she straightened the sheet and adjusted her hospital gown. When she was sure Cindy's appearance wouldn't frighten Ryan, she covered her hand with her own, her brown skin dark as ebony against Cindy's transparent, blue veined arm.

"Don't worry, baby doll," Ronnie told her. "There's been others made do with less. You'll get it together." She squeezed Cindy's hand before she left.

A few rooms down the hall, Jane Doe's parents sat grimly beside their daughter's bed. This was Ronnie's first opportunity to introduce herself. Before knocking lightly on the door, she reminded herself the girl's name was Jaime Gates, not Jane Doe, as she'd been called most of the day. Her parents motioned her in, whispering "Do you need us to leave?"

"No. I'm just checking in on her. My name's Rhonda, and I'm on duty tonight, if you need anything."

"Thank you. We appreciate that," said the man.

"What should we be doing?" the woman asked.

"Talk to her. Maybe put a tiny ice chip in her mouth every now and again. Has she been awake since you came?" Jane Doe, or Jaime, had come to a few times, but was completely incoherent, once even hysterical when they put her in the room with Cindy Swift.

"Yes, only once. She was talking about dead people in the graveyard," her mother fretted.

Ronnie shrugged. "I guess that's where dead people ought to be."

The parents smiled, and Ronnie felt better. She left them to visit the other, less famous patients on her floor. "Dead people in the graveyard," she muttered. What was that all about?

***

Ryan and Robby sat on the picnic table, staring at a board game more than playing it. In the house Robby's parents were cleaning up the dinner dishes. Robby's job was to entertain Ryan until time to go to the hospital. He had the hardest task of all. Ryan was too sad to get interested in anything, so Robby filled the empty air with talk about work. Just when he was convinced he was talking to himself, Ryan asked, "What's a Vanderkellen?"

Robby thought for a moment, trying to remember. "Who. Not what. He died a long time ago. You know, out at Vanderkellen. The cemetery."

"The cemetery?" Ryan paused. "Are there any Vanderkellens now? Like, uh, decadence?"

"Descendants," Mr. Canwell corrected, chuckling. He stood at the backdoor, a towel over his shoulder. "Have you guys been hearing ghost stories today?"

"No sir," Ryan answered too quickly.

"Well, they say Lucas Vanderkellen had no children. Some people think that's why we get an Itch every twenty years, because there are no Vanderkellens to keep Barker dead."

"Why does he come every twenty years then? Why doesn't he just stay?" Ryan asked.

"Ryan," Mr. Canwell came outside and sat on the table. "Do you know what superstition is?"

"Yeah. Like not stepping on cracks or walking under ladders."

"Those are examples, yes. But what it really is, is when people attribute unrelated events to a chance occurrence. Or even a natural phenomena."

"What?" Ryan's face knotted trying to follow this explanation.

"I'm sorry. It's like when you win a ball game and you think it's because of the underwear you have on, so you wear your lucky underwear to every game."

"It's in your head," Robby simplified.

"Right, son," Mr. Canwell said, smiling as if he had educated superstition out of young Ryan. "We'll be taking off in a few minutes." He patted Ryan's shoulder before going back inside.

"What was he talking about?" Ryan asked.

"There's no such thing as the Itch."

"I don't care about the Itch. Anna's mom said she was at my house this morning. She told the policeman. She knows what happened to Mom, she said she took her somewhere. I heard her." Robby noticed the sudden animation in his speech and frowned, skeptical. "I did. When I was in my house. And they said they were going to the cemetery—oh, forget it."

"Ryan, why would Mrs. Redmond go to the cemetery? No one goes out there. Maybe she was talking about seeing your mom at the hospital this morning. She's a nurse."

"She said she was at my house. She said she took my mom somewhere. Ask the policeman! He believed her."

"Maybe he was trying to make her feel better or something."

Ryan shook his head. "No, it wasn't like that."

Before Robby could argue, Mrs. Canwell called out the kitchen window for them to meet at the car. He shook his head sympathetically. Robby understood a lot more than he could verbalize, and he realized Ryan needed to know why his mother was sick.

"Just forget it," Ryan said again, and went back into his fog. Robby, feeling useless, put a hand on his shoulder and guided him to the car.

***

Forty miles west of Salem, Tim Swift was having dinner with Teena Ladd, or Teeny, as she preferred to be called. She was up to something, Tim could tell. He couldn't say she had something up her sleeve because she was wearing a strapless dress. Her hair was pulled high, and fell down her back in a cascade of curls. Candles lit the table and dinner came from Saltwater Slim's, a rib place he loved and she detested. Despite the food, Teeny would probably get what she wanted because she knew just how to ask.

He noticed her pushing her food around her plate, and prepared himself. She cleared her throat. He laid aside his fork.

"Have you checked on Cindy?" she said.

"I called before I left work. No change."

"I've been thinking that, given her unstable mental condition, now might be a good time to seek custody."

"Excuse me?"

"Well, it's inevitable. You may as well do it now and get it over with."

"Teen, that's cruel!"

"Cruel? No more than what she's done to you all these years, holding you back. It's bad enough that she continues to do so, using Wil—Ryan, but now what's going to happen? We'll have him while she recovers, then send him back? To some drug addict?"

"She's not a drug addict," he began, but she cut him off.

"These constant disruptions are making me crazy. Think, Tim, if we had him, we could move to New York."

"I don't need custody to move. I can't take him away from home anyway. You know that. His friends, his school, his mother," he reached for her hand, but she pulled away.

"But she's holding him back too, Tim! What does that town have to offer a child?"

"There's nothing wrong with that town."

"He deserves better. William is too bright and curious."

"Ryan," Tim said. "His name is Ryan."

"Oh, yes, I know. Ryan," she spat. They had gone rounds over Ryan's name. *Fifty percent of his graduating class will be named Ryan, and I'll bet Cindy believes she thought up that name herself!*

And William is original? he countered.

It certainly has more class. And there certainly aren't dozens of Williams in his dinky little school, she argued.

Don't you think there's a reason for that? Though the argument ended there, she constantly undercut him by 'forgetting' Ryan's name.

"Teeny, honey, why do you persist in this? I know you love Ryan, but he's not mine exclusively." She turned her back to him. "Have you been honest with me? I've told you it doesn't matter, and I mean it. Are you not able to have children?" he asked gently, as he had in the past.

"Of course I can have children," she turned on him, her eyes full of venom. "But why would I? For heavens sake, look what it did to your ex-wife's body. I'm not doing that to mine."

"Let's drop it, okay?" More and more he found himself defending Cindy, which he though was an odd thing for an ex-husband to do. Teen had been especially vicious lately, and not even Cindy's breakdown brought out a sympathetic word. If anything, it added fuel to her flaming opinions.

That was another thing he never understood. Why did she hate Cindy so vehemently? Cindy couldn't have been more accommo-

dating during their break up. He had a suspicion that Cindy's cooperation may have been the result of Teen's early threats to hire top
lawyers and sue for custody. Tim tried to smooth things over, and
thought Cindy was doing all right until today.

Teeny's face softened. "I'm sorry, darling. I get so angry when
I think of how stifled you are because of her. But this isn't about
her, it's about Ryan and what's best for him. She's unstable, Tim.
Unfit. The house is a mess and she's never home. Ryan practically
lives with the neighbors. It's not right, especially when we can
afford live-in help. Better schools. You know I'll do whatever it
takes to help financially - *if he's with you* - but I won't give a cent
to support her and whatever habits she's developed." He was about
to retort when she put her finger to his lips and a wineglass in his
hand. "Enough of that for tonight," she said, kissing his temple.
"But consider it, please?" She stepped behind him and began a
slow massage, setting the stage for what he had come to think of as
Act Two of her performance.

***

When seven o'clock passed with no word from Judy, Tom called
his sister. She didn't hesitate to come over to answer the phone in
case Judy called. Judy was wrapped up in the Itch, she agreed with
Tom, but when she entered the kitchen and saw the pots on the
stove and took the dried roast from the oven, she looked at him,
biting her lower lip. "Hasn't called?" she asked. Tom explained
about the phone lost in the yard and she nodded. Of course. She
shooed him out as she rummaged the cabinet for storage bowls.

He headed to Leslie's first. If she caught wind of the gossip at
the hospital, she would have first gone to Hartmann's. Because
Anna came home to drop off the car, he knew she hadn't made it
there before they left at five. Next she would have gone to Leslie's,
and hopefully tucked a note in the door. Where would she have
gone then? Maybe waiting at a neighbor's house? She had probably given up calling home after getting the busy signal so long.

The Vickers' house was deserted. There was no specific indicator, only an air of emptiness. He parked the car and went to the
door. No note stuck in the screen. Across the street, a door slammed.

"Can I help you? The Vickers aren't home right now." A woman
with dyed yellow hair came toward him.

"I'm Anna Redmond's father," he explained

"Oh, I see. Well, they were here, right after your wife left."

"Judy was here?" He was relieved.

"Yeah. She met the cop here. She was pretty rude," she informed him. "The Itch, I guess. It gets her pretty upset."

"Well, she worries about the girls," he said.

"And she should! I don't want to be a tattle, but do you know they're out with that old pervert Ed Philips tonight?"

"Pervert? Why do you call him that?" Tom asked. He liked Ed, and Leslie had always been fond of him, as had her mother. It neither surprised nor distressed Tom that they were dragging him along. Like Judy, Ed believed in the Itch and was probably doing his duty to watch over them.

"Why else would an old man like him be out with them girls?" the woman challenged. Tom decided she wasn't worth his time, so he answered the challenge with a thank you, and once again Dottie was left standing alone.

***

In the Vanderkellen Cemetery, Claire had already finished her work. With the help of the crowbar and the muscle of the woman, she had the door open and was now picking blackberries to quiet the woman's squalling belly. It was important to keep the woman healthy out here, because replacements were not going to come by frequently. To kill time, she picked the woman's brain. "Pick pick pick," she sang to both the bushes and Judy. Judy protected herself effectively. "Oh, tell me something!" Claire begged. "I'm so bored! It doesn't matter anymore. Do you have a husband? I know about your daughter. Are you the Vanderkellen? Your magic all dried up with your womb? Was it your daughter we felt at that house? Who is your mother? Do you know?" Claire prattled on, but Judy held tight. Some things did slip through, though. Claire stopped, paralyzed by joy at Judy's memory of holding baby Anna. She smelled the clean scent, felt the warm breath from the soft baby lips, met and held Anna's eyes.

"Oh Judy!" Claire gushed. "Will it be that way for me? Can you feel the weight of my baby? It's a boy. Are boys different? Do they stare that way? Why am I asking you? How would you know?" A handful of blackberries went in the mouth. Claire had covered Judy's face with the juice.

Another experience escaped. A man, asleep, and a feeling similar to that of holding the baby, affection just as strong, but different. Secure. Safe. Being loved. Needed. No, wanted. The baby needed, the man wanted. He chose to be with her, and she chose to be with him. Mutual love. Mutual need. Mutual want. So many emotions. More than Claire ever had with Walter. Not at all the same as she had with John. John did not choose her. He was stuck with her, and she knew he'd as soon throw her into that circle as the Vanderkellen. She patted her belly, his baby. The only thing they had in common anymore. The only reason he tolerated her. She sighed, sucking blood from multiple thorn wounds. "Judy, you are so lucky. I'm almost sorry it has to end for you."

***

In Salem, Alan Macklin lay on the bed in his small apartment. He had hoped Anna would call, but it was going on eight, almost too late for them to get together. He wasn't satisfied with the direction their relationship was taking. Seven months should bring people closer, but here he was, alone once more on a Friday night. He rolled on his stomach and stared at the phone on his night table. Her number was on the speed dial. She didn't know it.

The idea of calling her crossed his mind. It had crissed and crossed and ricocheted about his head most of the day. Their conversation last night drove him crazy. Sure, she said what he wanted to hear, but something was missing, the tone of her voice lacked, what? Desperation? Eagerness? Since school let out for the summer, she had cooled ever so slightly. With the competition gone she began to relax. His sly appraising looks at her classmates, the comments about Jessica Renniger, had less impact. More distressing was Anna's friendship with Leslie Vickers. During the semester Anna dedicated her spare time to studying in the Biology lounge while Leslie played with her little friends. Summer took Leslie's buddies home and put her to work along side of Anna. With Anna taking only one class, she found herself in Miltonville more than Salem, and Leslie was always waiting to nab each unoccupied moment. He wished that cow would get her own life.

It occurred to him then that she might be with Leslie tonight. A Friday night. Going to the meat markets in Westerville. Did Anna give other men the same innocent doe-eyed 'I'm not ready' speech?

Would she even remember it when she was falling down drunk? One glass of wine was her limit with him, but if Leslie arrived with pure grain alcohol and an intravenous feed, she would slap a vein. Leslie could talk her into anything, while Alan was expected to wait and be patient, to explain and reason his desires to her, to understand and respect her hesitance. Things had certainly changed since their early days.

She thought they met coincidentally because he worked in the Bio lab. She would never know how carefully he watched her the previous spring semester, how he thought of her during the summer, even while dating Jessica, and how he searched the fall class rosters for her name so he would know when to be where. He studied her, her clothing, her reading material, her friends. He talked to her in the lab occasionally, carefully bringing up topics he knew interested her, declaring adherence to issues he knew she supported. He even lied about his love of cats because he noticed cat hair on her coat. He said these things, then purposely kept a distance until she was fully enchanted. He asked her to a homecoming party, then didn't ask her out again for two weeks. They continued dating casually, according to his plan. At Christmas, he told her of his deep feelings for her. That's when she nailed him with the not-yet-speech. That was okay. He was dimly aware that it wasn't sex he wanted anyway. Devotion is what he sought, sex would be a bonus. The speech was good because it reinforced his belief in her character. She had the makings of a model wife: intelligent, presentable, adaptable. Her parents were of a very modest income, so not only would she appreciate the luxuries he would offer, she would have nothing to run home to.

It was going so well, until this summer.

He should call. She would be eating with her family tonight, or so she *said*. He was probably getting worked up over nothing. He hit button number 3 and in Miltonville a phone rang.

"Hello," came the strange voice.

"Um, I'm sorry. Is this the Redmonds'?"

"Yes," the voice said eagerly. "Who is this, please?"

"Alan Macklin, Anna's friend." He punctuated the word 'friend.'

"Oh, hello. I'm Barbara, Anna's aunt. Anna's mother was out driving that old green car, and it may have broken down, she's late coming home, and Tom's gone out—"

"I'm sorry to hear that," he poured cream into his voice. "Is Anna around?"

"No, she's out with a friend."

"Oh." He let a low chuckle roll. "Leslie, I suppose."

"Who else?" Barbara laughed with him. "Want me to tell her anything?"

"Well, um, no. She'll probably be home late," his good humor oozed.

"Actually, we don't expect her back tonight."

He couldn't stop the pause that followed. When he gathered himself, all he could muster was a short "Oh."

She heard his hesitation, he could tell because she babbled on about girls' nights out and slumber parties. He let her go on as he thought of a way to recover. Nothing came to him, and he mumbled, "Oh, yeah. I know. Girls." They said goodbye and he hung up, humiliated. Now big mouth Aunt Barbara would blab to the whole family about how Anna ran around behind his back. How could Anna do this to him? He couldn't blame it all on Leslie, either. Anna was just as responsible.

She should have called.

***

"I should have called Alan," Anna said in unison with Alan's thoughts.

"I was wondering when this would start," Leslie said. Behind her Ed smiled wryly, eager to keep their conversation going. They had been on the road for over an hour without asking him why he was there. He made Leslie go over the Bruce story again, and offered carefully worded theories. It worked, and now even the once skeptical Anna bit her nails fretfully. The next big hurdle would come when they made a call to the Everette home. They stopped to call once already, and still couldn't reach anyone. Did anything happen there? Perhaps, or then again, maybe the phone wasn't working. What would he do if they finally reached her parents and found out, no matter what had happened, they were okay? Then Ed would have to insist they continue because he must meet with Leslie's parents. It wasn't what he wanted, but it's what he had to do. He steeled himself for the inevitable meeting with Dan and Michele. Whatever their reaction, whether they agreed to keep

Leslie away from Miltonville or whether they had him arrested, Leslie's fate would be removed from his hands.

In the seat before him, Leslie chided Anna about Alan, her comments bringing giggles. Her voice touched only the periphery of Ed's attention, his focus was on her light brown hair. That curly hair had been passed down from Jerry, along with the attitude and the famous irresponsibility that might vanish with distance from Amberly County. Could he twist fate? Should he? If it were to end for her tonight, with no children to raise for Barker's slaughter, would it be over? Or would Barker's evil really be unleashed, as Virginia wrote? What would that mean? Amberly County would become corrupt? Decadence and violence would rule? *Welcome to the nineties, John Barker. Do you think you can handle it?*

Suddenly Leslie's hand was in his face, full of cookies. She was twisted in the front seat, grinning. "Sorry about dinner. We'll do it another night. Try these. They're non-fat for those of us who are metabolically challenged, but they aren't too bad. Crunchy, though, so chew hard and you won't hear Anna gush about Anal-er-Alan," she advised. "Believe me, if you listen you'll just throw 'em up." He took two, bit one and reassured her with a nod that they were tasty. Satisfied she turned around. So much like Jerry. So much like her mother. What would life have been like if he had stopped Barker from killing Holly? Ed had loved her, and his back, bent by guilt when Jerry died, had broken under the weight of Holly's death. If he let Leslie die, he would be crushed, and this time, he too would not survive. These things Leslie did not know, but he wished she did. It was not his place to tell her what he believed; that was better left to her parents.

To his relief, they kept themselves occupied. Anna was still talking about Alan and he encouraged her. "How long have you been going out with him? Where is he from? Big family?" Leslie, not as enthusiastic, was however polite. Ed started on the second cookie, smiled at Anna in the rearview mirror, and hoped like mad he was doing the right thing.

***

Anna was confused. This morning she found Leslie's account of Bruce's activities chilling, but she attributed that to Leslie's imagination and talent for exaggeration. As the day progressed, with each hour bringing more bizarre news, she fought the urge to blurt out in agreement with every tabloid toting customer that came through her check out: "It's the Itch!" Her mood was morbid, her thoughts nagged. This must be how it felt to be in Leslie's head. Be rational, she told herself. Then there was Ed, ready to dish more doomsday lore to satisfy Leslie's craving. But it was not the usual Ed babble. When Ed had information to share, he did so with a self-assuredness that at times came off as self-righteousness. Tonight was different. Tonight there was anguish on his face. It took little begging on Leslie's part to get her to agree to meet with him. People were dying and deranging all around, and with Ed promising them new information, her curiosity was aroused.

Besides Ed and his unusual demeanor, there was Robby Canwell. His behavior tonight troubled her. Once, a few years before, Robby told her about a movie he saw. He told her the monster, a zombie, was really scary and he was glad there was *no such thing*. He was capable of distinguishing fantasy and reality. This evening Robby was obviously being careful not to say much. Anna could tell he believed in Bruce. There was such a thing.

What are you thinking? she admonished herself. Was anything really going on? There had been no time for reason. The decision to go to Yellowbird was made in a split second. From Leslie she expected such haste, but Ed? The more he said, the more worried Leslie became. "It was Ray trying to scare everybody," Anna said. "Maybe, but..." Then more postulation. There *was* trouble in Yellowbird...no answer when they called, a report of gunshots. "But no animated mannequin," Anna countered. "So far as we know," Ed answered. "Mind control?" Leslie wondered. "Telekinesis," Ed speculated.

LET ME THINK! Anna wanted to scream. Make a list, a graph, anything. She didn't want to go to Yellowbird. She should discuss this with Alan. Her parents. They would certainly talk her out of it. Driving all the way to Yellowbird on a whim! And Ed! Why was he egging them on? What were they doing? If Ray had shot up Grandma Everette's house, what could they do? Why did Ed want to go so badly? Why did he keep bringing up Bruce, insinuating the mannequin was behind the shooting - if there really was a shooting? This was insane, but what could she say? She felt like a heel just for pointing out that she had to work the next day.

In spite of her worry over Leslie's family, Ed and Robby's

undisguised distress, and the possibility that a supernatural world full of spirits and curses may actually exist; or maybe because of those worries, the whole idiotic trip was kind of exciting.

***

The sky was losing its brightness. Inside the police station, the wall clock read 8:30. A uniformed woman sat behind the sliding glass window, a phone receiver squeezed between her ear and shoulder as she wrote. Finally, she hung up the phone and slid open the window. "Yes, sir?"

"Hi, um, I think I want to report my wife missing," Tom stammered.

The woman raised her eyebrows.

"Uh, I could be wrong. I'm worried or I wouldn't be here."

"Of course. Please," she attached a card to a clipboard and handed it to him. "Have a seat and fill this out. Someone will be with you as soon as they can. I'm sorry. It's been busy today."

"Yes, I know," he said. He sat in the lobby, the clipboard on his lap, and stared out the doors. Judy was all right, he was sure. She was out searching for Anna.

Okay, he debated himself, as he had done all evening, why hadn't she tried to call home again? Not even to check if Anna had stopped in? And why was the car at the hospital?

After leaving Dottie Geist on the Vickers' lawn, he had gone to Hartmann's to see if Judy had been there. No. Next he drove out to Thrifty's on the off chance he would know someone who might have seen Judy, but when he saw the vast parking lot of cars, he changed his mind. The hospital, maybe? She might have gone back. For what? He made up a dozen reasons: to look in on Cindy, to see if there was any more news, maybe she forgot something? Check her schedule?

He was relieved when he pulled into the employees' lot and saw the old car Anna referred to as the stink bomb. But no one in the hospital had seen her in hours. They looked everywhere, asked everyone.

He called home. Still no word.

So now he sat in the police station, a blank form on his lap, a blank stare on his face, trying to think of where else she might have gone.

"Hello, I'm Sergeant Grimes."

Tom looked up. A young, tired man had come into the lobby. "Tom Redmond," he introduced himself.

"Want to come with me?" Grimes said, and turned without waiting for an answer. Tom followed, uneasy about the blank card, feeling the need to explain it.

"Have a seat," Grimes indicated a chair next to an old wooden desk. Tom sat and waited nervously while Grimes rifled through a stack of forms.

"Okay, now. Did you fill out the—" He saw that Tom hadn't and nodded. "It's okay."

For half an hour Tom filled out forms and gave information. Grimes softened as they talked, interested in Judy's history as an Itch survivor, though Tom thought that was more out of curiosity than a quest for answers. At one point he offered coffee, and when he left to get it, Tom overheard him talking around the corner.

"Guy's wife is missing," Grimes said to a man Tom couldn't see.

"No kidding? Maybe she's with Wendell?" the man answered, not bothering to lower his voice.

"I don't know what to tell him."

"Don't look at me. Hey, Horn's wife called a few minutes ago."

"How is he?"

"He's better. He finally fell asleep, but he's still saying stuff like, 'leaves grow on trees, birds live in trees, birds build nests'..."

"I get it, I get it."

"She said if he hadn't stopped on his own, they would have put him out. He was driving everybody nuts."

When Grimes came back, Tom asked him, "Are there other people missing?"

The sergeant sighed. "Have you seen the news today? This town is chaos."

"But are other—"

"I can't say for sure. One was reported. Mostly today we have—" He stopped. "Well, you've probably heard. Believe me, though, the patrols will have this description and they'll be watching. There's not likely to be a lot of women out tonight. Not in Miltonville. She probably hooked up with a friend. You said yourself, she's probably upset, thinking it's the Itch and all."

"Well, she apparently already called or stopped a cop, because she was out in the Kitchen talking to one earlier."

"I told you, we'll look into that."

They worked together a bit longer before he dismissed Tom. "Look, you might want to go home in case she calls. You'll let us know?"

"Yes," Tom promised.

"Well, like I said, we'll check in with you later, maybe in an hour or so. You will go home?"

"I will."

"Good. I think tonight it'd be especially wise," Grimes said, sorting the forms. "Don't worry. It's been quiet the last few hours. I suspect the worse is over."

***

As night fell, Judy Redmond began to relax. Claire was still in control, but she was drifting somewhere in her own thoughts. Sleeping maybe. Judy heard nothing from her in the last half hour, but she was still careful. At least now she had a chance to rationalize her situation. From her first moments with Claire at the hospital, Judy stayed preoccupied with fighting her intrusions. It felt as if her brain were being probed with a dull needle. Claire searched around Judy without bothering to hide her own intentions and motives, which were horrifying. Several times Judy almost let go of everything, ready to admit defeat, unable to form a plan, or even conceive an idea of what was happening. With Claire asleep, or whatever she was doing, Judy had more freedom of thought.

It was a dream, she told herself. Her body was dreamlike; she could move around but touched nothing, affected nothing. She was light as air and heavy as lead at the same time. Was it a coma? Did she have a stroke? Was she actually lying in the hospital, hallucinating, going crazy like Cindy? Or was it real? It seemed real: she felt the air cooling and the itchy, dewy grass; smelled the evening; tasted the berries; heard the crickets. Through hazy eyes, she saw early stars, an airplane moving among them. Her senses worked, but she couldn't move her body; only the bizarre dream body moved. She could either look out through her eyes at the world, or she could turn around and see darkness, shapes and shades of memories, both her own and Claire's. She could hear with earth ears, or listen to Claire thinking. For what might have been hours and could have been minutes, she stared into the midst of Claire's cosmic daydreaming and watched the last two hundred years with an intrigued disgust. Her only consolation was the secret she kept successfully: John Barker left town to chase Anna and Leslie, and they were probably safe at home this very moment.

***

Ed and Anna hovered around Leslie as she punched the calling card number into the pay phone. "Wish I had a sweater," Anna said, probably more for talk than anything else. Ed nodded, staring off into the darkness. He had been quiet the last hour. Boredom, Leslie thought. After three hours on the road, conversation was becoming stale. A radio talk show amused them for a while, and every half hour they stopped to check the Vickers' messages and try Grandma Emily's. They called the sheriff's department around seven, but they claimed to have no information. Now they stood outside a mini market, seventy miles from Yellowbird, checking in again.

The Vickers machine picked up. Leslie pressed in the code. "Your Dad's message," she reported. She heard it each time she called, not remembering the code to erase old messages. "Sure you don't want to call?"

"No way. You know Mom wants us to stay at the house. Better to just act like we never heard it."

Leslie nodded her agreement. "Okay, there's a hang up call. Duh da da da da. Me checking. Da dum dum...another hang up. You cold?" she asked Anna. "There's some clothes in the trunk. Probably a jacket. Another hang up."

"You have clothes in the trunk?"

"I think I still have some from one time when I was going to stay at your house. And some Good Will stuff, too. Here," she held out the keys. "And *another* hang up." Anna walked from the bright sidewalk into the night. Ed didn't seem to notice. Just as Leslie opened her mouth to ask if he was okay, he turned around.

"Anything new?" he asked.

"A lot more hang ups. How much you want to bet it's Alan?" Ed smiled vaguely and looked off once more. "Ever wonder where the dark begins?" he said.

"What?"

"It's like daylight here on this sidewalk, and we can see the darkness everywhere around us, but how far into it can we walk before we realize we've left the light behind? Where does it start?"

"Uuuhhhhh..." Leslie waited for the right words. None came, but luckily, Anna broke the moment by shouting from the car. "I *cannot* believe this! You've got so much crap in here." She came back to the storefront, pulling a sweatshirt over her head. "I'm half afraid to wear—what's going on?"

"Nooootthhing." Leslie threw an exaggerated glance at Ed's back. "No new messages. I'm going to try Grandma's again."

"Ed, you want some chocolate milk or chips or something?" Anna offered.

"Oh, no. I'm fine."

"I'm really sorry we dragged you all the way out here. Maybe she'll find out everything's okay, and we can go home."

"Oh," Ed said, sounding defeated. He wandered away.

"No answer," Leslie said. "I'm going to try the sheriff's department again. Surely they've filed their stupid report by now." She dug into her purse for the number.

"Hurry," Anna whispered. "He's weirding out."

"Okay, yeah. This whole night is weird, have you noticed?" Once more she called the Jackson County Sheriff's Department.

"Hi, this is Leslie Vickers again. I called earlier—"

"Yes, I remember," a female voice replied.

"Well, uh, can you tell me anything yet?"

"Just a minute, please."

"I'm on hold again," she explained to Anna.

"Ms. Vickers? I'm sorry. I wanted to get a copy of the report. As you know, there was a shooting. The victim was treated and released, and a warrant has been put out for the assailant."

"The victim? Who was the victim?" Anna's eyes grew round, and Ed stopped pacing to join them.

"I really can't—"

"Please...my parents, my sister..."

The dispatcher was quiet for a minute. "Who is it you're concerned about?"

"Well, all of them."

"It really was not a serious injury..."

"My parents. Dan and Michele Vickers. Or Becky...uh, Rebecca Vickers."

"No," the voice said. "It wasn't one of them."

"Oh, thank you," Leslie muttered, not sure who she was thanking. Anna clasped her hands together and Ed sighed loudly.

"Ms. Vickers, why don't you call—"

"They don't answer," she whined. Then she remembered Bruce, and her brief relief was gone. "Was there anything on the report about a mannequin?" Anna's head dropped into her palms.

"Excuse me?"

"A mannequin. Like in a clothes store?"

"I wouldn't know anything about that. Why?"

"It's nothing. Really. But who? Who did it? Was it an accident?"

"You really should get the details from your family. Where did you say you lived?"

"Miltonville, Indiana."

"Well, I'm sure your parents will call you when everything settles down."

"But you haven't caught—"

"No, but he won't be hard to find."

"It was Ray, wasn't it?"

"You'll probably hear the whole story from your parents," the voice said, apparently reluctant to say any more. Leslie gave up.

"Thanks so much. Goodnight."

Anna squeezed Leslie's arm. "They're okay?" Leslie nodded. "Oh, good. What happened?"

"I don't know, but let's go," said Leslie.

"Home?" Anna asked hopefully.

"No. Let's go get Bruce first," Ed said quickly.

"What?"

"Don't you want to get him before your parents find him?"

"Ed, I'm sure I'll be able to get a hold of someone—"

"But the phones aren't working. Do you think that's a coincidence? Have you forgotten he walked to your bedroom last night? Why do you think he did that?"

"Ed, they will kill us."

"Will they sleep in the trailer tonight?"

"I don't know. I doubt it. They'll stay in the house."

"Then they won't know we were there."

"And if they're awake?"

"Then all the better. I need to talk to Dan and Michele."

"Why?" Anna interrupted. "You're just going to upset them."

"Do you think I want to?"

"We're almost there, Anna," Leslie grasped her arm and pulled her away. "Something's up. We have to go."

"Your dad doesn't need to hear more stories about the Itch. Neither does my mom, which is where this will all end up."

"Ed is freaking out about this, Anna. What am I supposed to do?"

Anna looked back at Ed. "Ed?" she called. "Do you really, honestly, truly think that Bruce is part of the Itch?"

"Yes," he said, joining them.

"Then why did the Itch go on while he was gone?"

"I can't explain. Maybe he just got it started."

"Okay, then, let's make a deal. Let's go to Yellowbird, try to sneak Bruce away, dump him, burn him, kill him or whatever, and never mention this to anyone ever again. Not my parents, not Leslie's. Tell us whatever you want, but leave them alone."

Ed looked hurt. "Okay. But we have to take him far. North maybe, so he can't get back."

Anna slumped, her mouth open, but Leslie agreed.

"Leslie, this is so stupid!" They argued their way back to the car, and Ed followed slowly.

***

"I'm really getting sleepy," Anna yawned.

"We're pretty close now. You can sleep all the way back," Leslie promised. They were riding in thick darkness, the starlight obscured by the forest lining Route 58. Leslie drove slower on the winding road, straining to see landmarks. Cool air flowed in the open windows drowning out the ballgame that no one was listening to. Everyone had been quiet since their last stop, and Ed thought Anna might have dozed off. Thankfully she had sulked too much to ask what it was he wanted to tell their parents. He said nothing, embarrassed by his behavior at the convenience store. He panicked when it looked like they would be going home, and all he could think to do was to frighten Leslie more. They couldn't return to Miltonville, yet. Or could they? Here again he came back to the question: How long did she need to stay away? His thoughts went the complete cycle until he once more doubted himself. The briefcase was full of fantasies and twisted truths. Still, it helped make sense of the Itch phenomenon. That is, if one chose to believe in the Itch.

Around and around his mind traveled until he actually felt his head spin. The thought of discussing any of this with Dan made him want to vomit, but he would insist on following through. His hands shook when he realized how soon they would arrive at Emily's. He reached into his jacket pocket and carefully pulled out the small flask hidden in the pocket. Concealed by the dark, he took a hurried pull, and let the wind carry the odor out the window. It was his third sip since night fell, not nearly enough to provide the courage he needed.

***

"Is that it?" Leslie said aloud to herself.

"What?" Anna answered.

"Big Fork Road." The car slowed and all three strained to read the washed out wooden sign as they cruised past. Then they shouted "It is!"

"This is country. The next time Alan complains about Salem, I'm going to bring him here," Anna said.

"This is nothing," Leslie told her, backing the car to Big Fork Road. "You should see where my cousins live in West Virginia."

"I remember when most of Amberly County was like this," Ed said from the backseat.

"I though you were asleep. You've been awfully quiet," Leslie stated, steering Bret onto the road. Big Fork followed a river, twisting beneath heavy trees that hid an occasional tobacco or soybean field. Battered mailboxes stood sentinel before gravel drives that might lead to large, tidy farmhouses, or rusted, weathered trailers.

"Just napping a little," Ed said. "I like the woods. It would be nice to live in a place like this."

"Don't get used to it," Anna said. "Won't be long before it's all golf courses and subdivisions."

"It's already started," Leslie told them. "I hate it. I had the best time playing in the woods. There's supposed to be a graveyard in them, we were always looking for it. And my great-uncle Delbert was killed by a bear out there. It was really gross. He and this other guy were hunting rabbits, and found a deer trail so they decided to go after deer instead, but they got lost. After a few days, I guess, people started searching for them, and when they found Delbert, he was being eaten alive by a bear. Turns out, while they were tracking the deer, the bear was tracking them. Nobody knows what happened to the other guy. Grandpa scared the bear away, but Delbert's legs were eaten off and he had gangrene or something and died."

"That's ridiculous," Anna said. "There aren't any bears around here."

"This was a long time ago. There could have been."

"Your grandpa told you there were bears to keep you out of the woods. It's scarier than saying Uncle Delbert was eaten alive by bunnies and squirrels."

"Demonic man-eating bunnies and squirrels," Leslie said.

"Man-eating bunnies that roam the forest seeking lost hunters," Anna said.

"That's why there aren't any bears. The bunnies ate them."

"There might have been bears," Ed said, loosening the cap on his bottle.

"Hey, Ed, now that you're awake, what was it you wanted to tell us?" Anna turned in her seat. Ed saw her face squinch and panicked. *She smells the bourbon. No,* he reasoned. *You're imagining things. You can't even see her face. It's too dark.*

"Oh," he floundered, but Leslie interrupted.

"Here we are."

Dim yellow lights flickered behind the trees, marking Emily's house. "There's a little bean field up here where we can park," Leslie said, and in a moment she pulled the car off the road and stopped in front of a gate. "Let's go survey. The trailer will be in the front. Quiet…quiet. Not a peep."

"You sure Bret's okay here?" Anna asked.

"He should be."

" Bret?" Ed asked, confusing the name with Bruce.

"The car," Leslie said. "Let's go. Lock up."

"Do you have the keys?" Anna pulled the passenger seat forward and held the door for Ed.

"I have them," Leslie said. "Now class, do we all know what to do if a car comes? Get into the trees."

In single file they made their way back to Grandma Emily's. Despite the order to keep quiet, they discussed their plan. Leslie said they should take Bruce to the quarry and fill his pockets with stones and drop him in. Ed insisted they take him farther away, but he wasn't going to win this argument. Anna said someone would have to wait in the field, otherwise Bruce would not fit in the car. Leslie said she might be able to find something in the trunk so they could strap him on top, but they weren't counting on it.

"Les? What if the trailer's locked?" Anna whispered.

"It won't be. They had to get pajamas and stuff out. They wouldn't have locked it. I don't think."

The lights from Grandma Emily's filtered through the trees. Leslie turned and held a finger to her lips. "Watch the gravel. She used to have a dog, but I think he stays inside."

"A dog. What kind of dog? A big dog? Are you sure it's inside?" Anna fired away with hushed tones.

"It's fine. A little dog. And that was years ago. Just be real quiet." They carefully skirted the noisy gravel and walked through the stand of trees beside the drive and into the clearing of the yard.

There was no trailer.

There were two trucks and a station wagon, but no trailer. Nor was the family car in the drive.

"Oh no," Leslie said.

"Could they park it in the back?" Anna asked.

"Shhhh" Leslie froze. Anna stopped, holding out her arm to halt Ed behind her.

A shadow appeared from behind the house and they heard the unmistakable sound of a shotgun being cocked.

***

"I'm glad Anna's out having a nice time tonight," Aunt Barbara whispered to Judy's sister. Joyce nodded her agreement as she wrapped the left over roast. Barbara continued, "There's no point in her being worried, too. Probably be all over soon, and here we are, fussing for nothing." She took the roast from Joyce, intending to put it in the refrigerator, but got lost along the way. It ended up back on the table.

That's how it had been all night. Joyce and Barbara fixing things, putting things away, cleaning up, messing up. Tom sat at the table, staring out the kitchen window at the driveway that led to the garage behind the house. Occasionally he joined the conversation, but every movement outside distracted him. He searched until ten, returning home when the darkness left him scared and bewildered and he knew of nowhere else to go. He came home to a house full of concerned family, and now, an hour later, they remained. There was measured commotion, a tightness that couldn't be hidden by Barbara's chatter, a grimness in the way Tom's brother, Dale, periodically got to his feet and paced. In the living room, two boys slept on the couch while the teenagers played cards around the coffee table and watched television, wondering and whispering among themselves.

Joyce dropped a glass in the sink and it shattered. It seemed even the ticking of the kitchen clock stopped for a long moment. "No," she said, "I don't think it's good that Anna is out. Tom, call her again. They've got to be home by now."

Tom shook his head. "Let her be. If they are home, they may as well get some sleep."

"But with all that's going on..."

"You mean the Itch?" Tom challenged her to say it. "If it weren't for all that superstition, Judy would be here right now. If more people had told her what nonsense it was instead of placating her, we'd all be in bed asleep."

"I'm sorry. I'm worried, okay? And I'm sorry, but someone had to bring it up. Whether or not you believe it, Tom, something is going on, and I think Anna should be home."

Before Tom could respond, the phone rang. Time stopped once more. Tom grabbed the receiver and said hello.

"They hung up," he announced.

"Again? That's the third time. Who would be doing that?" Barbara said.

"Who knows," Tom muttered.

***

Alan Macklin hung up the pay phone. Since nine o'clock he had visited every bar in Salem and Westerville. He circled the parking lot at Burke's Cinemaplex and cruised around the mall looking for that piece of crap car. He called both Leslie's and Anna's hoping she'd answer. Running out of options, he stood at the pay phone in Club West. Leslie liked this place, so he decided to stick around in case they showed up.

He ordered a drink, took a stool and leaned casually against the bar. Face after face appeared, some familiar, most not. None were Anna. He stewed. Had they already been here? Did Leslie meet someone and influence Anna to go along? Maybe Leslie met someone with a friend for Anna.

"Hey, I know you! You go to Salem," the girl beside him giggled. He turned and inspected her, raising one eyebrow.

"Yeah?" She was tall, taller than Anna, but not so skinny, curvy where Anna was bony. He could see the pooch of her belly under her tight dress. She noticed him looking and sucked it in. Her body was okay, but not the type to withstand children and age. "Who're you?" he asked.

"Shelly. You were the lab instructor in my biology class. Don't you remember?" she pouted.

"Oh," he said. "Of course. Shelly. How could I forget?" Her permed hair stood high, and the cheap perfume was no match for the odor of her hair spray. Anna had nice straight hair. Long, natural, never sprayed or stiff.

"So, why don't you buy me a drink to make up for that grade you gave me?" Shelly smiled woozily, shaking the ice in her glass.

"How can I be sure you're worth it," Alan sneered. Shelly, either too drunk or too dense to comprehend, winked as if to promise Alan his three dollars would be well spent. He shrugged and waved to the bartender.

"Aren't you gonna offer me your seat?" Shelly asked, wobbling closer. Alan leaned away, but didn't get up. He didn't want her next to him should Anna come in and get the wrong idea. Seeing him with someone else might, in her mind, justify her behavior.

"What's the matter? You afraid of me?" Shelly tried to purr.

"Just drink up," Alan ordered, and continued to watch the door.

***

"Robby?" Ryan asked from his twin bed.

"What?" Robby grunted. His sleep had been disrupted several times by Ryan's restlessness.

"How far away is the cemetery?"

"What?" Robby rolled over. "Vanderkellen Cemetery?"

"Yeah. Is it real far? I mean, can we ride our bikes there?"

"No. Haven't you ever been there?"

"Have you been there?"

"Once with my brothers."

"Where is it?"

"It's far. You need a car. Forget about it."

"My mom looked real sick," Ryan said so softly Robby barely heard him.

"Ryan, Mrs. Redmond doesn't know what's wrong with your mom. The doctor said she's better, anyway. She was even waking up some. She'll probably be okay tomorrow."

"I know." Ryan pulled the sheet to his chin. "Goodnight."

Robby closed his eyes against the shadows cast by the streetlights.

***

"Who's that?" the voice of the shadow demanded.

Leslie backed into Anna just as Ed ran into her. Suddenly the darkness disappeared in the glare of the porch light. "Who is it?" a second voice called.

"Leslie? Is that you?" The shadow became Uncle Joe. "What're you doing here?" A screen door creaked, and Joe was joined by his wife.

"Joe!" Leslie cried, then in unison with Joe said, "I thought you were Ray!"

A flurry of questions flew between them. Olivia ushered them inside. The bright kitchen pinched the eyes of Leslie, Anna and Ed, and the lingering aroma of the dinner leftovers set their bellies to growling. In the Everette family tradition, the visitors sat with Joe at the table while Olivia heated coffee and food. "If I know you," Olivia said to Leslie, "you're starved."

"What happened? Where's Mom and Dad? We heard someone got shot," Leslie asked the same questions for the third time. Everyone finally settled down enough to begin answering each other.

"What always happens?" Olivia said at the sink.

"How did you know?" Joe asked back.

"I was trying to call and no one answered, so I called the Sheriff's Department, and all they said was they sent someone out because shots had been fired," Leslie explained.

"So you drove out here?"

"Uncle Joe! What happened?"

He took a deep breath before he began: "Well, as usual, Ray came home drunk. Somebody said something to get him mad—"

"I brought a watermelon," Olivia muttered as she set out the coffee cups.

"Yeah, well, it was something stupid like that," Joe continued, leaning back while Olivia poured his coffee. "He started tearing stuff up. Tore the phone out of the wall. That's probably why you didn't get an answer. He went upstairs and started shooting at squirrels out the window—"

"Eeeuuuhhh," Anna groaned. Ed shook his head and clucked his tongue. Leslie was unfazed; she'd been to plenty of Everette family dinners.

"—and, it was an accident, I do really believe. He shot his own kid."

His audience gasped.

"He's okay. Grazed his arm, is all, but he was hurt. His mom came for him. At least she was sober. But the Sheriff is looking for Ray. He made Mama swear she wouldn't bail him out this time."

"Where is Grandma? And Mom and Dad?"

"Staying at Audrey and Lew's. Your Dad packed up the family and went on to the park." Joe stopped talking as Olivia set plates in front of them. " Now, tell me again why you came out here? If something had happened, you know we'd call."

"I told you..."

"You drove all this way instead of calling the hospital? Or one of your cousins?"

"I wasn't thinking very clearly," Leslie mumbled.

"And you?" Joe asked, his gaze on Ed.

Ed shrugged uncomfortably. "It's a, well, kind of a long story. You see—"

"We were on our way to dinner," Anna interrupted. "Leslie wanted to call and say hi before we left, and when she found out, we all panicked."

"Yeah," Leslie continued, "we thought if it was something really bad, they might never tell us anything, and I couldn't wait—"

"You know how impatient she is," Anna interjected.

"—and, well, we were kinda bored anyway so we decided 'Why not just go?'"

"She's impulsive, too," Anna said. Joe's eyes narrowed suspiciously. Olivia's expression mirrored his.

"And you? Ed, is it?"

"Well, like they said. We were all going out—" He looked to
Anna and Leslie who stared back like rabbits in headlights. "I wasn't
going to be able to talk them out of coming, so I thought I better
come along. Just in case."

"Ed's okay," Leslie defended. "I've known him all my life."

"I'm just asking."

"It's okay. Really, I'm only along in case there was trouble,"
Ed assured him.

"Trouble, huh?" Joe continued to stare at him.

"Soup's on, everyone," Olivia broke in. "I ain't the maid. This
is buffet off the stove."

***

They ate quickly, listening to Joe and Olivia retell stories of
Ray's past adventures. Anna had heard some of them before, and
had witnessed one event herself years ago when she had come with
Leslie to stay at Grandma Emily's. Ed pretended to be shocked,
but he wondered if his mother and sister ever had similar conver-
sations.

"And you oughta see his room," Olivia was saying. "We picked
up the rest of his mess, but I refuse to pick up that room."

"He went berserk after he shot Little Ray," Joe explained.

"Mom hasn't seen it yet, so I'm saving it," Olivia continued.
"The first time I hear the violins for Ray, I'm dragging her right in.
It's a disaster. Go see."

"Let's look," Leslie got up, followed by a reluctant Anna and
Ed. Behind them Olivia began clearing the table.

In the hallway, Leslie said, "Well, they didn't mention Bruce…"

"Who's Bruce?" Joe asked, coming around the corner.

Quickly, she said, "Oh, nobody."

"Long story," Anna said.

"Are you guys gonna tell me what's going on?" he asked as
they climbed the stairs.

"I told you—oh my gosh!" Leslie said when she flipped on the
light in Ray's room. The mattress was pulled off the bed, pictures
yanked off the walls, pillows exploded, a dresser overturned, the
mirror smashed, holes in the plaster walls. In one corner, an old
lamp, probably worth hundreds of dollars this morning, lay shat-

tered. She had seen Ray on a rampage, but never anything like this.

"He lost it this time. He's in trouble," Joe explained, bending over to pick up a bottle. It was half full of amber liquor. Disgusted, he looked around for a wastebasket. Realizing the futility, he tossed it onto the mattress.

After an uncomfortable moment during which Leslie thought Joe might cry, Anna looked at her watch. "Hey, it's almost midnight."

"Catch up, girl. It's more like one," Joe said, clearing his throat.

"Huh? Oh, we're an hour behind you guys. We aren't on Daylight Savings."

"Either way, we gotta go," Leslie said.

"I don't think so," Olivia appeared in the doorway. "You'll stay with us."

"I have to work tomorrow," Anna said.

"You can't drive home now. You'll fall asleep," Joe argued, leading the way out.

"We're going in shifts," Leslie said. "Besides, I never go to bed until morning anyway."

"Yeah, we really gotta go," Anna said, sounding a little frustrated.

Ed hung back in the room. He started to follow Anna out, but he hesitated.

The bottle lay on the mattress.

He opened his jacket and peeked in the breast pocket at his own flask. It was almost full. He didn't need any more.

Tomorrow or the next day, whenever they clean this room, they would take that bottle and throw it out. Maybe drain its contents into the sink. Or the toilet. It was going to be wasted. He didn't plan to drink it, but it was always nice to have liquor around the house for company.

He scooped up the bottle and hid it in his jacket pocket, keeping his hand over it to cover its shape.

***

The moonlight was eerie in the Vanderkellen cemetery, but Judy Redmond no longer saw it. Claire's eyes were closed, and Judy drifted behind her in the darkness. The floating sensation was almost pleasant, not distressing like the out of control, roller coaster motions she experienced when Claire opened her eyes. Here, in the chasm they shared, their memories and histories twisted through a maze of tight hallways. Unsure if she was actually in another dimension, or if she was simply visualizing, she wandered the hallways, opening doors behind which memories waited to be absorbed and brought to life. It was surreal, dream-like, but yet brutally real. Apparently Claire understood little of what was happening, or why. She followed John Barker, doing his bidding, carrying his child. Fascinated, Judy learned about her life in the settlement, everything from the mundane difficulties of washing clothes and preparing meals in the wilds of an unsettled Indiana to the bizarre behavior of the community. Judy saw the place where Claire was held after her death. She saw the Wethacanwee and other, uglier tormentors. She watched the three spirits in the early days of what became known as John Barker's Itch, shocked at the sight of the demons that appeared, sickened by Barker's hatred and the deviance of it all. Place to place and year to year, plot after plan, Judy learned the truth about the Itch.

"Oh, Judy! No!" a familiar female voice laughed, catching Judy's attention. Who was that? Was someone here? Don't wake Claire! Judy panicked. But Claire lay still, undisturbed. "That's her!" A male voice whispered, close by. "Which one?" a woman answered, and this voice was inside her own head.

"I dare you!" The first woman howled merrily, and then Judy recognized the voice. Her back prickled and tears stung her eyes. Odd that Claire shifted and rubbed her face. Did she feel the tears? Distracted by her influence on Claire, she didn't hear her own voice.

"You think I don't have the guts? I'd wear it."

The man's voice said into her ear, "Which one? They're too close together."

"Tom might like it." Judy whirled in the dark hallway, searching for the source of that voice. Her own voice.

She found herself. Young. As young as Anna. Her hair was long and straight, like Anna's, but dyed yellow. She was at a table in the old Woolworth's wearing a large floppy hat festooned with an enormous sunflower. "I think it's me," she was saying as she posed before the mirror. Behind her, Holly Vickers shook her head and turned away, catching Judy's eye. Not the old Judy, the happy, fun yellow haired Judy, but the trapped, bedraggled Judy who stood by helplessly. "Margo! I didn't see you."

"Holly," the present day Judy cried, but Holly didn't hear. Judy saw herself putting down the hat.

"Hello. Holly. Judy." Judy heard Margo Gentry say stiffly.

"Uhm...what's going on?" Holly smiled hesitantly.

"Oh, uh. I'm ill," Margo said and Judy realized what happened to Margo almost twenty years ago. Judy not only shared Claire's memories, but Margo's as well, at least, what Claire experienced as Margo. Claire's mind pounded Margo mercilessly, demanding information, and Judy both felt and saw Margo's confusion and what? Something else...something was wrong with her. She was stoned! Despite that, she had tried to protect Judy and Holly, Judy discovered, saddened by Margo's weak attempts to fend off Claire.

"Yes, ill" the man beside her agreed. Judy hardly remembered Steve. Margo had dated him a short time.

"Oh, I'm sorry. Hey, if you feel better later, we're playing cards at my house tonight," Holly told her. Judy watched herself looking uncomfortable. Did she feel it then? Although her memory of the night Holly died was always with her, her recollections of that day were dim.

"Cards?" She heard Margo saying. Suddenly Judy felt Claire's head fill with information from Margo: Card game, couples, snacks and beer.

"You don't look so good. Either of you," Judy said, her hand on Holly's shoulder.

"Do you need a doctor?" Holly reached out, and as her fingers brushed Margo's arm, an electrifying current ran between them. Margo jumped back, but Holly didn't seem to notice. Judy saw it register on her own face, however. Her jaw slackened, and her brow puzzled.

Claire, in Margo's body rushed away from Holly without another word, and Judy saw the streets of Miltonville as it existed twenty years ago. This morning, if anyone had asked, she would have sworn nothing in the town had changed; that it stood motionless while time marched around it. This sight surprised her. The cars were completely different: Little Beetles and gigantic gas hogs in hideous colors crowded the streets. The buildings were the same, but many of the names had changed. Sometime in the last twenty years new traffic lights had gone up, and the parking meters were painted red. Trees had grown, and she had completely forgotten Pepe's Pizza. Otherwise, it was pretty much the same. Judy had been right after all. Time had largely bypassed Miltonville.

"It was her! Why didn't you kill her?" Margo was all but screaming at Steve.

"I didn't know which one! I didn't have time to kill them both!" he yelled at Margo, who was actually Claire.

"The first one! She touched me and I felt it!"

"But the other one was touching her. It could be either," Steve said, now calmer. "These bodies, they know those women. We can take the time to plan. Where's Walter? We might need him." Looking closely at Steve, Judy understood why she and Holly had worried about their health. His normally pale skin was practically translucent, the flesh around his eyes and mouth puffy and brown. His long hair was greasy and his clothes were rumpled, but that wasn't unusual. Hippie, Tom had called him. He was, at one time, a student at Salem. Famous as a sophisticated drug user, his choice was synthetic drugs, and though Margo protested otherwise, rumor had it she was experimenting with him.

Judy was brought quickly back to Claire's memory by the phantom sensation of fingers clinching her arms. "Dig! Find it!" Steve demanded. There was an internal scramble as Claire beat Margo. Images rushed past, and Judy rolled into herself, not looking up until she heard the screaming. One mental eye opened and she saw Margo, small and huddled on a vast cracked plain. From nowhere, a giant boot came crashing down, barely missing her. The sound was brain splitting and Margo screamed, "What do you want!" over and over. Judy's experience had been bad, but nothing like this assault. Could Claire be tiring in the advanced state of her imagined pregnancy? Or was Judy not worth the effort?

"Who are they?" a voice boomed.

"I don't know!" Margo cried. She tried to get up, but staggered and fell. "I can't see! I can't move! Steve! Steve! What did you give me? I'm dying!"

Giant fingers came from above and squeezed Margo's form. "Do you want to live?" the voice asked. Margo answered with a terrified whimper. "Then cooperate!"

Margo soon gave in and told Claire who Holly and Judy were, where they lived, who their husbands were, how old their children were. "They have babies!" Steve growled as if it were her fault. Only he wasn't Steve. He was John Barker, and she, Claire Brandenburg. It wasn't legend, it was fact, and somehow Judy and the Vickers were involved. Could one of them actually be a descendant of Lucas Vanderkellen?

"A baby. Think John, if we would have killed those women, the child would have survived. This couldn't be more perfect."

"Yes," he said. "And they will be together this night."

"We must be careful, they won't be alone," she reminded him.

"We have to pick the right one immediately, we can't go to their home killing randomly and not expect someone else to stop us."

"We can kill them all at once, the babies, too, like we did with the fire—"

John yanked at her hair. "Did that work before? No. Now think."

"But how can we get the babies? We didn't—"

"We didn't before because we were careless."

"But we can't kill babies!"

"What point would it be to allow us out if we couldn't kill them, you idiot! Now shut up and think!"

And they did. At least Claire did. Judy watched her thought processes as one idea led to another; watched as ideas changed and were discarded. One idea might have worked, but lucky for them Barker had interrupted her thoughts to chastise her for some inconsequential act. It was difficult for Claire to think clearly with Margo's clutter and John's constant narration of his own plans. For this Judy was grateful. Their plan had been deadly, but in light of their intentions, it was fairly lame.

They prodded Margo for more information on Holly and Judy. As far as she knew, neither had dead parents. Both had one child. They discovered times when Holly and Judy had come to her rescue, that Margo sold cosmetics to them. They both placed orders recently. Claire spoke this aloud, and with that, she and Barker devised the plan. Margo tried to tip Holly off with the strange story of the old school friend wishing to see the babies, but why would Holly be suspicious?

Finally, Judy had the answers she sought for twenty years. She understood the events she had taken apart and analyzed again and again. Was it only yesterday, she asked herself, when she sat at her kitchen table reliving it once more? Only yesterday that her daughter and Leslie came to this very place?

She hoped Tom was watching over them, that they were home and not out looking for her. What they must be imagining.

At least John Barker was far away in Ohio. If nothing else, that bought them time.

***

Tim Swift lay awake next to Teena. Overcome by wine, she snored deeply. The darkness did not soften her features, nor did sleep, but she was beautiful.

So why was he lying next to this rich, beautiful woman, thinking about Cindy? Worried about her condition, he assured himself. He had no idea she was this unstable. Teena did, however. She told him long ago that Cindy had problems. Subtly at first. Today he had thought a lot about Teena's early, sly innuendoes.

In the beginning, he saw Teena only once a week, and then in the company of her father and the other members of the management team. Immaculate and tailored, she spoke graciously and intelligently. He often caught her glancing his way and easily returned her small, mischievous smiles. From there he went home to a riotous house, filled with Ryan and his friends, and littered with toys and bikes. Cindy would be frazzled from the activity of the day, be it her home nursing job, or volunteering at the Haven Rest Home, or baking for a fundraiser, or hauling children around town. It was always something for someone else, Teena pointed out. "Why did she insist on working that silly job?" Teena asked. "Just because she's uneducated doesn't mean she can't do something with her life. For instance, take care of you and raise your son." Tim never mentioned that Cindy's silly little job was helping pay off his student loans.

He wondered how she was surviving, even with two jobs. She had no medical insurance. How was she going to pay this hospital bill? She didn't have sick leave, either. And didn't Ryan say something about the car acting up? Tim, caught up in his new life, had not considered the impact his absence was having on Cindy.

With smooth, precise movements, he slid from the bed. Teena snored on. He wished she could see herself; her mouth partly open, drool catching the moonlight as it forged a path toward the pillow. Mascara was smeared under her eyes and the wine made her gassy. What a picture, Tim thought. If this had been Cindy, he would have put it on videotape for her morning hangover viewing embarrassment. With a slight pang of regret, he realized he could never pull a stunt like that on Teena. Unlike Cindy, she didn't have a sense of humor concerning herself.

He made his way downstairs. In the kitchen he picked up the phone, and relying on the light from the keypad, he punched in the number of Miltonville General Hospital. Having called five or six times that day, the number was committed to memory.

In a loud whisper, he inquired about Cindy. Relief washed over him when the nurse told him she had awakened and asked about Ryan. Still, she was very exhausted, confused and dehydrated, and was sleeping without medication.

When Tim returned to bed, he was not as careful. Laying with his back to Teena, he muttered a mute thank you into the air, and soon after fell asleep. Across the room, the red numbers of the alarm clock changed to 12:00.

SATURDAY

Miltonville after midnight was usually quiet, even on the weekend, and the Itch all but shut the town down. Dale's was busy, full of the county's bravest and most curious. Boonie's Tavern was open, but ready to close. The band quit early, and no one had been in for the last hour. Buddy, the bartender, was getting the creeps. This wasn't his regular shift. Patti Anne was supposed to be there, but what with Rubin being found dead in his jail cell this afternoon...

The excitement was over at the hospital. The evening was tense, the emergency staff waited, but there was nothing. On the third floor, one of the night nurses commented to another that Cindy Swift's ex-husband had called. *Again?* the other nurse replied...

A few doors away, Cindy was aware of nothing. The sleep was necessary, not only for her survival, but for her sanity. She dreamed vividly, mostly images of a cemetery, and a party, and a girl she had not seen before today. The girl who screamed at her...

Across the hall and three rooms down, Jaime Gates slept, but not the deep, dead sleep that Cindy experienced. Jaime woke with a start at every noise. She had wrapped herself in her blanket like a mummy, every prickle and itch a worry. Tomorrow she would go home, and she intended to beg her parents to send her to another school. Thoughts were occurring to her, memories that couldn't be real. Slowly, her mind revealed not only the events of the last twenty-four hours, but those of the last two centuries. The comprehension was painful and frightening, and Jaime believed she was losing her mind, especially the times she found herself wishing to scream

277

or crawl under the bed. Sandy and Theresa, they could help her straighten this out. They would tell her what happened. But did she really want to know? Tomorrow, she would think about it. For now, she thought, dropping back into her doze, she just wanted to get through this night...

Theresa Hoover stared at the ceiling, her paperback forgotten. No word about Whit. Rubin was dead. Sandy had gotten into a fight with her mother and taken off. Did Jaime remember what happened last night? At least she was okay, but were any of them safe? Was the master looking for them? She was afraid, but after all the she had been involved with, she was too ashamed to pray for help. So she lay and stared at the ceiling...

In a bar in Missouri, Sandy Cornett drained her drink and accepted an invitation to dance with the tall cowboy. Her cousin Lani winked her approval. It sure was nice of her to let Sandy stay at her place...

In another bar, Alan Macklin was relaxing. The nastier he was to Shelly, the sweeter she became. When he went too far, she would sulk, and he'd pretend to be apologetic, and the stupid thing would perk right up. He glanced at his watch. It was well after midnight. Maybe he'd try Anna again soon. Or maybe not. He was tired of hanging up on her father...

The Redmond house was quiet. Barbara's husband had taken the kids home with him, and she was in front of the TV, sleeping in a chair. Tom wanted her to go home, but she refused. Then he wanted her to go to bed, but she refused this also. She wasn't going to leave him alone. At least she was being quiet. Joyce took her kids home around eleven thirty. Since then, Tom sat at the kitchen window, waiting...

The campground in Colombia, Ohio, was still. It was well after one o'clock, and most of the trailers contained children anxious to sleep the night away because morning meant the Galaxy. Dan and Michele lay side by side in their claustrophobia-inducing bed, physically and emotionally worn out. After the blowup at Grandma Emily's, they had gone to the hospital with the family, leaving Ray on his own. Once they were sure Little Ray was all right, Dan suggested they go on to Colombia. It was difficult for Michele, but with pressure from the whole family, they were able to extract a promise from Emily that she would stay with Audrey and Lew. Joe and Olivia intended to spend the night at Emily's in case Ray showed up. When they left the hospital at nine o'clock, Dan and Michele went with them. Despite his desire to get Becky away from the farmhouse, the pathetic remains of Emily's spoiled dinner tugged at Dan's heart. They offered to stay and help clean up, but Joe and Olivia insisted they go on. Becky was irritable and tired, and Joe said they needed something to keep busy.

As usual, after a trip to Yellowbird, Becky was upset. Dan and Michele worked hard during the ride to Colombia to get her to talk. They tried to cheer her up by playing her cassette tapes and reading stories. At last, she fell asleep, her fears for Grandma Emily unallayed, the vision of her cousin's bloody arm in her mind, the blast of the gunshot still in her ears. Then Dan and Michele discussed the evening, growing more angry at Ray with each word.

They checked in at the Galaxy Motor Lodge around 11:30, relieved to find a vacancy since they were a night early for their reservation. All went smoothly until they began to clear off Becky's bunk and Michele found Bruce. Michele distracted Becky by taking her to the campground bathroom. While they were gone, Dan pulled Bruce off the bunk and dragged him outside, wondering who would have done this, and how. The garbage truck took him this morning. He carried Bruce to the fence at the edge of the campground and dropped him. What else could he do? Later, when he and Michele crawled onto the foam rubber mattress, encased in linens freshly laundered by Dan's sister-in-law, he asked Michele how Bruce could have gotten in the camper. Afraid Becky might hear, she shushed him. "Did you lock the door?" she asked. "Yes, dear," he assured her, hoping that would be enough...

Walter lay on his back where he had been dumped by the campground fence. What luxury to rest and enjoy the earth! John was nowhere! Had they fouled up once more? Did he care? Perhaps, with this distance from John Barker and without all the distractions of his mission, he might find a way out of this body...

***

In Yellowbird, Anna, Leslie and Ed had returned to the car. The food had a sobering effect on Ed, and put the girls in better spirits. Uncle Joe didn't believe a word they said, and Aunt Olivia begged them to stay, but to no avail. Leslie fumbled through a half-concocted explanation of why the car was parked down the road before they all waved goodbye to the doubtful couple.

"Home?" asked Anna.

"I guess. But what about Bruce?" Leslie said.

"I think we should go find your parents," Ed said matter of factly.

"Yes, let's go another hundred miles farther away," Anna retorted.

"Well, Bruce is still with them, apparently. How would you know..." He purposely let his voice drift off.

"Know what, Ed?" Anna asked, her good mood gone.

"It'll be the middle of the night by the time we get there. What'll we do?" Leslie unlocked the passenger door.

"Surely they've found him by now," Anna said.

"Yeah, you're right," Ed held the seat forward for Anna. She intended to lie down and sleep on the way home. "If they... I'm sure they're fine. What do you think they did with him, though? Maybe set him outside?"

"What are you getting at?" Anna asked. She already saw Leslie's wheels spinning.

"You know, that's probably what they did. Dad probably thinks someone played a joke on him—"

"Someone did," Anna reminded her.

"It's not really that far, is it?" asked Ed.

"No, a couple hours, maybe not even that."

"Great!" Anna snapped. "Do what you want. I'm calling in sick tomorrow, anyway. And I'll probably get fired, thank you."

"Oh, you won't. You never call off," Leslie started the car and pulled onto the road. "Come on, admit it. This is kind of exciting. We could be heroes."

"Yeah, I'm sure I'll enjoy telling my grandchildren all about how I stopped a department store mannequin from...what is it he does again? He, uh, walks? Yep, a hero."

Ed brightened as they bantered. Four more hours he'd bought, at least. He would wait to tell them his Itch stories until he could no longer scare Leslie with his increasingly weak innuendoes about Bruce. Truthfully, he had to admit he was ready to tell her now, anyway. If she believed all this Bruce stuff, why wouldn't she believe his Itch stuff?

***

A hundred miles north, the remains of Miltonville's Officer Fred Wendell pulled into a service station. His death had been so slow and quiet Barker hardly noticed he was gone. Poor dumb slob, Barker thought once he realized he was alone. Actually believed he would survive, even offered his eager help because he knew how to get to the Galaxy. *Just don't hurt me,* he pled. *I'll get you there.* Well, Barker thought, I didn't hurt him.

Driving was easier, although the night slowed him considerably. He seemed to be getting nowhere and reading the cluttered map was a chore. All this in Ohio? Cities close enough to walk between, linked by wide, tar roads. Sky-high buildings, massive bridges, big color photographs lining the way. For two hundred years, all he had known was Amberly County, and the newness gave him an exciting lift, the closest to freedom he had come in centuries.

The trip, for all its wonder, was wearing him out, and as much as he wanted to keep discovering, he knew he must keep on track or wither away. He didn't know how much time he had, or how far he could venture from the Wethacanwee before he wound completely down, so he forced himself to concentrate on how to get the Vanderkellen to the circle. The policeman suggested something he called 'over the counter drugs' to give the girl to make her sleep. *My treat*, he said, like a beaten puppy hoping for a scrap. He gave no indication of how Barker might get the tablets into the girl, but it wouldn't matter if he couldn't find her. He'd been in Columbus an hour without the faintest scent of the Vanderkellen. He couldn't even find the Galaxy, but it was a big city. He might have to ask for directions.

A gas station lit the darkness ahead, and Barker drove to it, knowing someone would be there. When he stepped inside, a bell jingled over his head, startling him. A greasy man in a sloppy sweatshirt looked up from a magazine and nodded.

"Evenin' officer," he said.

Barker approached the counter. He breathed deep and forced the air back up so he could speak. In Miltonville, he did this without much thought. Here, far away, it was a struggle.

"Where's the Galaxy?" he asked quickly, trying to conserve air.

"Huh?" the clerk asked. Barker did not want to expend the effort to speak again, so he waited. "Oh, okay. I'll play. Why, officer, it's there," the little man waved at the window, to the sky beyond.

"No. The Galaxy. It's, uh," he strained to remember the word Wendell had used, "an amusement park."

"What? Oh, you mean Grady's Galaxy—hey wait. What force are you on?" His answer was a blank stare. "You aren't from around here, are you?"

"I'm traveling."

"Why you dressed like that? You one of them weirdoes that pull women over and pretend to be a cop?"

"No. What? I'm going to the park. I have to find...my daughter."

"Oh, right, man. Well, if you're looking for the Galaxy you got some ways to go. It's all the way down by Kentucky. Colombia, I think. Or is it Columbiana? Here, I gotta map." The clerk turned around, squatting to search through a floor cabinet.

Barker glared at the man, filling his lungs and burning with the first flickers of rage. He might be ignorant of the new landscape, but he could read a map well enough to know Kentucky was south. Very far south. He wrapped Wendell's hand around a sharp wire rack and wished the cop were alive to feel the pain.

"Here," the clerk unfolded a worn out map. He spread it on the counter and studied it a few minutes. Barker leaned over it, too, seeing many tiny names.

"It's around here," the clerk said, pointing to an area a little to the east and a lot to the south. "There it is. Colombia. You can take 71 down to 13—"

"No," Barker interrupted. "This is Columbus, isn't it?"

"Yeah, but—Oh! You thought it was in Columbus! No man, Colombia. Big difference. But it ain't that far."

"How far?"

"Maybe three hours. I dunno about them old roads though. They're pretty curvy. Like I was saying, take—"

"You know the way?"

"Mister, here's the map. Look at it. It really—" He stopped when Barker's hands circled his throat.

"Hey," the man gurgled. Barker squeezed with the last of Wendell's strength. Having caught the man off guard, he had the advantage.

"Let me in," Barker uttered silently. The man apparently saw no alternative and complied.

***

Anna was not able to sleep. Resigned to the fact that she would miss work in the morning, she didn't feel the need to rest. She sat in the middle of the backseat, leaning against the front seat, her arms folded across the backrest, listening to Ed reminisce about his days at the university, as both student and instructor of architecture. The longer he talked, the heavier her eyes became. She wondered what it must have been like to go from teaching at Salem to cleaning at Miltonville High School. She would have thought it humiliating, but to hear him tell it, it was merely a different job. The pay was comparable, the hours about the same. *But Ed*, she wished she could ask, *weren't you embarrassed?* She thought about her father, how he missed out on his education and was stuck in a tedious job. He could only dream about the opportunities Ed drank away. Her father didn't complain, of course. That wasn't his nature. From all outward appearances, he seemed to enjoy his job. Anna knew better. That's why she grew up being told college was not an option but a requirement. The whole family sacrificed to put her through school because her parents obviously felt what they had wasn't enough. Her mother did have a two-year nursing degree, but how much respect had that garnered for her? The medical field was an ugly caste system where doctors ruled, treating the nurses like lower class servants, expecting them to keep their secret mistakes hidden. Her mother was probably as knowledgeable, and certainly as capable as any of the doctors at Miltonville General, yet she was treated like a maid. Of course, she would never complain either, but Anna knew. Neither of her parents got a tenth of the respect they deserved. That was why Anna worked hard to achieve high marks and learn as much as she could. She would make her parents proud by becoming the best in her field.

Trouble was, she wasn't sure what her field was. For the past two years she focused on genetics. But lately, to her disdain, she found herself growing more interested in medicine. How would her mother feel if she pursued medical degree, when most of the doctors she dealt with were kooks? More importantly, how would it look if she were to suddenly change her career goals?

There was a thump, and Anna jumped. Looking around, she realized she had fallen asleep.

"You okay?" Leslie asked.

"Yeah. I think I nodded off."

"Why don't you lay down?" Leslie suggested.

She tried, but her feet kicked something lying on the seat. Feeling around, she pulled Ed's briefcase to her lap. "Ed, what is this? You never did tell us."

***

It had to happen sooner or later. He'd been fortunate so far; each time they asked, an interesting diversion would occur on the road or on the radio. Without looking around, Ed answered, "Weren't you going to go to sleep?"

"I'll try to stay awake," she said. Ed imagined he heard a touch of sarcasm.

"Yeah, we still got a ways to go," said Leslie. "You may as well tell us now."

"Well," he hedged, "it *is* a long story. And like I said, it would be better if you could see the material I brought."

"We can't, so just tell us. We can see it later," Leslie said, and Anna voiced agreement.

"Well," he started. Chewing his bottom lip he looked out the window and wished for the opportunity to steal one more drink. "You see, my father spent a great deal of time researching the Itch. He uncovered some information that might prove the legend to be true—"

"The Vanderkellen-Barker thing? That's been documented," Anna said.

"I don't mean the incident itself. I'm talking about the reason for it...and subsequently, the reason for the Itch."

"You mean, the reason for the idea of the Itch," Anna corrected.

"No. No I don't at all. In that briefcase I have the majority of Virginia Drake's memoirs. You see, Anna, the 'Vanderkellen-Barker thing' was documented, but not accurately. And not in its entirety. Many of the things that happened weren't proper to report in that day." The tone of Ed's voice began to change. It surprised him. He felt as though he were lecturing, and because of that, he was incredibly confident. Just as he had once been an authority on architecture, he was now the world's only expert on the Itch. His audience was interested, albeit captive, and it was important to pass on this information. For once he wasn't arguing opinions so he didn't feel particularly defensive, despite Anna's attitude. He proceeded with measured words, mindful not to let his excitement wander into his speech. Most of the story he would save for Dan and Michele. This was a warm up.

"What Virginia wrote explains everything. Well, almost," he said.

"The myth says Barker is killing off descendants of Vanderkellen, but Dr. Hock said he wasn't married," Anna said.

"Since when does that matter?" Leslie said.

"It was kind of a big deal two hundred years ago," Anna retorted.

"He did have a child. One. Let me tell you first about Virginia..." He meant to give them the short version, but as generally happened with Ed, he launched into an elaborately detailed account. He became so involved with the story he didn't notice Leslie falling asleep at the wheel.

***

Leslie found herself caught up in Ed's tale of Virginia and her ordeal with John Barker. It was a fascinating story, but Ed's speech was lulling, not his usual animated, gravely voice. Maybe it was because she couldn't see his expressions and gestures, but he sounded as if he were delivering a lecture. Leslie, who always had difficulty staying awake during lectures, began nodding off before Lucas Vanderkellen made it to Indiana.

***

The trio would never have noticed little Bret the Maverick drifting to the left had not the right rear tire exploded. Ed stopped mid-sentence, Anna's head jerked up from where it rested on her arms, and Leslie's eyes snapped open, her muscles tensed, causing her foot to press hard on the accelerator. Not fully awake, she thought she heard a gunshot and panicked, remembering Uncle Ray. Barely digesting that thought, she realized she had dozed off. The car shook, swerving out of control toward the opposite side of the road. Her first reaction was to yank the wheel right. She grossly overcompensated, and this, combined with the blown tire, caused the car to veer wildly toward the embankment. It wasn't a large embankment, and in the slow-fast motion typical of car wrecks, Leslie had time to wonder what would happen when the car hit the small hill. Would they flip over? Hit a tree? Maybe just ride it out? Before she finished the thought, she screamed, Anna and Ed joining in. Little Bret shot up the embankment, went airborne, over and down and—*OHMIGOSH WE'REGOINGTODIE!*

***

Like Leslie, Anna had been lulled to sleep by Ed's tale. And also like Leslie, her first thought at the sound of the tire blowing was of Uncle Ray. By the time the situation registered it was too late to do anything but scream. They hit the embankment with enough force to pitch her into the front seat. Her head met the windshield, then her back slammed against the roof. She fell on Ed as the car skidded sideways down the hill. Suddenly it stopped with the tooth aching scrape of metal against the trees.

Then there was silence.

***

Ed spoke first. "Is anyone hurt?"

"My mouth," Leslie groaned.

"Anna?" His queasy stomach suddenly reminded him that at one point her body cushioned his head from the roof, and he repeated himself with more urgency. "Anna!"

"I'm okay," she said weakly from the backseat. She didn't sound okay.

Leslie fumbled around the dash and turned on the interior light. Ed tried not to panic when he saw Anna's blood streaked face.

"Anna!" Leslie cried.

"Don't move," Ed cautioned, now thinking of Judy and Holly. Had it followed them? He unbuckled his belt, and, using his shoulder, pushed open the crumpled car door. Leslie climbed out too, and together they pushed forward the front seat.

Despite Ed's warning, Anna pulled herself into a sitting position. Blood ran down her forehead, over her cheeks and nose. Ed thought her eyes were bleeding, and his heart walloped. How could they get her to the hospital? He reached to her, telling her to lie down, but Anna waved him away.

"Am I bleeding?" she asked. She wiped at her face and looked at her hands. "Oh no. I am bleeding."

"Where do you hurt?" Ed asked.

"I don't," Anna said.

"Ed, open the glove box and hit the trunk button," said Leslie. He did, and Leslie disappeared, returning a moment later with a handful of clothes.

"Hey, you aren't cleaning me up with your oil rags," Anna protested.

"This is a clean t-shirt. I swear," Leslie said, climbing in next to Anna. Carefully she began to dab away the blood. "This doesn't hurt?"

"No. My head stings. I must of cut it..."

Ed interrupted, "I'd say. Look at the windshield. I'll bet it was your noggin done that."

"You guys are okay?"

"I had on my seatbelt," Leslie said.

"Me too," Ed echoed.

"Geez," Anna said. "Have you ever known me to go without one? I was going to lie down."

Leslie was making progress on Anna's face. There were several cuts on her forehead, the worst of which was barely an inch long, with a nice goose egg under it. "It's a good thing you have bangs," Leslie told her.

"Give me a mirror," Anna said, feeling around for her purse.

"It's not bad. Really. I can't believe all that blood came out of those." Still she helped Anna find her purse, and watched as Anna frowned at her reflection.

"Don't fret," Ed said. "None of us look our best." Indeed, according to their body clocks, it was two AM and they were all pasty-faced and ghostly in the yellowish overhead light.

"Did you hurt your mouth?" Ed asked Leslie.

"I just bit my cheek," she said, apparently ashamed for complaining in light of Anna's bloody face and stoic demeanor. She shifted the attention back to Anna. "Nothing else hurts?"

Anna shook her head. It was a slow shake, but it was definite. "I'm just dazed. What happened?"

"I think I might have fallen asleep," Leslie admitted.

"I think I did, too," Anna said.

"Well, let's look at the damage," Ed suggested. When Anna moved to get out, Ed motioned her to sit. "Give your head a minute to adjust. Keep pressing that rag on it. You might be hurt and just not feel it yet." Anna nodded.

Leslie joined Ed in front of the car. The woods were spooky in the headlights. Ed crouched before the car, feeling around the grill.

"What do you think?" Leslie asked.

He shook his head. "I think you're asking the wrong person. Do you have a flashlight?"

"No. It looks okay, though. Maybe we can just drive back the way we came?" she asked.

Ed stood and looked over the roof into the darkness. Without answering, he made his way to the back of the car. The interior light shone out the open doors. He ran his hand along the side of the car. "You have a few dings," he said.

Leslie followed and jerked her fingers away from little Bret. He was mutilated. "Oh, man. Dad's going to shoot me."

The back of the car seemed all right. The glow of the taillights revealed all the scrubby trees they had taken down. If Bret's tires could find a hold, they might be able to drive back up the hill to the road.

"Let's try to turn it around," Ed said.

"Right," Leslie agreed quickly. They returned the to the car and explained their plan to Anna.

"Think you can stand a bumpy ride?" Ed asked.

"Compared to what? Really, I'm okay. Probably because I was asleep. I was pretty limber."

"Here goes," Leslie breathed and turned the ignition.

Dependable Bret started right away.

The three of them looked at each other and smiled.

"Direct me," she said. Ed rolled down his window as far as the crumpled door allowed so Leslie could hear him, and went behind the car. He waved her back. The rear wheels spun, but the car barely moved. "Go forward," he shouted. "You're hung up on something." She shifted. The car barely budged. "Rock it out," Ed called. Nothing. He came to the window. "You're in mud or something. Put it in reverse and I'll push from the front."

"No, Ed. You'll kill yourself. You drive and I'll push."

"Les, both of you push and I'll drive," Anna said from the backseat.

"You sure?" Leslie asked. Ed started to protest, but Anna was already climbing out of the back. Together Ed and Leslie succeeded in moving the car, but not far.

"I think you're in a hole," Anna called. "It's sitting really low on that side."

Once more Leslie followed Ed around the car. He knelt beside the rear tire. "Uh oh."

"What?" Leslie asked.

"Open the door."

She tugged at the passenger door, wincing with sympathy for poor Bret. Light spilled out - not enough to see well, but enough to show Leslie what Ed discovered.

"We're not in a hole, are we?" Anna stretched across the front seat so she could peek out the passenger side.

"We have a flat," Ed stated what they all knew.

"That's okay. There's a spare—" Anna began. She stopped because Leslie was shaking her head. "Leslie, I saw a spare when I got this sweatshirt out of the trunk."

"That wasn't a spare," Leslie said with a mournful voice. "Remember that time I had a flat coming home from school?"

Anna put her hands over her ears. "I can't hear you."

"It was a pretty long time ago. I think before Thanksgiving. Anyway, that's it. In the trunk. We've been driving on the spare."

"We've been driving on that old patched up tire my dad gave you!? Are you crazy?"

"I know! I kept forgetting. And it did okay for a long time. Besides, I never had any money—"

"What do you do with all your money? Leslie? Tell me! You don't pay for school. You didn't pay for this car. You don't pay insurance or food or rent."

"Okay!" Ed interrupted. "This isn't the time."

"I'm sorry," Anna went on, "but if my parents gave me a car, even an old one like this, I'd take care of it. She doesn't even change the oil..."

"Here we go again," Leslie wailed. "Poor Anna never gets anything! How many times do I have to hear this? Is it my fault my parents give me stuff?"

"I said stop it!" Ed shouted at them. They both quieted down. "Obviously this car isn't going anywhere. Leslie, do you have a map? Do you know were the next town is?" She shook her head.

"Do you know how far we are from the highway?"

"We're close. This road butts into Route 15 or 50 or something. Dad said it took an hour or two from Grandma's. We were probably driving at least an hour."

"Okay then. You two stay here. Turn off the lights and lock the doors."

"No, Ed," they both cried.

"You'll be okay, and I will too," he assured them.

"Ed!" Leslie said. "That's how every hook-hand man story I ever heard starts!"

Anna glanced at her watch and reported, "It's after three Ohio time. There's not going to be anyone out but drunks. Stay here. We'll get some sleep and go in the morning."

"It's not appropriate."

"Oh please. Like that matters. You should hear what Anna—"

"Leslie, shut up. We're all tired, Ed. Let's call it a night."

"I second that," Leslie chimed in. "No sleep's what got us into this mess to start with."

The debate continued until Ed admitted he wouldn't know what to do when he found the highway except keep walking farther away. They heard no traffic from the road above, and there wasn't likely to be a lot on the country highway either.

"I'll sleep outside, then," Ed said.

"Eeeuuuooohhh. Where?" Leslie asked.

"On the hood."

"Don't be silly," Anna started to argue, but he was already sitting on the hood. Bret popped and pinged as Ed lay back against the cracked windshield. "You girls don't understand how good this feels to an old back."

"Are you sure?" Anna asked.

"Go to sleep," he replied.

***

Inside the car, Anna crawled into the back seat with the pillow and gave Leslie the blanket Ed refused. Leslie shut out the lights and tried to stretch out in the front. Bret wasn't as wide as they were long, and the seatbelts poked them, but their bodies tingled as they relaxed.

"As weird as it is, this feels good," Leslie said.

"This whole night was weird."

"The whole thing with Bruce is weird."

"Yeah, well. Whatever," Anna yawned.

"We never did get to hear Ed's story."

"I'm sure we will."

"Yeah." Now it was Leslie yawning. "I'm sorry you got hurt. And about you missing work tomorrow."

"I know. And I'm sorry about what I said. It's not your fault you're spoiled," Anna said. "Go to sleep. We have to get going early so I can get to a phone and call in sick before they call looking for me. Mom'll freak out."

***

On the hood, Ed listened to the soft talk inside the car. Then it was quiet, all but the chirping insects and the call of far off bullfrogs. He took a long sip from his flask. Then he buttoned his jacket and stared up at the stars through the branches. Eventually, his eyes closed, and he fell asleep, thankful for the delay.

***

Claire slept serenely in the cemetery. Judy was not so comfortable. Angry and frustrated, she quit looking in on Claire's memories. If she learned anything, it was that she was going to die. Fear for Anna kept her hanging on. That, and the dread of what was waiting for her on the other side of life. Hell? She had never been a religious person, especially since the last Itch. Churches were lovely places for weddings and funerals and ignorant people who needed something to believe in, she once said. Now she felt foolish because she was certain God was watching. *Too late. If He cared at all to say anything, He'd say, "Too late."*

Horrendous pain brought her back in touch with her strange reality. Claire woke also, howling up to the early morning sky, clutching her belly as her labor began. Judy recognized the pain and thought of the children she never had, and the bitter irony of suffering through the birth of a ghost baby.

***

291

His body ached like never before, and he was freezing and sweating at the same time. Fever, Ed thought in his dream-wake state. As his eyes opened, he saw the orange light of the sun filtered through the trees, and remembered where he was. Groaning softly he raised his head and slowly pushed himself into a sitting position. Miraculously, he had not fallen off the car. Shivering, he pulled his hands into his sleeves.

He tried not to disturb the girls, but the hood popped when he slid off the car. Quietly, he sneaked off to relieve himself, and when he returned Anna and Leslie were both sitting up, looking around like lost children. The driver's door opened, and Leslie pulled herself out. Anna came after her, stepping gingerly on the soggy ground.

"Everything I have aches," she said.

"I'm sorry," Leslie apologized.

"I'm okay. Just stiff. How'd you do, Ed?"

He shrugged. "I've slept in worse places," he said honestly.

Leslie said, "Anna, you're all bloody."

"I need a bath," Anna said. "Do you have any clean underwear?"

"I doubt it. What time is it?"

"Ooh. We better go. It's almost six o'clock."

"Whose time?"

"Ours."

"We still should have plenty of time."

"The way you move..."

They muttered back and forth, digging through Leslie's trunk. The clothes they found were as rumpled as those they wore, and no, there was no underwear they trusted. Leslie decided on a wrinkled pair of boxers and turned her t-shirt inside out. There was another t-shirt that looked worn, but Anna preferred it to the blood-covered sweatshirt she slept in.

"Here, let's try to clean your face with these wet leaves," Leslie suggested.

"You'll give me poison ivy." They disappeared into the woods to change and clean up. When Anna brushed her hair and tied it back, she looked a hundred percent better. Leslie, whose hair, on a good day, resembled a bush faired less well, but looked better all the same. Ed was sure he looked used, but he always did anyway.

"I don't want to carry my purse. Do you think we can lock it in the trunk?" Anna asked.

292

"Yeah, I'll lock the glove compartment so no one can get to the latch." They both dug out their cash and driver's licenses and tossed their purses into the trunk. Anna also took her emergency-only credit card.

"Ed? What about your briefcase?" asked Leslie.

He decided against taking it when he thought of how far they might have to walk. He gestured for her to put it in with their purses. When they were satisfied Bret was secure, they made their way to the road.

"I hate to leave him," Leslie said of Bret.

"He'll be fine," Anna assured her, rolling her eyes.

"Look at all this! It's a wonder we weren't hurt worse," Leslie said when they came abreast of the embankment. Bret had traveled upwards about eight feet, and skidded down another hundred. His tracks were everywhere.

"Look," Ed pointed down the road where strips of rubber lay. "I thought I heard a shot or something."

"Did the tire blow?" asked Anna. Ed nodded.

They stepped onto the road and began walking toward the highway.

"You know what? If we died in that crash no one would even know. I mean, your parent's would know we were missing, but how long before they found us? I'd feel bad if they were out looking for us and found us way out here. They'd have no idea why," Leslie said.

"If we died, we wouldn't be feeling bad. We wouldn't be feeling anything," Anna countered.

"*You* think."

"Anna? You don't believe in an afterlife?" Ed questioned.

"I haven't seen any proof one exists."

"What kind of proof do you want?"

"I wouldn't know, since I don't believe it's there."

"I hope you're wrong," Leslie said, thinking of her mother. "I'm kinda counting on an afterlife."

"I haven't completely discounted it," Anna said. "I just said nothing has happened to convince me it's there. And if it is, is it just another dimension, or this Heaven and Hell thing? Face it, all we know is what we've been told. I haven't seen anything, myself."

"It's faith, Anna," Ed said.

"Are you religious?" Leslie sounded surprised.

"Not religious. But I think there's something after this."

"What do you think?" Leslie prodded, always eager for opinions on getting into Heaven that didn't involve going to church.

"Don't know. I think there are forces at work we can't see."

"But what do you think's going to happen when you die?" Leslie asked.

"Well, if those TV preachers are right, then I guess I don't want to know. I suppose I do believe in God. But I'm not sure what things will be like, or if there is an actual place like Heaven. Or Hell. Maybe we will just *be*."

"Like how? In space or something?" Leslie persisted.

"Haunting houses," Anna offered.

"Or graveyards," Leslie said, thinking of Vanderkellen.

"Yeah, maybe the ghosts are trying to find their tombstones," Anna added.

"Or they want to see if anyone comes to visit them," Leslie said.

"I'd like to hang around my grave. Maybe dance on it, just to see what that's like," Ed chuckled. "That is, if God will let me have a minute before I get sucked into the great yonder. Whatever yonder He might be sending me to."

"Oh Ed, you grave dancer, you." Leslie kicked a rock into the road.

"Stop kicking rocks," Anna said.

"Did you know I was quite a dancer when I was younger?" Ed continued.

"You may have mentioned it once or twice," Anna said as Ed prattled on.

"If I came back, I guess I'd want to dance too," Leslie agreed.

Anna stopped to tie her shoe. "If you were smart, you'd be doing your dancing now."

Ed and Leslie dismissed her and they continued their stiff, painful walk toward Highway 50.

***

Ed, Anna and Leslie weren't the only ones nearing Highway 50. John Barker, in the bedraggled body of Tony Farren was also approaching. He was tired and angry, having lost an hour due to a poorly marked detour. Now, with the sun rising he pressed to hurry.

Despite his fatigue, Barker felt smug. He could drive quite well, knew how to pump gas, and could read the map. Having learned about the Galaxy from Tony, he was prepared for the noise of the machinery and the visual cacophony. He couldn't yet feel the Vanderkellen but—what was that? Inside. Tony. What was he doing?

***

Tony Farren accepted the truth. He was not hallucinating or flashing or dreaming. Somehow this cop took his body. Possessed him, like that movie with the kid and the pea soup. His senses were in tact; he smelled the morning air, saw bleary images, felt his back ache from the drive, yet he was inside his head, really physically inside. How disappointing it was to find his head such an empty place. Corridors beckoned, dark and cavernous, and at first he turned from them in fear because he knew where they led. Finally, he ventured inside, ready to face his past. He had accepted the truth, and now he must accept responsibility. He saw himself as he once was, saw it as if he were that way still.

Slapping his mother during a drunken tantrum...

Leaving a girl alone in an abandoned building while she died from an overdose...

Shooting up with shaky hands in a dark room...

But no, that was over! He reminded himself again and again that he was three years clean, but the crazy cop kept taunting him. *You aren't clean, you're dirty. You're filth. Not even worthy of Hell. Now quit wallowing and tell me which way I should turn!* Since coming off the detour, the cop concentrated on his driving. Then Tony discovered the cop's corridors. They were hidden, and closed off with doors, but Tony persisted until one opened. Heat rushed out and Tony saw blood red darkness and hundreds of shapes. Riding the heat were the wails of tortured and mangled hearts that would not cease to beat. Tony suddenly wished strongly he had never abandoned the church. He wished strongly, crying out to God in fervent anguish.

***

Barker's eyes widened in pain. Releasing the wheel, he grabbed at his head, screaming in agony. Inside, Tony prayed, not the timid, token prayer of one long separated from God, but a true calling out for forgiveness. Tony's prayer rose from the pit of his stomach; his remorse and guilt washed Barker like lava, burning him so that he beat his arms, screaming *Stop!*

The car went off the road and into a field, taking down a barbed wire fence and a few rows of young corn. He was ready to combust! *They* were coming! No - they were *here!* Barker sprang from Tony like he was jumping out of a fire. For a few horrifying seconds he flitted wildly about, certain the Wethacanwee would pull him back into their world. A field mouse sufficed, and Barker rode it as long as he could, terrified of the hawk that was sure to sweep him away. Barker could handle the slow death of his victims, but the adrenaline rush and white blinding pain of violent death would leave him debilitated for hours.

Ahead, on a fence post sat an old crow. Barker let go of the mouse and went for it. Sensing danger, the crow took flight, but Barker over came it. He made it fly in search of humans. He must find one quickly; the terror of the crow was crushing his attempts at thought. Humans had that terror also, but they generally subdued it as they rationalized and protected themselves. He could almost ignore their reactions, they were so mundane. If his circumstances weren't so urgent, he would prefer to conquer the beast than the human. They were much more challenging.

Barker flew the crow high, leaving Tony Farren and his prayers miles behind.

***

Tom heard the stairs of the Redmond house creak under his sister's weight. A moment later, Barbara appeared in the kitchen, her hands full of the litter left in the living room by the children the night before.

"Still keeping watch?" She stuffed the empty chip bags into the garbage can.

Tom nodded, sitting at the table as he had throughout most of the night. "I made coffee."

"Thanks. Anything new?"

He shook his head and went back to staring out the window.

"When'd you call last?"

296

"Not long. I'm going to call Anna at seven thirty. She'll be up for work by then." He pushed his cup over and Barbara refilled it. The coffee was cloudy and strong.

"I think I'll make another pot," she said, moving to the counter. The rising sun warmed the kitchen and cast orange light and gaunt shadows across the room. "She's probably up now if she has to be at work at eight."

"I guess I should get this over with." He went to the wall phone and looked for Leslie's number on the list pinned next to it. There was only a #1 next to her name. Tom wasn't amused. He blamed these convenience phones on Judy's disappearance. If the cordless disconnected like a normal phone, she might have been able to call before heading into whatever trouble she had found.

Trouble. He did not want to use that word, but what else could he think? She hadn't been seen since five o'clock yesterday. Fourteen hours. He gave up the idea that she was out searching for Anna. Surely Anna hadn't stayed out late on a work night, and Judy would have eventually gone back to the Vickers' and found her. Unless—

Stop scaring yourself! he ordered. Anna was fine. In fact, he left a message on Leslie's machine last night, so she would probably be calling home soon, when she was sure he'd be awake. That's why she didn't call back last night, he assured himself. It was late. He punched the pound key and the 1.

The Vickers' phone rang three times. The machine picked up. *Probably in the shower,* he thought. The greeting was followed by a series of beeps. Two, three, four. He chewed his fingernail. Ten, eleven, twelve. He frowned, sixteen, seventeen, eighteen. His pulse quickened. Twenty two, twenty three. Long beep then pause.

"Anna!" he nearly shouted into the phone. "Are you there? Leslie? It's Tom. Pick up! Are you oversleeping? Anna, call home before you go to work. It's important."

Barbara turned away from the coffee maker, her face reflecting the panic he tried to hide. "What?" she asked when he hung up.

He shook his head. "I'm overreacting. It sounded like there were a hundred messages. For a minute I thought they didn't..." Unwilling to say it aloud, he offered a strained grin. "Tired, I guess."

Barbara also forced lightness onto her face. "They probably didn't even check the machine last night." Tom shrugged, not wanting to correct her. The answering machine was such an important part of Anna's life that she often checked it the minute she came home. This must have occurred to Barbara, for she hurried to add: "Or they probably saved the messages so they wouldn't have to write them down. You know, I do that sometimes."

"Didn't know Leslie was that popular," Tom grunted as he resumed his seat.

"I'm sure there were a lot of people concerned last night. Regardless of what you believe, there're lots who think the Itch is real."

He nodded his agreement.

"Uh, oh," Barbara gasped. "You don't think anyone would have left a message about Judy? I'd hate for Anna to hear—"

"No," he interrupted. "We would have heard from her."

"Still, don't you think we should go over?"

Turning back to the window, he sighed. He would feel better if Anna were home. Besides, things had changed since he left the message. At that time, Judy had only been gone a few hours. He should talk to Anna in person, and before someone else did. Remembering Dottie Geist, he made up his mind to catch Anna at Leslie's before she left for work.

* * *

The same sun that warmed the Redmond kitchen brightened the rooms of Miltonville General. It came in through the blinds and fell in bars over Cindy Swift. She struggled to stay asleep, but the puffing of a blood pressure cuff interfered. Reluctantly, her eyes opened.

"How're you feeling?" the nurse smiled.

"My head hurts," she croaked, her voice thick and hoarse.

"I'll bet it does. But you're a hundred percent better than yesterday."

"Yesterday? Where's Ryan?"

"I think your memory is going. You ask about him every time you wake up. Try to remember." The nurse made notes on a chart while Cindy strained to get past her mental block. It was one of the strangest feelings she ever had, and it was frightening. Suddenly she smiled. "MC's?"

"Good! Can you remember anything else?"

"Kind of. What did I do?"

298

"Mostly you slept. Dr. Chance will be in later. Are you hungry?" First Cindy shook her head, but changed her mind and nodded.

The nurse nodded back, made a notation on the chart, and hung it on the end of the bed. Cindy wanted to read the chart, but before the nurse was out the door, she had fallen back to sleep.

***

MC joined her husband at the kitchen table. He tossed the newspaper aside and accepted her good morning kiss. In the Canwell house, Big Mike was the early riser. Keeping to the routine, he had already made coffee and toast while MC stumbled around the bathroom.

She pointed at the paper. "What's the news?"

"Big day in Miltonville yesterday. General consensus is that the Itch returned right on schedule. They're analyzing dates and body counts," he said.

"Anything on the radio?"

"It was a quiet night. Apparently it's all over. Body count stands unofficially at four. There're always one or two turns up later."

"We really shouldn't joke about this."

"I'm not joking about the victims. It's the attitude. Some people really think there's a curse, and the news people eat that up. If anyone's guilty of perpetuating this myth, it's them. They completely overlook every reasonable explanation."

"To which 'reasonable' explanation do you subscribe, dear?" she asked, buttering her toast.

"The one that says there is no explanation. Things happen. People have embolisms and aneurysms and strokes. It happens all the time. It's just that every twenty years or so, people in Amberly County make themselves more aware of it."

"In any case, it'll pass," she said. Leaning back in her chair, she lifted the phone off the wall cradle and hit the redial. She checked on Cindy's condition, and was glad to hear her improvement was continuing. Her symptoms were almost identical to that of the now identified Jane Doe, the ward nurse confided, then happily reported that Jane Doe would likely be released today.

As she hung up, she heard the alarm go off in Robby's room. On Saturdays the Center opened later, so he was able to sleep in to seven-thirty.

"It looks like Cindy's all right," she told Mike.

"Hmm," Mike said. "I wonder if they'll ever figure out what she had."

"Well, I think they can rule out any pills or alcohol reaction, since the Jane Doe had the same thing."

"I'm not so sure they ruled out drugs in that student." They debated until Ryan and Robby lumbered in, yawning and rubbing their eyes.

"Good news," MC announced brightly. "Ryan's mom is doing much better, and I quote, is sleeping like a log."

"Really?" Ryan grinned. "Then I don't have to go with my dad?"

Mike and MC looked to each other for words, but Robby came to the rescue. "Your dad probably still wants you with him until she's all the way better," he said, placing a cereal bowl before his friend. "Flakes or oats?"

"Neither," Ryan grumbled. "And I don't want to go to my dad's either."

"Maybe we can talk him into letting—" MC was stopped by a warning kick from Michael. "We'll just have to see, Ryan. That's the best I can do."

"Why don't you want to go to your dad's anyway?" Robby asked, pouring flakes into both his and Ryan's bowls. "He's got all that cool stuff."

"Because I don't want to go, that's why." MC saw he was ready to erupt and wasn't sure how to avert it, or even if she should.

Mike changed the subject. "After you get dressed we can run over and see your mom."

He shook his head stubbornly, glaring into his cereal. Everyone held their breath, unsure what to say. Big Mike cleared his throat and looked at his wife, who shrugged and looked at Robby.

"Why don't you want to see your mom?" Robby asked.

Ryan didn't answer.

"You might hurt her feelings," Robby continued.

Ryan said nothing, still staring at his cereal, and Robby gave up.

"Can I go to the Center with you?" Ryan suddenly spoke up. Robby glanced at his parents for their reaction. Both seemed eager to please Ryan.

"I guess so. If you eat," Robby said. Ryan shoveled the cereal in his mouth, surprising everyone with his sudden enthusiasm.

***

Walter Brandenburg lay on the ground in the Galaxy Motor Lodge where Dan dropped him the previous night. The morning sun sat high on the horizon, drying the dew on the plaster encasing him. The comfort of leaving Miltonville waned, and a gnawing in his gut urged him to move on. Trapped with limited mobility, and practically no means of communication, his anxiety increased. Was Barker coming for him? Was the Vanderkellen dead?

Walter watched and sniffed, waiting for someone, anyone, to come along. He would reach into the mind of the first person he saw and convince them that he would be a wonderful addition to their household. It had worked years ago with Ralph Vickers, and he would make it work again.

***

Butch Mueller poked his way along Ten Mile Road, not in any particular hurry to be in any particular place. He'd already had coffee with Emma, but thought maybe he'd mosey on down to Betsy's Kitchen for another cup or two and catch up on the news.

The morning was pretty and bright, and he caught himself staring off into the trees, marveling at the way the sun lit up the leaves. So captivating it was, he almost didn't notice the dead animal in the road ahead. The third eye, the one he drove with, alerted him. What was it? Rabbit? Raccoon? Sad to see them like that, all smeared and mangled. It wasn't natural and it sure wasn't dignified.

No, wait. It wasn't an animal. Just a long strip of rubber. *Somebody had some bad luck,* he thought. As he came upon the remains of the tire, he saw skid marks leading toward the embankment. The brush was mashed and the tiny trees were broken down.

He slowed and pulled off. This was a sparsely traveled road only used by those going between the little signpost towns like Crooked Creek and Yellowbird. If he were in the city, he'd think twice about stopping, but this was light years from any big city. If anyone had problems here, it was likely to be someone he knew.

The climb up the small hill was treacherous for Butch, and he took it carefully. Can't be much of a hero with a broken hip. When he crested the hill, he saw Bret's blue back end about a hundred feet down the other side. Butch took precise steps, following the furrows left by the car. When he reached it, the first thing he noticed was the cracked windshield and the blood. He peered inside. There was dried blood everywhere, even on the ceiling.

The doors were all locked, so they must have made it safely away. Probably managed to walk the four miles to the highway. Probably called for help from Betsy's. He surveyed the woods. The car had been stopped by stronger trees where the forest grew denser. What if the occupants of the car crashed in the night and headed the wrong direction in the woods? Maybe they were lost out there. *Oh Butch, you're creating drama*, he could hear Emma saying.

Still, he hiked back to his car with a little more vigor.

***

"I'm exhausted," Leslie said, dropping her head into the sink.

"What?" Anna called over the noise of the hand dryer she used to dry her hair.

"Nothing," she sighed, rinsing away the last of the overpriced, cheap shampoo. They were in the rest room of Betsy's Kitchen, a large combination restaurant-gas-station-souvenir stand. It had appeared on the horizon at the highway entry ramp like a lighthouse in the storm, and not a minute too soon. Bret's remains were only four or five miles away, but it had taken the three of them over an hour to make the walk. They were tired and hungry and smelly and to them Betsy's Kitchen was Betsy's Oasis. From the rack of sundries they purchased the shampoo along with deodorant, toothpaste and a toothbrush to share. Unfortunately they did not sell underwear, but the clerk informed them there was a department store about a mile off the next exit. While Leslie paid, Anna had gone to the pay phone and called Hartmann's Grocery. Daisy Mier answered.

"Hi, Daisy," Anna attempted to sound feeble. "It's Anna. I'm real sorry but I can't make it in."

"Oh Anna. Are you sure? We're so short-handed today." Anna heard another voice in the background, and Daisy said, "Hold on a second." Anna waited, trying to prepare a convincing speech.

"Anna? You still there?" Daisy said.

"Yeah."

"I was wrong, we're covered today. Don't worry about a thing. Are you doing okay?"

"Yeah, I'm okay."

"Well, I won't keep you on the phone. Keep us posted and call if you need anything, okay?"

"Huh?" Anna was surprised by her concern. "Well, thanks."

"I mean it. We're here for you. We're family."

"Any problems?" Leslie had asked.

"No," she said. "In fact, they wanted me to stay home."

"I bet I know why. Bart scheduled too many people. They were probably going to send someone home anyway." Satisfied with that, they went to clean up. Ed had already gone to the men's room, stating that good old dispenser soap was all he needed.

The dryer stopped, and Anna came back to the mirror to 'organize,' as she called it. She re-wet her bangs.

"What did you think of his story?" Leslie asked, ringing her hair over the sink. Ed had continued his lecture on the Itch during the long walk.

"Hmm. Lets see. I guess I was wondering what any of it had to do with us."

"Yeah, he does tend to ramble. But it is kinda interesting. I sure didn't know all that. I'd love to see that journal."

"Me too," Anna admitted.

Ed's speech was livelier this morning. The walk went quickly as he told the story of Donald and Rebecca Bennett. He had just begun telling them about Jerry Templeton when Leslie shouted happily, "Look! Civilization!" Not that this Betsy's had been the first sign of life. Since stepping off Old 42 onto Route 50, cars had passed them without slowing down. Many of these had Salem University stickers on them, their destination undoubtedly the Galaxy because of the huge discounts offered this weekend. Ed sulked because no one would stop and give them a lift, until Leslie pointed out that no one they would *accept* a ride with would stop for two hags and a geezer.

Leslie tied her wet hair in a ponytail. Anna decided this was best for her too. The wounds on her forehead were ugly, but the bangs hid them well. Leslie said her cheek hurt, but she could live with it. They didn't look so bad for having slept barely three hours in a car. Anna shoved the comb they shared into her back pocket, and Leslie left the shampoo on the sink for the next drifter. They went out to the restaurant to meet Ed.

He looked no cleaner than when they left him. His hair was wetted down, but he was scraggly as ever. "Feel better?" he asked.

"Not really," Anna said.

"What now?" Leslie added.

"I need to finish telling you about the Itch."

Anna disagreed. "First we have to figure out how to get home."

"What about Bruce?" Leslie said.

"Don't forget him," Ed said.

"Come on you guys. This has gone *way* too far. I'll admit it was adventurous last night, but here in the harsh daylight I can see it was just plain stupid. I can't believe you want to go on with it."

"It's not that far. Let's just go make sure they made it okay," Leslie said.

"But *why*?"

"I want to see Leslie parents," Ed said.

Leslie was talking at the same time. "What if he did something on the way? Or if Dad just set him outside, he could still do something. If nothing else, I just want to get rid of him myself."

"Okay genius," Anna said. "Lets go. Oops! Silly me. I plumb forgot the car is dead in a ditch back in the boonies."

"We can get a tow truck to bring a tire and get Bret out. What's the problem? We're barely an hour from the Galaxy. We can sneak in the campground, check out the trailer and look for Bruce. I'm sure he's still around somewhere."

"But *why*? You still haven't told me why we have to go there," Anna begged for a reasonable answer. "We can call the campground right now and ask them to get your dad. The Galaxy isn't open yet. They're probably still asleep. Why do we have to go when we can call?"

"I'll tell you why," Ed answered. "I have to talk to Leslie's parents. Period. That's the end of it." He leaned across the table and stared into Anna's eyes. "You cannot go back to Miltonville yet."

Anna was speechless at his sincerity, but there was something else. For a second, she thought she caught the faint odor of alcohol, but when he lifted his coffee cup with a steady hand, she dismissed it. Anna was thankful when a waitress came and the subject was dropped.

After ordering coffee and muffins, Leslie said, "I guess we need to count our cash." They piled their bills and change onto the table. The grand total was thirty two dollars and eighty two cents. Bret's uncontrollable hunger had cost them a lot.

"Oh, and this." Anna tossed her credit card on the table.

"That'll get Bret out. I swear I'll pay for it," Leslie promised.

"You know it."

"I'll help," Ed offered, and Anna felt cheap. The waitress came back with their order, and Anna promptly pulled six dollars out for payment. The waitress would think she was cheap, too.

"Hey look," Leslie pointed out the window. "There's some Salem kids."

A decrepit van was parked at a set of gas pumps. Around it milled a small group, one of whom sported a green and gold Salem Knights t-shirt. Beside him a heavyset man in a knit cap fiddled with the pump. Three women separated themselves and headed inside.

"Going to Salem Day, I guess," Anna said wistfully.

"I'll bet we can hitch a ride!" Leslie turned away from the window. "Go ask 'em Anna."

"No way! I'm not begging a ride from strangers." She leaned closer to the window. "I've seen that guy before."

"All right! They aren't strangers then."

"I said I've seen him before. I don't know him. He works in the library or something."

Leslie looked again. "Which one?"

"Purple shirt."

"He works in the library? I've never seen him before."

"When have you ever been to the library? I'm not sure if that's it or not. He looks familiar though. Maybe I had a class with him."

"I think we should ask for a ride. Ed?" Leslie said, still looking outside. "Ed?" She turned around.

Ed was gone.

"Oh no!" Anna groaned. Outside, Ed was advancing toward the group at the pumps. Anna laid her head on the table. "Somebody shoot me."

"I can't believe him! Wave, Anna, they're all looking." Leslie waved, grinning, but Anna slapped her hand down.

"Stop it! You're embarrassing me!"

"Lighten up," Leslie grumbled, settling down in the booth. Beside her Anna slumped, elbows on the table, holding her head up by the ears. "Anna? It's not that bad. And we need a ride."

"So then how do we get home?"

Leslie sighed. "Well, then we call about a tire."

"Leslie," Anna growled, still hunched over her water. "We will be an hour away from Bret. Can you guess how much it would cost if we could even find someone to go that far in the first place? Have you thought about that? Have you thought about anything?"

"Um, excuse me," a new voice broke in. Startled, Anna's head snapped up and her face went red. "Hi," he said, "I'm Colin. Your uncle told us what happened."

"He did?" Leslie asked. Anna sat mutely, her mouth open. Colin was not too tall, not too short, not thin nor puffy. He was just right. His brown hair was pulled back from a face that she could only describe as sweet.

"Yeah, but the thing is, that's not my van. We found that guy on the ride board and we're all paying him to drive us, so he'll probably charge you, too. Think you can cover it?"

"Oh, man," Leslie said. "That's going to depend on the price."

"They're negotiating. If you can't swing it, I might be able to help. If it's not a lot. You know, broke college students," he grinned at Anna. "Do I know you?"

"I go to Salem, too," she said, almost stuttering.

"That's what your uncle said."

"He's not my uncle," Anna said. "He's hers."

"Well, I was on my way," he jerked his head toward the men's room.

"Uh huh," Anna breathed as he left. He looked back and smiled.

Leslie poked her. "Anna! He's *too* gorgeous!"

"Shut up!" Anna said, but her heart wasn't in it.

"Great news!" Ed called as he neared. "We have a ride. But it's gonna cost twenty dollars."

"Ed, that's almost all our money," said Leslie.

"We have it," Anna counted out twenty, leaving them six. "See, two bucks apiece left over." Leslie stared in obvious disbelief at Anna's sudden cooperation. Then Colin came out of the restroom, and Anna glanced his way, feeling a blush touch her cheeks. Leslie's face lit up with understanding. "Oh! I get it."

"Well?" Colin smiled.

"We're in," Anna smiled back.

"Let's roll!" Leslie grabbed the rest of her muffin, and when she saw Anna was leaving hers, she grabbed it too.

As they walked to the van, Anna heard Leslie behind them saying, "Good job, Ed." And then, to Anna's complete embarrassment, Leslie called, "Hey Colin? Can we stop at the next exit? We need to buy clean underwear."

***

Tom Redmond was disheartened when he did not find Leslie's old Maverick among the few cars in the small parking lot at Hartmann's Grocery. Perhaps Leslie dropped Anna off? Anna wasn't scheduled for almost half an hour, but maybe they called her in to work early. He was afraid to go inside.

After leaving Barbara, he had gone directly to the Vickers. The neighborhood was not yet awake. The yards sparkled with dew, the morning sun already yellow and warm, promising a perfect day for most.

Leslie's house was quiet, the doors locked. A newspaper lay in the driveway. He rang the bell. He knocked. He went around to the kitchen door and tried to peek in. He saw only still shadows.

When he went back to his truck he noticed movement in the Geist house as a curtain fell. Dottie might have answers, but she would only provide information if it were malicious. He wasn't up to dealing with her.

He went to knock once more, and heard the phone ringing in the empty house. He waited for it to stop, then knocked again. Rang the bell. Finally he gave up, and drove to town.

The reception in Hartmann's frightened him. The employees glanced from him to each other. He stepped to the nearest cashier.

"I'm Anna Redmond's father. Has she come in yet?"

"Um, let me get Ruta. She's supervisor this morning." The cashier left, as if anxious to be away from him. He gripped the handle of a shopping cart to steady his hands while he waited.

"Mr. Redmond?" A short, chubby woman stepped out of the service area. "Anna called in sick a little while ago."

A heavy, relieved sigh escaped him. "Did she say what was wrong? Where she was?"

"I didn't talk to her. Missy, go get Daisy," she said to the cashier. "I'm sorry. We assumed she was at home, you know...I mean, we heard about her mother. Has there...is she home?"

Unable to speak, he shook his head. If he dare utter the words, 'my wife is gone,' he would pass out, or throw up, or cry, or any number of things he didn't wish to do here in Hartmann's on a beautiful Saturday morning.

"Here comes Daisy," Ruta said. "Daisy, did Anna say where she was or anything?" Daisy shook her head, her round eyes showing her concern, her mannerisms expressing her discomfort.

"I really didn't ask. In fact, I was about to beg her to come in because no one told me." She shrugged apologetically.

"Did she say anything about her mom?" Tom prodded. Daisy thought for a minute before shaking her head once more. "I really can't say for sure. I think I asked. No, I asked her to call if she needed anything. That's all, I think."

"How long ago did she call?"

"Not too long. It was maybe, oh, almost seven thirty. Not long."

"Please, if she shows up, or calls again, tell her to call home right away," he made them promise.

"Of course. If there's anything else we can do, call us," Ruta offered.

Tom thanked her and left. Back in the parking lot he stood at his truck. Was Anna with Judy somewhere waiting for the Itch to end? Not likely; Anna would have called him, or at least told Daisy what was going on. But why did she call in sick? She was rarely sick, and even then she never called in. Should he file a report on Anna? Would she be considered missing if she called work thirty minutes ago? Should he check in at home? Drive around aimlessly?

He hadn't felt this helpless since those days long ago when Judy lay in the hospital, her organs mashed, her bones crushed. As horrible as things became financially and physically, the worst was over the day she opened her eyes. The waiting then, as now, was unbearable, and he was desperate for her, her words, her comfort, her love. She was the most important person in his life, the one he depended on during the bad times, the only one strong enough for him to lean on. His fears were the same today as they were nineteen years ago: would she come back? And if not, then what? He may as well be cut in half, ripped in two, gutted. All the precious pieces of his life were worthless without Judy.

Suddenly he realized that if Anna called work at seven thirty, she may also have called home. Some of his heart returned, and he headed toward home.

***

The Vickers' vacation had started out badly, and wasn't showing any signs of improving. Dan and Michele walked from the campground toward the Galaxy with a solemn Becky shuffling between them. Yesterday had been traumatic enough, but this morning put the final tarnish on the trip. Dan and Michele were awakened at seven by an ear-splitting scream of such volume it brought pajama-clad neighbors running.

Bruce's wig lay in Becky's bed. Last night it had gone unnoticed by sleepy eyes in the dim light of the camper, but it was the first thing she saw when she woke up. Her parents could not convince her that Bruce had not been there. They told her Leslie probably played a trick, even though they knew they shouldn't. Becky didn't believe them anyway. Half an hour of cooing and consoling calmed her down, but the unbridled joy she displayed yesterday morning had disappeared.

Michele tried to cheer everyone at breakfast by putting Dan to work flipping pancakes and teasing him about his style. Becky smiled, but was listless. She said she didn't feel good, but she did eat and showed some enthusiasm about the Galaxy. Anxious to get Becky out of the campground lest she wander about and discover Bruce, who Dan had confirmed was still laying out by the fence, they left for the park before it opened at nine.

Grady's Galaxy was across the street from the Galaxy Motor Lodge. A quarter mile east, an enclosed skywalk spanned the road allowing pedestrians to cross safely. Becky enjoyed waving at the traffic below. After descending the skywalk, they crossed acres of parking lot.

"Look there, Becky, they're waiting on us!" Dan said, mussing her hair. At the park entrance, cartoon characters mingled with the visitors. Banners hung between the kiosks "Welcome Nasta Employees!" read a blue one and next to it a yellow one exclaimed, "Welcome Cincinnati Investments!" The one Dan referred to was green and gold and read, "Welcome Salem University!"

A crowd gathered around the kiosks and lines began forming a few minutes before the park opened. The Vickers fell in behind a portly couple and their children. In the next line stood a man wearing a familiar green and gold SU ball cap.

"Hi," Dan said. "We're SU too!"

"Hi!" the man answered. The boy next to him smiled. "Did you drive in this morning?"

"No, we came in yesterday. We're over at the campground."

"Smart move. We had to get on the road at 5 am. I would have opted to arrive a little later, but you know kids." He slapped the bill of the boy's cap so it covered his face. The kid pushed it back, grinning. Dan introduced himself and Michele, and they all made small talk about the university. The line began to move.

"So have you been following the news in Miltonville?" asked the man, who turned out to be Steve from Housing Services.

"Which news would that be?"

"You obviously haven't heard or you wouldn't ask. They say there's another Itch. One of our professors died, and I think they said three or four others, but I didn't hear any names—hey? Are you all right?"

Dan felt his face freeze, and he wished he could cover Becky's ears. Michele's too. Maybe even his own. No, he didn't believe in the Itch in the form that Amberly County believed, but he did believe in deluded psychotics that murdered innocent people: wives and mothers and friends. And he believed in the power of suggestion that could start such a rampage.

He had to call Leslie. She was fine, he was sure, but he had to check. He couldn't wait another minute without hearing her voice. Michele obviously felt the same, for she was gripping his arm tightly, staring at him with wide eyes.

"Daddy," a tiny voice whimpered. Becky looked up with a quivering lip. "That's what killed Leslie's other mom."

"Oh honey," he dropped to his knees and Michele joined him. "There isn't any such thing." Steve hovered nearby, apologizing profusely and offering assistance. "It's all right," Dan assured him. "My other daughter is home alone, though, and well, the stories scare Becky. I think we might go call home so Becky can talk to her."

He forced himself not to run to the bank of pay phones. "Dan?" Michele asked, pulling Becky along with one hand and fishing in her purse with the other. "Here's the calling card."

"Thanks." He took the card when they reached the phones, but his hands were shaking. Michele plucked it from his fingers. "I'll read it, you dial."

He made the call and heard the long series of beeps. "I'll bet she stayed at Anna's. Do you have our code to listen to the messages?" She told him, and after the twenty-ninth beep, he pressed it in. He heard Tom calling, all the hang-ups, the tones where Leslie had called in to retrieve the messages, then Tom again, his message from that morning: "Anna? Are you there? Leslie? It's Tom. Pick up! Are you oversleeping? Anna, call home before you go to work. It's important." Dan's faced drained, and Michele noticed. Her hand fluttered to her heart and Becky tugged at her shorts. "Mommy? Can I talk to Leslie? Did she put Bruce in the trailer?"

The next message was Daisy Mier from Hartmann's asking if Leslie could work because Anna had called in sick. Then came the tone made when Dan called. That was it.

"What's Anna's number?" he asked casually for Becky's sake. Michele understood and recited it from memory.

The Redmond phone barely squeezed out one ring before it was picked up.

"Yes?" said a harried voice.

"Judy?" asked Dan.

The voice cooled. "Who's calling, please?"

"This is Dan Vickers, Leslie's father."

"Oh, I'm sorry, Dan. I didn't know your voice. This is Barbara Kelly, Tom's sister."

"That's okay. We're in Ohio, I can't get hold of Leslie. I was wondering if Anna knew where she was."

"Oh." Silence followed.

"What is it?" Dan pushed the words through his closed throat.

"Nothing, really. It sounds worse than it is. We just don't know where they are. Anna or Leslie. Or Judy," Barbara's voice broke. "Dan, we've had another Itch, and Judy's been gone since, since, oh I don't know! Her car's at the hospital and no one's seen her. And the girls, they were going out last night and staying at your house. They didn't call, but we thought they just got in late. They didn't know about Judy, but then they didn't answer this morning—"

"Barbara, Barbara," Dan tried repeatedly to interrupt.

"—and the police, they really can't do anything, but so many people died, and a couple of people went nuts just like the last time..."

"Barbara, calm down. So you think maybe the girls stayed out somewhere else? Could they be at Alan's?"

"Not likely. He called about every half hour last night. At least we think he did. Didn't say anything. But that's his way. He's strange. Oh, here comes Tom. Hold on."

Dan listened to Barbara explain to Tom that he was on the phone. "Dan? It's Tom. Where are you?"

"I'm in Colombia, about two hours past Cincinnati. Tom, what's going on?"

"I wish I knew. Judy left yesterday about four thirty. She went to the hospital, visited a patient, and left. Left her car and all. Dottie Geist saw her at your house talking to a cop, and that's it."

"What did the police say?" Dan regretted asking that in front of Michele and Becky. They both flinched.

"They don't have any records of Judy calling the police, or of the police being in the Kitchen. They're going to talk to Dottie this morning. She also happens to be the last to see Anna and Leslie. That was yesterday afternoon, too. Around dinner time. They were going to stay at your house, but it doesn't look like they did."

"They might have stayed at someone else's house. Maybe they drank too much or something."

"I don't know, but Anna did call in to work this morning, so they're probably okay. Dottie said they were with Ed Philips."

"Ed?"

"Yeah. He's not home, either. Or he's not answering his door, anyway."

"So, now what?"

"Barbara's going to stay here and wait. I'm going to keep looking. The only thing I can think is that Judy is hiding the girls until the Itch is over."

"Who—I mean, has anyone we know...?"

"So far, Troy Ivers, a guy named Mark Reynolds - he lives out by you. A guy named Lutz and Rubin Tanner. He works at the filling station. They found a girl out by your house, too. Wait, your neighbor, across the street, she went into the hospital yesterday..." Tom seemed to be making connections.

"We're going to start back as soon as I can pack up," Dan said with an eye on Becky, fearful of a tantrum over leaving the Galaxy. There was none. "I'll call as soon as we get in. About three, three and a half hours. Depends on traffic."

"Everybody outta be home by then," Tom said.

They said goodbye, then Dan touched his daughter's hair. "Sweetie, I'm sorry, but we have to leave. I promise we'll come back real soon."

"Where's Leslie?" she asked, with not a glimmer of disappointment.

"We're going home to find out."

They walked back to the campground. Dan hooked up the trailer while Michele and Becky repacked and secured their belongings. He then went to the campground office to explain they would be leaving and settle the bill. On his way back, he glanced down the row of trailers to the place where he left Bruce.

His heart fluttered. He almost tripped over his own feet in his haste to get back to the trailer. In answer to the questioning looks from his family, he gave Becky a pillow and told her to wait in the car, then he pulled everything out of the closet and off the beds.

"Dan? What's going on? Why are you tearing everything up?"

He stopped and shook his head as if to clear it. "It's nothing. Let's just get out of here." He nudged her gently to the door, stopping a moment to peek in the privy. Satisfied the trailer was safe, he locked up and followed Michele to the car, anxious to get going. He didn't tell Michele that Bruce was no longer lying by the fence.

***

Leslie swam in the warm, blue water. It was easy, gliding like a fish, the sun glistening on the ripples around her. The sound of water and birdsong relaxed her, but it was time to get out. She rode the momentum of her last strokes to the edge of the pool and started to climb out. When she saw Dr. Loomis's Western Civilization class in progress on the grassy lawn beside the pool, she let herself sink back into the water. She hoped Dr. Loomis hadn't noticed her over here, swimming happily, when she had promised to sign up for this special summer class.

Lying on her back, she propelled herself quietly to the other side of the pool. Her arms were tired and her nose was getting sunburned. When she was close to the side, she rolled over and again started to get out. But there were Mom and Dad! And Becky, pulling on Dad's arm. What a pest! What were they doing out here? Mom carried a laundry basket on one hip while she tended burgers at the grill. Dad kneeled before the lawn mower, fiddling with the motor, getting grease on his good shirt. Becky persisted in her pursuit or attention.

Leslie ducked before they spotted her. She was too tired for chores.

Pulling her way along the edge of the pool, she peeked over the third side. Oh no! Mr. Hartmann! Anna called in sick today, and if he saw her he'd make her work!

With out bothering to swim across the pool, she took her chances and raised up high enough to see what was happening on the lawn by the fourth side. Ah! Empty! She dove deep and swam toward freedom. As she began her ascent, a familiar figure appeared and sat on the edge of the pool. She was about to break surface when the figure stuck a foot out and placed it on her head, pushing her down. Leslie went a little left and made another attempt to rise, but once more, she was held under water. Farther left, and again. Her side began to ache, and she swam back toward the middle of the pool, but still she could not reach the surface. No matter how far she swam, the figure's leg stretched, its foot planted firmly on her head. Panic cramped her legs, and her lungs felt at once empty and ready to burst.

She clawed at the foot, but her ebbing strength and the weight of the water fought against her. Didn't Mom or Dad see? Dr. Loomis? Mr. Hartmann? But the figure sat so serenely, no one would ever guess it was in the process of drowning someone. The violent water distorted the features, but Leslie could see it was female. She leaned back on her arms, her face tilted toward the sky. A bird soared by and she followed its flight with gentle eyes. Leslie then recognized her, and her courage boiled. She grabbed the woman's toe and twisted it viciously.

The woman gasped and looked at Leslie. Leslie stared back into her own face.

***

A painful cramp in her toe yanked Leslie from her sleep. There was a long moment of disorientation as she assessed her surroundings. It wasn't dark, but it wasn't very light either. Gray. Rumbling. Low bass rhythm, subdued talking.

Oh, yeah, she remembered. They were on their way to the Galaxy with Crazy Sam, the van man. She was on the floor, stuffed in the corner against the quasi-couch-bed and the paneled van wall. Beside her, a couple slept, her head on his shoulder. On the bed behind her, a pale young woman laid out tarot cards, telling a young man his fate. He seemed more interested in the woman than her words. Next to them another girl slept, curled up.

Anna and Colin were sitting on the floor close to Leslie, chatting away like long lost friends. Leslie wanted to say something, but couldn't think of anything. Instead she tried to remember everybody's name. Colin had introduced them when they first climbed aboard, but he really didn't know anyone other than his friend Alex, the one who was having his fortune told. The pale reader was the driver's girlfriend, Cissy, or something like that. The sleeping couple, she totally blanked out on, but the girl sleeping on the bed was named Michelle. That was easy for Leslie to remember. Michelle was meeting friends at the park, as were Colin and Alex. Each passenger paid thirty dollars carfare. Leslie guessed that Crazy Sam had cut a deal with Ed since they were practically there and might not need a ride back. They were probably just an extra twenty bucks to Sam.

Rolling her head between her shoulders, she strained to see how Ed was getting along up front. He and Sam hit it off pretty well. Sam's head, protected by the knit cap, bounced above the neck rest. He passed a bottle to Ed. Leslie bit her lip. That was bad. Why was he drinking? Humoring Sam, maybe? Oh well, Ed was an adult.

Squirming deep into her corner, she let her eyes close again. The hum of the road lulled her, but a thought woke her for a second. This time yesterday she was at work, bored and wondering what to do this weekend. Just yesterday. This was a stupid idea. Bruce is a stupid mannequin. Robby did a silly thing, putting him in the trailer. And as far as the shooting at Grandma's, well, it would have been a bigger surprise if the evening had passed without an outburst from Ray. There hadn't been a lot of time to think about it, but now she understood why Ed had encouraged them to leave. From what he told them so far, he believed they were in danger from the Itch and wanted them out of Miltonville. The whole thing was moronic, Anna was right. Sighing sadly, trying to sort her thoughts, she fell into another dream, her last one forgotten.

***

Ed saw no point in going on. There was no need to finish telling Leslie about the Itch. It would get her anyway. Why distress her with details? He choked back more of the hot liquor before passing the bottle to Sam. He received a joint in return. He inhaled and watched the countryside fly past in a blur while Sam ranted about politics.

What a difference thirty minutes made. His spirits had been high, the bourbon was a reward. After making a deal with Sam, they piled into the van, and grudgingly stopped at the Smart-Mart before continuing east. Anna was suddenly enjoying herself; Leslie fell asleep as soon as they hit the road. Sam told Ed the Itch was over, and Ed was elated. There was no need to tell the Vickers the long, unbelievable tale of the Barker curse. All they had to do was find a way home.

He asked Sam if he could listen to the radio to catch up on the news. Sam obliged. Ed's mind had drifted so far that he almost missed the segment on Miltonville. It was short, reporting the last casualty had occurred around five Friday night. Ed's grin lasted but a moment

"In a related story, missing Miltonville Officer Fred Wendell's body was found in a convenience store about ten miles north of Columbus around three o'clock this morning. The cause of death is still under investigation. Officials say there was no indication of robbery or theft. The clerk on duty at the 1stOp, Anthony Farren, was missing, but his jacket and uncashed paycheck were still in the store. This morning brings another twist to the strange story: Anthony Farren was found unconscious in his car almost a hundred and fifty miles south of Columbus, on Rural Highway 13. He was transported to Carpenter Regional Hospital and at this time, his condition is unknown."

"Hey, Roger," a cheerful voice broke in. *"Are there any theories about similarities between the Wendell and Farren cases? A contagious virus, perhaps?"*

"Everything is speculation at this point, Wayne. There hasn't been an official statement released, but we will continue to provide details to this bizarre story as they become available..."

"Wow," Sam said.

"Do you have a map?" Ed asked.

"Why? You wanna see Highway 13?"

"I'm curious."

"We passed it about twenty miles back."

"It's here?" Ed gripped the worn armrests of the captain's chair. "You mean it goes from Columbus to Colombia?"

"I don't know. Relax man. There's a map around somewhere. Look under your seat." But Ed was silently repeating himself. Columbus. Colombia. It could be confusing. Whatever the process, the outcome was the same. A man disappears from Miltonville and dies in Columbus. Another man disappears from Columbus and turns up close to Colombia. Unconscious. Like the girl yesterday, the one they found in Leslie's neighborhood.

Ed uncapped his flask. "Hey man. You gotta share with the pilot," Sam scolded. Ed shrugged and handed it over, grateful for the second one in his jacket. "Don't worry, dude, I got some smoke." Ed took back the bottle while Sam lit up. He didn't care how he abused himself now. The Itch was coming. Leslie would die. He didn't wish to be conscious when that occurred.

***

The crowds were bustling at Grady's Galaxy, cars tight against one another, their motors rumbling. Music of every kind blended with chatter and laughter, charging the atmosphere. Fat lines of people led to the kiosks. Fathers lined up families for photos before the massive Galaxy emblem where gigantic costumed characters posed, hugging children and shaking hands. It was a happy place for everyone.

Everyone except John Barker. For him, things couldn't be worse.

From the moment Tony Farren sent him spiraling out of control, nothing had gone right. He rode mouse and bird and a rodent he was not able to identify, hanging tightly until he found a dying crow whose spirit had departed. He took its weak body, aware he would have it a short time, forced it high, then soared on the tired wings. Fueled by anger sharp and harsh, he couldn't appreciate the beautiful images left in the ancient crow's brain. Instead he looked downward, searching.

He found a large building beside a busy road, cars parked all around. Carefully, he brought the crow down, amazed at how smoothly the near lifeless body steered itself. Sleepy people milled about, but none distracted enough to overtake. In fact, they were so acutely aware of everything about them they practically sent

317

unconscious warning signals. Then, in a large truck, he found a man sleeping. He swooped in, and within six feet he was knocked away with a force that almost flipped him out of the bird.

Great! Another one! Hallelujah right back! Barker cast a few choice words toward the man and his protectors, then wisely flew away.

Again, he worked the wings, taking the bird higher. It tired him, but the wings were too stiff to keep flying low, and he couldn't maneuver around the many obstacles down there. Most people would be awake by now, he thought, not realizing that Saturday was a day for late sleepers. How could he find someone in an early morning reverie from this altitude?

Then, from his vantage point, he saw a vehicle parked among trees, a faded green station wagon with tinted windows. In a nearby clearing, he saw what he recognized as a children's park. There were tables and swings, a merry go round and a concrete building, all surrounded by ranks of tiny houses. The concrete building caught his attention, not the building itself, but rather the row of pink demons that sat on the roof waving at him. Dodging the trees with the last of his strength, Barker made it into the clearing, landing under the swingset. The demons, he now saw, were not pink, but burned. Parts of them had peeled away in black edged curls, exposing blood red blisters and wounds.

"What are you doing here?" three of the creatures squealed in unison.

"You are screwing it up!" another shouted.

Barker, not able to speak, cocked the crow's head.

"Get in there!" the fattest of the demons ordered, pointing at the building below. "Use him. But you better remember your promise to Mohar!"

"And don't kill this host! We want him back!" said another, leading a chorus of shrieks and threats.

Barker studied the square little building. Two open entryways were marked with figures, one with legs, and the other, in a dress. MEN. WOMEN. Between the roof and the walls were open vents, actually places where the cement blocks were left out for ventilation. Barker flew into one of them.

In one of the stalls, an old man sat cross-legged on a toilet, reading a magazine. He flinched at the sound of Barkers arrival, then leaned forward expectantly. Disappointed, he relaxed and looked again at the book. Within minutes, the man was miles away, his mind an open door. Barker leaped. The crow fell.

The man fought violently, and initially had the advantage, because Barker had been taken aback by what accosted him in this man's mind. The man was waiting—*Oh! You disgusting swine!* Barker bellowed, suddenly up to the fight. Barker wanted him. The old man, lost in his own murky spirit, confused by the sudden dissonance, obeyed the demons that had controlled him for so long, and gave in.

The station wagon belonged to him. It carried a smell similar to a rotting body, fitting for the old man's purpose. Pornographic magazines were spread across the front seat, and Barker swept them outside. When he climbed behind the wheel, he saw in the mirror the group of demons seated behind him

"Let him drive," the fattest one said. He seemed to be in a hurry. Light smoke tendrils drifted upwards from his body. Barker let the old man drive. The man, Albert Leehman, was under the delusion that Barker was from outer space, having sought him out because he was a superior human. Barker encouraged him, and was rewarded by Albert's determination to be a devoted escort. Squeezed between Albert's drooling allegiance and the screeching voices of the demons, Barker fumed, holding back an eruption. He tried to calm himself with visions of his life after the Vanderkellen.

Now they were in Colombia, riding beside the Galaxy. The scorched demons bounced around the car, kicking Barker in the head and wheezing in his ear, *Don't screw this up or you'll wish you'd had gone to Hell when you died the first time.* Barker was too distracted by the park to be annoyed by their threats. The sunlight danced upon colors, dazzling and dizzy, so much life and movement. He wanted to be a part of it, to absorb the energy, and he urged Albert to go faster, but the traffic inched ever slower the closer they approached. Barker opened his senses, breathing deeply, awaiting the scent of the Vanderkellen that was certain to be mixed among the aroma of waffles and chlorine and machine grease. Several times along the way, he fancied he smelled her, and he enjoyed the sensation. Leaning Albert's head toward the open window, he inhaled deeply, but instead of the noxious Vanderkellen he detected something else.

He slammed the brake, surprising the old man. *What? What are you doing? The park is ahead. You're in the wrong lane!* Horns honked behind him. A demon grabbed his hair. *Is it her? Did you find her?* it demanded to know.

"Shut up!" Barker snapped. Again, he inhaled. It was thick, pungent. A human would choke on it. It was terror he smelled, and he recognized its source. He let off the brake and they rolled ahead. Stronger, stronger, then it became weaker, and he knew he passed it. He stopped again and put Albert's head completely out the window, twisting and sniffing. More car horns, this time accompanied by shouts. Barker picked up the odor, to the right, behind them.

"Walter, you little cur," he said.

Inside, Albert begged, *Pull off! You'll get us killed!* Barker complied, pulling into an asphalt lot in front of a cabin. EXIT read the sign at the drive, GALAXY MOTOR LODGE read the sign atop the building. The same sign was high in the sky at either end of the parking lot. Barker's arrival created a stir as more car horns blared. Albert ranted, *You went in the exit! You almost killed us! Didn't you see that car coming? Didn't you read the sign?*

"Shut him up!" Barker said to the demons, who happily obliged.

Albert, writhing, was forced once again to drive. Barker told him the direction he wanted to go, and Albert complained, *This is a private campground! They have security!* But, in order to avert more pain, he drove to a gate. The sign said GUESTS. There was a glass booth, and a pole with another sign: INSERT KEY CARD. Before them, a striped bar blocked their path. Albert puzzled a moment. A man stepped from the booth, smile on his face, clipboard in hand. "Howdy. Are you a guest or a visitor?" He produced a white card with a number on it.

"Huh?" Albert uttered. "What's the difference?"

"Do you have a keycard?"

Barker took over. "Open the gate."

"Excuse me? I'm sorry, sir. Are you here to visit one of the guests? I have to log all visitors. Security."

Barker was aghast. Was this idiot deaf?

What are you doing? You're gonna get us thrown in jail! Albert blabbered. Barker turned on him, squeezing, killing. The demons around him revolted. "You weren't supposed to kill him!" they screamed, pummeling Albert's dead body.

"Stop it!" Barker shouted. The attendant stepped back.

"What are we supposed to do?" the fattest demon cried.

"I have to get through here!"

"Then we're latching onto you, brother, until you get us out of this mess," said one of them. Another flew out the window. Barker could no longer see him, but the attendant stopped as if hit with a sharp pain. With slow, shaky movements, he went inside the booth and the bar raised.

Cautiously, driving alone with at least ten hot, angry demons hanging off him like leaches, he passed through the gate. Beyond, rows of trailers and tents were set up, much like people set up their houses. Ignoring them, he followed the scent of Walter. He lost his way only once. At the end of a drive, he saw Walter.

And he knew Walter saw him.

Walter's terror drenched him like a luxurious bath. Barker laughed aloud at Walter's pathetic attempt to roll away. The demons howled. Barker parked the station wagon next to him.

"Well, old friend," he said, standing over the mannequin. "Are you ready to go home?" Walter's reaction radiated through the air in currents of electricity.

"Where on earth did that thing come from?" A man's voice surprised him. Barker turned, prepared for a confrontation. Behind him stood a tubby man in white shorts and a shocking flowered shirt. Thin hair was combed over a bald head and his black socks were pulled up to his knees. Barker raised his eyebrows, on the ready, but the man shrugged and waddled off, calling, "Have a good day," as he went. Barker turned his attention back to Walter.

"We'll talk later, Walter." Albert's body was frail, but it had sufficient strength to lift Walter into the station wagon. Barker would have preferred to take one of the massive mobile homes that surrounded him, but with Albert gone, he wasn't sure he could maneuver one. He needed to find a live body, but first he must locate the Vanderkellen.

Although Albert and his demons had worn Barker out, his vigor was renewed by Walter's emotional energy. The demons must have sensed this, for they grew quiet. One let go and drifted away. With heightened confidence, he retraced his way through the campground to the parking lot. He sat a moment at the exit, worried about the traffic. Part of the parking lot was directly across the street, surrounded by a high wire fence. It spread as far as he could see, but the park entrance was barely a quarter mile away. Several groups of people walked along side the road. Perhaps a daydreamer among them? Young and healthy? Maybe even the Vanderkellen itself, though he had not yet caught a whiff of it.

He backed away from the exit and drove to the parking slot farthest from the park office to diminish the likelihood of Walter grabbing someone going in or out. Checking the door locks, he remembered to remove the keys and put them in Albert's shirt pocket. He inhaled, drinking Walter's terror until there was no room left in his being. So invigorating! Without bothering to inform Walter of his plans, he left the car and headed toward the park, the demons still clinging to him. He was glad for their silence; he needed time to think. He had yet to figure out what to do with the Vanderkellen when he found her, but he assumed he could use any resource at his disposal, including whatever help he could coerce from the monsters riding on his back.

Rejuvenated by Walter's dread, he was up to the challenge. Albert's old corpse moved with a light step and a whistle on its lips.

***

The Vickers waited at the motor lodge exit for a chance to pull onto the road. Even though the Galaxy traffic had special lanes off the main road, a left turn was still fairly difficult with a trailer attached to the car. Dan said nothing, waiting for the nearest stoplight to change so he could claim a spot on the road. Becky had quit asking about Leslie and was staring out the window. Michele felt the burden of the anxiety, and in her maternal way, considered it her duty to distract everyone.

"Boy, look at that old man. He looks like he's sick," she said of the thin, balding man passing in front of the car. Dan and Becky cast vague glances at him. Michele sighed and watched for a clearing in the traffic.

***

A pothole jarred Leslie from her second nap. She felt as if she had slept for hours, but it couldn't be so. The entire trip to the Galaxy from Betsy's Kitchen only took an hour. She nudged Anna. "How far?"

"Hey sleepy head," Anna said. Leslie noted how coy she had become since Colin showed up. "We're about there."

Leslie yawned and tried to stretch without disturbing the couple next to her. She hoped her family was having fun. Surely they were at the park by now; it wasn't likely Becky would let go of one minute of ride time. She began to worry about what would happen next. Would Ed really insist on speaking to her parents? Did he have any concept of how upset they would be? She and Anna must talk him out of that. Why couldn't they just check the dumpster at the campground and make sure her father had thrown Bruce out? Being Saturday, last night's trash was probably still there. What if Bruce wasn't there? Well, of course he would be. Even if her father found him before they arrived at the campground, he wouldn't have just tossed him out on the highway, not when they were so close to a convenient - and legal - garbage dumpster. But then, when Leslie found him, what would she do with him? She wouldn't feel comfortable leaving him there, especially not after coming all this way. Dumping him in the Ohio River seemed the only logical option, if logic could be applied to the situation. Of course, they had to get him to the river. Leslie slumped back into her dismal corner.

Would Crazy Sam help? Maybe Ed was buttering him up. She peered around Anna and saw Ed passing a bottle to Sam. Great. Colin? He might help. He seemed to like Anna, but Anna would never tell him what they were doing. Leslie would, though. With his assistance and a little luck, they might accomplish their mission and make it home safely without anyone being the wiser.

"Man," Crazy Sam called back to them. "You could populate a small country with this crowd."

Good, thought Leslie. *That significantly decreases the odds of seeing my parents.*

Odds are strange. Had she been looking out the window, she would have seen her family passing in the westbound lane as they headed home.

***

"We have an idea," Anna told Leslie as they waited in traffic. "We?"

"Yeah, well, I told Colin what's going on," Anna looked at the floor, shyly. Colin smiled, nodding.

"You did? So I guess you think we're nuts?" Leslie asked.

323

Colin shrugged. "If it had been anyone else but Anna, I would."

"Uh huh," Leslie said, surprised by her irritable tone. "Did she tell you we're trying to kill a mannequin? That we wrecked the car and slept in the woods?" Colin nodded as she spoke. "And you're still here?" She scrunched her face and looked at Anna. "Gee, I wonder why?"

"Les, come on. Colin wants to help us." Leslie glanced away, ashamed by her crabbiness. "He's going to loan us money to get Crazy Sam to help us, uh, dispose of Bruce, then drive us back to the restaurant so we can get Bret pulled out and find a tire. If Sam won't help, then we'll rent a car. Colin has an ATM card."

"Let's hope a tire is all it needs," Colin added.

"What're you guys talking about?" Crazy Sam's girlfriend, Cissy, interrupted.

"Business," Colin said.

"Sam ain't taking you nowhere," she said with slurry words. "He promised to take me on the rides!" She stared at Colin a moment then burst into laughter. Everyone joined in, although Leslie felt as if she'd missed something. When a little giggle gnawed at her she understood what was so funny, and why Anna had told Colin about their ridiculous predicament: they were all stoned. Riding an hour in an unventilated van with at least two joints burning at all times, and who knew how much carbon monoxide, was having an effect on them all.

Colin got to his knees and shuffled to the front. Propped between the two captain's chairs, he talked to Sam while Anna and Leslie strained to hear. Sam's words were buried under the sound of the motor and music, but it was easy enough to understand that he wasn't interested. There was more talking; Leslie rose to her knees to look out the window. On the left side, the parking lot stretched endlessly in either direction. Out the front window, she saw they were in a long line of traffic. Cars heading for the Galaxy were being diverted into a special lane. A wide pedestrian skywalk spanned the road, permitting access to those staying at the numerous motels and campgrounds along the road, including Grady's Galaxy Inn and the Galaxy Motor Lodge, which Leslie could see coming up on the right.

"Here's what we'll do," Anna said, jerking Leslie's shirt so she would sit back down. "We'll go to the trailer park, find the trailer and search the whole stinking place. We'll check the dumpster and if he's not there we'll ask people it they've seen him. When we find him, we'll take him to the river and sink him."

"What if we can't find him?"

Anna sighed loudly as she thought about it. By now everyone was listening to their conversation, though it was doubtful anyone followed it. "Well, then that has to mean they already found him and pitched him somewhere."

Leslie nodded absently. She was thirsty and wanted fresh air.

Colin shuffled back. "Change in plans, folks. Seems Sam's all excited about the riding the Rocket. But, for a modest fee, he is allowing me to chauffeur you. Alex, I need you to loan me some cash until I can get to an ATM."

"You ain't leaving me here with these clowns," Alex said, pulling out his wallet.

"Then come with us. Besides, we might need you to check out the car. Three hours tops. We'll be back before two." When Alex started to whine again, Colin reasoned, "We're gonna be here till midnight."

"No," said the girl named Michelle. "Come with me, Alex."

Alex looked at Colin, his mind made up. "We're supposed to meet Lardo and Crane."

"Oh, go on," Colin waved him off.

"What's a modest fee?" Leslie asked, tugging Colin's shirt sleeve.

"It's probably cheaper than renting a car."

"How much?"

"Um, you don't want to know."

"If I have to pay you back, you better believe I want to know."

"A hundred bucks, plus it has to have a full tank upon return." Her jaw dropped.

"What else can we do?" Anna asked her. Leslie threw up her hands with indifference.

"Where are your folks staying?"

"The Galaxy Motor Lodge."

"There?" Colin pointed to the sign coming up on the right. She nodded. "Hey, Sam?" He knee-shuffled back to the driver, pleading as he went. Suddenly everyone and everything was flung left as Sam charged out of the Galaxy lane and onto the main road.

"What are you doing?" Cissy demanded to know.

"Don't worry about it!" Sam answered, his hand out to steady

Ed. Colin lost his balance, and landed on his rear. He scooted over to Anna.

"I think your uncle's wasted," he said to Leslie.

"He's not my uncle," Leslie muttered. Again they swayed left as Sam cut across another lane to the Galaxy Motor Lodge.

"Well, kids, here's where we part company. Everyone knows when and where to meet? The skywalk at 12:30. Colin, I trust I don't have to tell you what the consequences will be if you are not back. Suffice it to say, I will report the car stolen. Come on everyone, we're gonna take a little stroll."

"What?" Cissy groaned. "I'm not walking!"

"Yes, you are. Upsy daisy. Let's go." As everyone filed out, protesting, Sam held out his hands palm up; keys on one, the other empty. Colin placed the money on the empty hand and took the keys. Before leaving them, Sam slapped Ed on the shoulder. "Good luck, old timer. I don't know what you guys are up to, but don't bust up my bus. See ya back in Salem."

"I need some air," Leslie climbed out the side door. Ed stayed in his seat, his head back, eyes closed. Leslie waved a hand at him. "This is great."

"He'll be all right," Colin said. He opened the passenger door and rolled down the window.

"Look," Anna pointed to the visitor check in gate.

"I think we should walk through," Leslie said. "I need to stretch."

"But what if your folks see you?"

"They won't. You think Becky'd let them sit here when the park is open? They were probably first in line."

"But if we find Bruce, we'll need the van."

"Okay," Leslie conceded, getting back inside. On the floor, on their knees, she and Anna each took a window as Colin drove to the visitor gate.

"Morning," the guard said. "Can I help you?"

Colin sat dumbly. "Vickers," Leslie and Anna called. "Vickers," Colin repeated. "We're with the Vickers. They're staying here." The guard checked the list he was given when he went on duty at 8:00 AM. He produced a card and handed it over.

"They are in lot 12 F. There's a map on the back of the visitor's pass. Keep it on your dash." Colin nodded. "Have a good day!" the guard said as they pulled away.

They drove slowly through the campground, Anna and Leslie peeking out the side windows like periscopes. The map on the parking pass wasn't necessary, the campground was so well marked a chimpanzee could find its way to 12 F. There were trailers and tents in every lot, but it appeared devoid of people. At row 12, they turned in the direction marked A-N. The lot next to the big red F was empty.

"Anna," Leslie whimpered. "They didn't make it."

Anna hurried to put her arm around her. "We don't know that. The gateman said they were here."

"But they had reservations for today."

"Let's go ask at the office," Colin said. Leslie's face stuck to the glass, looking at the place her family should have been.

***

Across the street, Barker paced wildly through the crowds. He thought he smelled her, but the crowds were maddening, distorting his senses. How could he find anyone? Reluctantly, he stood in a line. She was here, somewhere.

In the next line, a child stared at him. His mother noticed, and admonished him with a jerk to a lock of his hair. When she looked into Barker's face, her eyes widened, and she turned her attention back to the boy. Albert must be showing signs of wear, Barker thought. He didn't need to attract attention; people were plentiful here, but not abundantly available. He rubbed at eyes that were likely to be drying up or rolling back. The fingers were stiff, but Barker had kept Albert moving, so he wasn't too decayed. Not yet. Still, he better start watching for a new body.

***

Leslie, Anna and Colin parked in front of the campground office. Inside the log cabin-style building was a souvenir shop stocked with a number of items bearing the Galaxy logo: Coffee mugs, floating ink pens, fly swatters, pennants, polished rocks, and an entire corner dedicated to aromatic cedar artwork.

Leslie stepped to the counter, smiling nonchalantly. The woman at the counter smiled back and offered her assistance.

"I'm here to visit the Vickers, but their lot is empty. Is 12 F right?" She held her tone steady.

"Hmm. Let's see." The woman tapped at a computer and after a moment said, "Aw, you just missed them. They checked out about half an hour ago."

"They did? Did they say why?"

"Well, I don't know for sure. Looks like Ben checked them out. He's around somewhere. Should I page him?"

"Do you mind? I mean, they're supposed to be at the Galaxy today, and I'm kind of worried."

"Oh, I bet I know what they did. Check out time is noon, so lots of people just drive across the street and pay to park over there. Otherwise they have to pay for another day here," she explained.

"Of course," Leslie spun around and grabbed Anna's elbow. "I'll bet that's exactly what they did! Dad didn't want to stay here another night because it's so expensive—" She realized the clerk was listening and she lowered her voice and ushered Colin and Anna to the cedar corner.

"He was complaining because the prices are so high. I'll bet he called Piney Grove and got a place there tonight."

"Would he do that?" Colin asked.

"Heck yeah. It wouldn't take long to get there from here. Believe me, one yawn from Becky and he'll move 'em out. Besides, if they stayed here tonight, then they'd have to go back to the Galaxy tomorrow or Becky'd have a fit."

"That means they've dumped off Bruce," Anna added.

"Oh, man. I feel better," Leslie said.

"Then let's go," said Colin.

On the way out, Leslie waved to the clerk. "Thanks," she said.

"It's okay, darlin'. Gonna go to the park?"

"I wish. Say, you didn't have a mannequin in your trash today?"

"A what?"

"Can we look in your dumpster?"

"Well, I guess. It's around back of here."

"Come on, Les," Anna dragged her from the store. They all waved goodbye to the clerk. Leslie led the way to the back of the building. Behind a maintenance shed were two large dumpsters where the trash from each campsite was deposited each day. Both were half full, and neither contained a mannequin. Leslie practically crawled inside to verify that he wasn't present.

"Les, they probably found him before they left your grandma's," Anna said.

"Yeah," Colin agreed. "At least you know they're okay."

As they walked to the van, Leslie kept looking over her shoulder toward the park. Finally she spoke her mind. "Can we drive around the parking lot? I mean, we're all the way here, and it's an ugly trailer. We can't miss it."

Colin harrumphed and made a face Anna understood. "Les, it costs five bucks just to drive through the gate."

"We can walk over," Colin suggested.

"Yeah," Leslie quickly agreed. "Let's scope the lot from the skywalk as long as we're here."

"Okay, but let's get moving." Anna's buzz had apparently worn off, but Leslie could tell she was trying to hide her frustration from Colin.

Because of Ed's snoring, and because they did not want Crazy Sam's van towed away, they drove to the farthest end of the Galaxy Motor Lodge's parking lot and pulled into a slot beside an old station wagon with tinted windows. It was their intention to hurry before the van was noticed. Parking pass or not, the Motor Lodge certainly wouldn't appreciate them leaving it there, even for a short time, according to the dozens of red lettered signs posted about the lot. They made their way to the sidewalk, scurrying quickly past the office, and fell in behind a small crowd. At the skywalk, the small crowd merged with another coming from the other direction. Any other day, the chatter of those around her and the view of the park from the skywalk would stir delight in Leslie, but she was preoccupied with finding the trailer. She needed reassurance that her family was enjoying themselves in the park, and not...what? Although Leslie had found the nerve to insist they look for the trailer, she could not cough up the courage to say what was really on her mind. Yes, she thought it likely that her parents had found Bruce last night and disposed of him. But not finding him in the dumpster worried her. Could he somehow make his way back to them? At least they had moved across the street, but was that far enough? If Ed was right and Bruce was connected in some way to the Itch, and if her family was related to the Vanderkellens, then Bruce would be determined to reach them. She thought about that, once more realizing the ludicrous turns her mind was taking. She decided to remain silent about her worries because Anna wasn't going to humor her any more.

She paused to look out the massive windows at the traffic below. Beyond, the park seemed to be a living creature, waving its flags, spinning the arms of a dozen rides, pushing the cars of the roller coaster up the first steep hill with a steady pulse, its voice a chorus of delirious screams. Leslie could almost feel its heartbeat, a *thump thump thump* under her feet.

"Is this thing shaking?" Anna asked.

***

The line where Barker waited grew shorter, as did his temper. How would he find the Vanderkellen in this mess? People pressed close, their smells suffocating, their voices irritating. His discomfort was further aggravated by Albert's frail corpse. After barely ten minutes standing in line, Albert began stiffening. And itching! That was odd, because his receptors were dead; the only electricity coursing through the body was that generated by Barker, and he was being conservative. Imagination, he assumed, helped along by the glutinous demons. He was also mortified because Albert's clothes were becoming tight. He had experienced this before, but never in a crowded place like this.

The decision to leave the line came too late. A large amount of gas escaped his body, first from one end, then the other. With no hope of remaining inconspicuous, he fled from the line, away from the people and into the parking lot.

That's when he smelled it. He sniffed at the air, excitedly inhaling the stench. Not his own, but that of the Vanderkellen. She was out here! He made his way across the parking lot, his nose high in the air.

There! Definitely. No, losing it. This way! *Move, people!* Weaving across the lot, bumping into cars, he tracked her energy. Once, it had protected her; now it announced her arrival. But this place! The people! Their signals infected the atmosphere, and her energy hit them and bounced away, touched them and blended so he couldn't pinpoint it.

He reached the edge of the parking lot, stopped by the high chain fence. Across the street was the Galaxy Motor Lodge. He could shout to Walter from here, but his voice would be obliterated by the shrieks and the cars and the horns.

He grabbed the fence and shook it, then let go, spinning in all directions, trying to get a fix on her. There! At the skywalk? No! A continuous flow of people dismounted the steps and filed to the ticket booths like ants to a picnic. Where was she? Where? But then what could he do with her in this rancid, bloated body? Even he couldn't stand the smell of himself.

"We told you not to kill him!" said a demon on his back.

"Such an idiot. Let's send him off."

"Leave me alone!" Barker cried. The itching drove him mad, the tight waistband made him angry, the odor gagged him. He pressed the heels of his hands against his eyes, trying to clear his thoughts, and the eyeballs sank deep into their sockets.

"Look at all the dumplings! Let's fix them!"

"Let's fix him, too!"

Barker's misery was interrupted by a jolt that sent him into the air. Below him, Albert's body slumped, then fell, while Barker kept rising, twisting, tumbling as his being was pulled apart. Faster he went, the demons dragging him high, gyrating him with a velocity that shook him to pieces. They hooted, pinching and scratching, then they let go, and off he went, shooting ever higher, screaming. The sound of his anguish exploded into thunder, the wind of his voice shook the ground. He squeezed the rage from his heart and it spewed across the sky. Around him, he saw demons streaking all about. Not the little ones, but big, ferocious, angry shapeless creatures that darkened the sky. The roller coaster shook and crumbled, the cars unzipping from the tracks. The Ferris wheel teetered against the blast, pieces of it snapping off, flying away like tissue. The skywalk convulsed, and Barker's scream was silenced by his own terror and confusion as he lost his buoyancy.

His fall was meteoric, but eventually slowed as he was caught in the breezes left by the attack. Were they still here? What had summoned them? Was his time up? Were they looking for him? Panicked, he searched for a host. Certainly there would be plenty now, but there was no time to locate one that wasn't broken.

Scanning the ground below, he saw *them* for the first time. The invisible ones. For a fleeting moment, they appeared before him, sharp points of light stabbing the atmosphere. He heard cries of agony, not of the humans, but of the demons, as they were cast out. Then the other world became silent.

A small gust carried him toward a stand of trees, and there, using more strength than he could spare, he grabbed onto a bird. *Please, please,* he begged. *Just let me rest.* The bird didn't understand, and flew from the tree, terrified. Barker bore down, holding tight, forcing it to land.

"Well, isn't this great," a voice said from above. Barker looked and saw one of the pink demons clinging to a branch. "Now they're mad at us for helping you. You better get this done and do it right!" Barker could only stare back mutely. "You idiot," the demon said. "Go back to Albert's car. There's a surprise for you. If you mess this up now, then you are even stupider than I thought." Barker sat still, needing a minute to digest everything, but the demon yelled, "Go!" sending the bird fluttering from the tree.

Beneath him, Barker saw the motor lodge with its rows of aluminum campers, and then, Albert's old station wagon. As much as he despised Walter, he was the only thing familiar to Barker in this horrible, noisy place. He brought the bird down, both of them confused and agitated, and sat on the station wagon. Breathing Walter's fear calmed him. Tightening his grip on the bird, he surveyed the damage as it could be seen from the roof of the station wagon. It would be easy to find a body now. As soon as he regained his composure, he would fly over and pick a nice, handsome boy to lure the Vanderkellen back to the cemetery.

Hoping to avoid going to the park to find a host, he scanned the people from the Motor Lodge who had come to the parking lot to see what had happened. They called out questions and exclamations, adding to the noise. Close by, Barker heard a groan.

Close?

A groan and a *snuffle?* And a *snort?* He turned the little bird's head toward the vehicle parked next to him. Inside, an old man twisted his body, stretching. A grizzly man with a straggly, yellow-gray beard and matching hair. He yawned, showing his discolored dentures, and opened his glassy eyes. Barker stared into his face.

***

Ed woke up slowly. Last night's adventure, trying to sleep on the hood of the car, and his frequent morning 'sips' left him wrung like a rag. He knew where he was, and had a faint memory of Leslie and Anna walking off with that boy. Where was Crazy Sam? What was that noise? Sirens? Had there been an accident?

His body ached when he stretched, his eyes burned as they opened. Outside the window was the queerest thing; a little bird cocked its head, staring straight at him.

At that precise moment the wind was knocked from his body. *Sucker punched!* he thought, but how? *An ambush! Crazy Sam had set him up!* He couldn't see! *Open your eyes!* But they were open! It was dark, so dark. He felt around, amazed by his fluid movement. The darkness was fading to—to nothing! Grayness, or dust, he couldn't tell which, enveloped him. He reached ahead, behind, beneath. Nothing! White speckles against black. Static. Death, he thought, surely this is death.

There came laughter! Crazy Sam? Where were Leslie and Anna? Was Crazy Sam a killer? Where were the others? What was happening?

It struck him then; the Itch had found them. It had known they were coming and waited. Somehow, it took hold of Crazy Sam, or maybe one of the others, and now they had her. He knew it was going to happen; after all, he spent the morning preparing for it. He just hadn't planned on regaining consciousness.

The laughter continued, closer now, and Ed suffered a brutal kick to the side. He yelped. All logic was stifled by that feral laughter that came from within, as if he wore headphones. A face appeared before him, darker than the grayness, and featureless.

"Take me to her and we'll be done with it," it said.

"What?" Ed whimpered. Another kick.

"You don't quite understand, do you, Ed?" There was a pause, then a chuckle. "Oh, yes. I see you do understand. But you are not *comprehending*! Tell me now Ed, where is she?"

Ed's head tightened, his bowels churned as though full of worms. The empty face fixed on him, *forced* itself on him, *invaded* him. Clammy tendrils prodded his confused thoughts, then pushed them away. Ed remembered his original mission, and realized what the face wanted from him.

"Where is she?" it demanded and Ed grit his teeth, and squeezed his eyes shut.

"Don't insult me with your pitiful attempts to keep me out. Nothing can stop me," the voice circled him. "Look."

Ed did. He saw himself, forty years younger, at a barstool with Jerry Templeton. Closer, closer. Jerry laughing, then falling. Ed shut his eyes again.

"Look!"

Ed refused, but he saw anyway. A door swinging open onto

the night. Holly Vickers's concerned face waiting, young Judy Redmond behind her. Holly slammed against the railing, falling, falling, her eyes round with surprise and pain.

"Any doubts who you're dealing with? Now show her to me!" Ed shook his head and wondered if he were really shaking his head. He bravely opened his eyes, but just barely. Everything was muddled, unfocused.

"I don't have time for this," the voice said. The world shifted, sending Ed reeling. His mind was cloudy from the alcohol, and he wished he could throw up. He needed a minute to assess things. The only thing he grasped so far was that he had become exactly what he had been running from.

Bracing himself in space, a mental trick he mastered unconsciously, he concentrated on his vision. Filtered light glowed above, illuminating rocky walls. A cavern? Could he manage a climb? He looked for an easy route and as he wished for it, there appeared a stair cut into the wall. Very surreal. Was he dreaming? He lifted his face toward the light, and wished to go. The mere idea rose him. Once in the light, he was able to see. But no, this was not his hand trying to open the door of a station wagon.

"Confounded thing!" said his own voice, miles distant. Then, inside, the other voice said, "Old man, we have some things to do before you show me the Vanderkellen."

Ed did not respond. He watched the street getting closer, and the chain link fence surrounding the big parking lot grew larger.

Think! Think! he told himself. Everything was happening too fast! He didn't have time to wonder about his predicament, let alone decide what to do about it. And what about Leslie?

No! He must not think about her! This entity was searching for her. Apparently it didn't know who she was…wait. It didn't know! It was inside him, it read some of his memories. It showed Ed things. But Ed had been able to shut him out. The entity claimed he hadn't, but obviously he did. That's why he was kicked.

Kicked? How could that have been? He was discorporate, yet still within himself. He thought of the stairs in the rock wall, the floating. He was creating his own physical reality. He looked at his hands. They were there, as he expected. He clapped them together. *Clap.* They don't have to clap, he thought. They aren't real. He did it again.

They passed through each other.

He made them clasp each other. He pulled, and his forearms stretched. He twisted his finger, twisted and twisted until it broke off.

No pain. When he looked again, his finger was back, his hand, normal.

In a way he was glad he had the bourbon. It made the whole insane situation easier to accept. A sober man would have gone mad.

Suddenly, he did feel pain in his hands! Not severe, but definite. How? He looked outside himself and saw his bloody fingers picking at the wire on top of the fence. They were climbing over and down. An old man lay on the asphalt.

They needed the keys.

Now how did he know that?

"Get out!"

Ed jumped back. Did the door swing both ways? Could he reach into his attacker and confirm his identity? Was he, as Ed suspected, John Barker coming to kill the Vanderkellen? Is this how the Itch worked?

He decided to take a chance. Concentrating on mentally manipulating his surroundings, he conjured up his earlier thought of the door swinging both ways. He held that image, crept closer to it, and said, "John Barker?"

"Who else did you expect?" came the angry reply, along with a blast that nearly blew the door in.

"Just asking," Ed timidly backed away. He looked outside himself. They were in the Galaxy's parking lot, next to the old man's body, surveying the crowd. What was going on? The sirens continued screaming. People scurried everywhere.

Pounding at the imaginary door interrupted his observations. The door bowed at the middle. Ed leaned against it, but the pounding went on, harder. He would not be able to keep this up. How could he secure the door? If it were a real door, he could use a chair under the knob.

Wait a minute. This is real. And if Leslie were really at his apartment, and Barker was at the door, he would hide her, or get her out. But there was no backdoor, and even if there were, Barker might catch her. He would have to hide her and every scrap of her being. Where in the apartment would she be safe? A safe. Of course! He made the door, and now he made a safe. As idiotic as it seemed, he took his briefcase full of Leslie's history and put it inside. Then he sat on it, just as he saw he hadn't locked the door.

It crashed inward, the wind whipping Ed fiercely. Parts of himself were hurled about and flung against make-believe walls, but he held to the safe and it remained strong. He gave up everything in order to keep it.

"Tell me where she is!"

There was no time for inspiration; he had to act in a hurry. Leslie would eventually head west, back to Miltonville. He would instruct Barker to head east. Or south. How much time did Barker have to find her? He couldn't roam the earth endlessly, could he? And if he could, what did that mean for Ed?

No matter now, he needed an idea. In its semi-drunken state, his mind was flexible, so outrageous schemes seemed almost feasible. Plotting a hasty strategy, he looked to see what Barker was up to. Barker was excited, sniffing the air, heading toward the skywalk. The skywalk? That couldn't be the skywalk. It was in pieces!

What happened here? He wondered, not remembering to keep his thought to himself. Barker didn't notice; his interest was elsewhere. Ed cringed, afraid to think all this destruction could have been caused by the Itch, that he may have inadvertently brought on this devastation by taking Leslie out of Miltonville. What had he done? Was her life worth all this?

"Whose life? What did you say?"

"I said, if you're looking for the Vanderkellen, what are you doing here?" Ed ventured, then carefully added, "Oh, I see. Never mind."

"Shut up you old fool. I smell her vile presence."

"Really? Interesting."

"Quit playing, old man." A pause. "What? What's so interesting?"

Ed squelched his excitement.

That's when he heard his name, and saw the boy from the van, the one Anna liked, running toward him. Ed shut his eyes and tried to disappear. That was one mental trick he couldn't perform.

***

When the skywalk started shaking, Anna, Leslie and Colin held tight to the metal railing inside the wall. When it became apparent it was not going to stop shaking, Anna let loose and shoved her friends back toward the stairs. The run down the two short flights was treacherous. A young couple gripped the handrail on the landing, and found themselves being swept away with the little group. They shouted that during a tornado the stairs were the safest place to be.

"It's an earthquake," Colin yelled back.

"Didn't you feel the wind?" the man argued. The woman screamed for everyone to shut up.

They stumbled off the steps as a whole and the wind pummeled them as soon as they were out of the shelter of the skywalk. Their eyes closed to slits. Debris flew in amazing spirals of mini-twisters, garbage sailed by, first low, then high. The man continued to bellow, but remained linked to his wife, the end of a chain that Colin pulled.

"We need a ditch!" Anna yelled, her voice riding away on the wind.

"What?" Colin yelled back.

"I told you we shoulda stayed put!" the man bawled while his wife colored the air blue.

"There!" Anna pointed to a grassy ditch, and the group changed direction.

They didn't make it.

The roaring gusts stopped abruptly. The five halted, one by one, running into each other. They stood, still holding hands, paper skittering at their feet. The wail of car alarms assaulted their ears, a bizarre accompaniment to the screams from the park.

The man and woman held each other. They all stared at the broken skywalk and the strewn banners, their joyful colors grotesque and obscene. The clouds overhead broke apart, and the sun set the cars in the parking lot to sparkling. Time compensated for its earlier speed by slowing to allow a small eternity to pass while they stood dumbly.

There was shouting from the skywalk and Anna was on her way before Leslie could speak, Colin on her heels. Leslie ran after them and they dashed up the steps.

The skywalk still bridged the road, but hunks had fallen out and parts of the roof and some of the glass wall sprinkled the highway. The walk was not crowded when the storm came up, but there had been several people crossing ahead of them. They found them, scattered like the litter left by the storm, bloody and bruised, crawling and calling for each other. Amid the groans and cries, a woman shrieked. All heads turned. Some people rose on unsteady legs. Anna sprinted past. Leslie started to follow, but stopped when she saw a woman struggling to stand. Her leg was not cooperating. Leslie bent down, not sure what to do.

"Just be still. Help's on the way," she said.

"No, my son and husband. Where are they?" the woman asked, her gaze fixed on a place where a wall had once been. Leslie went cautiously to the edge of the walk. A few minutes ago, this had been a big tunnel, the walls and roof sturdy glass and steel. Now it was a craggy bridge, and Leslie was afraid to look over the side. She approached the edge cautiously, partly in fear of her safety, mostly in fear of what might lay below. They were there, the boy and the man. The boy was on the hood of a car, the man on the ground nearby, sitting up shaking his head. There were others down there, too. Thankfully, people were leaving their cars and circling the victims, kneeling down to comfort those they could. To her surprise, she saw the couple that ran with them from the skywalk tending to the boy, the woman running her fingers through his hair, talking to him, gently forcing him to stay down. The man Leslie assumed to be the father joined them. He held the boy's hand while looking around, dazed. Leslie waved until she caught his eye.

"They're okay," she shouted happily back to the woman, then shouted, "She's okay!" to the man. Either he didn't hear or it didn't register, because he continued staring.

"They fell?" the woman cried. "Help me get down there."

"Stay there. They're okay. It's a mess down there, but there's help everywhere. I'll get someone." Leslie impressed herself with her calmness. She began calling for help, unnoticed by those below.

***

Anna reached the shrieking woman with no idea what to do. The woman seemed to be all right physically. A little girl stood behind her, her white jumper splattered with blood. A man knelt before her, fighting several large pieces of glass and steel beneath which a boy lay in a growing pool of blood.

Another man approached from the other direction. Without words the two men, joined by Anna and Colin, worked at the glass, a huge segment of what was once the wall. It had landed on the child, pierced his midsection, and held its place, balanced on the remains of a metal frame that smashed the child's leg. Only a miracle had kept the boy from being cut in half.

Each took a corner. Colin said, "Anna? Is it going to be too heavy?" She tested it and shook her head. She wasn't offended; the consequences were not worth the risk of proving her strength against that of the men. "I'm pretty sure I can hold it," she said.

"Hurry!" the woman begged.

"Bring it around this way," said the man who knelt next to Anna, holding up the bottom corner. Everyone nodded. On three they lifted. It was very heavy, but worse than that, it was slick. Anna squeezed so tight her fingers cramped. She thought they would never lift it high enough, or be able to hold it long enough, to get it safely away from the boy. Mercifully, the metal frame on the boys leg clunked to the ground and wasn't an obstacle. She sucked her lips in and bit down, holding her breath. Again time slowed and her fingers ached all the way up her forearms. They all rose from their bent and half-squat positions and took mincing steps. Once they cleared the boy, they swung the glass around and leaned it against the wall.

The boy's mother practically threw herself on him, patting his face. He was bleeding heavily from both his leg and stomach. Page after page of anatomy class notes flipped through Anna's mind. She looked to Colin.

"Should we put a tourniquet on his leg?" she asked him. He looked at her helplessly. "I think so," he said.

"A belt?" Anna asked, but Colin had already removed a leather cord from around his neck and was tying off the leg. Anna was frightened because she remembered hearing somewhere this could be dangerous if not done correctly.

His mother had been gently prodding his stomach, and she pulled her shirt over her head and wadded it up. She pressed it against the wound, all the while talking to the unconscious boy. Her shrieking was over. The little girl stayed behind her, wearing a blank expression. The father knelt on the other side of the boy, telling him over and over he was going to be all right.

I should be doing something, Anna thought. Last year there had been a six week emergency medical training course. Basic, but intense. It had caught her attention, but she passed it up in order to devote time to a Theories in Biological Engineering seminar series. Not that she thought emergency medical training wasn't important, it was just impractical for her. Her career goals did not include direct patient care. She had chosen the safe and respectable field of genetics in order to avoid these calamities.

She looked from the bleeding boy to Colin, who was looking back at her with worried eyes, blood on his hands and face. Why couldn't this have been a genetic emergency?

"Here comes help!"

Anna turned and saw Leslie leading two women through the rubble. They didn't hesitate a second when they saw the boy. Gently, they backed the parents and spectators away and went to work, speaking softly to the boy and his family.

"What's his name?"

"How old is he?"

"Give me that? Hmm, here, Kate, hold...right there. Good!"

Anna watched them, fascinated by their cool demeanor as they went about their care. "Are you doctors?" she asked.

"Not quite," the first woman answered without taking her eyes off the boy. "Nurses. I'm Jane."

"I'm Anna." It was a stupid thing to say, but she was at a loss for words.

"Do me a big favor, Anna," said Jane. "Run down and tell one of the medics to get a stretcher up here. Pronto. Clue him in, okay?"

"I'll go with you," Colin said. Naturally, Leslie followed.

Finding a medic with a spare minute was more difficult than Jane insinuated it would be, but more emergency vehicles were arriving and eventually they found a team and led them to the boy.

"Anna?" Colin asked. She was mesmerized by the activity, by how smoothly Jane and the other nurse worked with the medics. "Hey, are you okay?" She didn't want to talk, so she nodded.

"Are you sure?" She nodded again. The boy was being placed on the stretcher, gingerly but with astonishing speed. Colin and Anna stepped back to make room when the paramedics brought the boy by. Jane patted Anna's shoulder and said, "Good job, Anna." Then they were off, following Leslie to tend to others.

Does my mom do that?!

"Anna?" Colin again interrupted her thoughts.

"Yeah?" She returned to reality and it smacked her hard. Her preoccupation with the little boy had distracted her from the surrounding tragedy. The view from the skywalk gave a clear perspective of the extent of the damage. The top of the building facade that disguised the ticket booths had disappeared. Rides missing arms stood ominously motionless amid the trees. Here and there smoke billowed on the park horizon.

"Look, I don't want to sound cold," said Colin. "I really want to see if I can find Alex."

"Yeah," she agreed. "We need to find Leslie's folks, too."

"Hey," Leslie made her way back to them. "This is really bad."

"Let's go see what's going on," Anna said, and they descended the skywalk. When they stepped onto the sidewalk inside the parking lot, they stood still, unsure where to go.

"How will we find anyone?" Anna asked. Colin shrugged. Leslie stared off into the park.

"Mom and Dad are probably back where the kiddy rides are. What about Ed? Think he's all right?" Leslie asked, just as Colin said, "Hey! There's your uncle!" Colin shouted his name, jogging away. A few yards distant, a dazed Ed walked toward them, his path crooked, his nose in the air, blood on his hands.

"He better be sober," Leslie said. Anna shook her head, doubtful.

Ed saw them when Colin called his name, but he looked as if he'd never seen them before. Then he smiled, a wide smile that didn't include his eyes. His gait became steady and he sped up to meet them.

"Are you okay? What happened to your hands?" Colin asked. Ed ignored his questions.

"We have to go," he said.

"Not yet!" Leslie said. "We have to find Mom and Dad."

"They're fine. Come on. We have to get Walter," he paused for a long time before finishing. "I mean, Bruce back to the cemetery."

"The cemetery? Bruce? What are you talking about? What happened to you? Why are you bleeding?" Leslie asked.

"We can't leave yet," Anna insisted. "We have to find Dan and Michele and Becky. And Colin has to find Alex."

"I'm not leaving until I see they're okay," Colin agreed.

"*Colin* does not have to go." Ed spat the name at them.

"Hey, man," Colin spat back. "*Colin* has the keys."

Ed dangled Albert's keys and shook them. "I have Bruce in the car." He seemed to be choosing his words slowly. Anna and Leslie cast each other a sideways glance.

"You have Bruce?" Leslie gasped. "Where was he?"

"Across the street. I think he was rather angry, wouldn't you say?" Ed waved his hand absently.

"Please don't insinuate he did this," Anna warned.

"Remember the story I was telling you? Here's the end: We have to put him in the building at that cemetery. You do."

"*What?*" Anna and Leslie said simultaneously. Colin, thoroughly confused, said over and over, "What's he talking about?"

"The last remaining Vanderkellen has to put him in the circle."

"The what? You mean the church?" Leslie interrupted.

"Whatever you call it. I believe that mannequin contains the spirit of John Barker. You know the story."

"Who's the last remaining Vanderkellen?" Leslie demanded.

Ed paused, looking first at Leslie, then Anna. Finally he said, "One of you. I'm not sure which. You'll both have to carry him in, I suppose, and lock him up."

"Oh come on!" Anna said. "This is ridiculous and we've got real problems this time."

"We'll do it, as soon as we find Mom and Dad," Leslie promised.

"No! We have to go now! There isn't time!"

"It's been two hundred years, Ed. It can wait a few hours," Anna said.

"Don't fight!" Leslie said. "She's right, Ed, it can wait. We're doomed anyway, once everyone finds out we're here."

"Excuse me folks," a police officer joined them. "I'm afraid we're going to have to ask you to go across the street. We need to clear the area."

"But my family is in there," said Leslie. "We have to find them."

He shook his head. "I'm sorry, but we have too many folks getting in the way. We can't get our crews through. Besides, they can use help over there. The motels are setting up wait stations. They need help tending to people and matching up lost people. Stuff like that. That'd be the best place for you now." Without giving them time to argue or agree, he ushered them toward the big gate. It was crowded with people picking their way around stuck cars.

"Let's go over there," Ed suggested, indicating the motor lodge. The place was bustling with volunteers. Colin led the way, anxious to get busy.

In front of the office, a pile of blankets and first aid supplies was accumulating. Many campers had left the Galaxy and raided their gear for anything of use. A table had been brought around, and was filling up with packages of donuts and cookies, complements of the guests. The clerk Leslie and Anna had spoken to earlier was there, bringing chairs from the big recreation lodge. Colin tapped her on the shoulder, "What can we do?"

She started to answer, then recognized them. "Hey, I'm glad you're back. I have news for you. I guess it's good, I don't know."

"What?" Leslie asked eagerly.

"Ben," she said as she scanned the faces milling about. "I don't know where he is. Anyway, Ben talked to, was it your dad? Vickers, right?" Leslie nodded. "Well, he came in right after you left. I didn't say anything to you, but he forgot to finish out the paperwork, so I guess it's good you asked or I wouldn't have noticed and there would have been a screw up with the credit card stuff. Ben hates that computer. Anyway, when I was showing him, I told him about you asking and all. He said they were heading *home*. Problems at home. I guess that part ain't so good."

Leslie blanched while Ed's grin widened.

"Did he say what?" Leslie persisted, ignoring Ed and his strange inappropriate smile.

"I don't know. If I see Ben, I'll ask and let you know." The clerk turned away to give instructions to a group of women.

"Problems at home," Leslie said, dismayed. "Do you think they found out we're gone? Maybe they think something happened? Like the Itch?"

"Maybe something happened in Yellowbird? Maybe Joe shot Ray?" Anna offered, hopefully.

"We better get going."

"I agree," Ed said.

"Should we call?" Leslie wondered.

"No, what if it is a problem in Yellowbird? Then they'll never know we were gone."

"No matter what," Ed cut in, "we need to go. You don't realize how dangerous Bruce is."

"But what about Bret?" Leslie cried.

"Who?" Ed asked, his face contorted.

Colin spoke up, "We'll be back in Salem tomorrow. I have a friend with a truck, between him and Alex, we might be able to get it home. If it hasn't been towed already."

"Thanks Colin," Anna said.

"Okay," Leslie decided. "We came for Bruce. Let's take care of him and then worry about explaining this to our folks."

"Hey Ed," Anna said as he steered them toward the car. "Whose car is this?"

"Yeah, you didn't steal it, did you?" Leslie questioned.

"No. I got it from an old pervert named Albert."

"So where is he?" Colin asked.

"Who?"

"The pervert."

"Over there somewhere," Ed tipped his head toward the park.

At the car, Colin peered into the dark windows at Bruce's still form. Ed unlocked the car, and Leslie looked inside. "Yep, that's him. How on earth did you find him?"

"Long story," he started to climb in the driver's seat.

"Ed?" Leslie stopped him, incredulous. "You're going to drive?"

"Would you rather?"

Anna stepped in. "It's my turn."

"Fine," Ed said curtly. "I'll sit in the back and keep watch over Walter. I mean Bruce." He unlocked the back door and slid in.

"Whew," Leslie said over the roof of the car. Anna grimaced and shrugged.

"Well guys, it's been a real adventure," Colin smiled at Anna. She smiled back.

Leslie shook her head. "It really has, hasn't it?"

"Um, can I have your number? I mean about tomorrow, I can take you to the car and all. If you're up for another road trip," he said, his eyes on Anna.

"Excuse me!" Leslie spoke up. "It's *my* car! Why do you want to call Anna about *my* car?" Both their faces went red, and Leslie noted her objective had been achieved. "Oh, I'm kidding. See ya later, Colon."

"It's *Colin!*" Anna hissed, but Leslie was already in the car, belting up.

"Anyway, Colin, my number's in the book. And the school directory."

"Okay. Tomorrow then."

"Definitely. I hope Alex is okay. And the rest of them."

"Me too."

"Let me know..."

"I will."

"Come on!" Leslie and Ed chorused from the car.

"I'm sorry about all this," she said. "Be careful, all right."

"I'll be fine. You take care. I'm not real sure about your Uncle Ed."

"He's not my uncle," she reminded him.

He winked at her. "I know. Be extra careful."

***

It was slow getting onto the road, but once they wove their way into the westbound lane, the going was easier. Most of the clogged traffic was headed toward the park. Anna made up for her uptight attitude in other areas by being an absolute maniac behind the wheel. After they turned from Galaxy Boulevard to Pendelton, the road that took them to the highway, she drove heedless of the speed limit.

"Careful Anna! We're in a stolen car," Leslie warned.

"I think the cops are too busy to be watching speeders today. Ed, how did you get this car? If I do end up in jail, I'd like to have my story straight at least."

"Don't worry. If Albert reported me, I'd have to report him. It was a fair deal."

"I don't like this," Anna said. "If I weren't so tired and sore and—"

"Freaked out?" Leslie finished for her. "Can you believe what's happening? All those people hurt and we should be helping, not taking Bruce to the cemetery. I think I've lost the trail of reason somewhere."

"We were lucky to meet Colin."

"Yes Anna, *we* were very lucky to meet Colin," Leslie said. "You definitely owe Ed one. I do, too, actually. I'd be thrilled if you dumped Anal for Colon."

"It's Col*in*!" Anna growled, but laughed anyway. Her laughter was cut short when she caught sight of Ed in the rear view mirror.

He was glaring at the back of her head.

She remembered Colin's warning, and mashed the pedal farther.

***

While Dan Vickers tried to call Leslie from the Galaxy, Ryan Swift sat on the edge of Robby's bed watching MC refold his clothes. Robby paced impatiently in the hall. "Mom, we're gonna be late for the bus," he complained.

"You have time," she told him for the second time. After breakfast, she sent Ryan to his house to feed the cat and pack because he would be staying with his father. Ryan did so, careful to bring enough clothes to convince her he believed he would be going away. He was also careful to leave the back door unlocked.

"I guess you're all set," MC said to Ryan. "Are you sure you don't want to go with me to see your mom this morning?"

"No. You said she was okay. Besides, she's probably sleeping. I'll go at lunchtime." Ryan hated to lie to Mrs. Canwell, and especially hated for her to think he'd rather go swimming than see his mother, but he saw no other choice.

"Okay, then. I'll pick you up around quarter of twelve. Robby, make sure he's out of the pool and dressed."

"He will be. Come *on*," Robby ordered from the doorway.

"Okay," Ryan hopped off the bed and followed him down the steps.

"Ryan?" MC stopped him. "Won't you need these?"

"Huh? Oh, yeah. Thanks," he said, embarrassed, and snatched his swim trunks from her hands.

He caught up with Robby at the front door, and after calling goodbye to Mr. Canwell, they stepped out into the fresh morning. Robby breathed deeply, commenting, "It's a good day to swim."

"Yeah," Ryan answered vaguely. Robby filled the silence with a variety of observations about the morning. When they reached the bus stop, Ryan interrupted him. "You know what?"

"No, what?"

"I think I want to go see my mom."

"What? You better make up your mind, I hear the bus." Ryan heard it too.

"It might hurt her feelings if I don't visit her." He walked backward, waving. "I'll see you when my dad brings me back."

Robby threw his hands up in resignation.

The bus pulled off the highway into the Kitchen and rumbled slowly to where Robby waited. Ryan watched him climb aboard before running off Apple Street to Raisin. He found the house be-hind his and cut through the yard. Once safely home he sat on the floor and received a lonely Misty into his arms. After a few com-forting nuzzles, he sat her down, then went to look up the Redmond's number.

Someone picked up the phone on the first ring. A woman said an anxious hello. "Mrs. Redmond?" he asked.

"Who's calling?" her voice stiffened.

"Ryan Swift, ma'am," he said politely.

"Oh," the voice softened. "Mrs. Redmond isn't home yet, Ryan."

"Oh." He was never very good on the phone. There was a brief silence while he composed his next sentence. "I'll call back later."

"Maybe you shouldn't. We're trying to keep the phone open. But I'll tell her you called. It'll make her happy that you were concerned."

"Okay," he replied, not entirely sure what it was he okayed. Before he could venture any further, the phone clicked in his ear.

Next he called the hospital switchboard. Maybe Mrs. Redmond was at work. A cheerful voice greeted him.

"Is Mrs. Redmond there?" He was about to volunteer more information, but the cheery voice cut him off.

"I'm sorry. She's not here. May I ask who's calling?"

He panicked. He didn't want them telling his mother he was bugging Mrs. Redmond. Unable to fabricate a name, he hung up. Now what? His plan had been to talk to Mrs. Redmond and then go back to the Canwells, full of answers. He couldn't go back now, not with his dad coming in a few hours. Maybe he could hide here until his dad went home.

He wondered about the cemetery. Was Mrs. Redmond still there? Where was it? Robby said it was far, but Robby thought uptown was far, too, and Ryan could ride his bike there in five minutes if he was allowed on the highway.

His dad probably left a map around somewhere. Ryan set about searching. If he could figure out where the Vanderkellen cemetery was, he could ride his bike there. It may be for nothing, but he was curious. It was that, or go home with his dad.

***

Tom Redmond was again sitting at the kitchen window. Help-less. Nine thirty AM and already out of ideas. His home was full of relatives. They paced, snacked, chatted, their movements cautious and voices low.

"Well, she's taken the girls and run off," Barbara said, repeat-ing what everyone else had expressed at one point or another. "She'll be home as soon as she's sure the Itch is over."

"What do you think Wendell was doing up in Columbus?" Cousin Bill chimed in.

"Hmm hmm. Still in his uniform, I heard."

"Speaking of uniforms," Tom muttered as a cruiser came up the long gravel lane. He pushed back his chair. "Stay here."

He waited on the front porch, fighting for composure. The of-ficer left his car in the crowded drive, hitched his belt and nodded toward Tom. "Morning, Tom."

"Matt. Do you have news?" Tom asked half-eagerly, half-fear-fully.

"Maybe. Tell me what you think. We had a call this morning from Chester County, in Ohio. They found a car in the woods. They figure it blew a tire and went over an embankment. The car registers to Dan Vickers, but no one can reach him. Anna's purse was in the trunk. They called us to try and track him down. Make sure the car wasn't stolen or anything."

"Anna's purse?"

"Had her checkbook and wallet. Now don't panic, but one of them hit the windshield, and there was a lot of blood, but they apparently walked away. The thing is, no one has called for a tow yet."

"Anything else?" Tom asked mostly to conceal his worry.

"Well, I told them you had filed a missing persons on your wife, and asked him to check for any indication that she might be with them. Leslie Vickers's purse was there, too, and some clothes, and a briefcase full of newspaper clippings and stuff, really old. Weird stuff."

"It's not too weird if you know Leslie. She's a pack rat."

"Do you think Judy and the girls have taken off because of the Itch?"

"Seems that's the popular consensus, but no matter what ev-eryone believes, my wife does trust me enough to call."

"I'm just asking," the officer kicked at the dirt. "Look, Chester

County is looking around. I'll keep checking and I'll call the minute I hear anything."

"Thanks for stopping out. Sorry I bit your head off."

"It's okay. Hasn't been easy on anyone," Matt admitted.

"Yeah. We heard about Wendell. And the detective that—well, kind of got sick," Tom tapped his temple.

"Horn? At least he's better. Stopped talking, anyway. Doesn't really remember anything. Doctor said it was stress." A voice crackled over his radio. "I'll get back with you later." He left Tom standing in the drive with eight pairs of eyes watching from the kitchen window.

***

Red darkness covered him.

Alan Macklin hoped it was a dream. Clarity came, and when it did, he still hoped it was a dream.

Soft breathing on one side, the tick tick tick of an old fashioned alarm clock on the other. Oppressive heat, thick head, heavy limbs. Blond hair on the pillow next to him, smelling of stale smoke and sticky hair spray.

What was her name?

He rolled away from her and took in his surroundings. Heavy drapes filtered the sun into a room the color of a dying pink rose.

Sun! He searched out the alarm clock. Ten o'clock!

A princess phone sat next to the clock. He reached for it, and blindly pressed the number to his apartment. There were no messages.

Anna would be at work by now. He punched in the number, having memorized it although he never called her at work. With no regard to the sleeping female beside him, he asked for Anna.

"Anna's not here today," he was told. He hung up without explanation. Where was she? What had she done last night?

The blankets rustled. "Who you callin'?"

"No one. Go back to sleep." Was it Mandy? Micky?

He tried Leslie's house. The answering machine rewound for almost five minutes. He hung up. He would wait before calling Anna's house.

Fumbling around the dark room, he scooped his clothes from the floor. Quietly, he opened the door and stole down the hall. Find-

ing the cluttered bathroom, he dressed, preparing for a swift get-
away.

As he passed through the living room, he was surprised to find
children watching cartoons. A woman appeared in a doorway,
dishtowel in her hands.

"Hi, sleepyhead. Can I get you some breakfast?"

Alan stared at her, stunned.

"I'm Shelly's mom." When he didn't answer, she added, "You
know, Shelly. The girl you were sleeping with?"

"Oh," he stammered. "Sorry. I'm kinda out of it."

"That's all right. Coffee? I'm sorry, I didn't get your name."

"Steve. And thanks, but I'm late for work," he backed away.

"Stop back later, then," she invited, but he was gone, out the
door, pretending not to have heard. His car was at the curb, half on
it, actually. He had not the slightest idea where he was. Oakdale,
maybe, judging by the number of toys and broken cars lying about.
He drove off in a hurry, not worried about the direction he was headed.

The adrenaline rush lowered and his hangover rose. Thoughts
of where Anna might have spent the night heightened the headache
and caused his stomach to cramp. This would not be a good time for
a confrontation. He decided to go home and nurse his hangover before talking to her.

***

The hospital room was bright, even with the lights off. Jaime's
headache had ebbed slightly. If only her parents would leave for a
while. She could no longer convince herself that the dreams she
experienced throughout the night were self-concocted. How wonderful it would be to have some time to herself without the distraction of her parents' worry.

Unfortunately, it looked as if she would be at their mercy for
the next few days. After her horrible night alone in the hospital,
she told them she wanted to come home. They were extremely
agreeable. The doctor might release her today; it depended on her
feet. They were raw and sore, and she spent yesterday hooked up
to an antibiotic drip to fight infection. Walking was painful without support, and not recommended. Since waking, a wheelchair
was parked beside the bed and she was encouraged to use it. This
morning the nurse who changed her bandages assured her she had

improved much in the short time since her arrival.

Physically, she was better. But her insides ached with frustration. She wanted desperately to discuss her experience, but with whom? Everyone kept asking what she remembered, but if she told them the tiniest bit, they would call a psychiatrist.

Then also, there was that thing with Whit.

She wasn't sure what happened to him, everything went so fast. Vaguely, she could see him being flung through the air. She had no recollection of seeing him get to his feet. Rubin running, yes. Theresa and Sandy arguing with her, yes. The Master calling her Claire and brushing her off, yes. Of course, he was not the Master. His name was John Barker, the man in the legend. At first, she thought there was another woman there, until she discovered the other woman was herself. She had become John Barker's married mistress, come to kill the Vanderkellen.

There was one person she could talk to. The woman across the hall. The woman who became Claire. The white haired nurse, Betty, said she was doing well, but was very achy and sleepy, just as Jaime had been.

"Do you remember being in the room with her?" Betty asked. Jaime lied and said no. "You were sure upset."

"Has anyone else come down with it?"

"Can't tell. We had an Itch, did you know?"

"My parents told me. Is that what was wrong with me?"

"No," the nurse smiled. "There's no such thing. I was kidding."

"But people died. Did they have what I did?" Jaime persisted. "Was anyone a Vanderkellen?"

Betty's expression showed surprise. "You've heard too many stories. I don't think you're going to die any time soon."

When her parents returned bearing balloons, the nurse disappeared. Since then, Jaime dozed while her parents chatted and watched television. It was almost ten. The doctor was due to dismiss her between 12:30 and 2:00. If she really wanted to talk to Cindy Swift, she should do it soon.

***

The same nurse who had earlier tended to Jaime's feet now flipped through Cindy Swift's chart. A weak voice said, "Nurse?" Betty put the chart down and went closer to the bed.

"Good morning," she said, watching Cindy carefully. "How do you feel?"

"My head hurts. Dry," she smacked her lips together. Betty poured a glass of water from the pitcher and poked a straw in the glass. "Go slow," she warned. "Could you go for some green gelatin?" Cindy nodded.

"Have you heard from my son? Ryan? Has he called?"

"I think. Tell you what, I'll go fetch you a little bite and on the way I'll check the desk and see what kind of messages were left."

Cindy nodded again. "Oh, wait. What is today?"

"Saturday. You asked that twice already today, did you know?"

"Sorry."

"Oh pish," Betty waved the apology away. "I'll be back in a few minutes."

Cindy attempted to push herself up, but it hurt her head. Then she discovered the magic button that controlled the bed, and she raised herself until she was practically sitting. She wished for a pencil and paper, but decided it was better if she didn't find one. Best not to record what she thought had occurred. A document like that could be used in court; Tim would rejoice to discover such an essay. A judge would have no choice but to have her put away.

Maybe they should. What had she been doing? Drinking so much with Ryan in the house? Did she take Mr. Willus's pills? Is that what put her here? Had yesterday been a hallucination? Or did she really loose control and fight with Ryan? With MC? It was more than losing control; it had been taken from her. Her entire body had been taken from her.

There were other things, images, memories of events she had never experienced. Was it some kind of reincarnation dream? Claire. Her name was Claire. Pregnant. Cindy could feel the heavy, bulging belly. Claire. Angry, hurt.

Much like she, Cindy, was angry and hurt.

Is this what multiple personality disorder was like? To be out of control, taken over, doing things totally alien? She remembered fighting Claire, afraid for Ryan.

Afraid she was going to do something to him.

Afraid *who* was going to do something to him?

It hurt to think. Sleep would be good. Sleep covered her like a blanket, wrapping her, taking her back to memories that belonged to another.

***

John Barker was delighted. Finally! Things weren't only going his way, they were absolutely carrying him along. He rested comfortably in the back seat of Albert's station wagon. Beside him, the plaster legs of Walter's body stuck up from the back, his toes pointing to the roof. The aroma of Walter's fear complemented the stink of the Vanderkellen. The moment could not be more perfect. Barker relaxed and almost enjoyed the scenery speeding past.

So far, the drunken sot Ed had not revealed the identity of the Vanderkellen, but so what? Both girls would carry him into the building, and maybe, somehow, he could get Claire to follow them.

During the ride, Barker observed Ed's personality and was now able to act more naturally. He watched Ed's past, saw his interest in Barker's history and his plan to save the Vanderkellen. *All for naught, old Ed! Now you'll die too, thanks to the silly Vanderkellen you love so much.*

And silly was a fitting term for the two women in the front seat. Their chatter was banal, their concerns inane. *Poor Bret*, sighed the fuzzy headed one. *He'll be fine*, promised the skinny one. They were talking about a car! Women their ages should be raising families, keeping households. These two had no substance in their lives; they talked of education (imagine!) and boys and food. Barker was doing the world a favor by ridding it of them.

"Your turn, Ed," Leslie turned around. "Who's your favorite?"

"Huh?" he grunted, caught off guard.

"Sorry. Were you asleep?" He shook his head, yawning for show. "Who's your favorite star?"

"Hmm. The north star, I suppose." How amusing, these two discussing astronomy.

"Oh, ha ha," Leslie smirked.

He chuckled along, wondering why. Had the north star disappeared? "Try again. Movie star? Or TV star?"

He kicked at Ed for help with these unfamiliar terms. Moving stars? Tevee stars? Ed gave him no help. He had drifted away, ignoring Barker and the conversation. Playing it safe, he shrugged. "I don't know."

"Me either," she said.

"We're close to 'E'," Anna announced. "Start looking for a gas station."

Barker knew gas stations. He'd been to several on this trip. He reached into Ed's jacket for the money he'd lifted off Albert. When he handed it over the seat, Leslie whooped.

"Have you been holding out on us?"

"Where'd you get that?" Anna asked.

"It came with the car. Don't worry about it."

"And exactly why did this guy give you money and a car? You still haven't told us."

"You don't want to know. He was a sick man." With that, he leaned his head against the window and pretended to nap.

***

Inside his own mind, Ed was rediscovering things long forgotten. At first, he believed he could manipulate Barker. Unfortunately, that reasoning was the result of his inebriation. Those effects were wearing off, though the aches lingered. As the futility of his situation sank in, he gave up. The safe he guarded containing his secrets about Leslie shrank first to the size of a shoe box, then to the size of a ring box, holding only the identity of the Vanderkellen, which Barker could easily guess should he bother to piece together the information available. Discouraged, Ed envisioned a bed and climbed in, stuffing the ring box under the pillow, wishing only for oblivion.

It didn't come. There would be no peace, no sleep.

He heard his mother. His ears perked at the music of her voice and he searched for the source. Clutching the ring box, he began to explore. This place within himself was cave-like, with tunnels running in all directions. Tunnels led into more tunnels and he followed them, in awe of what he found.

There was his sister, a vivacious little brat, years before the cancer devoured her. She marched about the living room, chanting, while he tried to read. *Yes, that's me!* The image startled him. Lanky and dark, his white shirt tucked into stiff jeans that were rolled at the cuffs. "*Susan shut up!*" he growled from his chair without raising his stare from the book. She didn't, and despite the aggravation she aroused in him as a child, he wished for her comfort right now.

Further he went, peering at grandparents and cousins long forgotten, picnics and holidays, school dances and girlfriends. One glance and suddenly he was living it over.

Eventually a young Jerry Templeton appeared. Ed saw him pushing Susan in a swing and urging her to *jump! jump! jump!* She whined that it was too high, but then she let go, the swing a catapult and she, a shrieking fireball. To a child, it must have seemed miles high - to him, it certainly did. Susan tumbled in the grass, landing first on her feet, then falling to her knees, stunned. When she realized she hadn't broken any bones, she laughed and shouted, "Eddie! Did you see me jump? I wanna go again!"

Then Susan again, older, thin, dying. "Why should I be mad at God?" she was saying. "Eddie, I've lived a blessed life."

"Blessed? You have cancer. Your husband left you—"

"Which was a blessing," she laughed. "Really, I still love God, cancer or not. I asked Him years ago to use me, and maybe He is. Who knows?"

"Yeah, I can see how dying is putting you to good use."

"If you knew God, you would understand. I wish you would find Him."

"If He wants me, He'll find me."

"Oh, He wants you, all right. But believe me, it's easier to find Him now than wait for Him to come after you."

"Save it for the angels, sis. It's too late for me."

"As long as you're breathing, it's not too late." She said it as if it were a promise. Her pale face faded into the bed sheets and she was gone. Would he see her again? Was there a place, other than memories, where the dead congregated? Or was this it? No, not for his sister. If Barker survived death, then surely she had passed through to Heaven. She was not dead, but maybe he was. Maybe he *had* waited too late, and now he was in Hell, his fate to relive every mistake he ever made, over and over.

***

Barker pressed his ear against the men's room wall at the gas station, listening to the conversation in the next room.

"Do you think I should call home and leave a message for Mom and Dad? So they know we're okay? Just in case they went home instead of Yellowbird? Or if Uncle Joe ratted us out?"

"Hmm. I forgot about Uncle Joe. Maybe you should. Maybe call your grandma's too." That was the skinny one talking.

"I'll wait and see what's going on at home first. Either way, I guess I'm busted. I hope they went to Yellowbird and end up staying there awhile. Then maybe I can get the car back before they find out I wrecked it."

"I hope so too. I don't want your mom and dad to be home when we get there."

"I'll call the house and leave an evasive 'I'm okay' kind of message. You know, 'heard you were heading home, don't worry, blah blah.' If they are going to Miltonville, we'll probably beat them home, as fast as you're driving."

"Yeah, well..."

"Do you think he's on medication? You know, when we left, we expected to be home before morning. He probably didn't bring any pills."

"I don't know. He's acting weird though. This thing with the car bugs me."

"Think he'll let me borrow it to get to work this afternoon?"

"If your dad hasn't killed you, you mean?"

"I'll be glad to get home and get this over with," the frizzy haired girl said.

Barker would be glad to get them home, too.

***

Barker was waiting in the car when the girls came out of the station. Leslie carried a plastic bag, which she began to unload as soon as she settled in the car.

"I didn't know what you wanted, Ed, so I got you a pop and some cookies and some potato chips." She passed the items back to him. Not wanting to attract attention, he tore open the cookies and stuffed them into his mouth.

Scrumptious! He munched them all, then fought with the potato chip bag. Leslie laughed and opened it for him. They were delicious! Barker hadn't tasted much of food in two hundred years, and he didn't remember it ever being so wonderful! Salty and sweet! No wonder Anna and Leslie talked about it so often. The soda pop can was another mystery that Leslie solved for him. He didn't care for it at all. The bubbles stung his nose.

"No," he said, handing it back to Leslie.

"No? I thought you liked that."

"No," he repeated.

She rolled down the window and held the can upside down, spilling the liquid as they drove. Then she put the empty can in the bag.

"Had enough?" He nodded and burped. "Gross! Go back to sleep," she ordered. He leaned back and listened to them babble on, plotting schemes that would never come to pass.

"Sleep sounds good right now," Anna said. "A hot bath, first. My shoulders and legs are so stiff."

"Maybe you should go to the doctor?"

"Nah, it's just strained muscles. Only time can heal."

"You should let me drive."

"I'm okay. Oh, crap!" She smacked her forehead. "I just remembered! Dad left a message for me last night."

"Oh, yeah," Leslie said. "I wonder if he called back."

"Probably. But he might have thought your machine was broken."

"Yeah. I think it beeped fifty times when I just called." There was a moment of quiet, then Leslie piped up, "Here's what we'll do. We'll get home at, say one-ish? Thank heaven for Daylight Savings! Call home and tell them you're sick and have been sleeping and didn't feel up to driving home."

"That'll work. If no one figures out we've been gone, anyway."

"Even if they know we didn't go home last night, they probably think we stayed at Alan's or something. They don't worry about us big girls anymore."

Barker smiled. He wasn't worried anymore, either.

***

Anna's father dozed in his easy chair while the family tiptoed around him. It relieved everyone to have him sleeping. His temper had grown short. Obviously Judy had taken Anna and Leslie away without telling him because he would have tried to persuade her to stay. But what about Ed Philips? Did he go along? Ed would have been supportive; he believed in the Itch. It made sense to the family, but they dare not speak of it. To Tom it seemed an accusation that Judy did not trust him, though this is not what they meant.

So they didn't talk about it. The fact that he was dozing, no matter how lightly, could mean that, perhaps, he too thought Judy and the girls were together.

That didn't necessarily mean they were safe.

Without a sound, Barbara glided past her sleeping brother and into the kitchen. She gathered snacks for the kids, who were playing exceptionally well together in the yard. The phone rang while her head was in the fridge, and she almost dropped the pitcher of tea in her haste to answer it before it woke Tom.

"Hello?" she whispered.

"Hello, is Anna there?" came a male voice.

"No, she's not. Can I ask who's calling?"

"Alan Macklin. Is she still at Leslie's?"

"Oh, Alan. We don't know. Have you heard from her at all?"

"No. But I haven't been home much."

"Well, they found Leslie's car over in Ohio and—"

"What?"

"In Ohio. And her mother's gone, too. We're so worried. The police—"

"The police? I'm coming over," he said.

"Oh, please, don't. She might try to reach you..."

"My roommate's here. I want to be there if she needs me," he insisted over her protest. When she hung up, Tom was behind her.

"Alan?"

"Yes."

"He's not coming over, is he?" Tom made no attempt to hide is displeasure.

"Looks so," she said, and tried to smile.

***

Judy Redmond wanted to die. It wasn't as though she hadn't tried. The tremendous pain went beyond agonizing. Unbearable might describe it, if not for the fact that she was bearing it. Occasionally there came a brief but welcome lack of consciousness, but the sharp contractions brought her back. Even her ability to travel through memories was lost to the pain.

Of course, Claire made it more difficult. She fought her labor, determined to keep the baby inside. Judy pushed against her, against the baby, trying to get it out. The baby kept her here, kept her from dying. Claire did not realize that the baby was her weakness; she saw it as a strength, a way to hold on to John Barker. Judy, observing Claire's history in much the same way one watches a movie, picked up things Claire missed.

Years ago, Claire had been very powerful, easily influencing people and killing them without a wince. She was as wicked as her husband in her devotion to John Barker, that's why she still existed as she did. But as the baby grew, he removed much of that evil and replaced it with something Claire didn't understand. A goodness, a disdain for causing ill on others. Claire could no longer pinch the life from a victim, nor could she endure the death of a host. It hurt her physically because the child could not stand it. The baby did not share the evil of its parents. It was its own entity, its own soul. And now, ready for birth, it sapped Claire and Judy both.

So the battle raged, Judy pushing, Claire restraining, and the baby waiting for nature to do what it would.

It was, after all, just a baby.

***

Cindy yawned, opening eyes that no longer ached. Her head did still, but not as much as before.

Reaching for the phone attached to the bed, intending to call Ryan, she caught sight of the gelatin the nurse left on her nightstand. Her stomach called for it. After dialing, she gobbled much of it before she even tasted it. When MC answered, Cindy had to gulp a mouthful before speaking.

"It's Cindy. Thanks so much for keeping Ryan."

"Cindy? My Lord, you sound great. Are you feeling okay?"

"Kinda groggy. And very embarrassed! I kind of remember yesterday. I'm really sorry. I honestly...well, I can't explain...well, I could, but you'd think I was crazy," she rambled.

"We have a lot to talk about," MC said, and her tone pierced Cindy's heart.

"What's going on? Is Ryan with you?"

"I sent him swimming with Robby this morning, but he's okay. Yesterday was hard on him. The problem is going to be Tim."

Cindy swallowed hard, waiting for MC to continue.

"Tim's coming for Ryan today at one. At the hospital, I better warn you. I couldn't talk him out of it. He's worried about you, and so am I. Why did I find Mr. Willus's pills in your robe?"

More silence while Cindy remembered why she had stolen the

pain medication from her patient. The bills. The divorce. Her tooth. The car. Her glasses. Now there would be hospital expenses. She hoped MC left the pills at the house.

"Cindy? We have to talk. Okay?"

"Yes," Cindy admitted, weakly.

"I'm bringing Ryan by at noon to see you before his dad comes. Is that okay?" MC's voice softened.

"Yes. Thanks for...thanks," Cindy said, biting back tears.

"Don't mention it. If you'd like, I can get him earlier so you can have more time. I didn't think you'd be feeling well enough."

"I'm not sure I am," she said weakly. "It's probably best if he spends the weekend with Tim. Just until I get myself together. I'm real sorry, MC." She thanked her again, and hung up, ready to cry, when she saw a young woman peeking around the door at her.

"I'm sorry," she apologized. "Can I talk to you?"

"Come in." The woman advanced, walking as if on hot coals, and sat in the cold vinyl chair.

She spoke hesitantly, "Do you know about Claire?"

Cindy felt the blood drain from her face. "Do you?"

Jaime nodded, her lip trembling.

"Then it's real?" Cindy asked, and Jaime all but leapt to the bed and they hugged and sobbed together.

"Glad to see you two have made up," Nurse Betty said as she passed by the door.

***

An extra hour of sleep caught at his apartment did wonders for Alan's disposition. Yes, he was still ticked at Anna, but he was able to recognize the opportunity her irresponsibility had laid at his feet. For some reason he couldn't fathom, he had always sensed a slight distaste for him from the elder Redmonds. Eventually it dawned on him that they were jealous of the things he could offer Anna. How petty. They should be happy that, as his wife, Anna would never have to work; she would be free to stay home and raise children - children who would never have to work in a dirty grocery store to pay for their education.

Today, he would take advantage of the situation and endear himself to the family. Let them see how concerned and caring he could be, how much Anna put him through, and how patient he was with her. If she was in trouble, he would offer to pay her way out. If she came stumbling in, bedraggled and hungover, he would admonish her for worrying them so, then help clean her up and tuck her in bed. Her parents would see how lucky she was to have him in her life.

***

"Okay, Darling, I'm ready," Teena announced as she waltzed into the living room. Tim caught his breath. No wonder it had taken her so long. The hairdo alone must have taken hours! Her dark hair, sleek in front, was pulled into a loose bun from which curls fell in strategic chaos. She wore a black suit, conservative and smart on top, short and daring at the bottom, ending in treacherous heels. Stunning.

"You're wearing *that* to the hospital?" he asked.

"I know, it's an old suit," Teena pouted.

"Hmm." He put aside his paper and guided her toward the door, feeling underdressed. "I really appreciate you coming, but you know you don't have to."

"Why do you keep saying that?" Her lower lip protruded. Within a blink her face lit into a smile. "I have an idea! Why don't we take Ryan to that new video-slash-pizza parlor for dinner tonight?" On the way to the car, she rattled off plans that seemed to pop into her head spontaneously.

Tim trailed behind her, not listening, wondering how he was going to get her to wait in the car while he visited Cindy in the hospital.

***

Jaime and Cindy spent an hour comparing notes on Claire. By noon they were certain of their sanity. There was only one thing Jaime held back from Cindy; her experience at the cemetery.

"I'm so glad you came," Cindy said to her. "I really thought I was nuts."

"I almost didn't. I was afraid you would think I was nuts."

"But who is the Vanderkellen?" they wondered together.

"It must be the girl across the street," Cindy deduced. "Her mom died in the last Itch. Everyone kind of forgets, because she calls her step-mother 'mom.'"

"She didn't know where she was going," Jaime thought back. "By morning I was so tired, I wanted to die. I was out of it a lot of the time. Everything hurt, and my stomach cramped from her baby, and even she was ready to give up. Then she sorta picked up the scent, I guess. My skin got prickly. And she knew she was close, and her husband was somewhere close, too."

"Yeah, she was screaming at him," Cindy jumped in, "but I didn't see him, and I was so worried about Ryan—"

"Oh gosh, I was so tired! I barely remember, but I think I just fell down—"

"What are we going to do?" Cindy stopped suddenly. It was wonderful to have someone to discuss this with, but now what?

"What do you mean? Tell someone?" Jaime asked.

"Well, we know all about the Itch. John Barker..."

"...and Claire..."

"...possessing sleeping people..."

"I wasn't asleep," Jaime corrected, then clammed up. She steered the conversation in a different direction. "I wonder where she is now?"

"Oh," Cindy bit her lip. "I don't know. Maybe that's when the Itch ended? Anyway, how did it happen with you?"

Jaime turned away. "I really don't want to talk about it."

"Why?" Cindy leaned toward her, concerned. "Was it...was it really bad? I was sort of, well, this will sound horrible, but so what? I was hungover when she hit me, maybe even still a little drunk. I didn't know what was going on."

Jaime turned back, her words reluctant. "I was drinking too. But it was worse than that. You'll hate me when I tell you, but I've gotta tell someone. Please, please don't tell anyone else." Cindy promised, and slowly the story of the weird cult came out.

***

MC was running late. It was after noon when she reached the Miltonville Activity Center. Ryan was supposed to be waiting. She didn't see him out front, so she went to the lobby. He wasn't there either.

A teenager sat behind a long counter, talking to a friend. She noticed MC and offered help.

"My son is Robby Canwell. He brought a friend today to swim."

"He did? He didn't have him check in," the girl said, excusing herself from her friend. "Let me go find Robby, okay?" MC found a seat and picked up an information brochure. Almost ten minutes went by before Carol Murphy, the program director, came into the lobby.

"Hi MC," Carol smiled, more in her eyes than on her face. "Robby's on the way. He's helping Mrs. Stewart in the cafeteria."

"Oh, I don't need to see him. I have to pick up Ryan," MC explained.

"Ryan?"

"Yes. Ryan Swift? He came with Robby today." Carol was shaking her head. "Carol, please tell me there's a little boy in there swimming."

"Let me get Robby." Carol started away, but Robby was already there.

"What's wrong Mom?" He wanted to know.

"Robby, I'm here to pick up Ryan," MC said, grasping all her patience.

"Ryan?" Robby's eyes grew wide. "Mom, he didn't come with me. He went home before the bus came. He said he wanted to go to the hospital."

"The hospital?" Carol asked.

"Are you sure Ryan said he was going home?" MC pressed.

"Yes. The bus was coming and he said he changed his mind."

"Robby," MC said as calmly as she could, "he didn't come back this morning. Did you see which way he went?" He shut his eyes, trying to visualize the morning.

"Uh oh," Robby opened his eyes. "I bet I know where he went."

"Where?" Carol and MC urged together.

"The Vanderkellen Cemetery."

"What?" MC exclaimed.

"Where?" Carol cried.

"You know, that old—"

"I know, I know! But why?" MC urged.

"Because last night he saw a policeman talking to Anna's mom, and Mrs. Redmond said she was at Ryan's house when Mrs. Swift went...got sick. So Ryan wanted to ask her what happened."

"Judy Redmond?" Carol asked, unbelieving.

"That's what Ryan said."

"But what does Vanderkellen Cemetery have to do with it?" MC asked.

"Well, the policeman was going to meet her there. They were going to do something. I don't know what. Neither did Ryan, but he kept asking me where it was."

"Did you tell him?"

"I don't know where it is. I told him it was a dumb idea."

"You were right," Carol said. "MC, Judy Redmond is missing."

"Can I use the phone?" MC asked her. Carol pointed the way, and stayed with Robby.

***

As they passed the entrance to the Kitchen, Leslie waved. "Hi, house," she called mournfully. "Hi, bed."

"We'll be right back," said Anna.

"Hurry," Ed urged.

"Hey, they strictly enforce the speed limit here," Anna told him. "I can't afford a ticket on top of everything else."

***

Barker forced himself to sit still. Walter's fear was strong enough to overwhelm the Vanderkellen's smell. Pleased, Barker reached up and tickled one of Walter's plaster feet and thought about Claire. What if she hadn't gotten that door unlocked? He shrugged, not caring that the skinny girl was watching in the mirror. Things were going so well, he knew the rest would fall into place.

***

Tom Redmond stared into the cup. He was sick of coffee, but someone kept refilling his cup. The morning was dragging. There was no more news about the car, but that wasn't surprising. The radio was constantly breaking in with news from Grady's Galaxy. Emergency crews were being called in from everywhere, including Chester County. No one there would have time to follow up on an old abandoned car.

For a fleeting instant, he had an awful vision of his wife luring Anna and Leslie away on the pretense of visiting the park. After all, it was Salem University Day. That was a ridiculous thought. Even if Judy talked them into such a thing, Anna would have called him. It disturbed him that she hadn't yet, but he didn't let his mind stray in that direction.

At least the Vickers had left the park. Dan had checked back in a while ago, but Tom hadn't spoken with him. Barbara didn't tell him about Bret. She didn't want that on his mind while driving with the camper.

The phone rang again. Tom left the answering to his sister; most of the calls were concerned friends and family. The routine of answering the same questions repeatedly wore Tom out. This time Barbara was in the yard, feeding her brood. Tom reached behind him and picked up the phone.

"Hello," said a harried voice. "My name is MC Canwell. Forgive my brashness, but I may have news about Judy Redmond. That is, unless she's home."

Tom stood up so fast the chair fell backward. Barbara came to the back door.

"Go ahead," he said, prepared for a hoax.

"My son said a friend of his saw her talking to a policeman last night."

"Yes, we know that," Tom said, not mentioning that the policeman she was speaking with might have been the infamous late Officer Wendell.

"Well, it's a long story, but they think she went to the Vanderkellen Cemetery."

"Where?"

"I'm not sure of the details, but he said, well, never mind what he said. They didn't know she was missing so they didn't say anything until now."

"I'll look into it. Thank you," he said and hung up.

"What?" Barbara asked urgently.

"Somebody named Canwell. Says her kid said Judy was going to the Vanderkellen Cemetery. I'm going. Will you call the police and let them know?"

He left her nodding and scurrying about the house. When he pulled onto the road, he passed Alan Macklin and didn't bother returning his wave.

***

"Jaime, you have to call the police." Cindy squeezed the frightened girl's hand.

"I can't. My parents would die if they knew I was out there."

365

"They're going to find out eventually. Somebody will find Whit. Do you think your friends will protect you when the police go to them?"

"I can fake like I don't remember," Jaime sobbed.

"Can you?"

The phone rang then. Cindy glanced at the wall clock. "Wow, it's almost one o'clock." They had been talking for hours, lunch had come and gone, nurses did cursory checks, Jaime's parents, who she had earlier begged to take a stroll around town, came back and stopped in to say hi, only to be sent out again. Jaime tried to make them understand they were appreciated, but she needed time to talk to Cindy. They left to get lunch with puzzled, hurt faces.

Cindy excused herself to answer the phone as Jaime wept softly over her dilemma. She came to attention the instant she heard Cindy whisper hoarsely into the phone: "Vanderkellen Cemetery?" A faint voice chattered on the phone. While she couldn't understand the words, she understood Cindy's face.

"Did you call her husband?" Cindy was asking. She appeared calm, but her hand gripped the bed rail tightly. "I'm going out there right now, MC...I'll find a way...Oh, Tim's here, he'll take me." Jaime turned to see a tall man and a petite, scowling woman in the doorway.

***

"This place isn't so creepy in the daytime, is it?" Leslie commented as they rode through the sun-speckled shade from the trees that lined Nepowa Road.

"No," Anna agreed. "It's a pretty day, too."

Behind them, Ed chuckled.

"What?" Leslie demanded.

"Oh nothing," he crooned, poorly imitating Ed. "You two just crack me up."

***

"You two just crack me up." The sound of his own voice made Ed's skin crawl. Barker took everything from him, his phrases, his gestures, and mastered them casually. Ed, back in the bed with his ring box hidden beneath the pillow, pulled the covers over his head.

Barker might intend to kill them, but Ed didn't have to watch. Besides, there were worse things in store for him. Earlier, he had thought he might already be dead and in Hell, but he knew better now. He saw the demons in Barker's memories, not red cartoon devils, but hideous scaly creatures, and he realized Hell was yet to come, and when it did, he would long for this misery.

***

MC drove back to the Kitchen, a sullen Robby beside her.

"Maybe we should go, too," he suggested, talking about the cemetery.

"We will, but I want to get your father. Let's see if Ryan took his bike."

"Why?"

"So if the police ask, I mean, if we can't find him out there," she struggled to find words that wouldn't upset him.

"Oh, I get it. If he's on his bike, he took the road. If he walked, he took shortcuts," Robby supplied his own answer.

"Exactly. He was wearing blue, wasn't he?" she wondered aloud as they pulled onto Apple Street. "Dad might have seen him while he was working in the yard. The neighbors, too."

"Ugh. Not Mrs. Geist, please."

"I'll handle her."

They parked in the Swift's driveway. "Let's check the garage windows to see if his bike's in there," she said, getting out of the car.

"It's usually just laying around the yard," Robby said. He led the way toward the house. "Mom!" he hissed, placing his finger to his lips. She hurried to him. "Listen."

At first she heard nothing, but then, faintly, came the sound of laughter. Fake laughter. From inside the house.

"The TV!" she exclaimed. Running past Robby, she beat the door with her fist. "Ryan!"

"Ryan!" Robby called, trying to peer in the front window.

"Ryan, are you in there?"

"Maybe he's asleep. Is the door locked?"

MC twisted the handle. "It's locked." She pounded on the door again.

"I'll check the back door," Robby disappeared around the house.

"MC! Oh, MC!" Dottie Geist ran across the yard, her curlers

bouncing on her head. "What's going on?"

"Nothing, Dottie. I'm picking up Ryan."

"What's he doing here? I thought he was staying with you."

"Dottie, please, I'm in a hurry," MC continued to pound on the door.

"How could you leave that kid here all alone? With his mom all whacked out like that. Drugs, I bet. It has to be. No wonder Tim took off—"

The door opened, and Ryan stood there, glaring past MC at Dottie.

"My mother is not whacked out! She does not take drugs! My Dad left because he's a jerk!" Ryan rushed at her. MC, too stunned to get in the way, sighed with relief when Robby appeared in the living room, running after him, and grabbed Ryan around the waist. He held Ryan, soothing him the way MC and others had soothed Robby in the past when he lost control.

"The back door was unlocked," he told the women, hanging on to the sobbing child, pulling him into the house. MC left Dottie outside and shut the door on her.

"Ryan? You scared us to death. What's going on?" she asked. Before he answered, the door behind her opened.

"Dad!" Robby said.

MC looked, grateful to see Michael.

"What happened?" he asked.

"You wouldn't believe. I have to call Cindy," she said. "Ryan, what are you doing here?"

"What are you all doing here? Robby?" asked Michael.

"Dad, we thought Ryan went to the cemetery to find his mom!"

"The cemetery? Ryan, your mother didn't die—"

"No," Ryan said, calmer, wiping his cheeks. "I wasn't going to go. Well, I was, but I don't know where it is."

MC waved for them to be quiet while she was on the phone. "Can you catch her?" she was saying. "Oh, my. Okay." When she hung up, she told Michael, "We have to go. I'll explain on the way."

They herded Ryan, still clinging to Robby, into the car, and sped away, leaving an agitated Dottie Geist in the front yard.

***

The nurse hung up after speaking to MC, and greeted the two police officers standing before her. "We're here to see Jaime Gates," the female officer informed her.

"You have to see her doctor first."

"I'm here," Jaime limped into the hall. "Let's hurry, before my parents get back."

***

Ed and Anna stood in front of the car, gazing at the church. The door swayed inward, touched by the breeze that stirred the trees and pushed the high grass in waves. Leslie, anxious to be done, was at the back of the car, intent on removing Bruce.

"Hey, the church door's open," Anna said.

"Look!" Leslie shouted, frantically. "You guys, come here!"

Anna hurried to her, and after a short moment, Ed joined them. They stood staring, Anna and Leslie shocked, Ed grinning wickedly.

In the car, Bruce's quivering body bounced up and down.

"Ed, you were right," Leslie whispered. Anna watched silently, her mouth open. Ed moved ahead of them and grabbed Bruce's head in both hands, dragging the convulsing form out of the car. He dropped it on the ground, where it continued to quake.

"It's up to you two," Ed said solemnly.

"No way!" Leslie said.

"I'm not touching him," Anna backed her up.

"You will! This is what we're here for! Finish it!" His voice climbed on the rising wind. "Now! Come on!"

Anna and Leslie traded a glance. With a loud sigh, Anna touched a cautious finger to the head of the mannequin. It jumped. She reached again, and this time held it.

"Come on Les. Let's run for it," she said bravely.

Leslie bent for the legs, picking them up much the same way she used to pick up Becky's diapers. "Let's go!"

They ran for the church, Anna in the lead, carrying the top half of the mannequin at her side, her arm wrapped around its neck and chest. Leslie stumbled trying to keep up with her longer legged friend.

***

Ed watched helplessly. Anna and Leslie ran up the steps toward their death. He'd hoped to be dead by now. He didn't want to see this; he needed no more kindling for his home in Hell.

He felt the wind kicking up, heard it high above, blowing through the treetops. And then he heard screaming.

***

Anna had just stepped inside the church when the shouting began. Leslie stopped on the top step, outside the door, Bruce's trembling legs still in her arms. Looking back, they saw a woman staggering in the grass.

"Anna! It's your mom!" With a mighty shove, Anna heaved most of Bruce into the church, and they ran again, away from the church to where Judy Redmond teetered on wobbly legs, swaying in the wind.

"John! Oh John! It's happening!" she cried over and over.

***

Barker bellowed against the wind, in agony because the Vanderkellen was running away, running to Claire! So close, almost there, and that witch Claire drew them away!

At least now he knew which was the Vanderkellen because the tall one had been inside the circle and still lived. He leapt into action after the other one. He'd throw her in himself. He hadn't come this far to stop now. He chased her, unnoticed.

***

"Mom! Mom!" Anna called as she ran. Leslie, close behind, saw something was seriously wrong. Judy looked right past them, crying for John. Who was John? There was a long, throat scraping scream, and Leslie thought she heard Anna's mother saying *The baby's coming! I'm having the baby!*

Then Leslie was tackled from behind, her head jarred hard enough to shake her teeth.

***

370

Anna reached for her mother only to be met with a brutal punch to her face. She stumbled backward, stunned, arms wheeling for balance. Judy bent forward, holding her belly, wailing. Anna shook away the punch, then circled her mother and put her arms around her, trying to grab her hands. A sharp elbow hit her like a piston, knocking her to the ground. Her mother then assaulted her with a string of words Anna never realized she knew.

"Kill her!" Ed yelled. Anna looked up to see him pulling Leslie by the hair. Leslie's arms flailed, slapping at his arms, clutching at the grass, her feet kicking. Anna tried to get up, but she was grabbed from behind. She went to her knees, digging into her own flesh, prying her mother's fingers from her throat.

***

Ed wished he could visualize a gun and shoot himself. He was killing her. Since recovering from the first blow, she struggled ferociously. Now she was pinned, his knee on her chest, choking her while she pressed her nails into his wrists, fighting for release. Ed gazed out at her face. It was red, then purple. Her mouth was round in its effort to gasp air and her eyes, first wide, were now tightly closed, no doubt still seeing the last image they beheld; him, Ed, her friend, killing her. They would die together.

What then? With her gone what would Barker do? Destroy another amusement park? Blow up a few buildings? With the Vanderkellens gone, what would his capabilities be?

But wait—he wasn't the antichrist. Ed knew enough of Barker's situation to realize that he was a low spirit among the lowest. Still, he was more than Ed could handle. Then again, Barker seemed powerless against the good spirits. Angels. While roaming Barker's mind, he saw many occasions where certain people were protected from Barker's intrusion. In fact, Barker was fairly intimidated by these protectors, though he misread that intimidation as hatred. Were those angels close? Was God close? Would God help them? Why should He? This was probably as close to a church as any of them had been in years, and this building wasn't even a church.

If that wasn't enough reason for God to look away from their predicament, a bigger one, Ed realized sorrowfully, was that he had never been completely convinced in the actuality of God. Until now, anyway. Ed had seen, through Barker's memories, that

Barker's spirit world was a horrible, bloody, acrid place. A hateful place. The only way the earth survived the existence of such a place was because another, beautiful, loving realm operated in opposition. It was up to mankind to choose sides. Ed had made the wrong choice.

***

Tom Redmond ran the truck off the road when he saw what was happening in front of the church. The tall grass obliterated most of his view, but he was sure he saw Ed Philips dragging something. No, somebody! If Ed were here, then maybe the caller had been right about Judy being here. He jumped from the truck and ran toward Ed. The wind blew the grass away and for a moment Tom saw Leslie. Ed pulled her through the grass by one arm.

Even though he felt as if all the air had been sucked from his lungs, Tom ran, screaming, at Ed. Ed didn't look up, and Tom knocked him away. Leslie fell, one arm up, the other under her back. She didn't move. Tom had barely assessed the situation before Ed came at him. He ducked, and spun. Before Ed launched at him again, Tom stumbled away. He didn't look back at Ed, and may have even pushed him off. He would not remember because a few yards away, he saw his wife was strangling his daughter. He raced to separate them, leaving Ed alone with Leslie.

"Judy! Anna!" he shouted, not knowing if they could hear him in the wind. As he closed in, he heard Judy growling. He pushed her away, more gently than he had pushed Ed, partly because he loved her, and also because Anna seemed to be holding her own. Judy fell easily, and rolled into a ball, screaming in agony. Anna fell also, spitting and choking.

***

Judy had no strength. She couldn't even keep her own hands from strangling her daughter. Crippled by the pain of childbirth, Judy could only scream as Claire acted on John's wishes, and with each contraction, she squeezed Anna's neck harder.

She didn't know how to feel when Tom arrived, relieved or ashamed. She was going to die, and he would never know what happened. He pushed her down, she heard Anna coughing. *Thank you*, she thought.

The baby began to leave her body. Claire wailed, holding her stomach, forcing it to stay. The pain was horrendous. Judy closed her eyes and waited for death.

***

Death wasn't coming soon enough for Ed, despite the torment awaiting him. How stupid he had been. How lazy and irresponsible. Had he acted sooner—no, he knew that probably wouldn't have changed things. But he might have been able to do something now if he had listened to his mother and his sister and turned to God while he still had the chance.

He turned from Leslie's slack body and looked behind him.

There was Susan, as he had seen her earlier, near her own death, saying "As long as you have breath, it's not too late."

Oh, Lord, he thought. It can't be true. Can it?

"No it can't!" came the voice Ed knew as John Barker's.

Ed continued to stare at Susan. He felt the warmth of her sincerity, her certainty, her contentment.

"It is too late, you fool! It's over!" Barker's voice interrupted. Ed looked outside. They were almost to the church, Barker again dragging Leslie by the arm. Ed fell to his knees, crushed by discouragement, until he once more heard Susan's words; *"As long as you have breath, it's not too late."*

He looked at her peaceful face, remembered her faith, her goodness. Tears rose in his eyes and then he smiled because he realized God *had* used her. His breathing sped up as he began to understand. God was using her now! Her words came back to him and he raised his arms to the sky and cried out: *"Please, Lord, use me too! Jesus, you know all my sins, more than I do, and I am just now realizing how bad they were and what awful things they caused! Had I turned to you sooner..."*

Ed's prayer filled him with a mixture of remorse and joy, the resulting sensation like being washed by a wave of hot water. Barker felt it too, because Ed sensed his panic. Before Barker could flee, Ed wrapped his arms about him and prayed harder, straight from his belly. *Forgive me Lord! Forgive me!*

As Ed prayed, it occurred to him how crazy he'd been to have believed in this curse and not in God! His head was clearer now than ever in his life, his direction set. He pulled Barker so close they became one. Ed shouted, "Thank you, Jesus!" Then he jerked hard. Suddenly it was Barker who was trapped. Ed beamed, feeling as if the brightness of this moment would last for eternity. He thanked God again and again for saving him.

***

Anna had just gotten to her feet when the she heard Ed. First he said, "Thank you Jesus!" Then he howled, "Let me gooooo!" His words rode the gale, blending and stretching until she couldn't tell his voice from the wind. Tom heard him too, and he and Anna watched Ed let go of Leslie and wrap his arms around his head. He left Leslie on the church steps and began backing up them awkwardly, twisting and turning like a cat trapped in a burlap sack. Before he entered the church, he stooped to push something inside. Tom didn't know what, but Anna knew he had pushed Bruce's feet across the sill.

Ed bent, arms back over his head, swaying. Then he reached out, grabbing the doorframe. He looked their way, his eyes hard, his voice firm.

"Get them away!"

He disappeared inside the church.

***

Time seemed to slow for some; for others it raced. Judy sat up, reaching toward the church, calling "John!" before collapsing back into the grass. The church door slammed shut and the building shook. Incredibly, the wind picked up, beating Tom so that he had to raise his arm to protect his eyes. He rushed to where Leslie lay drooped on the steps and picked her up, terrified of causing further damage, yet afraid the building would collapse atop her. Not knowing where to go, he ran behind the old station wagon and laid her on the ground. Then he ran to help Anna get her mother to safety.

Around them, leaves and branches swirled and the earth rumbled. Ancient shingles peeled from the roof of the old church. Tom lay flat, covering his ears, trying to convince himself that the squealing laughter he heard in the wind was a trick of the storm.

***

"It's just that I can't believe you left the child with someone who's so irresponsible," Teena was saying.

"Tim," Cindy cut her off.

"Teena," Tim said impatiently.

They were on Hopeful Road, a mile shy of Nepowa. Teena was unhappy about sharing the car with Cindy. She practically raced for the front seat, almost tripping on her high heels. Cindy didn't care where she sat, or even how she got there, but she was going to the cemetery, and she was going to get there fast. Betty and the other nurses had done what they should to keep her at the hospital, but, being mothers themselves, they didn't do all they could.

"Oh great Tim!" Teena whined, "Now we're being chased by the cops!"

Cindy turned around. Oh yes, behind them was a car with a light bar, but the lights weren't flashing and the sirens weren't sounding, so they were hardly being chased. Tim slowed the car.

"Don't slow down!" Cindy said. "Jaime called them. They're coming because of the body. Hurry!"

"Body?" Teena shrieked. "What body? You *are* involved in drugs!"

"Teena," Tim repeated, his teeth gritted.

They turned onto Nepowa fifteen miles an hour faster than they should have, and Tim lost control. Teena screamed. After a brutal fishtail, he caught the road and floored it.

"It's up there. Couple of miles," Cindy tried to direct him.

"Slow down, Tim!" Teena ordered.

"On the right, isn't it?" he said just as the siren whooped behind them.

***

Officers Matt Michaels and Dave Mitchell were on their way to meet County at Vanderkellen Cemetery concerning a report of a missing Miltonville woman when dispatch called to say the Jane Doe may have witnessed a murder there. The dispatcher had just finished relaying the information when the car ahead of them, which had been speeding, made a reckless turn onto Nepowa Road.

"What have we got here?" Dave asked.

"I hate working Saturdays," Matt said, sounding the siren and slowing to maneuver the car safely onto the gravel road. A cloud of dust obscured their view of the speeding car. On either side of the road, trees swayed and a low cloud grew amid their tops. They sped on, and soon the trees were almost bent, large limbs hanging. One hit the car. Matt backed off the pedal, holding the wheel tight. "Hang on," he said, staring wide-eyed at the road ahead.

"What's going on?" Dave held the dashboard.

"Tornado!" Matt began braking but Dave urged him on.

"Get out of these trees! There's a clearing ahead."

"We don't need a clearing! We need a ditch!"

"We don't need to be hit by a tree! Go!"

Matt, having never seen a tornado, trusted Dave's judgment and pressed the gas. A moment later they arrived at the clearing. Grass and branches circled the church like a cyclone. In the center, the old building broke apart bit by bit, the pieces flying high into the air. The sedan, along with a truck and a station wagon were parked off the road, and several people had taken shelter behind them.

"Get out of here! Get back in the trees!" Dave ordered, and Matt obeyed.

***

Tom cradled Judy while Anna hovered over Leslie. Frustrated and frightened, Anna pinched Leslie's wrist feeling for life. Her own pulse beat so hard, she couldn't tell whether Leslie had one or not. She gave up and held her hand close to Leslie's open mouth, but the wind touched her palm, so she couldn't tell if Leslie was breathing, either. It didn't appear she was, Anna thought, tears touching her cheeks. Leslie's neck was too swollen, her face too blue. Anna wanted to straighten her neck, but what if she made it worse? Then again, maybe it would save her life. Just as with the injured boy at the Galaxy, Anna was helpless.

A voice came to her on the wind, telling her what to do. It was Cindy Swift, shouting from where she squatted next to Tom and Judy. Tim Swift held Cindy's shoulder, then, after a firm squeeze, he ran into the windstorm.

"CPR, Anna! Now!" Cindy yelled.

"I don't know how!" Anna bawled.

Cindy squat-jumped to Anna and moved her away from Leslie.

"No! Don't move her! You'll hurt her!" Anna screamed over the wind.

"She's dying! I have to!" Cindy gently tilted Leslie's head back, felt inside her mouth, then blew into it. Anna crawled away to watch as Cindy puffed again and waited. Puffed and waited. It was useless. Two policemen appeared and huddled around Leslie, taking over as Cindy took off into the wind in search of Ryan. Anna closed her eyes, not able to bear Leslie's bloated face, or the policemen's futile attempts to breath life into her limp body.

***

The church crumbled, bricks flying light as tissue, wood splitting and soaring. Tim ran aimlessly through the churchyard, screaming for Ryan. Suddenly Cindy was there, tugging his arm, pointing to the road at the Canwells' car. Ryan's face pressed against the window. The wind pushed Tim and Cindy to the car.

By the time they found shelter, the church had vanished.

***

There was no explosion, no fire. Not even a spark. The church was gone. The wind died, leaves and branches dropping to the ground. The bricks and the roof and the beams of the church never did fall. They just ceased.

While Matt Michaels continued CPR on Leslie, Dave Mitchell called for an ambulance. Anna stood alone, fighting to be strong, holding back tears, wishing to do something but ignorant as to what. To her left, her mother breathed normally, but did not respond to her father, who held her head and smoothed her hair. To her right, the big policeman pushed on Leslie's chest.

"Anna?"

Robby stood next to her, his eyes wet with tears. Leslie was his friend, too. Anna broke, actually felt herself falling apart, and Robby hugged her.

"I knew it!"

She looked over Robby's shoulder and saw a livid Alan striding their way.

***

The paramedics arrived. County police arrived. Alan blustered on psychotically. Misunderstanding medics were ready to sedate him.

Anna ignored him. Teena ventured from the car, unsteady on her heels, and wobbled toward the policeman, pleading her innocence in the earlier car chase.

Leslie and Judy were loaded into the ambulances. Tom and Anna hopped in the truck and raced after them, leaving the red-faced Alan stomping around indignantly, apparently not realizing nor caring what happened. Tim led Cindy and Ryan to the sedan, and drove off after Tom and Anna, planning to talk with the police at the hospital. Teena, forgotten, saw them leave and joined Alan in a rampage.

"He left me here!" she hissed.

"She'll pay for this!" he hissed.

A few threats and several obscenities later, Alan offered Teena a ride home.

MC, Michael, and Robby answered questions for the police, and were there when Whit's body was discovered. When they were excused, they went to the hospital. The Vickers were already there. Upon arriving home from the Galaxy, they had called the police station to ask for help in locating Leslie. Before long, an officer arrived not to take a report, but to give them news that their daughter was en route to Salem Medical Center. He escorted them the entire twenty-five miles.

After a dangerous rush to the hospital, it was a long, long wait.

Epilogue

The young assistant pastor stood before the congregation, reading the notes on the podium. Dan put his arm around Michele. Becky held her mother's hand and scanned the crowd.

"Before we begin today's service, I want to ask you all to remember Leslie Vickers in your prayers," the pastor began. Becky squeezed Michele's hand. The pastor continued.

"She will certainly need them to get through graduate school."

There was laughter, and Becky turned to smirk at Leslie, who was sitting nearby with Anna.

"Ha ha," Leslie said, nodding at her tormentors. "Very funny. You're a great bunch. Ha."

"Your dad told him to say that," Anna said, laughing at Leslie's humiliation.

Someone patted Leslie's shoulder and she smiled at Nate Kingston. "Good luck, kid," he said, and the way he said it reminded her of Ed.

"You're coming to the cookout, aren't you?" she asked him. He nodded and winked.

The church service continued, with no further mention of Leslie. Everyone knew her story, or some version of it. After three years, she was old news.

That wasn't the case at first. While Leslie lay unconscious in the hospital, having been twice resuscitated, rumors began to spread. It started with Anna, who told the story of Bruce and the trip to the Galaxy. Cindy and Jaime were talking of their experience, and Cindy identified Bruce as Walter. Days later, when a groggy, achy

Judy Redmond filled in the gaps, they pieced together the events that brought about the Itch. In the weeks following, they studied the papers Ed collected, and Nate came forward with his knowledge, mostly to protect Ed, whom Anna had been especially viscous toward.

Those first days, while her mother was unconscious, had been confusing and painful for Anna. It was one thing for Ed to turn on them, but how could her own mother? Cindy and Jaime tried to explain the situation to Anna; nurses verified that Judy visited Cindy before she disappeared. Anna wanted to believe them rather than think her mother wished to kill her. Her father wanted to believe it, too. But when they spoke of it, it sounded ridiculous. The facts, according to Tom and Anna, were that Anna had been duped by Ed while Judy had succumbed to the same mysterious sickness that afflicted Cindy Swift and Jaime Gates.

***

Mercifully, Judy regained consciousness after two days. She wept hysterically at the sight of Anna. Together the family talked of those hours, and, Tom and Anna could offer no alternative explanation. The story of the curse was not nearly as strange as Tom and Anna's attempts to explain it logically.

"Leslie? What happened to Leslie?" Judy had asked, fresh tears in her eyes.

"We don't know yet," Tom said. "They lost her, but she came back. Her neck is broken. She has a skull fracture..." His voice trailed off.

"Oh, no," Judy sobbed. "After what Ed did for her..."

"What he did *for* her? Tried to kill her?" Anna exclaimed.

"Oh, honey, no," Judy took her hands. She tried to tell her daughter, but there were no words to properly define what she saw that day. It was much like describing a dream. Judy saw John Barker, not Ed Philips, strangling Leslie, trying to get her inside the church. He was frantic. Suddenly there came a light, and Ed stood in Barker's place. They were the same, yet they were separate, and they struggled like reflections in glass. While Tom and Anna surmised Ed might have been attacked by a swarm of bees, he was actually in battle with John Barker. Around him, pink formless creatures dove and screamed. The light grew stronger as Ed pulled

380

Barker into the church. Before the door shut, Claire shouted for John, and was gone. Sucked away, it felt like. Judy remembered no more.

So she said.

A week later, Cindy mentioned the baby. Judy begged her secrecy before telling her that when Claire went, there were no more efforts to keep the baby inside. The last thing she actually remembered was the squalling baby leaving her body.

She did not know where it was and she didn't want to speculate.

***

Leslie's coma lasted a week. Her awakening was slow, and after that she spent an additional month in the hospital. For almost six months she had to wear a halo, held in place by steel bolts. Her family had, in the meantime, discovered the First Miltonville Christian Church. The members received them warmly, and visited Leslie often. Dan and Michele credited them greatly with Leslie's recovery.

More miraculous than her complete recuperation was the change in her attitude. Leslie herself could not understand it, and she wasn't comfortable talking about it. When she was able to return to school, she took a full load of difficult courses, much against the recommendation of her advisor. She finished that semester at Salem University on the Dean's list and remained there until her graduation. Now she would begin working on her master's degree in special education.

***

Anna also went through a transformation after that strange Saturday. She made some serious decisions based on that experience. Alan's behavior determined his fate; after numerous phone calls, letters and visits, he gradually disappeared. She heard he was dating Teena Ladd, and she and Cindy laughed over that; they both had what they deserved. The following year Alan took a job in Oregon. Teena went to New York.

The Sunday after the Itch, Anna woke from a nap at the hospital to find Colin in deep discussion with her father. She smiled then, and smiled now at the memory. Her romance with Colin blossomed then faded, but their friendship remained. Colin had stayed at the Galaxy after the storm, helping with the relief effort throughout the day and most of the night. Crazy Sam and the others had survived unscathed. They did what they could, made coffee, cleared traffic, stayed out of the way. Later, Crazy Sam would be saddened to hear of the death of his new buddy, Ed Philips.

Colin and Anna both changed their majors to pre-med. If ever, ever, they should be in another position to save a life, or at least bring comfort, they wanted to be prepared. Together they took basic emergency medical training and they utilized Judy's knowledge and experience as a nurse. Anna was very proud of her mother.

Anna looked around the church for Colin. He and Tracy usually sat closer to the front. She didn't see him, but Maureen Russell, surrounded by her overly pierced, much tattooed and highly peroxided friends, caught her looking and waved.

***

Cindy Swift, sitting behind Maureen, also saw Anna glancing around, but didn't catch her attention. Cindy sat between her husband and son. Tim had moved home last year, and though things were rough, they were improving. There was a lot to work through, even without Cindy's bizarre experience with Claire Brandenburg. Cindy and Jaime Gates and Judy Redmond talked often, constantly in the beginning, but now less and less frequently. Last year they worked on recording their stories. They had yet to decide what to do with them, but they determined they must stay in touch and keep all the material for at least the next thirty years.

John Barker was destroyed, but they worried about his son.

***

The Itch touched everyone in the vicinity of Grady's Galaxy that Saturday. Eight people died in the storm, including one Albert Leehman. Weather experts shook their heads, unable to concur. They only agreed on their amazement that more hadn't died. The damage and injuries were of a magnitude never before seen in that county. Work and rescue crews from neighboring areas came to the scene, and the cooperation was magnificent. The injured were taken to the six closest hospitals, and the nearest high school gymnasium was converted to a recovery post. Luckily, the area housed mostly tourists, and no one lost a permanent home. Still, it was a horrendous week.

The park was operating again before the Fourth of July. Lawsuits were filed, and one named Leslie and the County of Amberly, Indiana, as defendants. It was tossed, along with many others.

***

Some things would never change. Uncle Ray spent sixteen months in jail, but still lived with Grandma Emily. The Vickers rarely visited, and begged Grandma Emily to come live with them or Uncle Joe. Grandma refused, insisting she could take care of Ray.

Sandy Cornett stayed in Missouri for a while, then moved on to Florida. There she married a man she met at a party. She found out three days after they were married that he was a paranoid schizophrenic who was missing from the Winter City Mental Heath Facility.

Theresa Hoover left school and also married. Her husband bossed her around much as Sandy did, and she complained and whined, but did nothing about it, except have more babies.

The Geists still lived on Apple Street, Dottie meddling and Artie staying invisible. The Canwells also still lived on Apple Street. Robby had helped Leslie with several classes by teaching her how to work with special needs children.

***

Miltonville Cemetery was bustling this Sunday. Kids skated along the asphalt trails, passing joggers and dog walkers, disappearing and reappearing on the hills. Leslie pulled the car over to the side of a drive and parked. Bret the Maverick had been retired after his accident; this car was a cast-off of Michele's. She popped the trunk and met Anna behind the car. There were two bouquets, and they each took one and carried them down the hill in silence. They were both very melancholy. Leslie put the flowers on her mother's grave, and knelt to converse with her. A few feet away, Anna did likewise at Ed Philips' memorial marker.

"Will any of this ever seem real?" Anna said. She said it all the time, so much that it was no longer a question. She could only believe it as long as she didn't think about it.

"I have a harder time believing that I'm moving away tomorrow," Leslie said. Anna helped her to her feet.

"It won't be forever," Anna consoled.

"And then you'll be in med school for ten years."

"Not that long! Besides, I'm just going to be across the river." Anna put her arm around Leslie and steered her toward the car.

"Everything's so different."

"Yeah, but it's better, too."

"Yeah. I guess it could be worse."

"The worst is over."

"You know, this reminds me of the day we went out to the Vanderkellen Cemetery that first time. Remember? When we thought the devil worshippers were coming. That was funny. Have you been back?"

"Just once."

"Me, too. You know, now that it's all over, we might ought to drive out there—"

"Oh no, we ought not," Anna protested, pushing Leslie into the car.

"Just for kicks. I don't get scared anymore."

"Then what's the point in going?"

Leslie thought for a moment, then shrugged. "I guess there isn't one."

***

As they walked to the car, the trunk of a tree bulged slightly, the grooves of its bark bending. Ed Philips emerged, watching Anna and Leslie, his heart full of affection. They would be all right.

Time had passed for them, he could tell, but he didn't know how long it had been since that day at the Vanderkellen Cemetery. For him, it was only a moment, a long moment filled with energy and light and comfort. There was no time here, not like he remembered before. There was only up and out and far and near. He stood close to comprehension, and it was exciting.

He stepped away from the tree where he had hidden and looked down on the graves. A black marker bore his name. It did not chill him; instead he was happy that Anna left flowers for him. He walked to his grave, smiling. The sound of fading voices caught his attention, and he looked up to see Leslie and Anna getting into a car. Didn't Leslie drive an old car? He couldn't remember. He then realized he didn't know how he came to be in the cemetery. Something good had happened, he felt. No, something good was about to happen.

There was a tug at his sleeve. The boy was there, holding a rose he'd plucked from the grave. The boy was growing; he was just a baby when Ed last saw him. When was that? The boy's face was blissful, round and golden, fresh as it was when he was newborn. Ed took the rose from him, and then, suddenly, he understood. Winking, he put it between his teeth, and raising his eyebrows, he stepped on his grave. The boy laughed. Ed did likewise. Bending his knees, he moved his elbows in and out like chicken wings. The boy clapped and sang a beautiful melody in strange words. Ed's stomach tingled and he began shuffling his feet, dancing atop his grave, laughing and singing, the rose falling to the ground as he opened his arms to spin. He was dimly aware of Anna and Leslie driving off. The pang of their departure barely bit him.

"OH!" the boy cried, and when Ed turned to him, he was not a boy, but a young man. They were both young men. The boy joined Ed's dance as light fell from the sky, touching them softly like misty rain. All about them it glittered and sparkled, enveloping them, filling them. Dancing, singing, spinning, they were lifted, their joy too great for earth. Up and up they went, off to join family and friends, the world behind them forgotten.

Below, squirrels chattered wildly to one another, the birds sang with excitement. They felt the warmth of the light and the pleasure of the moment and they tried to share it, but their jubilant clamor went unnoticed. The skaters and joggers glided past without looking up, going on with their days.

About the Author

Deanne Devine has always loved writing and all things writing related, such as twisting paperclips and doodling on phonebooks. She wrote her first short story at eight years old. Her teacher gave her a D for penmanship, then suggested she give some thought to the motivation of her protagonist. Deanne spent the next thirty years thinking about this, and as a result produced many neatly written short stories and one novel.

These days she lives in cozy contentment with her husband while working on a second novel and doodling all over their phonebooks. She continues to work on her penmanship.